MYSTERY AT LYNDEN SANDS

MYSTERY AT LYNDEN SANDS

J. J. Connington

COACHWHIP PUBLICATIONS

Greenville, Ohio

CONTENTS

INTRODUCTION
CURTIS EVANS

Alfred Walter Stewart (1880-1947)
Alias J. J. Connington

DURING THE GOLDEN AGE of the detective novel, in the 1920s and 1930s, "J. J. Connington" stood with fellow crime writers R. Austin Freeman, Cecil John Charles Street, and Freeman Wills Crofts as the foremost practitioner in British mystery fiction of the science of pure detection. I use the word "science" advisedly, for the man behind J. J. Connington, Alfred Walter Stewart, was an esteemed Scottish-born scientist who held the Chair of Chemistry at Queens University, Belfast for twenty-five years, from 1919 until his retirement in 1944. A "small, unassuming, moustached polymath," Stewart was "a strikingly effective lecturer with an excellent sense of humor, fertile imagination, and fantastically retentive memory," qualities that also served him well in his fiction. During roughly this period, the busy Professor Stewart found time to author a remarkable apocalyptic science fiction tale, *Nordenholt's Million* (1923), a mainstream novel, *Almighty Gold* (1924), a collection of essays, *Alias J. J. Connington* (1947), and, between 1926 and 1947, twenty-four mysteries (all but one true tales of detection), many of them sterling examples of the Golden Age puzzle-oriented detective novel at its considerable best. "For those who ask first of all in a detective story for exact and mathematical accuracy in the construction of the plot," avowed a contemporary

7

London Daily Mail reviewer, "there is no author to equal the distinguished scientist who writes under the name of J. J. Connington."[1]

Alfred Stewart's background as a man of science is reflected in his fiction, not only in the impressive puzzle plot mechanics he devised for his mysteries but in his choices of themes and depictions of characters. Along with Stanley Nordenholt of *Nordenholt's Million*, a novel about a plutocrat's pitiless efforts to preserve a ruthlessly remolded remnant of human life after a global environmental calamity, the most notable character that Stewart created is Chief Constable Sir Clinton Driffield, the detective in seventeen of the twenty-four Connington crime novels. Driffield is one of crime fiction's most highhanded investigators, occasionally taking into his hands the functions of judge and jury as well as chief of police. Absent from Stewart's fiction is the hail-fellow-well-met quality found in John Street's works or the religious ethos suffusing those of Freeman Wills Crofts, not to mention the effervescent novel of manners style of the British Golden Age Crime Queens Dorothy L. Sayers, Margery Allingham, and Ngaio Marsh. Instead we see an often disdainful cynicism about the human animal and a marked admiration for detached supermen with superior intellects. For this reason, reading a Connington novel can be a challenging experience for modern readers inculcated in gentler social beliefs. Yet Alfred Stewart produced a classic apocalyptic science fiction tale in *Nordenholt's Million* (justly dubbed "exciting and terrifying reading" by the *Spectator*), as well as superb detective novels boasting well-wrought puzzles, bracing characterization, and an occasional leavening of dry humor. Not long after Stewart's death in 1947, the Connington novels fell entirely out of print. The recent embrace of Stewart's fiction in recent publishing is a welcome

---

[1] For more on Street, Crofts and particularly Stewart, see Curtis Evans, *Masters of the "Humdrum" Mystery: Cecil John Charles Street, Freeman Wills Crofts, Alfred Walter Stewart and the British Detective Novel, 1920-1961* (Jefferson, NC: McFarland, 2012). On the academic career of Alfred Walter Stewart, see his entry in *Oxford Dictionary of National Biography* (London and New York: Oxford University Press, 2004), vol. 52, 627-628.

event indeed, correcting as it does over sixty years of underserved neglect of an accomplished genre writer.

Born in Glasgow on September 5, 1880, Alfred Stewart had significant exposure to religion in his earlier life. His father was William Stewart, longtime Professor of Divinity and Biblical Criticism at Glasgow University, and he married Lily Coats, a daughter of the Reverend Jervis Coats and member of one of Scotland's preeminent Baptist families. Religious sensibility is entirely absent from the Connington corpus, however. A confirmed secularist, Stewart once referred to one of his wife's brothers, the Reverend William Holms Coats (1881-1954), principal of the Scottish Baptist College, as his "mental and spiritual antithesis," bemusedly adding: "It's quite an education to see what one would look like if one were turned into one's mirror-image."

Stewart's J. J. Connington pseudonym was derived from a nineteenth-century Oxford Professor of Latin and translator of Horace, indicating that Stewart's literary interests lay not in pietistic writing but rather in the pre-Christian classics ("I prefer the *Odyssey* to *Paradise Lost*," the author once avowed). Possessing an inquisitive and expansive mind, Stewart was in fact an uncommonly well-read individual, freely ranging over a variety of literary genres. His deep immersion in French literature and supernatural horror fiction, for example, is documented in his lively correspondence with the noted horologist Rupert Thomas Gould.[2]

It thus is not surprising that in the 1920s the intellectually restless Stewart, having achieved a distinguished middle age as a highly regarded man of science, decided to apply his creative energy to a new endeavor, the writing of fiction. After several years he settled,

---

[2] The Gould-Stewart correspondence is discussed in considerable detail in *Masters of the "Humdrum" Mystery*. For more on the life of the fascinating Rupert Thomas Gould, see Jonathan Betts, *Time Restored: The Harrison Timekeepers and R. T. Gould, the Man Who Knew (Almost) Everything* (London and New York: Oxford University Press, 2006) and the British film *Longitude* (2000), which details Gould's restoration of the marine chronometers built by in the eighteenth-century by the clockmaker John Harrison.

like other gifted men and women of his generation, on the wildly popular mystery genre. Stewart was modest about his accomplishments in this particular field of light fiction, telling Rupert Gould later in life that "I write these things [what Stewart called tec yarns] because they amuse me in parts when I am putting them together and because they are the only writings of mine that the public will look at. Also, in a minor degree, because I like to think some people get pleasure out of them." No doubt Stewart's single most impressive literary accomplishment is *Nordenholt's Million*, yet in their time the two dozen J. J. Connington mysteries did indeed give readers in Great Britain, the United States, and other countries much diversionary reading pleasure. Today these works constitute an estimable addition to British crime fiction.

After his 'prentice pastiche mystery, *Death at Swaythling Court* (1926), a rural English country house tale set in the highly traditional village of Fernhurst Parva, Stewart published another, superior country house affair, *The Dangerfield Talisman* (1926), a novel about the baffling theft of a precious family heirloom, an ancient, jewel-encrusted armlet. This clever murderless tale, which likely is the one that the author told Rupert Gould he wrote in under six weeks, was praised in *The Bookman* as "continuously exciting and interesting" and in the *New York Times Book Review* as "ingeniously fitted together and, what is more, written with a deal of real literary charm." Despite its virtues, however, *The Dangerfield Talisman* is not fully characteristic of mature Connington detective fiction. The author needed a memorable series sleuth, more representative of his own forceful personality.

It was the next year, 1927, that saw "J. J. Connington" make his break to the front of the murdermongerer's pack with a third country house mystery, *Murder in the Maze*, wherein debuted as the author's great series detective the assertive and acerbic Sir Clinton Driffield, along with Sir Clinton's neighbor and "Watson," the more genial (if much less astute) Squire Wendover. In this much praised novel, Stewart's detective duo confronts some truly diabolical doings, including slayings by means of curare-tipped darts in the double-centered hedge maze at a country estate,

Whistlefield. No less a fan of the genre than T. S. Eliot praised *Murder in the Maze* for its construction ("we are provided early in the story with all the clues which guide the detective") and its liveliness ("The very idea of murder in a box hedge labyrinth does the author great credit, and he makes full use of its possibilities"). The delighted Eliot concluded that *Murder in the Maze* was "a really first-rate detective story." For his part, the critic H. C. Harwood declared in *The Outlook* that with the publication of *Murder in the Maze* Connington demanded and deserved "comparison with the masters." "Buy, borrow, or—anyhow get hold of it," he amusingly advised. Two decades later, in his 1946 critical essay "The Grandest Game in the World," the great locked room detective novelist John Dickson Carr echoed Eliot's assessment of the novel's virtuoso setting, writing: "These 1920s . . . thronged with sheer brains. What would be one of the best possible settings for violent death? J. J. Connington found the answer, with *Murder in the Maze.*" Certainly in retrospect *Murder in the Maze* stands as one of the finest English country house mysteries of the 1920s, cleverly yet fairly clued, imaginatively detailed and often grimly suspenseful. As the great American true crime writer Edmund Lester Pearson noted in his review of *Murder in the Maze* in *The Outlook*, this Connington novel had everything that one could desire in a detective story: "A shrubbery maze, a hot day, and somebody potting at you with an air gun loaded with darts covered with a deadly South-American arrow-poison—*there* is a situation to wheedle two dollars out of anybody's pocket."[3]

Staying with what had for him worked so well, Stewart the same year produced yet another country house mystery, *Tragedy at Ravensthorpe*, an ingenious tale of murders and thefts at the ancestral home of the Chacewaters, old family friends of Sir Clinton Driffield. There is much clever matter in *Ravensthorpe*. Especially fascinating is the authors inspired integration of faerie folklore into his plot. Stewart, who had a lifelong—though skeptical—interest

---

[3] Potential purchasers of *Murder in the Maze* should keep in mind that $2 in 1927 is worth over $26 today!

in paranormal phenomena, probably was inspired in this instance by the recent hubbub over the Cottingley Faeries photographs that in the early 1920s had famously duped, among other individuals, Arthur Conan Doyle.[4] As with *Murder in the Maze*, critics raved this new Connington mystery. In the *Spectator*, for example, a reviewer hailed *Tragedy at Ravensthorpe* in the strongest terms, declaring of the novel: "This is more than a good detective tale. Alike in plot, characterization, and literary style, it is a work of art."

In 1928 there appeared two additional Sir Clinton Driffield detective novels, *Mystery at Lynden Sands* and *The Case with Nine Solutions*. Once again there was great praise for the latest Conningtons. H. C. Harwood, a critic who, as we have seen, had so much admired *Murder in the Maze*, opined of *Mystery at Lynden Sands* that it "may just fail of being the detective story of the century," while in the United States author and book reviewer Frederic F. Van de Water expressed nearly as high an opinion of *The Case with Nine Solutions*. "This book is a thoroughbred of a distinguished lineage that runs back to 'The Gold Bug' of [Edgar Allan] Poe," he avowed. "It represents the highest type of detective fiction." In both of these Connington novels, Stewart moved away from his customary country house milieu, setting *Lynden Sands* at a fashionable beach resort and *Nine Solutions* at a scientific

---

[4] In a 1920 article in *The Strand Magazine* Arthur Conan Doyle endorsed as real prank photographs of purported fairies taken by two English girls in the garden of a house in the village of Cottingley. In the aftermath of the Great War Doyle had become a fervent believer in Spiritualism and other paranormal phenomena. Especially embarrassing to Doyle's admirers today, Doyle also published *The Coming of the Faeries* (1922), wherein he argued that these mystical creatures genuinely existed. "When the spirits came in, the common sense oozed out," Stewart once wrote bluntly to his friend Rupert Gould of the creator of Sherlock Holmes. Like Gould, however, Stewart had an intense interest in the subject of the Loch Ness Monster, believing that he, his wife and daughter had cited a large marine creature of some sort in Loch Ness in 1935. A year earlier Gould had authored *The Loch Ness Monster and Others*, and it was this book which led Stewart, after he made his "Nessie" sighting, to initiate correspondence with Gould.

research institute. *Nine Solutions* is of particular interest today, I think, for its relatively frank sexual subject matter and its modern urban setting among science professionals, which rather resembles the locales found in P. D. James' classic detective novels *A Mind to Murder* (1963) and *Shroud for a Nightingale* (1971).

By the end of the decade of the 1920s, the critical reputation of "J. J. Connington" had achieved enviable heights indeed. At this time Stewart became one of the charter members of the Detection Club, an assemblage of the finest writers of British detective fiction that included, among other distinguished individuals, Agatha Christie, Dorothy L. Sayers and G. K. Chesterton. Certainly Victor Gollancz, the British publisher of the J. J. Connington mysteries, did not stint praise for the author, informing readers that "J. J. Connington is now established as, in the opinion of many, the greatest living master of the story of pure detection. He is one of those who, discarding all the superfluities, has made of deductive fiction a genuine minor art, with its own laws and its own conventions."

Such warm praise for J. J. Connington makes it all the more surprising that at this juncture the esteemed author tinkered with his successful formula by dispensing with his original series detective. In the fifth Clinton Driffield detective novel, *Nemesis at Raynham Parva* (1929), Alfred Walter Stewart, rather like Arthur Conan Doyle before him, seemed with a dramatic dénouement to have devised his popular series detective's permanent exit from the fictional stage (read it and see for yourself). The next two Connington detective novels, *The Eye in the Museum* (1929) and *The Two Tickets Puzzle* (1930), have a different series detective, Superintendent Ross, a rather dull dog of a policeman. While both these mysteries are competently done—the railway material in *The Two Tickets Puzzle* is particularly effective and should have appeal today—the presence of Sir Clinton Driffield (no superfluity he!) is missed.

Probably Stewart detected that the public minded the absence of the brilliant and biting Sir Clinton, for the Chief Constable—accompanied, naturally, by his friend Squire Wendover—triumphantly returned in 1931 in *The Boathouse Riddle*, another well-constructed criminous country house affair. Later in the year came *The Sweepstake Murders*, which boasts the perennially popular tontine multiple murder plot, in this case a rapid succession of puzzling suspicious deaths afflicting the members of a sweepstake syndicate that has just won nearly 250,000 pounds.[5] Adding piquancy to this plot is the fact that Wendover is one of the imperiled syndicate members. Altogether the novel is, as the late Jacques Barzun and his colleague Wendell Hertig Taylor put it in *A Catalogue of Crime* (1971/1989), their magisterial survey of detective fiction, "one of Connington's best conceptions."

Stewart's productivity as a fiction writer slowed in the 1930s, so that, barring the year 1938, at most only one new Connington appeared annually (because of the onset of serious health maladies, Stewart was unable to publish any Connington novel in 1936). However, in 1932 Stewart produced one of the best Connington mysteries, *The Castleford Conundrum*. A classic country house detective novel, Castleford introduces to readers Stewart's most delightfully unpleasant set of greedy relations and one of his most deserving murderees, Winifred Castleford. Stewart also fashions a wonderfully rich puzzle plot, full of meaty material clues for the reader's delectation. *Castleford* presented critics with no conundrum over its quality. "In *The Castleford Conundrum* Mr. Connington goes to work like an accomplished chess-player. The moves in the games his detectives are called on to play are a delight to watch," raved the reviewer for the *Sunday Times*, adding that "the clues would have rejoiced Mr. Holmes' heart." For its part, the *Spectator* concurred in the *Sunday Times'* assessment of the novel's masterfully-constructed plot: "Few detective stories show such sound reasoning as that by which the Chief Constable brings the crime home to the culprit." Additionally, E. C. Bentley, much

---

[5] A tontine is a financial arrangement wherein shareowners in a common fund receive annuities that increase in value with the death of each participant, with the entire amount of the fund going to the last survivor. The impetus that the tontine provided to the deadly creative imaginations of Golden Age mystery writers should be sufficiently obvious.

admired himself as the author of the landmark detective novel *Trent's Last Case*, took time to praise Connington's purely literary virtues, noting: "Mr. Connington has never written better, or drawn characters more full of life."

With *Tom Tiddler's Island* in 1933 Stewart produced a different sort of Connington, a criminal gang mystery in the rather more breathless style of such hugely popular English thriller writers as Sapper, Sax Rohmer, John Buchan and Edgar Wallace (in violation of the strict detective fiction rules of Ronald Knox, there is even a secret passage in the novel). Detailing the startling discoveries made by a newlywed couple honeymooning on a remote Scottish island, *Tom Tiddler's Island* is an atmospheric and entertaining tale, though it is not as mentally stimulating for armchair sleuths as Stewart's true detective novels. The title, incidentally, refers to an ancient British children's game, "Tom Tiddler's Ground," in which one child tries to hold a height against other children.

After his fictional Scottish excursion into thrillerdom, Stewart returned the next year to his English country house roots with *The Ha-Ha Case* (1934), his last masterwork in this classic mystery setting. (For elucidation of non-British readers, a ha-ha is a sunken wall, placed so to delineate property boundaries while not obstructing views.) Although *The Ha-Ha Case* is not set in Scotland, Stewart drew inspiration for the novel from a notorious Scottish true crime, the 1893 Ardlamont murder case. From the facts of the Ardlamont affair Stewart drew several of the key characters in *The Ha-Ha Case*, as well as the circumstances of the novel's murder (a shooting "accident" while hunting), though he added complications that take the tale in a new direction.[6]

---

[6] At Ardlamont, a large country estate in Argyll, Cecil Hambrough died from a gunshot wound while hunting. Cecil's tutor, Alfred John Monson, and another man, both of whom were out hunting with Cecil, claimed that Cecil had accidentally shot himself; but Monson was arrested and tried for Cecil's murder. The verdict delivered was "not proven," but Monson was then—and is today—considered almost certainly to have been guilty of the murder. On the Ardlamont case, see William Roughead, *Classic Crimes* (1951; repr., New York: New York Review Books Classics, 2000), 378-464.

In newspaper reviews both Dorothy L. Sayers and "Francis Iles" (crime novelist Anthony Berkeley Cox) highly praised this latest mystery by "The Clever Mr. Connington," as he was now dubbed on book jackets by his new English publisher, Hodder and Stoughton. Sayers particularly noted the effective characterization in *The Ha-Ha Case*: "There is no need to say that Mr. Connington has given us a sound and interesting plot, very carefully and ingeniously worked out. In addition, there are the three portraits of the three brothers, cleverly and rather subtly characterised, of the [governess], and of Inspector Hinton, whose admirable qualities are counteracted by that besetting sin of the man who has made his own way: a jealousy of delegating responsibility." The reviewer for the *Times Literary Supplement* detected signs that the sardonic Sir Clinton Driffield had begun mellowing with age: "Those who have never really liked Sir Clinton's perhaps excessively soldierly manner will be surprised to find that he makes his discovery not only by the pure light of intelligence, but partly as a reward for amiability and tact, qualities in which the Inspector [Hinton] was strikingly deficient." This is true enough, although the classic Sir Clinton emerges a number of times in the novel, as in his subtly sarcastic recurrent backhanded praise of Inspector Hinton: "He writes a first class report."

Clinton Driffield returned the next year in the detective novel *In Whose Dim Shadow* (1935), a tale set in a recently erected English suburb, the denizens of which seem to have committed an impressive number of indiscretions, including sexual ones. The intriguing title of the British edition of the novel is drawn from a poem by the British historian Thomas Babington Macaulay: "Those trees in whose dim shadow/The ghastly priest doth reign/The priest who slew the slayer/And shall himself be slain." Stewart's puzzle plot in *In Whose Dim Shadow* is well-clued and compelling, the kicker of a closing paragraph is a classic of its kind and, additionally, the author paints some excellent character portraits. I fully concur in the *Sunday Times* assessment of the tale: "Quiet domestic murder, full of the neatest detective points. . . . These [characters] are not the detective's stock figures, but fully realised human beings."[7]

Uncharacteristically for Stewart, nearly twenty months elapsed between the publication of *In Whose Dim Shadow* and his next book, *A Minor Operation* (1937). The reason for the author's delay in production was the onset in 1935-36 of the afflictions of cataracts and heart disease (Stewart ultimately succumbed to heart disease in 1947). Despite the grave health complications that beset him at this time, Stewart in late 1936 was able to complete *A Minor Operation*, a first-rate Clinton Driffield story of murder and a most baffling disappearance. A *Times Literary Supplement* reviewer found that *A Minor Operation* treated the reader "to exactly the right mixture of mystification and clue" and that, in addition to its impressive construction, the novel boasted "character-drawing above the average" for a detective novel.

Alfred Stewart's final eight mysteries, which appeared between 1938 and 1947, the year of the author's death, are, on the whole, a somewhat weaker group of tales than the sixteen that appeared between 1926 and 1937, yet they are not without interest. In 1938 Stewart for the last time managed to publish two detective novels, *Truth Comes Limping* and *For Murder Will Speak*. The latter tale is much the superior of the two, having an interesting suburban setting and a bevy of female characters found to have motives when a contemptible philandering businessman meets with foul play. Sexual neurosis plays a major role in *For Murder Will Speak*, the

---

[7] For the genesis of the title, see Macaulay's "The Battle of the Lake Regillus," from his narrative poem collection *Lays of Ancient Rome*. In this poem Macaulay alludes to the ancient cult of Diana Nemorensis, which elevated its priests through trial by combat. Study of the practices of the Diana Nemorensis cult influenced Sir James George Frazer's cultural interpretation of religion in his most renowned work, *The Golden Bough: A Study in Magic and Religion*. As with *Tom Tiddler's Island* and *The Ha-Ha Case* the title *In Whose Dim Shadow* proved too esoteric for Connington's American publishers, Little, Brown and Co., who altered it to the more prosaic *The Tau Cross Mystery*.

ever-thorough Stewart obviously having made a study of the subject when writing the novel. The somewhat squeamish reviewer for *Scribner's Magazine* considered the subject matter of *For Murder Will Speak* "rather unsavory at times," yet this individual conceded that the novel nevertheless made "first-class reading for those who enjoy a good puzzle intricately worked out." "Judge Lynch" in the *Saturday Review* apparently had no such moral reservations about the latest Clinton Driffield murder case, avowing simply of the novel: "They don't come any better."

Over the next couple years Stewart again sent Sir Clinton Driffield temporarily packing, replacing him with a new series detective, a brash radio personality named Mark Brand, in *The Counsellor* (1939) and *The Four Defences* (1940). The better of these two novels is *The Four Defences*, which Stewart based on another notorious British true crime case, the Alfred Rouse blazing car murder. (Rouse is believed to have fabricated his death by murdering an unknown man, placing the dead man's body in his car and setting the car on fire, in the hope that the murdered man's body would be taken for his.) Though admittedly a thinly characterized academic exercise in ratiocination, Stewart's *Four Defences* surely is also one of the most complexly plotted Golden Age detective novels ever written and should delight devotees of classical detection. Taking the Rouse blazing car affair as his theme, Stewart composes from it a stunning set of diabolically ingenious criminal variations. "This is in the cold-blooded category which . . . excites a crossword puzzle kind of interest," the reviewer for the *Times Literary Supplement* acutely noted of the novel. "Nothing in the Rouse case would prepare you for these complications upon complications. . . . What they prove is that Mr. Connington has the power of penetrating into the puzzle-corner of the brain. He leaves it dazedly wondering whether in the records of actual crime there can be any dark deed to equal this in its planned convolutions."

Sir Clinton Driffield returned to action in the remaining four detective novels in the Connington oeuvre, *The Twenty-One Clues* (1941), *No Past Is Dead* (1942), *Jack-in-the-Box* (1944) and *Commonsense Is All You Need* (1947), all of which were written as

Stewart's heart disease steadily worsened and reflect to some extent his diminishing physical and mental energy. Although *The Twenty-One Clues* was inspired by the notorious Hall-Mills double murder case—probably the most publicized murder case in the United States in the 1920s—and the American critic Anthony Boucher commended *Jack-in-the-Box*, I believe the best of these later mysteries is *No Past Is Dead*, which Stewart partly based on a bizarre French true crime affair, the 1891 Achet-Lepine murder case.[8] Besides providing an interesting background for the tale, the ailing author managed some virtuoso plot twists, of the sort most associated today with that ingenious Golden Age Queen of Crime, Agatha Christie.

What Stewart with characteristic bluntness referred to as "my complete crack-up" forced his retirement from Queen's University in 1944. "I am afraid," Stewart wrote a friend, the chemist and forensic scientist F. Gerald Tryhorn, in August, 1946, eleven months before his death, "that I shall never be much use again. Very stupidly, I tried for a session to combine a full course of lecturing with angina pectoris; and ended up by establishing that the two are immiscible." He added that since retiring in 1944, he had been physically "limited to my house, since even a fifty-yard crawl brings on the usual cramps." Stewart completed his essay collection and a final novel before he died at his study desk in his Belfast home on July 1, 1947, at the age of sixty-six. When death came to the author he was busy at work, writing.

More than six decades after Alfred Walter Stewart's death, his "J. J. Connington" fiction again is available to a wider audience of classic mystery fans, rather than strictly limited to a select company of rare book collectors with deep pockets. This is fitting for an individual who was one of the finest writers of British genre fiction between the two world wars. "Heaven forfend that you should imagine I take myself for anything out of the common in

---

[8] Stewart analyzed the Achet-Lepine case in detail in "The Mystery of Chantelle," one of the best essays in his 1947 collection, *Alias J. J. Connington*.

the tec yarn stuff," Stewart once self-deprecatingly declared in a letter to Rupert Gould. Yet, as contemporary critics recognized, as a writer of detective and science fiction Stewart indeed was something out of the common. Now more modern readers can find this out for themselves. They have much good sleuthing in store.

MYSTERY AT LYNDEN SANDS

CHAPTER I
THE DEATH AT FOXHILLS

PAUL FORDINGBRIDGE, with a faintly reproachful glance at his sister, interrupted his study of the financial page of *The Times* and put the paper down on his knee. Deliberately he removed his reading-glasses; replaced them by his ordinary spectacles; and then turned to the restless figure at the window of the private sitting-room.

"Well, Jay, you seem to have something on your mind. Would it be too much to ask you to say it—whatever it is—and then let me read my paper comfortably? One can't give one's mind to a thing when there's a person at one's elbow obviously ready to break out into conversation at any moment."

Miss Fordingbridge had spent the best part of half a century in regretting her father's admiration for Herrick. "I can't see myself as Julia of the *Nightpiece*," she complained with a faint parade of modesty; and it was at her own wish that the hated name had been abbreviated to an initial in family talk.

At the sound of her brother's voice she turned away from the sea-view.

"I can't imagine why you insisted on coming to this hotel," she said, rather fretfully. "I can't stand the place. Of course, as it's just been opened, it's useless to expect everything to go like clockwork; but there seems a lot of mismanagement about it. I almost burned my hand with the hot water in my bedroom this morning—ridiculous, having tap-water as hot as that! And my letters got into the wrong pigeon-hole or something; I had to wait ever so long for them. Of course the clerk said he was sorry—but what good does that do? I don't want his sorrow. I want my letters when I ask for them."

"No doubt."

"And there was a wasp in my room when I went up there a few minutes ago. If I'd wanted a double-bedded room with a wasp as a room-mate, I would have asked for it when we booked, wouldn't I? And when I rang the bell and told them to put the thing out, the chambermaid—so it seems—was afraid of wasps. So she had to go and get hold of someone else to tackle it. And meanwhile, of course, I had to wait about until my room was made habitable. That's a nice kind of hotel!"

"Oh, it has its points," Paul Fordingbridge advanced soothingly. "One can get quite decent wine; and this chair's not uncomfortable."

"I don't sit in a chair and drink wine all day," his sister retorted, querulously. "And that jazz band downstairs is simply appalling— I can feel my ear-drums quiver whenever it starts playing."

"It amuses the children, at least. I haven't heard Stanley or Cressida complaining about it yet; and they seem to dance most of the time in the evenings."

"So like the younger generation! They get married—and they dance. And that's almost all you can say about them."

"Oh, no. Let's be fair," her brother corrected her mildly. "They both play bridge a good deal; and Cressida's not bad at golf. I can't say, taking her over all, that I'm ashamed of her as a niece. And Stanley's a great improvement on her first husband—that fellow Staveley."

Miss Fordingbridge made a gesture of irritation.

"Oh, of course, everything's simply splendid, by your way of it. A fascinating niece, a nice-looking nephew-in-law, and a wonderful hotel to live in for a month or so; what more could one want? The only thing I can't understand is what this family party is doing in an hotel just now, when we've got Foxhills standing empty almost within a stone's-throw. You know how I hate hotels; and yet you won't reopen Foxhills and let us live there. What's the use in coming to Lynden Sands at all, if we don't stay at our own house and get privacy at least?"

Her brother's brows contracted slightly.

"Foxhills isn't going to be reopened. You know quite well the size of staff you'd need to run it properly; and I don't propose to pay on that scale merely in order to stay at Foxhills for a month or so and then shut it up again. Besides, Jay, this new golf-course has changed things a bit. I'm trying to let Foxhills; and if I got a tenant, we might have to clear out of the place before we'd got well settled down in it. This hotel and the new course between them are going to make Lynden Sands more popular before long. There's a fair chance of getting Foxhills leased."

Miss Fordingbridge was manifestly taken aback by this information.

"You're trying to let Foxhills—our old house? Why, it isn't yours to let! It belongs to Derek."

Paul Fordingbridge seemed to be flicked on the raw. There was a certain asperity in his tone as he replied.

"Whether it *belongs* to Derek or merely *belonged* to Derek is an open question. He hasn't turned up to let us decide the point one way or the other."

He glanced at his sister's face and apparently read something in her expression, for he continued with a faint rasp in his tone.

"I thought I'd made the position clear enough to you already, but, as you don't seem to grasp it even yet, I'll go over it once more. But this must be the last time, Jay. I'm really tired of making the thing clear to you when you evidently won't take the trouble to understand how I'm placed."

He paused for a moment, as though to put his facts in order before stating his case.

"Since this is the last time I'm going to discuss the thing with you, I'll go right back to the beginning; and you'll be good enough to give me your attention, Jay. I'm tired of the subject; and specially tired of explaining it to you, as you never listen.

"Under our father's will, the major part of the family property—including the Foxhills estate—went to his eldest son, brother John, on a life-tenancy. After John died, it was all to go without restrictions to the next eldest—brother Rufus, out in Australia—or to his son, Derek. Failing Derek, it was to go to the next eldest—Cressida's father; or, if he died first, then to Cressida. If she didn't live to come into it, then it fell to my share; and, finally, if we all died off, then you were to get it. Of course, he'd left each of us enough to keep us going comfortably in any case. Foxhills and the investments that went along with it were extras, over and above that. You see that part clearly enough, I suppose?"

Miss Fordingbridge nodded; but it seemed doubtful if she had given the narrative much attention. She appeared to be treasuring up some thought which made her brother's statement of little real interest to her. Paul glanced again at her face and seemed to hesitate slightly. He decided to continue.

"None of us had seen Derek until just before the war. Then he came to Foxhills for a while with us. You took to him more than I did. He seemed to me a very ordinary young fellow. Meanwhile, John came into his life-rent of the estate and the rest of the property, after our father died.

"Then came the war. Derek had a commission in some Australian regiment. We saw little of him, naturally. I wish we'd seen less. He brought home that friend of his, Nick Staveley, on leave; and he got round Cressida and married her—the worst day's work our family's done for a good while. Lucky for her that he got wiped out, that day when Derek was captured."

Miss Fordingbridge winced at the name of her niece's first husband. Even after all these years, the very thought of Staveley had its sting for the family. Apart from this, however, she showed no interest in her brother's narrative, which was obviously an old tale to her, and important only as it concerned her brother's motives of action.

"Meanwhile, Rufus had a paralytic stroke out in Australia and died. Then, a little later, John got killed in that motor accident. Under the will, that left Derek in possession of the estate. I can't claim that I foresaw that exact state of affairs; but I'd been afraid of something of the sort happening. During the war, things needed a careful eye on them; and I didn't care to see Foxhills in the hands of lawyers. So before Derek went off to the Front, I got him to give me a power of attorney to deal with all his affairs. Are you listening, Jay?"

Miss Fordingbridge nodded absently. She still had the air of reserving a surprise for her brother.

"You know what happened next," Paul Fordingbridge went on. "Derek was captured and sent to Clausthal. Almost immediately, he got away from there, and nearly scraped over the Dutch frontier. The Germans caught him there; and as a result he was sent on to Fort 9, at Ingolstadt. We know he got away from there—it must have been almost immediately, as we got no letters from him—and after that all trace of him was lost. Whether he got shot in trying to get over the frontier, or whether he lost his memory, or what happened to him, no one can tell. He's vanished, so far as we're concerned."

Miss Fordingbridge repressed a faint smile, evidently with some difficulty; but her brother failed to notice the fleeting expression on her face.

"Now I want you to see the position that I'm left in, with all this muddle," he went on. "Derek may be alive, or he may be dead, for all we know. If he's alive, then Foxhills belongs to him; and, until we have evidence of his death, that's the state of affairs. Meanwhile, with his power of attorney, I have to manage things, fix up the investments, get the best return I can on his money, and look after the up-keep of Foxhills. I daresay we could go to the Courts and ask leave to presume his death; but I think it's fairer to wait a while yet, before doing anything in that direction. He might turn up, in spite of everything."

It was evident from his tone that he thought this contingency a most unlikely one, though not altogether impossible.

"In any case, I've got to do the best I can for his interests. That's why I propose to let Foxhills if I can find someone to take it on a short lease. We can't afford to let Derek's property stand idle—if it is his property. Besides, a place of that size is far better occupied. It's more or less all right just now, with old Peter Hay looking after it and living in the cottage; but it would be far better if we had someone living there permanently and keeping it heated. I'm afraid of dry-rot setting in sometime or other. Now, do you understand the state of affairs, Jay? Can't you see that's the best course to take?"

Miss Fordingbridge paid no attention to either query.

"I've listened to you," she said, perhaps with a slight lapse from strict accuracy, "and now it's your turn to listen to me, Paul. It's no use your trying to persuade me that there's any doubt about Derek at all. I know perfectly well he's alive."

Paul Fordingbridge made no effort to restrain his involuntary gesture of annoyance. Quite evidently he saw what was coming.

"Now, Julia, it's no use bringing up this stuff of yours again. I've told you fifty times already that I don't believe it in the slightest. Since you went in for this table-turning, and spirit-rapping, and planchette, and all the rest of the wretched business, you've hardly been sane on the subject. I daresay you adored Derek when he was here. No doubt you think you're justified in all this *séance* business, trying to get in touch with him, and the rest of it. But frankly, it leaves me as it leaves every other sensible person—completely sceptical."

Miss Fordingbridge was evidently well-accustomed to this kind of reception when she broached the topic. She ignored her brother's protest and continued as though he had not interrupted her.

"I remember quite well how you laughed at me when I came back from that wonderful *séance* and told you how I had been assured that Derek was still alive. That was five years ago, but I can recall it perfectly. And I know it was true. And if you had been there yourself, and had heard it with your own ears, you'd have believed it too. You couldn't have disbelieved. It was far too convincing. After the medium went into a trance, the control spoke to me. And it told me all about Derek—what regiment he'd been in; when he was captured; how he'd disappeared; how anxious I'd been about him; and how we'd lost all trace of him. You'd have been quite convinced yourself, if you'd been there and heard it all."

"I *am* quite convinced," her brother replied drily. "That's to say I'm quite convinced that they'd looked up Derek's name in the casualty lists and got together all the data they could gather beforehand. I expect you gave away a good deal yourself by your questions, too. You're about the easiest person to pump, if one goes about it in the right way."

Miss Fordingbridge smiled in a superior fashion, as though she knew that she held a trump card still.

"Would it convince you if I said that I'd *seen* Derek?"

"Some more of their confounded mummery? No, it wouldn't convince me. A child could deceive you, Jay. You *want* to be deceived. You can't bear the idea that Derek's dead—that's what vitiates this stuff that you dignify by the name of evidence."

"Vulgar abuse never hurts a spiritualist. We're used to it," Miss Fordingbridge replied with simple dignity. "But you're wrong as usual, Paul. It wasn't at a *séance* that I saw Derek. It was here, at Lynden Sands. And it was last night."

From the expression on her brother's face it was clear that he hardly knew how to take this news.

"You saw him here, last night? In a dream, I suppose?"

"No, not in a dream. I met him by appointment down at that rock on the beach—the one we used to call Neptune's Seat. And I saw him close enough to make no mistake—as close as I am to you this moment. And I talked to him, too. It's Derek; there's no doubt about it."

Paul Fordingbridge was evidently taken aback. This latest tale of his sister's seemed to have something more solid behind it than her earlier ventures.

"You said nothing to me about this. Why was that?"

Miss Fordingbridge recognised that she had scored a point and had startled her brother out of his usual scepticism. She had her answer ready.

"Naturally you'd hardly expect me to discuss a thing like that over the breakfast-table, with half-a-hundred total strangers sitting round and craning their necks so as to hear better? If you will insist on staying at hotels, you must put up with the results. This is the first time I've been alone with you since I met him."

Paul Fordingbridge acknowledged the justice of her view with a nod.

"Quite so," he admitted. "And you had a talk with this fellow, had you?"

Miss Fordingbridge's temper showed unmistakably in her tone as she replied.

"Kindly don't call Derek 'this fellow,' if you please. It's Derek himself. He talked to me for quite a long time—all about things that had happened at Foxhills when he was here before the War, and other things that happened at the times he was home on leave. And part of the time he told me about Clausthal and Fort 9, too."

Her brother's scepticism again made itself evident.

"Plenty of people were in Fort 9 and at Clausthal besides Derek. That proves nothing."

"Well, then, he mentioned a whole lot of little things as well. He reminded me of how Cressida dropped her bouquet when she was signing the register after her wedding. And he remembered which wedding march they played then."

"Almost anyone in Lynden Sands could have told him that."

Miss Fordingbridge reflected for a moment or two, evidently searching her memory for some crucial piece of evidence.

"He remembered that we used to bring up some of the old port from Bin 73 every time he went off to the Front. He said often he wished he could have had some of it just before zero hour."

Paul Fordingbridge shook his head.

"One of the servants might have mentioned that in the village and he could have got hold of it. If you've nothing better than this sort of tittle-tattle to prove it's Derek, it won't go far."

He reflected for a moment, then he asked:

"You recognised his face, of course?"

A flicker of repulsion crossed his sister's features.

"I saw his face," she said. "Paul, he's horribly disfigured, poor boy. A shell-burst, or something. It's dreadful. If I hadn't known it was Derek, I'd hardly have recognised him. And he was so good-looking, in the old days. But I know it's Derek. I'm quite sure of it. That medium's control never makes a mistake. If Derek had passed over, she'd have found him and made him speak to me at that *séance*. But she couldn't. And now he's come back in the flesh, it shows there is something in spiritualism, in spite of all your sneers. You'll have to admit it, Paul."

Her words had evidently started a fresh train of thought in her brother's mind.

"Did you recognise his voice?" he demanded.

Miss Fordingbridge seemed to make an effort to recall the tones she had heard:

"It was Derek's voice, of course," she said, with a faint hesitation in her manner. "Of course, it wasn't quite the voice I'd been expecting. His mouth was hurt in those awful wounds he got. And his tongue was damaged, too; so his voice isn't the same as it used to be. It's husky instead of clear; and he has difficulty in saying some words, I noticed. But at times I could quite well imagine it was Derek speaking just as he used to do, with that Australian twang of his that we used to tease him about."

"Ah, he has the twang, has he?"

"Of course he has. Derek couldn't help having it, could he, when he was brought up in Australia until he was quite grown-up? Last night he laughed over the way we used to chaff him about his accent."

"Anything more about him that you can remember?"

"He's been dreadfully hurt. Two of his fingers were blown off his right hand. It gave me such a start when he shook hands with me."

Paul Fordingbridge seemed to reflect for a moment or two on the information he had acquired.

"H'm!" he said at last, "It'll be difficult to establish his identity; that's clear. Face unrecognisable owing to wounds; voice altered, ditto; two fingers gone on right hand, so his writing won't be identifiable. If only we had taken Derek's fingerprints, we'd have had some sort of proof. As it is, there's very little to go on."

Miss Fordingbridge listened scornfully to this catalogue.

"So that's all the thanks you give Derek for suffering so horribly for us all in the war?"

"Always assuming that this friend of yours is Derek. Don't you understand that I can't take a thing of this sort on trust? I'm in charge of Derek's property—assuming that he's still alive, I can't hand it over to the first claimant who comes along, and then, if Derek himself turns up, excuse myself by saying that the first fellow had a plausible yarn to tell. I must have real proof. That's simply plain honesty, in my position. And real proof's going to be mighty hard to get, if you ask me, Jay. You must see that, surely."

"It *is* Derek," Miss Fordingbridge repeated, obstinately. "Do you think I can't recognise my own nephew, when he's able to tell me all sorts of things that only we in the family could know?"

Her brother regarded her rather ruefully.

"I believe you'd go into the witness-box and take your oath that it's Derek," he said, gloomily. "You'd made up your mind that Derek was coming back sooner or later; and now you're prepared to recognise anything down to a chimpanzee as your long-lost nephew, rather than admit you're wrong. Damn this spiritualism of yours! It's at the root of all the trouble. It's led you to expect Derek; and you mean to have a Derek of some sort."

He paused for a moment, as though following out a train of thought; then he added:

"And it's quite on the cards that if it ever came before a jury, some chuckleheads would take your word for it. 'Sure to know her nephew,' and all that sort of stuff. They don't know your little fads."

Miss Fordingbridge glanced up at the note of trouble in her brother's voice.

"I can't see why you're trying to throw doubt on the thing, Paul. You haven't seen Derek; I have. And yet you don't wait to see him yourself. You come straight out with a denial that it is Derek. And you say I've got a preconceived idea about the affair. It seems to me that you're the one with a preconceived notion. One would think you'd made up your mind already on the subject."

Paul Fordingbridge acknowledged the counterthrust.

"There's something in what you say, perhaps, Jay. But you must admit the whole business is a trifle unexpected. It's hardly taking the line one might expect, if everything were square and above-board. Let's assume that it *is* Derek, and then you'll see what a lot's left unexplained so far. First of all, it's years since the war. Why hasn't he turned up before now? That's a strange affair, surely. Then, when he does reappear, why doesn't he come to me first of all? I'm the person he left in charge of his affairs, and I should think his first step would be to communicate with me. But no, he comes down here unannounced; and he fixes up some sort of clandestine meeting with you. That's a rum go, to my mind. And there's more than that in it. He meets you last night and has a talk with you; but he doesn't suggest coming to see me. Or did he give you any message for me?"

"He didn't, as it happens. But you seem to think we were talking as if it was all a matter of business, Paul. It was a shock to me to have him back again. And I daresay I did most of the talking, and he hadn't time to give me any message for you. I was very shaken up by it all, and he was so kind to me."

Her brother seemed to find little pleasure in the picture which she drew.

"Yes, I expect you did most of the talking, Jay. He wouldn't interrupt you much. But, aside from all that, it's getting near lunch-time now. He's had the whole morning to break into the family circle; and yet he hasn't come near. From what I remember of him, shyness wasn't one of his defects. Whatever you may think about it, that seems to me a bit fishy. Damned strange in fact. I'm not taking up any definite stand in the matter; but there are things that need a bit of explaining."

Miss Fordingbridge seemed for a moment to be staggered by her brother's analysis; but she recovered herself almost at once and fastened upon his last point.

"Didn't I tell you that he was horribly disfigured? Even in the moonlight he was a dreadful sight. Do you expect him to come marching into this hotel in broad daylight this morning, so that everyone can stare at him? You really have very little common sense, Paul. I think it shows that he wants to spare us all the tittle-tattle he can. You know what hotels are, and how the people in them are simply on the look-out for something to chatter about. And when they got a chance like this—missing heir returns, and so forth—you can guess for yourself what it would be like. We'd have no life of it, with people staring at us and whispering behind our backs as we passed. And I think Derek has shown a great deal of tact and common sense in behaving as he has done. Naturally he asked to see me first. He knows how fond of him I was."

Her brother seemed to consider this fresh view of the affair for a longer time than he had devoted to any of her other statements. At last he shook his head doubtfully.

"It might be as you say, of course," he conceded grudgingly. "We must wait and see what turns up. But you can take it from me, Jay, that I shan't be satisfied unless I get something a good deal better in the way of evidence. It looks very like a parcel from a shop in Queer Street, so far as it's gone."

Miss Fordingbridge seemed content to drop that side of the matter, at least for the time. But she had something further to say.

"Of course you'll drop this absurd idea of letting Foxhills now, Paul?"

Her brother seemed irritated by this fresh turn given to their conversation.

"Why should I? I've told you often enough that it's my business to do the best I can for Derek; and the rent of Foxhills would be worth having, even if Derek did come back. You're not suggesting that he should stay there, are you? It's far too big a place for a single man, even if he wanted to live down here at Lynden Sands."

Miss Fordingbridge was plainly put out by this suggestion.

"Of course he would stay there. When he went away, didn't I keep his rooms in order, just as he left them? He could go back to-morrow and find his study exactly as it was when he left us. Everything's there just as it used to be: his books, his pipes, his old diary, his ashtrays—everything. When we shut up Foxhills, I wanted to have everything ready so that when he came back from the war he'd find everything in its usual place. He could walk straight in and feel that things were just the same and that we hadn't forgotten him. And now you want to let Foxhills just at the moment when he comes back again—rob the poor boy of the only place on this side of the world that he can call a home. I won't have it, Paul!"

"Whether you have it or haven't it, Jay, is a matter of total indifference. Until the power of attorney is revoked, I shall do exactly as seems best to me; and letting Foxhills is one of the things I shall certainly do."

"But I know Derek doesn't want it," cried Miss Fordingbridge. "Last night I told him all about how I'd kept his things for him so carefully; and if you'd seen how touched the poor boy was! He said it was the thing that had touched him most. And he was ever so grateful to me. And now you propose to spoil it all, after those years!"

She switched off on to another subject.

"And what do you propose to do about poor old Peter Hay? If you let Foxhills, it won't need a caretaker; and I suppose you'll turn poor Peter adrift? And, if you remember, Peter was one of the people that Derek liked best when he was here before. He was always going about with Peter, and he said he found him companionable. And he's learned a lot from Peter about beasts and so on—all new to him—since he came from Australia. But I suppose Peter's to go at a week's notice? That's a nice way to serve people."

Her brother seemed to consider things before replying.

"I'll try to find something for Peter. You're quite right, Jay. I didn't mean to turn Peter adrift, though. If I have to sack him from the caretaker business, I'll pay him out of my own pocket till something else turns up. Peter's too decent a man to let down, especially after he's been at Foxhills all his life. If it had been that last valet we had—that fellow Aird—I'd never have thought twice about throwing him out at a day's notice. But you can trust me to look after Peter."

Miss Fordingbridge seemed slightly mollified by this concession on her brother's part; but she stuck to her main point.

"Well, you can't let Foxhills in any case. I won't have it!"

But apparently her brother had wearied of argument, for he made no reply.

"I shall be going up to Foxhills some time to-day. I always go up to dust Derek's rooms, you know," she continued.

"What on earth do you do that for?" her brother demanded in an exasperated tone. "Are you training for a housemaid's place? I hear there's a shortage in that line, but you hardly seem to be a useful kind of recruit, Jay."

"I've always looked after Derek's rooms. When he was here at Foxhills in the old days, I never allowed anyone to lay a finger on his study. I knew just how he liked his things kept, and I wouldn't have maids fussing round, displacing everything."

"Oh, of course you doted on the boy," her brother retorted. "But it seems a bit unnecessary at this time of day."

"Unnecessary? Just when Derek has come back?"

Paul Fordingbridge made no attempt to conceal his gesture of annoyance; but he refrained from reopening the sore subject.

"Well, if you come across Peter, you can send him down to me. I haven't seen him since we came here, and I may as well have a talk about things. Probably there are one or two repairs that need considering. Perhaps you could go round by his cottage and make sure of getting hold of him."

Miss Fordingbridge nodded her assent.

"I'll be quite glad to have a talk with Peter. He'll be so delighted to know that Derek's back at last. It was only the other day that we were talking about Derek together. Peter thinks there's no one like him."

"All the more reason for saying nothing, then. If it turns out that it isn't Derek, it would disappoint Peter badly if you'd raised his hopes."

Then, seeing that his scepticism had again roused his sister's temper, he added hastily:

"By the way, how's Peter keeping? Has he had any more of these turns of his—apoplexy, wasn't it?"

"He seemed to be quite well when I saw him the other day. Of course, he's got to be careful and not excite himself; but he seemed to me as if he'd quite got over the slight attack he'd had in the spring."

"Still got his old squirrel?"

"It's still there. And the rest of the menagerie too. He insisted on showing me them all, and of course I had to pretend to be frightfully interested. Poor old man, they're all he has now, since his wife died. It would be very lonely for him up there, with no one within a mile of him. His birds and things are great company for him, he says."

Paul Fordingbridge seemed relieved that the conversation was edging away from the dangerous subject. He led it still further out of the zone.

"Have you see Cressida and Stanley this morning? They'd finished breakfast and gone out before I came on the scene."

"I think they were going to play golf. They ought to be back presently."

She went to the window and gazed out for a moment or two without speaking. Her brother took up *The Times* and resumed his study of the share market, with evident relief.

"This hotel spoils Lynden Sands," Miss Fordingbridge broke out after a short silence. "It comes right into the view from the front of Foxhills—great staring building! And, wherever you go along the bay, you see this monstrosity glaring in the middle of the view. It'll ruin the place. And it'll give the villagers all sorts of notions, too. Visitors always spoil a small village."

Her brother made no reply, and when she halted in her complaints he rustled his newspaper clumsily in an obvious effort to discourage further conversation. Just then a knock at the door was heard.

"Come in!" Miss Fordingbridge ordered.

A page-boy appeared.

"Message on the telephone for, you, sir."

Paul Fordingbridge rose reluctantly and left the room. He was absent for a very short time; and when he came back his sister could see that he was disturbed.

"That was a message from the doctor. It seems poor old Peter's gone."

"Gone? Do you mean anything's happened to him?"

"He's had another attack—some time in the night or earlier. They didn't find out about it until the morning. The doctor's just been up at the cottage, so there's no doubt about it."

"Poor Peter! He looked so well when I saw him the other day. One would have thought he'd live to see eighty. This will be a dreadful disappointment for Derek. He was so fond of the old man."

She paused for a moment, as though she could hardly believe the news.

"Are you sure there's no mistake, Paul?"

"None whatever. It was the doctor himself who rang up. Peter had no relations, you know, so naturally we'll need to look after things. He served us well, Jay."

"I remember when he came to Foxhills, and that's years and years ago. The place won't seem quite the same without him. Did the doctor tell you anything about it, Paul?"

"No details. He just rung up to let us know, he said, as we seemed to be the only people who had any real connection with the old boy. Now I come to think of it, that sawbones seemed a bit stuffy over something. A bit abrupt in his manner over the 'phone. He's a new man, apparently. I didn't know his name. Perhaps that was what put him out."

CHAPTER II
A BUS-DRIVER'S HOLIDAY

Sir Clinton Driffield, after a careful examination of the lie, deliberately put down a long putt on the last green of the Lynden Sands course. His opponent, Stanley Fleetwood, stooped and picked up his own ball.

"Your hole and match," he said, handing his putter back to his caddie.

Sir Clinton nodded.

"Thanks for the game," he said. "We seem to be fairly even. Much more fun when the thing's in doubt up to the last green. Yes, you might clean 'em," he added in reply to his caddie's inquiry. "I shan't want them until to-morrow."

A girl had been sitting on one of the seats overlooking the green; and, as the caddie replaced the pin in the hole, she rose to her feet and came down towards the players. Stanley Fleetwood waved to her, and then, in response to her mute question, he made a gesture of defeat.

"This is Sir Clinton Driffield, Cressida," he explained, as they met.

Sir Clinton had trained himself to observe minutely without betraying that he was doing so; and he had a habit of mentally docketing the results of his scrutiny. Mannerisms were the points which he studied with most attention. As Cressida Fleetwood came slowly towards them, his apparently casual glance took in mechanically the picture of a dark-haired girl still in her twenties, slim and graceful; but his attention fastened mainly on a faint touch of shyness which added to her charm; and in the expression of her eyes

39

he believed he read something more uncommon. It seemed as
though a natural frankness had been overlaid by a tinge of mis-
trust in the world.

"I hope I didn't rob you of a game this morning by taking your
husband away, Mrs. Fleetwood," he said, as they turned up the path
leading to the hotel.

Cressida reassured him at once.

"As it happened," she explained, "I didn't feel inclined to play
to-day, so he was left at a loose end; and when you took pity on
him, I was very glad to have my conscience cleared."

"Well, it was lucky for me," Sir Clinton answered. "The friend
who's staying with me just now wouldn't come out this morning.
He strained his foot slightly yesterday. So I was left in the lurch, and I
was very fortunate in finding Mr. Fleetwood free to take me on."

They entered the grounds of the hotel, and, at a turn in the
path, Cressida Fleetwood bowed to a girl who passed their group.
The newcomer was handsome rather than pretty; and there was a
hint of hardness in her face which detracted a little from her charm.
She was dressed with a finish rather unusual at that time of day in
a golfing hotel; and her walk lacked the free swing characteristic
of the athletic English girl. Written fairly plainly on her were the
signs of a woman who has had to look after her own interests and
who has not always come out a winner in the game.

When she had passed out of earshot, Cressida turned to her
husband.

"That's the French girl I told you about, Stanley—Mme Laurent-
Desrousseaux. I found her in some difficulty or other at the hotel
desk—her English isn't quite perfect—so I helped her out a little."

Stanley Fleetwood nodded without comment; and Sir Clinton
had little difficulty in seeing that he had no desire for his wife to
extend her acquaintance with Mme Laurent-Desrousseaux. He
could not help speculating as to the cause which had brought the
Frenchwoman into this quiet backwater, where she had no amuse-
ments, apparently, and no acquaintances.

Before he had time to turn the matter over in his mind, however, his train of thought was interrupted by the appearance of a
fresh figure.

"How's the strain, squire?" he greeted the newcomer; and, as Wendover came up to the group, he introduced him to his two companions.

"I hope you enjoyed your round," said Wendover, turning to Stanley Fleetwood. "Did he manage to work off any of his special expertise on you this morning?"

"He beat me, if that's what you mean."

"H'm! He beats me usually," Wendover confessed. "I don't mind being beaten by play; but I hate to beaten by the rules."

"What do you mean, Mr. Wendover? You seem to have a grievance," Cressida asked, seeing a twinkle in Wendover's eye.

"The fact is," Wendover explained, "yesterday my ball rolled up against a large worm on the green and stopped there. I'm of a humane disposition, so I bent down to remove the worm, rather than putt across its helpless body. He objected, if you please, on the ground that one may not remove anything growing. I don't know whether it was growing or not—it looked to me remarkably well grown for a worm, and had probably passed the growing age. But, when I urged that, he simply floored me by quoting a recent decision of the Royal and Ancient on the point."

"If you play a game, you must play *that* game and not one you invent on the spur of the moment, squire," Sir Clinton warned him, with no sign of sympathy in his tone. "Ignorance of the law is no excuse."

"Hark to the chief constable!" Wendover complained. "Of course, his mind dotes on the legal aspect of things, and he's used to keeping all sorts of rules and regulations in his head. His knowledge of the laws of golf is worth a couple of strokes on his handicap on any average round."

Cressida glanced at Sir Clinton.

"Are you really a chief constable?" she asked. "Somehow you aren't like the idea I had of chief constables."

"I'm on holiday at present," Sir Clinton answered lightly; "perhaps that makes a difference. But I'm sorry to fall below your ideal—especially in my own district. If you could tell me what you miss, perhaps I could get it. What's wanted? Constabulary boots, or beetle-brows, or a note-book ready to hand, or a magnifying glass, or anything of that sort?"

"Not quite. But I thought you'd look more like an official somehow."

"Well, in a way that's a compliment. I've spent a fair part of my existence trying hard not to look like an official. I wasn't born a chief constable, you know. I was once a mere detective sort of person at the other end of the world."

"Were you really? But, then, you don't look like my idea of a detective, either!"

Sir Clinton laughed.

"I'm afraid you're hard to please, Mrs. Fleetwood. Mr. Wendover's just as bad. He's a faithful reader of the classics, and he simply can't imagine anyone going in for detective work without a steely eye and a magnifying glass. It jars on his finer feelings merely to think of a detective without either of them. The only thing that saves me is that I'm not a detective nowadays; and he salves his conscience by refusing to believe that I ever was one."

Wendover took up the challenge.

"I've only seen you at work once in the detective line," he confessed, "and I must admit I thought your methods were simply deplorable, Clinton."

"Quite right," Sir Clinton admitted: "I disappointed you badly in that Maze affair, I know. Even the success in the end hardly justified the means employed in reaching it. Let's draw a veil, eh?"

They had reached the door of the hotel, and, after a few words, Cressida and her husband went into the building.

"Nice pair they make," Wendover remarked, glancing after them as they went. "I like to see youngsters of that type. They somehow make you feel that the younger generation isn't any worse than its parents; and that it has a good deal less fuss about it, too. Reinstates one's belief in humanity, and all that sort of thing."

"Yes," Sir Clinton concurred, with a faint twinkle in his eye. "Some people one takes to instinctively. It's the manner that does it. I remember a man I once ran across—splendid fellow, charm, magnetic personality, and so on."

His voice died away, as though he had lost interest in the matter.

"Yes?" Wendover inquired, evidently feeling that the story had stopped too soon.

"He was the worst poker-sharp on the liner," Sir Clinton added gently. "Charm of manner was one of his assets, you know."

Wendover's annoyance was only half-feigned.

"You've a sordid mind, Clinton. I don't like to hear you throwing out hints about people in that way. Anyone can see that's a girl out of the common; and all you can think of in that connection is card-sharps."

Sir Clinton seemed sobered by his friend's vexation.

"You're quite right, squire," he agreed. "She's out of the common, as you say. I don't know anything about her history, but it doesn't take much to see that something's happened to her. She looks as if she'd taken the world at her own measure at first, trusted everybody. And then she got a devil of a shock one day. At least, if that isn't in her eyes, then I throw in my hand. I've seen the same expression once or twice before."

They entered the hotel and sat down in the lounge. Wendover glanced from the window across the links.

"This place will be quite good when the new course has been played over for a year or two. I shouldn't wonder if Lynden Sands became fairly popular."

Sir Clinton was about to reply when a page-boy entered the lounge and paraded slowly across it, chanting in a monotonous voice:

"Number eighty-nine! Number eighty-nine! Number eighty-nine!"

The chief constable sat up sharply and snapped his fingers to attract the page-boy's attention.

"That's the number of my room," he said to Wendover, "but I can't think of anyone who might want me. Nobody knows me in this place."

"You number eighty-nine, sir?" the page-boy demanded. "There's somebody asking for you. Inspector Armadale, he said his name was."

"Armadale? What the devil can he be wanting?" Sir Clinton wondered aloud. "Show him in, please."

In a minute or two the inspector appeared.

"I suppose it's something important, inspector," Sir Clinton greeted him, "otherwise you wouldn't have come. But I can't imagine what brings you here."

Inspector Armadale glanced at Wendover, and then, without speaking, he caught Sir Clinton's eye. The chief constable read the meaning in his glance.

"This is a friend of mine, inspector—Mr. Wendover. He's a J.P. and perfectly reliable. You can speak freely before him, if it's anything official."

Armadale was obviously relieved.

"This is the business, Sir Clinton. This morning we had a 'phone message from the Lynden Sands doctor. It seems the caretaker at a big house hereabouts—Foxhills, they call it—was found dead, close to his cottage. Dr. Rafford went up to see the body; and at first he thought it was a case of apoplexy. Then he noticed some marks on the body that made him suspicious, and he says he won't give a death certificate. He put the matter into our hands at once. There's nobody except a constable hereabouts, so I've come over myself to look into things. Then it struck me you were staying at the hotel here, and I thought I'd drop in on my way up."

Sir Clinton gazed at the inspector with a very faintly quizzical expression.

"A friendly call?" he said. "That's very nice. Care to stay to lunch?"

The inspector evidently had not expected to find the matter taken in this way.

"Well, sir," he said tentatively, "I thought perhaps you might be interested."

"Intensely, inspector, intensely. Come and tell me all about it when it's cleared up. I wouldn't miss it."

Faint signs of exasperation betrayed themselves in the inspector's face.

"I thought, perhaps, sir, that you'd care to come over with me and look into the thing yourself. It seems a bit mysterious."

Sir Clinton stared at him in well-assumed amazement.

"We seem to be rather at cross-purposes, inspector. Let's be clear. First of all, I'm on holiday just now, and criminal affairs have nothing to do with me. Second, even if I weren't on holiday, a chief constable isn't specially attached to the find-'em-and-grab-'em branch of the service. Third, it might cause professional jealousy, heart-burnings, and what not, if I butted into a detective's case. What do you think?"

"It's my case," Armadale said, abandoning all further attempt at camouflage. "The plain truth is, from all I heard over the 'phone, that it seems a rum business; and I'd like to have your opinion on it, if you'd be so good as to give me it after you've examined things for yourself."

Sir Clinton's face relaxed.

"Ah," he confessed. "Now I seem to have some glimmerings of what you're after; and, since there's no question of my having interfered without being asked, I might look into the affair. But if I'm doing you a favour—as you seem to think—then I'm going to lay down one condition, *sine qua non*. Mr. Wendover's interested in detective work. He knows all the classics: Sherlock Holmes, Hanaud, Thorndyke, etc. So, if I come in, then he's to be allowed to join us. Agree to that, inspector?"

The inspector looked rather sourly at Wendover, as though try-ing to estimate how great a nuisance he was likely to prove; but, as Sir Clinton's assistance could evidently be secured only at a price, Armadale gave a rather ungracious consent to the proposed arrange-ment.

Sir Clinton seemed almost to regret his own decision.

"I'd hardly bargained for a bus-driver's holiday," he said rather ruefully.

A glance at the inspector's face showed that the expression had missed its mark. Sir Clinton made his meaning clearer.

"In the old horse-bus days, inspector, it was rumoured that when a bus-driver got a holiday he spent it on somebody else's bus, picking up tips from the driver. It seems that you want me to spend my holiday watching you do police work and picking up tips from your methods."

Inspector Armadale evidently suspected something behind the politeness with which Sir Clinton had turned his phrase. He looked rather glumly at his superior as he replied:

"I see I'm going to get the usual mixture, sir—help and sarcasm, half and half. Well, my hide's been tanned already; and your help's worth it."

Sir Clinton corrected him with an air of exactitude

"What I said was that I'd 'look into the affair.' It's your case, inspector. I'm not taking it off your shoulders, you understand. I don't mind prowling round with you; but the thing's in your hands officially, and I've nothing to do with it except as a spectator, remember."

Armadale's air became even gloomier when he heard this point of view so explicitly laid down.

"You mean it's to be just the same as the Ravensthorpe affair, I suppose," he suggested. "Each of us has all the facts we collect, but you don't tell me what you think of them as we get them. Is that it, sir?"

Sir Clinton nodded.

"That's it, inspector. Now, if you and Mr. Wendover will go round to the front of this place, I'll get my car out and pick you up in a minute or two."

CHAPTER III
THE POLICE AT THE CARETAKER'S

WENDOVER, SCANNING HIS FRIEND'S FACE, could see that all the carelessness had vanished from its expression. With the prospect of definite work before him, Sir Clinton seemed to have dropped his holiday mood completely.

"I think the first port of call should be the doctor," he suggested as he turned the car into the road leading to Lynden Sands village. "We'd better start at the beginning, inspector; and the doctor seems likely to have been the earliest expert on the spot."

They found Dr. Rafford in his garden, tinkering at a spotless motor-cycle; and Wendover was somewhat impressed by the obvious alertness of the young medico. Armadale introduced his companions, and then went straight to the point.

"I've come over about that case, doctor—the caretaker at Foxhills. Can you give us something to go on before we start to look into it up there?"

Dr. Rafford's air of efficiency was not belied when he told his story.

"This morning, at about half-past eight, young Colby came hammering at my door in a great state. He does some of the milk delivery round about here; and Peter Hay's house is one at which he leaves milk. It seems he went up there as usual; but when he got to the gate of the cottage he saw old Hay's body lying on the path up to the door. I needn't describe how it was lying; you'll see for yourself. I didn't disturb it—didn't need to."

47

Inspector Armadale's nod conveyed his satisfaction at this news. The doctor continued:

"Young Colby's only a child; so he got a bit of a fright. His head's screwed on all right, though; and he came straight off here to get hold of me. Luckily I hadn't gone out on my rounds as early as that, and he found me just finishing breakfast. I got my bike out and went up to Foxhills immediately.

"When I heard young Colby's tale, I naturally concluded that poor old Hay had had a stroke. I'd been doing my best to treat him for high blood-pressure, off and on; but I hadn't been able to do much for him; and once or twice he'd had slight attacks. He was bound to go, some time or other; and I concluded that he'd had a final attack through over-exertion or something of the sort."

He paused in his narrative for a moment and glanced from face to face in the group.

"You'll see, from this, foul play was the last thing that entered my mind. I got up to his cottage and found him, just as young Colby had said, lying face down on the garden path. From the look of him he'd obviously died of congestion. It seemed all plain sailing. In fact, I was just going to leave him and hunt up some assistance when my eye caught something. His arms were stretched out at full length above his head, as if he'd gone down all of a piece, you know; and his right sleeve had got rucked up a little, so that it showed a bit of his arm. And my eye happened to catch a mark on the skin just above the wrist. It was pretty faint; but there had evidently been some compression there. It puzzled me—still puzzles me. However, that's your affair. It struck me that I might as well have a look at the other arm, so I pushed up the coat-sleeve a little—that's the only thing I did to alter things in any way around the body—and I found a second mark there, rather like the first one."

He paused, as if to give the inspector the chance of putting a question; but, as none came, he went on with his story.

"The impression I got—of course, I may be wrong—was that marks of that sort might be important. Certainly, after seeing them, I didn't care to assert that poor old Hay's death was due entirely to natural causes. He'd died of congestion, all right. I'm dead sure that a P.M. will confirm that. But congestion doesn't make marks on a man's wrists. It seemed to me worth ringing you up. If it's a mare's nest, then it's a mare's nest, and I'll be sorry to have troubled you. But I believe in having things done ship-shape; and I'd rather trouble you than get into hot water myself, if there's anything fishy about the affair."

Inspector Armadale seemed rather dubious about how he should take the matter. To Wendover it almost looked as though he was regretting the haste with which he had brought Sir Clinton into the business. If the whole thing turned out to be a mare's nest, quite evidently Armadale expected to feel the flick of his superior's sarcasm. And obviously a couple of marks on a dead man's wrists did not necessarily spell foul play, since the man had clearly died of cerebral congestion, according to the doctor's own account.

At last the Inspector decided to ask a question or two.

"You don't know of anyone with a grudge against Hay?"

Rafford made no attempt to restrain a smile.

"Hay?" he said. "No one could possibly have a grudge against Peter. He was one of the decentest old chaps you could find any-where—always ready to do a good turn to anyone."

"And yet you assert that he was murdered?" demanded the in-spector.

"No, I don't," the doctor retorted sharply. "All I say is that I don't feel justified in signing a death certificate. That ends my part. After that, it's your move."

Armadale apparently realised that Rafford was not the sort of person who could be bluffed easily. He tried a fresh line.

"When do you think the death took place?"

The doctor considered for a moment.

"It's no good giving you a definite hour," he said. "You know as well as I do how much the symptoms vary from case to case. I think it's quite on the cards that he died some time about the middle of the night or a little earlier. But you couldn't get me to swear to that in the box, I warn you."

"I've often heard it said," the inspector commented in a disconso-late tone, "that you scientific people make the worst witnesses. You never will say 'yes' or 'no' plainly like ordinary people. You're always hedging and qualifying."

"Had a training in accuracy, I expect," Rafford replied. "We don't feel inclined to swear to things until we're convinced about them ourselves."

Armadale evidently decided not to pursue the subject further.

"What about the body?" he asked.

"I sent Sapcote up to look after it—the village constable. He's up at Foxhills now. If it was to be left for your examination somebody had to be there to see it wasn't disturbed."

The inspector nodded approvingly.

"Quite right. And I suppose I can get hold of this youngster—Colby's his name, isn't it?—any time I need him?"

Rafford gave him the boy's address, which he took down in his note-book.

"Anything else you can think of that might be useful?" he inquired, putting the book back into his pocket.

The doctor shook his head.

"Nix. I suppose the coroner will want a look in?"

"I expect so," Armadale replied.

He glanced at Wendover and Sir Clinton to indicate that he now left the field to them. Wendover took advantage of the tacit permission.

"You didn't see anything that suggested poison, did you?" he asked the doctor.

Rafford's faint smile put an edge on his reply:

"I believe I said that if it hadn't been for the marks on the wrists, I'd have certified congestion of the brain. I don't think poison marks the wrists."

Wendover, feeling that he had hardly shone by his interposition, refrained from further questions and glanced at Sir Clinton. The chief constable appeared to think that further inquiries could be allowed to stand over for a time.

"I think we'd better be moving on," he suggested. "Thanks for your help, Dr. Rafford. Once we've seen the body, perhaps something fresh may turn up, and we may have to trouble you again. By the way," he added, "did you notice if there was a heavy dew last night? I was playing bridge at the hotel and didn't go out after dinner; but perhaps you were out and can tell me."

"The dew did come down fairly heavy," Rafford said, after a pause for recollection. "I happened to be out at a case, and I noticed it. Are you thinking about the possibility of Hay's death being due to exposure?"

"Not exactly," Sir Clinton answered, with a faintly ironical smile. "As you would say, doctor, exposure doesn't mark a man's wrist—at least not so quick as all that."

Rafford acknowledged the dig good-humouredly and accompanied them to the garden gate as they went out.

"I hope I haven't started you on a wild-goose chase, inspector," he said on parting. "But I suppose that sort of thing's all in your day's work, anyhow."

Armadale digested this in silence as the car spun along towards Foxhills; then at last he uttered his views in a single sentence:

"That young fellow strikes me as uncommonly jaunty."

And having liberated his soul, he kept obstinately silent until they had reached their destination.

"This is the place, I think," Sir Clinton said a few minutes later, pulling his car up on the Foxhills avenue at a point where a side-road led off towards a little cottage among some trees. "I can see the constable in the garden."

Getting out of the car, they made their way along the by-lane for a short distance, and, as they came to the garden gate, Armadale hailed the constable. Sapcote had been sitting on a wooden chair beside the body, reading a newspaper to while away the time; but at the sound of the inspector's voice he rose and came forward along the flagged path.

"Things have been left just as they were, I suppose?" Armadale demanded.

Sapcote confirmed this and at once fell into the background, evidently realising that he had nothing to report which would interest the inspector. He contented himself with following the proceedings of his superior with the closest interest, possibly with a view to retailing them later to his friends in the village.

Armadale stepped up the paved path and knelt down beside the body, which was lying—as the doctor had described it—face downwards with the arms extended above the head.

"H'm! Looks as if he'd just stumbled and come down on his face," the inspector commented. "No signs of any struggle, anyhow."

He cast a glance at the paved path.

"There's not much chance of picking up tracks on *that*," he said disparagingly.

Wendover and Sir Clinton had come round to the bead of the body and the chief constable bent down to examine the wrists. Armadale also leaned over; and Wendover had some difficulty in getting a glimpse over their shoulders. Constable Sapcote hovered uncertainly in the rear, evidently anxious to see all he could, but afraid to attract the inspector's attention by pushing forward. Wendover inferred that Armadale must have a reputation as a disciplinarian.

"There seem to be marks of a sort," the inspector admitted grudgingly, after a brief study of the skin. "Whether they mean anything in particular's another matter. He might have had a fall at the gate and banged his wrists against a bar; and then he might have got up and staggered on until he fell here and died."

Sir Clinton had been studying the marks with more deliberation. He shook his head at the inspector's suggestion.

"The gate-bars are rounded, if you look at them. Now at one point this mark—see it?—shows a sharp line on the flesh. It's only at one place, I admit; the rest of the marking is more like something produced by general pressure. But still, you can't mistake that bit there."

Armadale re-examined the mark with more care before replying.

"I see what you mean," he admitted.

"Then go and try your own arm against the gate-bars and I think you'll admit it won't work."

The inspector moved off to the gate, slipped his sleeve up, and pressed his forearm hard against the most convenient bar. While he was thus engaged, Wendover stooped down to examine the markings for himself.

"What made you so ready with gate-bars, Clinton?" he inquired. "I never noticed what sort of a gate it was when I came in."

"Obvious enough. Here's a man been falling. Marks on his wrists. We learned that from the doctor. Naturally when I heard it, I began to wonder if he hadn't fallen against something; and as soon as we got out of the car, I kept my eye open for anything that Hay could have bruised himself on. The gate-bars seemed a likely thing, so I noted them in passing. One keeps one's eyes open, squire. But as soon as I saw this"—he indicated the edge on the marking where the indentation in the flesh was almost straight— "I gave the gate-bars the go-by. They couldn't have done it."

He glanced up.

"Satisfied, inspector?"

Armadale removed his arm from the bar, examined the mark left on it by the pressure, and nodded gloomily.

"This didn't do it. It leaves a mark deep in the middle and fading out on each side."

He came back to the body and scanned the mark once more.

"This thing on the wrist hasn't got any middle. It's fairly even, except for that sharp section."

A thought seemed to strike him and he pulled a magnifying glass from his pocket, adjusted the focus, and made a minute inspection of the dead man's wrist.

"I thought it might have been a rope," he explained as he put away his lens with a disappointed air. "But there's no regular pattern there such as a rope leaves. What do you think of it, Sir Clinton?"

"Got a piece of chalk in your pocket, inspector?" the chief constable inquired.

Armadale's face showed some astonishment, which he endeavoured to conceal as well as he could.

"No, Sir Clinton, I haven't."

"Are you thinking of bringing a photographer up here to take a souvenir picture?"

The inspector considered for a moment or two. "No," he said at last. "I don't see much use in that. The body's lying quite naturally, isn't it?"

"It looks like it; but one never knows."

Sir Clinton's fingers went mechanically to his waistcoat pocket.

"No chalk, you said, inspector?"

"No, I haven't any."

"Ah, and yet some people tell you that playing pool is a waste of time; and that the habit of chalking your cue and then pocketing the chalk is reprehensible. We now confound them."

He produced a cube of billiard-chalk as he spoke and, taking out a penknife, trimmed the paper away.

"Just chalk around the outline of the body, please, inspector. This paved path will show the marks excellently. If we need the marks later on, we can always lay some boards over them to keep the rain off."

While the inspector, obviously much against the grain, was chalking his lines, Sir Clinton turned to the constable.

"Perhaps you could give us some help, constable. Did you know Peter Hay?"

"Knew him well, sir."

"You can't throw any light on this business?"

"No, sir. It's amazing to me, sir, if there's anything in what the doctor says."

"Ah! And what does the doctor say?"

"Swears it's foul play somehow, sir."

"Indeed? He didn't go so far as that when he spoke to me about it."

The constable seemed rather confused to find himself taken so literally.

"Didn't quite mean that, sir. What I meant was I could see from his manner that something's amiss."

Sapcote, conscious that he had let his tongue run away with him, glanced anxiously at Sir Clinton's face. The expression on it reassured him. Evidently this wasn't the kind of a man who would eat you if you made a slip. The chief constable rose considerably in his subordinate's estimation.

"Nice little garden, this," Sir Clinton remarked, casting his eyes round the tiny enclosure. "A bit on the shady side, perhaps, with all these trees about. Did you ever come up here to visit Peter Hay, constable?"

"Often and often, sir. Many's the time we've sat on that seat over there when I've been off duty; or else in the house if it got too cold for my rheumatism."

"Suffer from rheumatism, constable? That's hard lines. One of my friends has some stuff he uses for it; he swears by the thing. I'll write down the name for you and perhaps it'll do you some good."

Sir Clinton tore a leaf out of his pocket-book, jotted a name on it, and handed the paper over to the constable, who seemed overwhelmed by the attention. Decidedly this superior of his was a "real good sort."

"Peter Hay was getting on in like," Sir Clinton went on, with a glance at the silvering hair of the body before him. "I suppose he had his troubles too. Rheumatism, or something like that?"

"No, sir. Nothing of the kind. Barring these strokes of his, he was sound as a bell. Used to go about in all weathers and never minded the rain. Never seemed to feel the cold the way I do. Kept his jacket for the church, they used to say about here. Often in the evenings we'd be sitting here and I'd say to him: 'Here, Peter, shirt-sleeves must keep you warmer than my coat keeps me, but it's time to be moving inside.' And then in we'd go and he'd begin fussing about with that squirrel of his."

"What sort of a man was he?" Sir Clinton asked. "Stiff with strangers, or anything like that? Suppose I'd come wandering in here, would he have been grumpy when he came to turn me out?"

"Grumpy, sir? That's the last thing you'd have called him. Or stiff. He was always smiling and had a kind word for everyone, sir. One of the decentest men you could ask for, sir. Very polite to gentlefolk, always; and a nice kindly manner with everyone."

"Not the sort of man to have a bad enemy, then?"

"No, indeed, sir."

Inspector Armadale had finished his work with the chalk and was now standing by, evidently impatient to get on with the task in hand. His face betrayed only too plainly that he thought Sir Clinton was wasting time.

"Finished?" the chief constable inquired.

"Quite," Armadale replied, in a tone which hinted strongly that there was much more to be done.

"In that case, we can turn the body over." Sir Clinton said, stepping forward as he spoke and beckoning to the constable.

Handling him gently, they turned the dead man on his back; and, before rising, Sir Clinton ran his hand over the front of the body. As he stood up, he motioned to Armadale to follow his example.

"His waistcoat and trousers are a bit damp," the inspector said, after he had felt them. "Is that what you mean?"

Sir Clinton nodded in confirmation. An expression of comprehension flitted across the inspector's face.

"So that was why you asked about the dew last night?" he observed. "I wondered what you were after, sir."

"Something of the sort was in my mind," the chief constable admitted. "Now have a look at the face, inspector. Has there been any bleeding at the nose? Or do you see anything else of any interest?"

Armadale bent down and inspected the dead man's face closely.

"Nothing out of the common that I can see," he reported. "Of course, the face is congested a bit. That might be the stroke, I suppose."

"Or else the settling of the blood by gravity after death," Sir Clinton pointed out. "Well, I hadn't expected to find any nose-bleeding. If he'd bled at the nose it might have saved him from apoplexy."

Armadale looked up inquiringly.

"You think it's merely apoplexy, sir?"

"I'm afraid this is a 'place' within the meaning of the Act, inspector; otherwise I'd be quite ready to bet you a considerable sum that if Dr. Rafford carries out a post mortem, he'll report that death was due to congestion of the brain."

The inspector seemed to read some hidden meaning into Sir Clinton's words, for he nodded sagely without making any vocal comment.

"What next, sir?" he asked. "Shall we take the body into the cottage and go over it there?"

Sir Clinton shook his head.

"Not yet. There's just one thing I'd like to be sure about; and it may not be easy to see. There's a better light out here. Turn up the trousers from the ankle, inspector, and have a good look for marks—probably on the front of the shins. It's a long shot, but I've a notion you'll find something there."

Armadale did as he was bidden.

"You're right, sir. There's a very faint mark—far fainter than the ones on the wrists—on the front of each shin, just as you said. It's more like a very faint bruise than a mark made by stumbling against anything. The skin's not broken. Of course it shows up after death, otherwise I'd hardly have seen it."

Sir Clinton nodded without making any comment. He was stooping over the dead man's face, examining it closely. After a moment or two, he signed to Wendover to come to his side.

"Smell anything peculiar, squire?"

Wendover sniffed sagaciously once or twice; his face lighted up; and then a look of perplexity came over his features.

"I know that smell, Clinton. I recognise it well enough; but I can't put a name to it somehow."

"Think again," the chief constable advised. "Go back to your early days and you'll probably recall it."

Wendover sniffed several times, but remained baffled. A look of interest passed over Sapcote's face. He came forward, bent down, and sniffed in his turn.

"I know what it is, sir. It's pear-drops—these sweets the children eat. Peter always had a bag of sweets in the place for youngsters that came to see him."

"That's it," Wendover exclaimed with some relief. "I knew I hadn't smelt that perfume for ages and ages; and yet it used to be familiar once upon a time."

Sir Clinton seemed to have passed to an earlier line of thought. He turned to the constable.

"Peter Hay suffered from apoplexy, the doctor told me. Had he any other troubles? Bad digestion? Asthma? Anything you can think of?"

Sapcote shook his head decidedly.

"No, sir," he said without hesitation. "Peter was as sound as a bell, barring these turns of his. I never heard tell of his having anything else wrong with him these last ten years."

The chief constable nodded, as though the information had satisfied him, but he refrained from comment.

"I think we'd better get him carried into his own bed now," he suggested with a glance at the body. "After that, we can look round the place and see if there's anything worth noting."

They carried the remains of Peter Hay into the cottage and laid the body on the bed, which had not been slept in.

"You'd better examine him, inspector," Sir Clinton suggested.

As the inspector set to work, the chief constable invited his companions to come into the second room of the cottage; and he left the bedroom door open, so that the inspector could hear anything of interest while he made his examination.

To Wendover, the tiny room seemed to offer little of interest. It was obviously kitchen and living-room in one. An oil cooking-stove; a grate; a sink; a dresser; two chairs and a table—these made up the more obvious contents. His eye wandered upwards and was caught by the movement of a tame squirrel in its cage on one of the walls.

"I heard he kept some pets," he remarked to the constable who had gone across to inspect the squirrel with a rather gloomy expression on his face.

"Yes, sir," Sapcote answered. "He took a lot of pleasure in the beasts. Some of them are in cages out behind the cottage."

He reflected for a moment, then added:

"Somebody'll have to look after the poor beasts, now he's gone. Would there be any objection to my taking them away, sir? They'll have to be fed."

Sir Clinton, to whom the question was obviously addressed, gave permission at once.

"We mustn't let the beasts starve. You'll have to take the cages too, of course?"

"Yes, sir. I can put them in my backyard at home."

The constable paused for a moment, then, a little shamefacedly, he added:

"Peter was a good friend to me; and I wouldn't like to see his pets fall into anybody's hands that might be cruel to them or neglect them. He was real fond of them."

Wendover's eye fell upon a small white paper bag on one of the dresser shelves. He stepped across, opened the parcel, sniffed for a moment, and then handed the thing to Sir Clinton.

"Here's where the perfume comes from, Clinton—a bag of peardrops, just as the constable said. He must have been eating some just before he died."

The chief constable looked at the crumbled paper.

"Not much chance of getting any fingerprints on *that*, even if we wanted them. You'd better hand the bag over to the inspector. We may as well get them analysed. Poison's always a possibility— Ah, inspector, you haven't been long over that."

Inspector Armadale emerged from the bedroom and stolidly made his report.

"Nothing that I can see on the body, sir, except the marks we noted already. No wounds of any sort, no bruises—nothing suspicious whatever. It almost looks like a mare's nest, except for these four marks."

Sir Clinton nodded as though he had received confirmation of some very doubtful hypothesis. He moved across the room and seemed to become engrossed in a study of the squirrel's antics. In a few moments he turned to the constable.

"You knew Peter Hay well, constable. I want some notions about his habits and so forth. What did he do with himself all day?"

The constable scratched his ear, as though to stimulate his memory by the action.

"To tell you the truth, sir, he didn't do much. He was only care-taker here, you understand? When the weather was fine, he'd go up to Foxhills and open some of the windows in the morning, to air the rooms. Then he'd take a look round the grounds, likely, just to see that all was as it should be. He might have to go down to the village for tea, or butter, or something like that. Then he'd come home and take his dinner. In the afternoon he'd have a bit of a sleep for a while—he was getting on in years—and then perhaps he'd dig a while in his garden here; look after his flowers; then he'd have his tea. Some time or other, he'd go up and look round Foxhills again and shut any windows he'd opened. And then he'd come back here; water his garden, most likely, if it needed it. And perhaps some of us would drop in for a chat with him. Or else he might take a walk down to see me or somebody else in the village. Or sometimes he'd read."

Sir Clinton threw a glance round the barely furnished room.

"He had books, then? I don't see any."

"He read his Bible, sir. I never saw him read anything else."

"There's a Bible in the bedroom, Sir Clinton," Armadale confirmed.

"An uneventful life, apparently," the chief constable commented, not unkindly. "Now I want to hear something about what sort of man he was. Polite in his manners, you said?"

"Very polite," Sapcote insisted. "I remembered hearing some visitor once saying that Peter was a natural gentleman, sir."

"They do exist, here and there, even nowadays," Sir Clinton admitted. "Now let's come down to dots, constable. I want to get a picture of him in my mind and you seem to have known him well enough to help. Let's see, now. Suppose I'd met him somewhere and offered to come and see him—or that he'd asked me here. What would happen? I suppose I'd knock at the door and he'd come and let me in. Which chair would he give me?"

"Whichever you liked best, sir. They're much the same. If there'd been any difference he'd have given you the best one."

"Quite so. I'm beginning to see him better. Now go on, constable. He'd have been easy and natural, too, if I can gauge him.

He'd just have met me in his shirt-sleeves as he used to meet you? No fuss?"

"He'd have made no fuss, sir. But he'd have put on his jacket for you, you being a strange gentleman coming to his house on a special visit; and perhaps he'd have offered you a cup of tea if the time was right for it."

"And if it was later in the evening? Some whiskey, if he had any?"

"No, sir. Peter was a strong teetotaller."

Sir Clinton glanced over the dresser on which all the dishes were neatly stacked.

"He was a tidy man, I see?"

"Very, sir. Always had everything ship-shape. He never could bear to have things lying about. Sometimes he used to anger me because he'd wash up his tea-things when I wanted to talk to him. Of course, if it had been you, I expect he'd wait till you'd gone. It wouldn't have been polite to wash up with a stranger there."

"You're helping me a great deal, constable," said Sir Clinton encouragingly. "Now, another thing. I suppose he must have saved some money. He seems to have lived very simply—no expenses to speak of?"

"That's right, sir. He put all he could spare into the savings-bank at the post office. All he kept in the house was what he needed to buy things in the village."

"So I expected. You see how well you've pictured him, constable. Now where did he keep his money—his loose cash?"

"In that drawer in the dresser," the constable said, pointing to one of the larger drawers which had a lock on it. "He carried the key about with him."

"See if you can get the key, inspector, please. You'll find it in his pocket, I expect."

Armadale produced the key almost at once, and Sir Clinton opened the drawer. As he did so, the constable uttered a cry of astonishment. Wendover, leaning forward, saw that the drawer held more than a little money—some silver articles were in it as well.

Sir Clinton warned them back with a gesture.

"Don't touch. We may have to look for fingerprints here. These things seem to have a crest on them," he continued, after scrutinising them.

"That's the Foxhills' mark, sir," the constable hastened to explain. "But it beats me what Peter Hay was doing with these things. That one there"—he pointed it out—"comes from the Foxhills' drawing-room. I remember seeing it, one time Peter and I went round the house when he was shutting the windows for the night. It's valuable, isn't it, sir? Peter told me these things were worth something—quite apart from the silver in them—and I suppose he'd learned that from somebody or other—one of the family, most like."

Sir Clinton left the silver articles alone and picked up the money which lay in one corner of the drawer.

"One pound seven and four pence ha'penny. Would that be more or less what you'd expect to see here, constable?"

"Somewhere round about that, sir, seeing it's this time in the week."

Sir Clinton idly picked up the savings-bank book, looked at the total of the balance, and put the book down again. Evidently it suggested nothing in particular.

"I think you'd better take charge of these ornaments, inspector, and see if you can make anything out of them in the way of fingerprints. Handle them carefully. Wait a moment! I want to have a look at them."

The inspector moved forward.

"I may be short of chalk, sir, but I've a pair of rubber gloves in my pocket," he announced with an air of suppressed triumph. "I'll lift the things out on to the table for you, and you can look at them there."

Slipping on his gloves, he picked up the articles gingerly and carried them across to the table. Sir Clinton followed and, bending over them, subjected them to a very careful scrutiny.

"See anything there?" he demanded, giving way at last to the inspector.

After Armadale had examined the silver surfaces from every direction, Wendover had his turn. When he raised himself again, he shook his head. Sir Clinton glanced at the inspector, who also made a negative gesture.

"Then we all see the same," Sir Clinton said finally. "One might assume from that, without overstraining probability, one thing at least."

"And that is?" demanded Wendover, forestalling the inspector.

"That there's nothing there to see," Sir Clinton observed mildly. "I thought you'd have noticed that for yourself, squire."

Behind Wendover's back the inspector enjoyed his discomfiture, thanking providence the while that he had not had time to put the question himself. The chief constable turned to Sapcote.

"I suppose Peter Hay kept the keys of Foxhills—those that he needed, at any rate—somewhere handy?"

"He kept them in his pocket, always, sir; a small bunch of Yale keys on a ring, I remember."

"You might get them, inspector, I think we'd better go up there next and see if we can find anything worth noting. But, of course, we can't go rushing in there without permission."

He turned back to Sapcote:

"Go off now, constable, as soon as we've locked up this place, and get hold of some of the Foxhills people who are staying at the hotel. Ask them to come up here. Tell them we want to go over Foxhills on account of something that's been taken from the house. Explain about things, but don't make a long yarn of it, remember. Then leave a message for Dr. Rafford to say that we'll probably need a P.M. When you come up here again, you'd better bring a cart to take away these beasts in their cages."

He gave Sapcote some further instructions about the disposal of Peter Hay's body, then he turned to the inspector.

"I suppose, later on, you'd better take Peter Hay's fingerprints. It's only a precaution, for I don't think we'll need them; but we may as well have them on record. There's nothing more for us to do here at present so far as I can see."

He led the way out of the cottage. The constable locked the door, pocketed the key, produced a bicycle from behind the house, and cycled off in haste down the avenue.

Sir Clinton led his companions round to the back of the cottage; but an inspection of the dead man's menagerie yielded nothing which interested any of them, so far as the matter in hand was concerned.

"Let's sit down on the seat here," the chief constable suggested, as they returned to the front garden. "We'll have to wait for these people from the hotel; and it won't do any harm to put together the facts we've got, before we pick up anything further."

"You're sure it isn't a mare's nest then?" Armadale inquired cautiously.

"I'm surprised that Dr. Rafford didn't go a bit further with his ideas," Sir Clinton returned indifferently. "In any case, there's the matter of that Foxhills' silver to be cleared up now."

CHAPTER IV
WHAT HAPPENED IN THE NIGHT

Sir Clinton took out his cigarette-case and handed it to his companions in turn.

"Let's have the unofficial view first," he suggested. "What do you make of it all, squire, in the light of the classics?"

Wendover shook his head deprecatingly.

"It's hardly fair to start with the amateur, Clinton. According to the classical method, the police always begin; and then, when they've failed ingloriously, the amateur steps in and clears the matter up satisfactorily. You're inverting the order of Nature. However, I don't mind telling you what I think are the indisputable points in the affair."

"The very things we want, squire," declared Sir Clinton gratefully. "Indisputable points will be no end of use to us if the case gets into court. Proceed."

"Well, to begin with, I think these marks on his wrists and round about his ankles show that he was tied up last night. The wrist-marks are deeper than the marks on the shins; and that's more or less what one would expect. The ligatures would rest on the bare flesh in the case of the wrists; but at the ankles the cloth of his trousers and his socks would interpose and make the pressure less direct."

Inspector Armadale nodded approvingly, as though his opinion of Wendover had risen a little.

"Suppose that's correct, then," Wendover continued, "it gives the notion of someone attacking Peter Hay and tying him up. But

65

then Peter Hay wasn't a normal person. He suffered from high blood-pressure, the doctor told us; and he'd had one or two slight strokes. In other words, he was liable to congestion of the brain if he over-exerted himself. Suppose he struggled hard, then he might quite well bring on an attack; and then his assailant would have a corpse on his hands without meaning to kill him at all."

Armadale nodded once more, as though agreeing to this series of inferences.

"If the assailant had left the body tied up, then the show would have been given away," Wendover proceeded, "so he untied the bonds, carried the corpse outside, and arranged it to look as if death had been caused by a heart attack."

He paused, and Sir Clinton put a question.

"Is that absolutely all, squire? What about the silver in the drawer, for instance."

Wendover made a vague gesture.

"I see nothing to connect the silver with this affair. The assailant may have been after it, of course, and got so frightened by the turn things took that he simply cleared out without waiting for anything. If I'd gone to a place merely to rob a man, I don't think I'd wait to rob him if I saw a chance of being had up on a murder charge. I'd clear out while I was sure I was safe from discovery."

"Nothing further, then? In that case, inspector, it's your turn to contribute to the pool."

Armadale had intended to confine himself strictly to the evidence and to put forward no theories; but the chance of improving on the amateur's results proved too much of a temptation, as Sir Clinton had anticipated.

"There's not much doubt that he was tied up," the inspector began. "The marks all point that way. But there was one thing that Mr. Wendover didn't account for in them. The marks on the legs were on the front only—there wasn't a mark on the back of the legs."

He halted for a moment and glanced at Wendover with subdued triumph.

"So you infer?" Sir Clinton inquired.

"I think he was tied up to something so that his legs were resting against it at the back and the bands were round the legs and the thing too. If it was that way, then the back of the legs wouldn't have any marks of the band on them."

"Then what was he tied up to?" asked Wendover.

"One of the chairs inside the cottage," the inspector went on. "If he'd been sitting in the chair, with each leg tied to a leg of the chair, you'd get just what we saw on the skin."

Sir Clinton acquiesced with a nod.

"Anything more?" he asked.

"I'm not quite through," Armadale continued. "Assume he was tied up as I've explained. If it had been a one-man job, there would have been some signs of a struggle—marks on his wrists or something of that sort. Peter Hay seems to have been a fairly muscular person, quite strong enough to put up some sort of show if he got a chance; certainly he'd have given one man enough trouble to leave some marks on his own skin."

"More than one man, then?" Sir Clinton suggested.

"Two, at least. Suppose one of them held him in talk while the other took him by surprise, and you get over the difficulty of there being no struggle. One man would pounce on him and then the other would join in; and they'd have him tied up before he could put up any fight that would leave marks on him."

"That sounds all right," Wendover admitted.

Sir Clinton put an innocent question.

"If it had been a one-man affair and a big struggle, then surely Peter Hay would have had his attack while the fight was going on, and if he'd died during the struggle there would have been no need to tie him up? Isn't that so, squire?"

Wendover considered the point and grudgingly agreed that it sounded probable.

"Go on, inspector," Sir Clinton ordered, without taking up the side-issue any further.

"I can't quite see what they did when they'd got him tied up," the inspector acknowledged. "They don't seem to have done much

in the way of rummaging in the cottage, as far as I can see. Whatever it was that they were after, it wasn't the cash in the drawer;
and it wasn't the two or three bits of silver, for they left them intact, although they could easily have got them if they'd wanted
them. That part of the thing beats me just now."

Wendover showed a faint satisfaction at finding the inspector
driven to admit a hiatus in his story.

"However it happened, Peter Hay died in his chair, I think,"
Armadale went on. "Perhaps it was the excitement of the affair.
Anyhow, they had a dead man on their hands. So, as Mr. Wendover
pointed out, they did their best to cover their tracks. They untied
him, carried him outside, laid him down as if he'd fallen unconscious and died there. But they forgot one thing. If he'd come down
all of a heap, as they wanted to suggest, his face would have been
smashed a bit on the stones of the path. They arranged him with
his hands above his head, as if he'd fallen at full length. In that
position, he couldn't shield his face as he fell. Normally you fall
with your hands somewhere between your face and your chest—
under your body, anyhow. But his hands were above his head; and
yet his face hadn't a bruise on it. That's not natural."

"Quite clear, inspector."

"Then there's another point. You called my attention to the
moisture on the front of his clothes, under the body. Dew couldn't
have got in there."

"Precisely," Sir Clinton agreed. "That dates the time when they
put the body down, you think?"

"It shows it was put down on top of the dew, therefore it was
after dew-fall when they brought him out. And at the other side
you've got the fact that his bed wasn't slept in. So that limits the
time of the affair to a period between dew-fall and Peter Hay's
normal bedtime."

"Unless he'd sat up specially late that night," Wendover interposed.

Armadale nodded a rather curt acknowledgment of this suggestion, and continued:

"Two points more. They've just occurred to me, sir. The silver's the first thing."

"Yes," Sir Clinton encouraged him, since the inspector seemed to feel himself on doubtful ground.

"I'm not sure, sir, that robbery can be ruled out, after all. It may be a case of one crime following on another. Suppose Peter Hay had been using his position as caretaker to get away with any silver left at Foxhills, and had got it stored up here for removal at a convenient time. The men who did him in last night might quite well have nailed the main bulk of it and overlooked those stray bits that he'd put away in his cash-drawer. For all we can tell, they may have made a good haul."

"And the next point, inspector?"

"The next point's the marks on the skin. They weren't made by ropes. Well, you can tie a man up with other things—strips of cloth, handkerchiefs, or surgical bandages. The edge of a surgical bandage would leave a sharp line on the flesh if it was pulled tight enough, or if the man struggled against it once he'd been tied in the chair. You understand what I mean?"

Wendover interposed:

"You mean a rope leaves its mark mainly at the middle, because it's a cylinder and the convex curve cuts into the flesh; whereas a flat bandage gives even pressure all over except at the edge, where the flesh can bulge up alongside the fabric?"

"That's what I mean," the inspector confirmed.

Sir Clinton volunteered no immediate criticism of either of the inspector's points. Instead, he seemed to be considering his course of action. At last he made up his mind.

"We've got a bit away from our original agreement, inspector. But, since you've put your cards on the table, I'll do the same, so that we're still level. But you're not to take this as a precedent, remember. I don't care about expounding airy theories formed as we go along. It's much better to go on the old lines and consider the evidence as we pick it up, each of us from his own point of view. Pooling our views simply means losing the advantage of three different viewpoints. You and Mr. Wendover came to slightly different conclusions about the basic factor in the business; and, if you hadn't put your ideas into words, then he'd have gone forward looking for one criminal, whilst you'd have been after two or more men; and so we'd have had both possibilities covered. Now, I think, the chances are that you've come round to the inspector's view, squire?"

"It seems to fit the facts better than mine," Wendover admitted.

"There you are!" Sir Clinton said. "And so we've lost the services of one man keeping his eye on the—always possible—case that it was a single-handed job. That's why I don't like pooling ideas. However, inspector, it wouldn't be fair to take your views and to say nothing about my own, so I'll give you mine. But it's no precedent, remember."

Armadale made a gesture of grudging agreement.

"Then here's what I make of things, so far," Sir Clinton continued. "First of all, one at least of the men mixed up in this affair was a better-class fellow. And he, at any rate, did not come on Peter Hay unexpectedly. He was paying a friendly call, and Peter knew he was coming."

"How do you make that out?" Wendover demanded.

"Easy enough. Hasn't the body a jacket on? I knew that when the doctor told us he had to push up the sleeves to see the marks; and, of course, when we saw the body, there was the coat, right enough. Now men of Peter Hay's class don't wear jackets as much as we do. They like to feel easy when they sit down after work's done—take off their collars and ties and so forth in the evening. The question was, whether Peter Hay varied from type. Hence my talk with the constable, inspector. I saw your disapproving eye on me all through it; but out of it I raked the plain fact that Peter Hay would never have had a jacket on unless he expected a visitor—and, what's more, a visitor of a class higher than his own. See it now?"

"There might be something in it," the inspector conceded reluctantly.

Sir Clinton showed no particular sign of elation, but went on with his survey.

"The next point that struck me—I called your attention to it—was the nature of the marks: the sharp edge. There's no doubt in my mind that some strip of cloth was used in tying him up. Now, one doesn't find strips of cloth on the spur of the moment. A handkerchief would answer the purpose; but here you had each leg tied to the chair and a fetter on the wrists as well. Unless there were three people in the attack, they'd only be able to rake up two handkerchiefs on the spur of the moment, since most people normally content themselves with a handkerchief apiece. Strips torn off a bed-sheet might answer; but I can't quite see Peter Hay standing idly by while they tore up his sheets in order to tie him up later on. Besides, his bedclothes were intact, so far as I could see—and he doesn't use sheets."

"I see what you're driving at, Clinton," Wendover interrupted. "You want to make out that it was a premeditated affair. They brought the apparatus in their pockets ready for use, and didn't tie the old man up on the spur of the moment with the first thing that came handy?"

"Things seem to point that way, don't they?" Sir Clinton continued. "Then there's the question of how it was done. I agree with you, inspector, that it was a job for more than one man. Quite evidently they had force enough to pin Peter Hay almost instantaneously, so that he hadn't a chance of struggling; and it would take two men—and fairly powerful fellows—to do that successfully. Also, if there were two of them, one could hold him in talk whilst the other sauntered round—perhaps to look at the squirrel—and got into position to take him unawares from the rear."

Armadale's face showed a certain satisfaction at finding the chief constable in agreement with him on his point.

"Now we'll assume that they had him overpowered. If it was a case of simple robbery, the easiest thing to do would be to tie his hands together and fetter his ankles, and then leave him on the floor while they looted the place. But they tied him in a chair—which isn't so easy to do, after all. They must have had some reason for that, or they wouldn't have gone to the extra trouble."

"Even if you tie a man's hands and feet, he can always roll over and over and make himself a nuisance," the inspector suggested. "If you tie him in a chair you have him fast."

"Quite true," Sir Clinton admitted. "But would you go to the extra trouble yourself, inspector, if the case happened to be as I've stated it? No? Neither should I. It seems as if there might be a likelier solution. Ever visit a sick friend?"

"Yes," said Armadale, obviously puzzled by the question.

"Did you ever notice, then, that it's easier to talk to him if he's sitting up in bed and not lying down?"

"There's something in that," the inspector admitted. "I've never paid any attention to it; but, now you mention it, sir, I believe you're right. One gets more out of a talk with a man when he's not lying down in bed. I suppose one's unaccustomed to it."

"Or else that when he's sitting up you can follow the play of expression on his face," Sir Clinton supplied, as an alternative.

Wendover evidently saw the drift of the chief constable's remark.

"So you think he was tied up that way, Clinton, because they wanted to talk to him; and they wanted to see his face clearly while they talked?"

"Something of that sort might account for things. I don't press the point. Now we come to the next item—the smell of pear-drops."

"But that's accounted for all right, surely. I found the bag of sweets on the dresser myself," Wendover protested. "Peter Hay had been eating them. There's nothing in that, Clinton."

Sir Clinton smiled a little sardonically.

"Not so fast, squire. You found a bag of pear-drops, I admit. But who told you that Peter Hay bought them and put them there?"

"It stands to reason that he did, surely," Wendover protested. "The constable told you he kept a bag of sweets in the house for children."

"Quite so. And there wasn't a second bag there, I'll admit. But let's confine ourselves to the pear-drops for a moment. One can't deny that they've got a distinctive perfume. Can you think of anything else that smells like that?"

Inspector Armadale's face lighted up.

"That stuff they use for covering cuts—New-Skin, isn't it? That stuff smells like pear-drops."

The look of comprehension faded slowly as he added: "But I don't see how New-Skin comes into the affair, sir."

"No more do I, inspector," Sir Clinton retorted blandly. "I should think New-Skin had nothing whatever to do with it."

"Then what's the point?" Armadale demanded.

"It's plain enough, if you'd keep your ears open. When I encouraged the constable to babble at large about Peter Hay, I was on the look-out for one thing. I found out that he didn't suffer from asthma."

"I don't see it yet, sir," the inspector admitted in perplexity.

Wendover had the information which Armadale lacked.

"Now I see what you're after, Clinton. You're thinking of amyl nitrite—the stuff asthmatics inhale when they get a bad turn? You wanted to know if Peter Hay ever used that as a drug? And, of course, now I come to think of it, that stuff has the pear-drop odour also."

"That's it, squire. Amyl nitrite for asthma; the solvent that evaporates and leaves the collodion behind when you use New-Skin; and the perfume of pear-drops—they're all derived from a stuff called amyl alcohol; and they all have much the same smell. Eliminate New-Skin, as it doesn't seem to fit into this case. That leaves you with the possibilities that the body smelt of pear-drops *or of amyl nitrite.*"

Inspector Armadale was plainly out of his depth.

"I don't see that you're much further forward, sir. After all, there are the pear-drops. What's the good of going further? If it's poison you're thinking of— Is this amyl nitrite poisonous, and you think it might have been used in the pear-drops so that their perfume would cover its smell?"

"It's a bit subtler than that, inspector. Now I admit quite frankly that this is all pure hypothesis; I'm merely trying it out, so to speak, so that we can feel certain we've covered all the possibilities. But here it is, for what it's worth. I'll put it in a nutshell for you. Amyl nitrite, when you inhale it, produces a rush of blood to the brain."

"And Peter Hay suffered from high blood-pressure in any case," Wendover broke in, "so an extra flood of blood rushing to the head would finish him? Is that what you mean?"

"Well, it's always a possibility, isn't it?" Sir Clinton returned. "Even a slight dose—a couple of sniffs—will give you a fair head-ache for the rest of the afternoon. It's beastly stuff."

Inspector Armadale ruminated for a moment or two.

"Then you think that when they'd done with him they dosed him with this stuff and gave him an apoplectic stroke, sir?"

"It could be done easily enough," Sir Clinton said cautiously. "A teaspoonful of the stuff on a bit of cotton-wool under his nose would do the trick, if he was liable to a stroke. But they didn't do it in the cottage. They must have carried him out here, chair and all, and dosed him in the open air, or else we'd have smelt the stuff strongly in the room, even after this time. Perhaps that's what suggested leaving him outside all night, so that the stuff would evaporate from him as far as possible. We'll know for certain after the P.M. His lungs ought to have a fair amount of the nitrite in them, at any rate, if that notion's correct."

He paused for a time, then continued:

"Now I don't say that it *is* correct. We don't know for certain yet. But let's assume that it is, and see if it takes us any further. They must have procured the amyl nitrite beforehand and brought it here on purpose to use it. Now amyl nitrite won't kill an ordinary man. Therefore they must have known the state of Peter Hay's health. And they must have known, too, that he kept some sweets in the house always. My impression is that they brought that bag of pear-drops with them and took away Peter's own bag—which probably hadn't pear-drops in it. You'd better make a note to look into Peter's sweet-buying in the village lately, inspector. Find out what he bought last."

Sir Clinton pitched his cigarette-end over the hedge and took out his case.

"You see what these things point to?" he inquired, as he lit his fresh cigarette.

"It's easy enough to see, when you put it that way," Wendover replied. "You mean that if they knew about Peter's health and Peter's ways to that extent, they must be local people and not strangers."

"If one works from the premises, I think that's so," Sir Clinton confirmed. "But remember, the premises are only guesses so far. We need the P.M. to confirm them. Now, there are just three more points: the time of death; the lack of wounds on the face or any-where; and the matter of the silver in the drawer. As to the first two, the amyl nitrite notion fits in quite well. The murderers, if it was murder, made their first slip when they laid him down so care-fully and forgot to arrange the hands under the body. I suppose they thought they were giving a suggestive turn to things by the attitude they chose—as though Peter Hay had collapsed under a thunderbolt attack. As to the time of the assumed murder, all we really know was that it was after dew-fall. They may have talked for hours before they finished the old man, for all we can tell; or they may have given him the nitrite almost as soon as they got him tied up. We can't tell, and it's not so very important, after all."

He flicked some ash from his cigarette.

"Now we come to the real thing that a jury would want to know about: the motive. What were they after?"

He glanced at his two companions, as if inviting an opinion.

"I suggested a possible motive, sir," the inspector reminded him.

"Yes, but from the jury point of view you'd have to do two things to make that convincing. You'd have to prove that Peter Hay was helping himself to stuff from Foxhills; and you'd have to establish that the murderers got away with the bulk of it. That's almost a case in itself. If you ask me, inspector, I think that silver repre-sents the usual thing—the murderer's attempt to make things too darned convincing."

Armadale's face betrayed some incredulity.

"Don't you see the slip?" Sir Clinton continued. "What sort of man was Peter Hay? You heard me pumping the constable, didn't you? And what did I get? That Peter Hay was a simple old chap who read his Bible and practically nothing else. Now, just recall the fact that there wasn't a fingerprint on any of those things; and silver will take a fingerprint more clearly than most surfaces. Whoever handled these ornaments knew all about the fingerprint danger. He wore gloves, whoever he may be. You'll hardly persuade me—after hearing the constable's report of Peter Hay—that he was a person likely to think of a precaution of that sort."

The inspector looked doubtful.

"Perhaps not, sir; but you never can tell."

"Well, my guess is that Peter Hay never handled the stuff at all. It was put there by his murderers; and they took good care not to leave their visiting-cards on it. Doesn't its presence suggest something else to you people?"

"You mean," said Wendover, "that they may have burgled Foxhills themselves, Clinton, and put these things into Peter Hay's drawer to lay the scent in his direction, while they got away with the main bulk of the stuff?"

Sir Clinton seemed disinclined to endorse this heartily.

"It's a possibility, squire. We needn't brood over it just yet, however. When we get into Foxhills, we'll see if anything's missing except these things."

He glanced at his wrist-watch.

"Time's getting on. These people might be here any minute, if the constable didn't waste time. Let's finish up this symposium. Suppose we eliminate robbery as a motive, then—"

He broke off abruptly in the middle of the sentence as a car came along the avenue and drew up at the entrance to the lane which led down to the cottage. Paul Fordingbridge was driving, and his sister sat beside him. Followed by his two companions, Sir Clinton walked down the lane to where the car had halted.

CHAPTER V
THE DIARY

"I suppose the constable explained things more or less, Mr. Fordingbridge?" Sir Clinton asked, as he came abreast of the car.

Miss Fordingbridge did not wait for her brother's reply.

"It's really dreadful, Sir Clinton," she broke out. "I can hardly believe that it's true. And who could want to kill poor Peter Hay, who hadn't an enemy in the world, is beyond me altogether. I simply can't imagine it. And what made them do it? I can't guess. I must try at my next *séance* to see if I can get any light on it. Perhaps you've found out all about it already."

Sir Clinton shook his head.

"We've found out next to nothing, I'm sorry to say."

Miss Fordingbridge regarded him with marked disapproval.

"And aren't you going to arrest the man who killed him?"

"In the end, I hope," Sir Clinton answered patiently. Then he turned to Paul Fordingbridge. "These are the keys of Foxhills that Peter Hay kept. I haven't a search-warrant; but we must get into the house, if you'll let us go over it. Would you mind showing us round the place? You see, you know all about it, and your help would be of value to us in case there's anything wrong up there."

At the word "search-warrant," Paul Fordingbridge seemed to prick up his ears; and there was a perceptible pause before he answered the chief constable's inquiry.

"Certainly, if you wish it," he replied smoothly. "I shall be only too glad to give you any assistance that I can. But what makes you think there's anything wrong at Foxhills? The constable told us that Peter Hay was found at his own cottage."

At a gesture from Sir Clinton, the inspector went over to the chief constable's car and, first drawing on his rubber gloves, he brought back one of the silver ornaments taken from Peter Hay's drawer.

"You recognise that?" Sir Clinton asked.

"Yes, indeed," Miss Fordingbridge replied, without hesitation. "That's one of the things we left behind when we shut up Foxhills. It's of no great value, and so we didn't send it to the bank strong-room with the rest of the stuff."

"Peter Hay told someone it was valuable," the inspector broke in.

"Oh, so it was, in a way," Miss Fordingbridge replied. "It was a present to me from an old friend, and so it had a sentimental value. But in itself it's worth next to nothing, as you can see."

Evidently Peter Hay had misunderstood something which he had heard. Armadale, rather disgusted by the news, carried the article back to the chief constable's car.

"We'll need to keep that and the other things in our charge for a time," Sir Clinton said apologetically. "They were found at Peter Hay's cottage. Perhaps you could suggest some reason for their removal from Foxhills?"

"There's no reason whatever that I can see," Miss Fordingbridge replied promptly. "Peter Hay had nothing to do with them, and he'd no right to take them out of the house. None at all."

"Possibly he mistook them for things of value, and thought they'd be safer in his cottage," Wendover suggested.

"He had no right to touch anything of mine," Miss Fording-bridge commented decidedly.

"Suppose we go up to the house?" Paul Fordingbridge suggested in a colourless voice. "You'll take your own car? Good. Then I'll go ahead."

He pressed the self-starter and took his car up the avenue. Sir Clinton and his companions got into their own car and followed.

"You didn't get much out of *him*," Wendover commented to the others.

Sir Clinton smiled.

"I don't think he got much chance to volunteer information," he pointed out.

They reached Foxhills as Paul Fordingbridge was opening the main door of the house; and he invited them with a gesture to come in.

"I suppose you merely wish to have a general look round?" he asked. "Do just as you like. I'll go round with you and answer any questions that I can for you."

Miss Fordingbridge attached herself to the party, and they went from room to room. Sir Clinton and the inspector examined the window-catches without finding anything amiss. At last Miss Fordingbridge noticed something out of the common.

"We left a few silver knick-knacks lying about. I don't see any of them."

Inspector Armadale made a note in his pocketbook.

"Could you give me a list of them?" he asked.

Miss Fordingbridge seemed taken aback.

"No, I couldn't. How could you expect me to remember all the trifles we left about? I daresay I could remember some of them. There was a silver rose-bowl; but it was very thin, and I'm sure it wasn't worth much. And a couple of little hollow statuettes, and some other things. They weren't of any value."

"What room is this?" Sir Clinton inquired, cutting her eloquence short, as they paused before a fresh door.

"The drawing-room."

She went in before the others and cast a glance round the room.

"What's that?" she demanded, as though her companions were personally responsible for a sack which stood near one of the windows.

Armadale went swiftly across the room, opened the mouth of the sack and glanced inside.

"It looks like the missing loot," he remarked. "I can see something like a rose-bowl amongst it, and the head of one of your statuettes. You might look for yourself, Miss Fordingbridge."

He stood aside to let her inspect the contents of the sack.

"Yes, these are some of the things," she confirmed at once.

Sir Clinton and Wendover in turn examined the find. The chief constable tested the weight of the sack and its contents.

"Not much of a haul," he said, letting it settle to the floor again. "Taking pure silver at eight shillings an ounce, and allowing for alloy, there's less than twenty pounds' worth there—much less."

"I suppose this means that the thieves must have been disturbed, and left their swag behind them," Paul Fordingbridge suggested.

Sir Clinton seemed intent on an examination of the window-fastenings; but Inspector Armadale curtly agreed with Paul Fordingbridge's hypothesis.

"It looks like it."

The chief constable led the way to a fresh room. "What's this?" he asked.

Miss Fordingbridge seemed suddenly to take a keener interest in the search.

"This is my nephew's room. I do hope they haven't disturbed anything in it. I've been so careful to keep it exactly as it used to be. And it would be such a pity if it were disturbed just at the very moment when he's come back."

Sir Clinton's eye caught an expression of vexation on Paul Fordingbridge's face as his sister spoke of her nephew.

"He's been away, then?" he asked.

It required very little to start Miss Fordingbridge on the subject; and in a few minutes of eager explanation she had laid before them the whole matter of her missing relation. As her narrative proceeded, Sir Clinton could see the expression of annoyance deepening on her brother's features.

"And so you understand, Sir Clinton, I kept everything in his room just as it used to be; so that when he comes back again he'll find nothing strange. It'll just be as if he'd only left us for a week-end."

Wendover noticed something pathetic in her attitude. For a moment the normal angularity and fussiness seemed to have left her manner.

"Poor soul!" he reflected. "Another case of unsatisfied maternity, I suppose. She seems to have adored this nephew of hers."

Paul Fordingbridge seemed to think that enough time had been spent on the family's private affairs.

"Is there anything more that you'd care to see?" he asked Sir Clinton, in an indifferent tone.

The chief constable seemed to have been interested in Miss Fordingbridge's tale.

"Just a moment," he said half-apologetically to Paul Fordingbridge. "I'd like to be sure about one or two points."

He crossed the room and examined the window-catches with some care.

"Now, Miss Fordingbridge," he said, as he turned back after finding the fastenings intact like the others, "this is a room which you're sure to remember accurately, since you say you looked after it yourself. Can you see anything missing from it?"

Miss Fordingbridge gazed from point to point, checking the various objects from her mental inventory.

"Yes," she said suddenly, "there's a small silver inkstand missing from his desk."

"I saw an inkstand in the sack," Armadale confirmed.

Sir Clinton nodded approvingly.

"Anything else, Miss Fordingbridge?"

For a time her eyes ranged over the room without detecting the absence of anything. Then she gave a cry in which surprise and disappointment seemed to be mingled. Her finger pointed to a bookshelf on which a number of books were neatly arranged.

"Why," she said, "there's surely something missing from that! It doesn't look quite as full as I remember it."

She hurried across the room, knelt down, and scanned the shelves closely. When she spoke again, it was evident that she was cut to the heart.

"Yes, it's gone! Oh, I'd have given almost anything rather than have this happen! Do you know what it is, Paul? It's Derek's diary—all the volumes. You know how carefully he kept it all the time he was here. And now it's lost. And he'll be back here in a few days, and I'm sure he'll want it."

Still kneeling before the bookshelves, she turned round to the chief constable.

"Sir Clinton, you *must* get that back for me. I don't care what else they've taken."

The chief constable refrained from making any promise. He glanced at Paul Fordingbridge, and was puzzled by what he read on his features. Commiseration for his sister seemed to be mingled with some other emotion which baffled Sir Clinton. Acute vexation, repressed only with difficulty, seemed to have its part; but there was something also which suggested more than a little trepidation.

"It's a rather important set of documents," Paul Fordingbridge said, after a pause. "If you can lay your hands on them, Sir Clinton, my sister will be very much indebted to you. They would certainly never have been left here if it had not been for her notions. I wish you'd taken my advice, Jay," he added irritably, turning to his sister. "You know perfectly well that I wanted to keep them in my own possession; but you made such a fuss about it that I let you have your way. And now the damned things are missing!"

Miss Fordingbridge made no reply. Sir Clinton interposed tactfully to relieve the obvious strain of the situation.

"We shall do our best, Miss Fordingbridge. I never care to promise more than that, you understand. Now, can you see anything else that's gone a-missing from here?"

Miss Fordingbridge pulled herself together with an effort. Clearly the loss of the diary had been a severe blow to her sentiment about her nephew's study. She glanced round the room, her eyes halting here and there at times when she seemed in doubt. At last she completed her survey.

"I don't miss anything else," she said. "And I don't think there's anything gone that I wouldn't miss if it had been taken away."

Sir Clinton nodded reflectively, and led the way in an examination of the rest of the house. Nothing else of any note was discovered. All the window-fastenings seemed to be intact; and there was no sign of any means whereby thieves could have entered the premises. An inspection of the contents of the sack in the draw-ing-room yielded no striking results. It was filled with a collection of silver knick-knacks evidently picked up merely because they were silver. Neither Paul Fordingbridge nor his sister could recall anything of real intrinsic value which might have been stolen.

"Twenty pounds' worth at the most. And they didn't even get away with it," Sir Clinton said absentmindedly, as he watched the inspector, in his rubber gloves, replacing the articles in the sack in preparation for transporting them to the car.

"Is that all we can do for you?" Paul Fordingbridge asked, with a certain restraint in his manner, when the inspector had finished his task.

Sir Clinton answered with an affirmative nod. His thoughts seemed elsewhere, and he had the air of being recalled to the present by Paul Fordingbridge's voice.

"Then, in that case, we can go, Jay. I'm sure Sir Clinton would prefer things left untouched at present, so you mustn't come about here again, shifting anything, until he gives permission. Care to keep the keys?" he added, turning to the chief constable.

"Inspector Armadale had better have them," Sir Clinton an-swered.

Paul Fordingbridge handed over the bunch of keys, made a faint gesture of farewell, and followed his sister to the car. Sir Clinton moved across to the window and watched them start down the av-enue before he opened his mouth. When they had disappeared round a bend in the road, he turned to his two companions again. Wendover could see that he looked more serious even than at Peter Hay's cottage.

"I may as well say at once, inspector, that I do not propose to extend my bus-driver's holiday to the extent of making a trip to Australia."

Armadale evidently failed to follow this line of thought.

"Australia, sir? I never said anything about Australia."

Sir Clinton seemed to recover his good spirits.

"True, now I come to think of it. Shows how little there is in all this talk about telepathy. I'd made certain I'd read your thoughts correctly; and now it turns out that you weren't thinking at all. A mental blank, what? Tut! Tut! It's a warning against rushing to conclusions, inspector."

"I don't see myself rushing to Australia, anyhow, sir."

"H'm! Perhaps we'll get along without that, if we're lucky. But think of the platypus, inspector. Wouldn't you like to see it at home?"

The inspector gritted his teeth in an effort to restrain his temper. He glanced at Wendover, with evident annoyance at his presence.

"It's going to be a pretty problem, evidently," Sir Clinton continued in a more thoughtful tone. "Now, what about the evidence? We'd better pool it while it's fresh in our minds. Civilians first. What did you see in it all, squire?"

Wendover decided to be concise.

"No signs of entry into the house. Bag of silver odds and ends in drawing-room, as if ready for removal. Set of volumes of diary removed from nephew's study. Strange story of missing nephew turning up. That's all I can think of just now."

"Masterly survey, squire," said Sir Clinton cordially. "Except that you've left out most of the points of importance."

He nodded to Armadale.

"See anything else, inspector? The credit of the force is at stake, remember."

"Mr. Fordingbridge didn't seem overmuch cut up by Peter Hay's death, sir."

"There's something in that. Either he's a reserved person by nature, or else he'd something of more importance to himself on his mind, if one can judge from what we saw. Anything more?"

"Mr. Fordingbridge and Miss Fordingbridge seemed a bit at cross-purposes over this nephew."

"That was more than obvious, I admit. Anything else?"

"Whoever packed up that silver must have come in with a key."

"I think that goes down to Mr. Wendover's score, inspector. It follows directly from the fact that the house wasn't broken into in any way."

"The silver here and the silver at Peter Hay's link up the two affairs."

"Probably correct. Anything further?"

"No more evidence, sir."

Sir Clinton reflected for a moment.

"I'll give you something. I was watching Mr. Fordingbridge's face when the loss of the diary was discovered. He was more than usually annoyed when that turned up. You weren't looking at him just then, so I mention it."

"Thanks," Armadale responded, with some interest showing in his voice.

"That missing diary would be a useful weapon," Sir Clinton continued. "You could check statements by it; or you could produce false statements from it, if you were a swindling claimant."

"That's self-evident," Wendover interjected.

"So it is," Sir Clinton admitted blandly. "I suppose that's why you didn't mention it yourself, squire. To continue. There's one point which strikes me as interesting. Supposing that Miss Fordingbridge hadn't come up here to-day, do you think we'd have discovered that the diary was missing at all?"

"No, unless Mr. Fordingbridge had noticed the loss."

"Naturally. Now I'll give you a plain hint. What is there behind Mr. Fordingbridge's evident annoyance? That seems to me a fruitful line for speculation, if you're thinking of thinking, as it were."

Wendover reflected for a moment.

"You mean that the diary would be invaluable to a claimant, and hence Fordingbridge may have been angry at its loss. Or else you mean that Fordingbridge was mad because the loss had been discovered. Is that what you're after, Clinton?"

Sir Clinton's gesture in reply seemed to deprecate any haste.

"I'm not after anything in particular, squire," he assured Wendover. "I simply don't see my way through the business yet. I merely recommend the subject for you to browse over. As they say about Shakespeare, new perspectives open up before one's eyes every time one examines the subject afresh. And, by the way, hypophosphites are said to be sustaining during a long spell of intense cogitation. I think we'll call at the druggist's on the way home and buy up his stock. There's more in this affair than meets the eye."

The inspector picked up the sack. Then, apparently struck by an after-thought, he laid it on the floor again and took out his note-book.

"Would you mind giving me any orders you want carried out immediately, sir?" he asked. "Anything in the way of information you need from the village?"

Sir Clinton looked at him in mock surprise, and answered with a parody of the "Needy Knifegrinder":

"Orders! God bless you! I have none to give, sir. This is your case, inspector, not mine."

Armadale succeeded in finding a form of words to turn the flank of his superior's line:

"Well, sir, suppose you were in my place, what would you think it useful to find out?"

"A deuce of a lot of things, inspector. Who killed Peter Hay, for one. Who stole the diary, for another. When I'm likely to get any lunch, for a third. And so on. There's heaps more of them, if you'll think them up. But, if I were in your shoes, I'd make a beginning by interviewing young Colby, who found the body; then I'd investigate the sweet-shop, and find out who bought pear-drops there lately; I'd make sure there are no fingerprints on any of the silver; I'd get the P.M. done as quickly as possible, since amyl nitrite is volatile, and might disappear if the body's left too long; and I think I'd make some very cautious inquiries about this long-lost nephew, if he's anywhere in the vicinity. And, of course, I'd try to find out all I could about Peter Hay's last movements yesterday, so far as one can discover them from witnesses."

Inspector Armadale had been jotting the chief constable's advice down in shorthand; and, when Sir Clinton finished speaking, he shut his note-book and put it back in his pocket.

"Peter Hay puzzles me," Wendover said thoughtfully, as they made their way to the car.

"Perhaps Peter Hay knew too much for his own safety," Sir Clinton answered, as he closed the door of Foxhills behind them.

A fresh line of thought occurred to Wendover.

"This missing nephew came from Australia, Clinton. I'm playing golf to-morrow morning with that Australian man who's staying at the hotel. He isn't the missing heir by any chance, is he?"

"I shouldn't think so, from Miss Fordingbridge's story. This claimant was pretty badly disfigured, whereas Cargill's rather a nice-looking chap. Also, she's sure to have come across Cargill in the hotel; he's been here for a week at least; but the claimant-man only presented himself to her last night, if you remember."

CHAPTER VI
THE BEACH TRAGEDY

Wakened abruptly by the trilling of a bell beside his bed, Sir Clinton bitterly regretted the striving of the Lynden Sands Hotel towards up-to-dateness, as represented by a room telephone system. He leaned over and picked up the receiver.

"Sir Clinton Driffield speaking."

"I'm Armadale, sir," came the reply. "Can I see you? It's important, sir, and I can't very well talk about it over the 'phone."

Sir Clinton's face betrayed a natural annoyance.

"This is an ungodly hour to be ringing anyone up in his bed, inspector. It's barely dawn. However, since you're here, you may as well come up. My room's No. 89."

He laid down the receiver, got out of bed, and put on his dressing-gown. As he moved across the room and mechanically began to brush his hair, a glance through the window showed him that the rain of the previous night had blown over and the sky was blue. The sun had not yet risen, and a pale full moon was low on the western horizon. A murmur of the incoming tide rose from the beaches; and the white crests of the waves showed faintly in the half-light.

"Well, inspector, what is it?" Sir Clinton demanded testily. "You'd better be brief, be businesslike, and be gone, as they say. I want to get back to bed."

"There's been another murder, sir."

Sir Clinton made no effort to conceal his surprise.

"Another murder! In a place this size? They must be making a hobby of it."

The inspector observed with satisfaction that his superior had given up any thoughts of bed, for he was beginning to dress himself.

"This is what happened, sir," Armadale continued. "Shortly after midnight a man appeared at the house of the local constable—Sapcote, you remember—and hammered on the door till Sapcote came down. He began some confused yarn to the constable, but Sapcote very wisely put on his clothes and brought the fellow round to me. I've got a room in a house near by, where I'm staying till this Hay affair is cleared up."

Sir Clinton nodded, to show that he was paying attention, but went on swiftly with his dressing.

"I examined the man," Armadale continued. "His name's James Billingford. He's a visitor here—he's rented old Flatt's cottage, on the point between here and Lynden Sands village. It seems he sometimes suffers from sleeplessness; and last night he went out rather late, hoping that a walk would do him some good. He strolled along the beach in this direction, not paying very much attention to anything. Then he heard the sound of shooting farther along the beach."

"Does that mean one shot or several?" Sir Clinton demanded, turning from the mirror in front of which he was fastening his tie.

"He was a bit doubtful there," Armadale explained. "I pressed him on the point, and he finally said he thought he heard two. But he wasn't certain. He seems to have been mooning along, not paying attention to anything, when he heard something. It wasn't for some seconds that he identified the sound for what it was; and by that time he was quite muddled up as to what he had really heard. He doesn't seem very bright," the inspector added contemptuously.

"Well, what happened after the Wild West broke loose on the beach?" Sir Clinton demanded, hunting for his shoes.

"It appears," pursued Armadale, "that he ran along the beach close to the water's edge. His story is that he couldn't see anything on the beach; but when he came level with that big rock they call Neptune's Seat he saw a dead man lying on it."

"Sure he was dead?"

"Billingford was quite sure about it. He says he was in the R.A.M.C. in the war and knows a dead 'un when he sees one."

"Well, what next?"

"I didn't question him much; just left him in charge of Sapcote till I came back. Then I hunted up a couple of fishermen from the village and went off myself along with them to Neptune's Seat. I made them stick to the road; and when I got within a couple of hundred yards of the rock, I left them and went down to the very edge of the water—below Billingford's marks, as the tide was still falling—and kept along there. There was enough moonlight to save me from trampling over anyone's footmarks and I took care to keep clear of anything of that sort."

Sir Clinton gave a nod of approval, but did not interrupt the story by any verbal comment.

"The body was there all right," Armadale continued. "He'd been shot through the heart—probably with a small-calibre bullet, I should think. Dead as a doornail, anyhow. There was nothing to be done for him, so I left him as he was. My main idea was to avoid muddling up any footprints there might be on the sand."

Again Sir Clinton mutely showed his approval of the inspector's methods. Armadale continued his narrative:

"It was too dim a light to make sure of things just then, a bit cloudy. So the best thing seemed to be to put the men I had with me to patrol the road and warn anyone off the sands. Not that any-one was likely to be about at that hour of the morning. I didn't think it worth while to knock you up, sir, until it got a bit brighter; but as soon as there seemed any chance of getting to work, I came up here. You understand, sir, the tide's coming in; and it'll wash out any tracks as it rises. It's a case of now or never if you want to see them. That's why I couldn't delay any longer. We've got to make the best of the time we have between dawn and high tide."

Armadale paused, and looked at Sir Clinton doubtfully.

"I understand, inspector." The chief constable answered his unspoken query. "There's no room for fooling at present. This is a case where we're up against time. Come along!"

As he stood aside to let the inspector leave the room in front of him, Sir Clinton was struck by a fresh idea.

"Just knock up Mr. Wendover, inspector. He's next door—No. 90. Tell him to dress and follow on after us. I'll get my car out, and that will save us a minute or two in getting to the place."

Armadale hesitated most obviously before turning to obey.

"Don't you see, inspector? All these tracks will be washed out in an hour or two. We'll be none the worse of having an extra witness to anything we find; and your fishermen pals would never understand what was important and what wasn't. Mr. Wendover will make a useful witness if we ever need him. Hurry, now!"

The inspector saw the point, and obediently went to wake up Wendover, whilst Sir Clinton made his way to the garage of the hotel.

In a few minutes the inspector joined him.

"I waked up Mr. Wendover, sir. I didn't wait to explain the thing to him; but I told him enough to make him hurry with his dressing. He says he'll follow in less than five minutes."

"Good! Get in."

Armadale jumped into the car, and, as he slammed the door, Sir Clinton let in the clutch.

"That tide's coming in fast," he said anxiously. "The Blowhole up there is beginning to spout already."

Armadale followed in the direction of the chief constable's glance, and saw a cloud of white spray hurtling up into the air from the top of a headland beside the hotel.

"What's that?" he asked, as the menacing fountain choked and fell.

"Sort of thing they call a *souffleur* on the French coast," Sir Clinton answered. "Sea-cave gets filled with compressed air owing to the rise of the tide, and some water's blown off through a landward vent. That's what makes the intermittent jet."

About a mile from the hotel the inspector motioned to Sir Clinton to stop at a point where the road ran close to the beach, under some sand-dunes on the inland side. A man in a jersey hastened towards them as the car pulled up.

"Nobody's come along, I suppose?" the inspector demanded when the newcomer reached them. Then, turning to Sir Clinton, he added: "This is one of the men who were watching the place for me."

Sir Clinton looked up with a smile at the introduction.

"Very good of you to give us your help, Mr.—?"

"Wark's my name, sir."

". . . Mr. Wark. By the way, you're a fisherman, aren't you? Then you'll be able to tell me when high tide's due this morning."

"About half-past seven by God's time, sir."

Sir Clinton was puzzled for a moment, then he repressed a smile slightly different from his earlier one. "Half-past eight by summer time then?" he queried.

He glanced at his wrist-watch, and then consulted a pocket diary.

"Sunrise is due in about a quarter of an hour. You gauged it neatly in waking me up, inspector. Well, we've a good deal less than two hours in hand. It may keep us pretty busy, if we're to dig up all the available data before the tracks are obliterated by the tide coming in."

He reflected for a moment, and then turned to the fisherman.

"Would you mind going into Lynden Sands village for me? Thanks. I want some candles—anything up to a couple of dozen of them. And a plumber's blowlamp, if you can lay your hands on one."

The fisherman seemed taken aback by this unexpected demand.

"Candles, sir?" he inquired, gazing eastward to where the golden bar of the dawn hung on the horizon.

"Yes, candles—any kind you like, so long as you bring plenty. And the blow-lamp, of course."

"The ironmonger has one, sir."

"Knock him up, then, and quote me for the price—Sir Clinton Driffield—if he makes any difficulty. Can you hurry?"

"I've got a bicycle here, sir."

"Splendid! I know you won't waste time, Mr. Wark."

The fisherman hurried off in search of his cycle; and in a very short time they saw him mount and ride away in the direction of the village. The inspector was obviously almost as puzzled as Wark had been, but he apparently thought it best to restrain his curiosity about the candles and blow-lamp.

"I think we'll leave your second patrol to watch the road, inspector, while we go down on to the beach. I suppose that's the rock you were speaking about?"

"Yes, sir. You can't see the body from here. The rock's shaped rather like a low chesterfield, with its back to this side, and the body's lying on what would be the seat."

Sir Clinton glanced towards the bar of gold in the east which marked the position of the sun below the horizon.

"I don't want to go blundering on to the sands at random, inspector. What about a general survey first of all? If we climb this dune at the back of the road, we ought to get some rough notion of how to walk without muddling up the tracks. Come along!"

A few seconds took them to the top of the low mound. By this time the dawn-twilight had brightened, and it was possible to see clearly at a fair distance. Sir Clinton examined the beach for a short time without making any comment.

"That must be my own track, coming along the beach from the village, sir. The one nearest the water. I kept as close to the waves as I could, since the tide was falling and I knew I was sticking to ground that must have been covered when Billingford came along."

"What about the fishermen?" Sir Clinton asked.

"I made them keep to the road, so as to leave no tracks."

Sir Clinton approved with a gesture, and continued his inspection of the stretch of sand below.

"H'm!" he said at last. "If clues are what you want, inspector, there seem to be plenty of them about. I can make out four separate sets of footprints down there, excluding yours; and quite possibly there may be others that we can't see from here. It's lucky they aren't all muddled up together. There's just enough crossing to give us some notion of the order in which they were made—in three cases at least. You'd better make a sketch of them from here, now that there's light enough to see clearly. A rough diagram's all you'll have time for."

The inspector nodded in compliance, and set about his task. Sir Clinton's eye turned to the road leading from the hotel.

"Here's Mr. Wendover coming," he announced. "We'll wait till he arrives, since you're busy, inspector."

In a few moments Wendover clambered up the dune. "Did you turn back to the hotel for anything?" he inquired, as he came up to them.

"No, squire. Why?"

"I noticed a second track of motor-wheels on the road at one point as I came along. It faded out as I got nearer here, so I thought you might have gone back for something or other."

"That would have made three tracks, and not two; one out, one back, and a final one out again."

"So it would," Wendover admitted, evidently vexed at having made a mistake.

"We'll have a look at that track later on," Sir Clinton promised. "I took care not to put my own tracks on top of it as we came along."

"Oh, you saw it, did you?" said Wendover disappointedly. "Confound you, Clinton, you seem to notice everything."

"Easy enough to see the track of new non-skids on a wet road, especially as I didn't see my own track while I was making it. We'll have no trouble in disentangling them, even if they do cross here and there, for my tyres are plain ones, and a bit worn at that. I think I ought to mention that our patrols report no traffic on the road since they came on to it; and, as I remember that there was no rain in the early evening, that gives us some chance of guessing the time when that car made its tracks in the mud."

"The rain came down about half-past eleven," the inspector volunteered as he finished his sketch. "I heard it dashing on my window just after I'd gone to bed, and I went up stairs about twenty past eleven."

Sir Clinton held out his hand for the inspector's notebook, compared the diagram with the view before him, and passed the book to Wendover, who also made a comparison.

"Better initial it, squire," the chief constable suggested. "We may need you to swear to its accuracy later on, since we'll have no visible evidence left after this tide's come in."

Wendover obeyed, and then returned the note-book to the inspector as they began to descend from the dune towards the road. Halfway down, Sir Clinton halted.

"There's another set of tracks which we couldn't see from the place we were," he said, pointing. "Behind that groyne running down towards the rock. The groyne was in the line of sight up above, but we've moved to the left a bit and you can just see one or two footprints. Over yonder, inspector. You'd better fill them in when we get to the road and have a clear sight of them."

The inspector completed his diagram, and handed it to his companions in turn for verification.

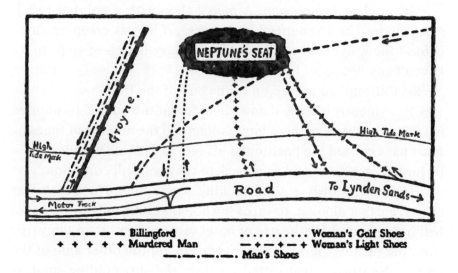

"We may as well start with this track," Sir Clinton suggested. "It's a fairly short one, and seems isolated from all the others by the groyne."

He stepped down on to the sand, taking care to keep well away from the footmarks; and his companions followed his track. They walked on a line parallel to the footprints, which ran close under the groyne. At first the marks were hardly defined; but suddenly they grew sharp.

"This is where he hit the sand wetted by the tide, obviously," said Wendover. "But the trail looks a bit curious—not quite like a normal man's walk."

"Suppose he'd been crouching under the groyne as he went along," Sir Clinton suggested. "Wouldn't that account for it? Look!"

He moved on to a piece of untouched sand, bent almost double, and began to move cautiously along. Wendover and the inspector had to admit that his tracks were very like those of the trail beside the groyne.

"Somebody spying on the people on the rock?" Wendover hazarded. "If you can get hold of him, Clinton, he ought to be a useful witness."

The inspector stooped over the footprints and scanned them closely.

"It's a clear impression. A man's shoe with a pointed toe, it seems to be," he announced. "Of course, if he was creeping along behind the groyne we can't get his ordinary length of step, so we haven't any notion of his height."

Sir Clinton had moved on to the end of the trail.

"He evidently crouched down here for quite a while," he pointed out. "See the depth of these impressions and the number of times he must have shifted the position of his feet to ease his muscles. Then he turned back again and went back to the road, still crouching."

He swung slowly round, looking about him. The beach was empty. Farther along it, towards the hotel, a group of bathing-boxes had been erected for the use of hotel visitors. Less than ten yards from the turning-point of the footprints, on the other side of the groyne, Neptune's Seat jutted up from the surrounding sand. It was, as the inspector had said, like a huge stone settee standing with its back to the land; and on the flat part of it lay the body of a man. Sir Clinton bent down and scrutinised the surface of the sand around the turning-point of the track for some minutes, but he made no comment as he completed his survey. When he rose to his full height again, he saw on the road the figure of the fisherman, Wark; and he made a gesture forbidding the man to come down on the sand.

"Just go up and see if he's got the candles and the blow-lamp, inspector, please. We may as well finish off here if he has."

Armadale soon returned with the articles.

"Good fellow, that," Sir Clinton commented. "He hasn't wasted time!"

He turned and gazed across at the advancing tide.

"We'll have to hurry up. Time's getting short. Another half-hour and the water will be up near that rock. We'll need to take the seaward tracks first of all. Hold the blow-lamp, will you, inspector, while I get a candle out."

Wendover's face showed that even yet he had not grasped the chief constable's object. Sir Clinton extracted a candle and lit the blow-lamp.

"Plaster of Paris gives a rotten result if you try to take casts of sand-impressions with it," he explained. "The classics pass rather lightly over the point, but it is so. Therefore we turn to melted wax or tallow, and by dropping it on very carefully in a thin layer at first, we get something that will serve our purpose. Hence the candles and the blow-lamp. See?"

He suited the action to the word, making casts of the right and left footprints in the sand from the sharpest impressions he could pick out.

"Now we'll take Mr. Billingford's track next," he said, as he removed the two blocks of wax from their beds. "His footmarks will be the first to be swamped by the tide, so we must get on to them in a hurry."

He led his companions back to the road and turned round the landward end of the groyne.

"This is where he landed on the road, evidently. Now step in my tracks and don't wander off the line. We mustn't cut up the ground."

He moved along the trail, and soon reached the tidal mark, after which the footprints grew sharper. A little farther on, he reached a point where Billingford's marks crossed an earlier track—the prints of a woman's nail-studded shoes.

"Golfing-shoes, by the look of them," he pointed out to his companions. "We can leave them alone just now. The tide won't reach here for long enough yet, so we've plenty of time to come back. Billingford's the important thing at present."

Billingford's track ran down to Neptune's Seat, where it was lost on the hard surface of the rock. Sir Clinton, without halting, directed his companions' attention to a second trail of male footprints running up towards the rock from the road, and crossed just at the landward side of Neptune's Seat by the traces of Billingford.

"There's no return track for these, so far as I can see," he pointed out, "so it looks as if the murdered man made them."

Without a glance at the body, he stepped up on to the rock, picked up the farther trail of Billingford, and began to follow it as it led along the beach towards Lynden Sands village. The footprints ran along the top of a series of slight whale-backs of sand, behind which lay a flatter zone running up towards the high-tide mark. Nearer the sea, a track showed the inspector's line of advance during the night. After following the trail for nearly a quarter of a mile, Sir Clinton pointed to a change in its character.

"This is where he began to run. See how the pace shortens beyond this."

Rather to the surprise of his companions, he continued to follow the trail.

"Is it really necessary to go as far as this?" Wendover demanded after a time. "You've come the best part of three-quarters of a mile from the rock. What are you trying to do?"

"I'm trying to find out the earliest moment when Billingford could have reached the rock, of course," Sir Clinton explained, with a trace of irritation.

A few yards farther on, Billingford's track was neatly interrupted. For twenty feet or so there were no tracks on the sand; then the footprints reappeared, sharply defined as before. At the sight of the gap Sir Clinton's face brightened.

"I want something solid here," he said. "Stakes would be best, but we haven't any. A couple of cairns will have to do. Bring the biggest stones you can lift; there are lots up yonder above the tide-mark."

He set them an example, and soon they had collected a fair number of heavy stones. Sir Clinton, with an anxious eye on the tide, built up a strong cairn alongside the last of Billingford's footprints which was visible.

"Now the same thing on the other side of the gap," the chief constable directed.

Wendover suppressed his curiosity until the work in hand was over; but as soon as the second cairn had been erected at the point where Billingford's footprints reappeared on the sand he demanded an explanation.

"I'm trying to estimate when Billingford passed that point last night," Sir Clinton answered. "No, I haven't time to explain all about it just now, squire. We're too busy. Ask me again in twelve hours or so, and I'll tell you the answer to the sum. It may be of importance or it mayn't; I don't know yet."

He turned and glanced at the rising tide.

"Jove! We'll need to look slippy. The tide's getting near that rock. Look here, inspector. Get hold of one of these fishermen and ask them to pounce on the nearest boat and bring it round to the rock. Then we can leave everything on the rock to the last moment and spend our time on the sands, which haven't got permanent traces and must be cleared up first of all. If we get cut off by the tide, we can always get the body away on a boat, if we have one handy."

The inspector hurried off, waving to attract the attention of the fishermen. In a few moments he was back again.

"They say, sir, that the nearest boat is at Flatt's cottage, just on the point yonder. They're off to bring it round. By the way, they warned me against going near that old wreck there, farther along the bay. It seems there's a patch of bad quick-sand just to the seaward side of it—very dangerous."

"All right, inspector. We're not going any farther along in this direction for the present. Let's get back to the rock where the body is. We've still got the other trails of footmarks to examine."

They hurried off towards Neptune's Seat, and at the edge of the rock Sir Clinton halted.

"Here's a set of prints—a neatly-shod woman, by the look of them," he pointed out. "She's come down to the rock and gone back again almost on the same line. Take a cast of good ones, inspector, both left and right feet. Be careful with your first drippings of the wax."

Wendover inspected the line of prints with care.

"They don't tell us much," he pointed out. "Billingford's tracks don't cross them, so there's no saying when they were made. It might have been a visitor coming down to the beach yesterday afternoon."

"Hardly," interrupted Sir Clinton. "High tide was at half-past eight; and obviously they must have been made a good while after that or else this part of the sands would have been covered. But it was a moonlight night, and it's quite possible someone came down here to look at the sea late in the evening."

"It's a small shoe," Wendover pursued, without answering the criticism.

"Size 3½ or thereabouts," Armadale amended, glancing up from his work. "I shouldn't make it bigger than a 3½, and it might be even smaller."

Wendover accepted the rectification, and continued. "The step's not a long one either. That looks like a rather small girl with a neat foot, doesn't it?"

Sir Clinton nodded.

"Looks like it. Have you a tape-measure, inspector? We ought to make a note of the length of the pace, I think. It might turn out useful. One never knows."

The inspector fished a tape-measure from his pocket; and, with the help of Wendover, Sir Clinton made measurements of various distances.

"Just twenty-four inches from one right toe-mark to the next," he announced. "And it seems a very regular walk. Now if you're ready, inspector, we'll go on to the next trail. It's the single one, so it's probably the murdered man's."

They moved round the rock a little. The inspector's face lighted up at the sight of the footprints.

"Rubber soles, sir; and a fairly well-marked set of screws to check anything with. If they do belong to the murdered man, we'll have no trouble in identifying them."

Sir Clinton agreed.

"Don't bother taking casts of them yet. We may not need them. Let's go on to the next tracks."

They had to cut across Billingford's trail and walk to the far end of the rock before they reached their objective.

"This is the other end of the track we noticed before," Wendover pointed out. "It's the woman in golfing-shoes who came down from the road near the groyne."

The inspector fell to work on his casting, whilst Sir Clinton took another series of measurements of the length of pace shown by the footprints.

"Twenty-six and a half inches," he reported, after several trials of comparison. "Now, once the inspector's finished with his impression-taking, we can have a look at the body. We've just done the business in time, for the tide's almost washing the base of the rock now."

CHAPTER VII
THE LETTER

FOLLOWED BY WENDOVER and the inspector, Sir Clinton mounted the platform of Neptune's Seat, which formed an outcrop some twenty yards long and ten in breadth, with the landward part rising sharply so as to form a low natural wall. The body of the murdered man lay on the tiny plateau at the end nearest the groyne. It rested on its back, with the left arm slightly doubled up under the corpse. Blood had been welling from a wound in the breast.

"Anybody claim him?" inquired Sir Clinton. "He isn't one of the hotel guests, at any rate."

Armadale shook his head.

"I don't recognise him."

Sir Clinton lifted the head and examined it. "Contused wound on the back of the skull. Probably got it by falling against the rock as he came down." He turned to the feet of the body.

"The boots have rubber soles with a pattern corresponding to the tracks up yonder. That's all right," he continued. "His clothes seem just a shade on the flashy side of good taste, to my mind. Age appears to be somewhere in the early thirties."

He bent down and inspected the wound in the breast. "From the look of this hole I guess you're right, inspector. It seems to have been a small-calibre bullet—possibly from an automatic pistol. You'd better make a rough sketch of the position before we shift him. There's no time to get a camera up here before the tide swamps us."

Armadale cut one or two scratches on the rock as reference points, and then, after taking a few measurements, he made a rough diagram of the body's position and attitude.

"Finished?" Sir Clinton asked; and, on getting an assurance from the inspector, he knelt down beside the dead man and unfastened the front of the raincoat which clothed the corpse.

"That's interesting," he said, passing his hand over a part of the jacket underneath. "He's been soaked to the skin by the feel of the cloth. Did that rain come down suddenly last night, inspector?"

"It sounded like a thunder-shower, sir. Dry one minute and pouring cats and dogs the next, I remember."

"That might account for it, then. We proceed. I can see only one wound on him, so far as the front's concerned. No indication of robbery, since his raincoat was buttoned up and the jacket also. Help me to lift him up, inspector, so that we can get his arm free without scraping it about too much. If he wore a wrist-watch, it may have stopped conveniently when he fell, for he seems to have come rather a purler when he dropped."

Armadale raised the left side of the body slightly, and Sir Clinton levered the twisted arm gently into a more normal position.

"You're right, sir," the inspector exclaimed, pointing to the strap on the dead man's wrist. He bent forward as though to turn the hand of the body, but the chief constable stopped him with an imperative gesture.

"Gently, inspector, gently. We may need to be cautious."

Very carefully he manoeuvred the dead man's wrist until they could see the face of the watch.

"It's stopped at 11.19," Armadale pointed out. "That gives us the moment when he fell, then. It doesn't seem of much use to us yet, though."

Wendover detected a flaw in the inspector's assumption.

"Some people forget to wind up their watches now and again. Perhaps he did, the night before last; and it might have stopped of its own accord at 11.19, before he was shot at all."

"Dear me, squire! This is a break-away from the classics with a vengeance. I thought it was always taken for granted that a watch stopped conveniently at the very moment of the murder. But perhaps you're right. We can always test it."

"How?" demanded Wendover.

"By winding it up now, counting the clicks of the rachet as we do it; then let it run fully down and wind up again, also counting the clicks. If the two figures tally, then it's run down naturally; if they don't it's been forcibly stopped. But I doubt if we'll need to bother about that. There must be some better evidence than that somewhere, if we can only lay hands on it."

Wendover's eyes had been ranging over the surface of the rock; and, as Sir Clinton finished his exposition, Wendover drew his attention to a shiny object lying at the other end of Neptune's Seat.

"Just have a look at it, squire, will you? I'm busy here just now. Now, inspector, it seems to me as if some of this watch-glass is missing. There doesn't seem enough to cover the dial. Let's have a look under the body and see if the rest's there."

Armadale raised the dead man sufficiently to enable Sir Clinton to examine the spot where the watch had struck the rock.

"Yes, here's the rest of the glass," the chief constable reported. "And there's a faint scrape on the rock surface to show that he must have come down with a bit of a thud. Thanks, inspector, you can let him down again."

When Armadale had let the body drop back into its original position, Sir Clinton knelt down and unstrapped the wrist-watch, after which he wrapped it carefully in his handkerchief. The fragments of glass he handed to the inspector, who stowed them away in an envelope.

Meanwhile Wendover had made a discovery.

"Come here, Clinton. That yellow thing was the brass case of a discharged cartridge."

Sir Clinton stepped across the rock and picked up the tiny object, marking its position as he did so by scoring a cross on the stone with his penknife.

"It's a .38 calibre, apparently," he commented, after a glance at it. "You'd better keep it, inspector. Hullo! Here's the boat coming in."

A rowing-boat manned by the two fishermen was approaching Neptune's Seat.

"That's good. We can finish our examination on the spot now. The tide won't rise to the level of the rock for a while yet; and it doesn't matter if we do get cut off, now that the boat's here. Bring her close in, please, if there's water enough."

The fishermen, nothing loath to get a closer view of the proceedings, brought the boat's bow up to the natural quay formed by the rock; and then, shipping their oars, they sat down to watch what was going on.

"We may as well go through his pockets next," Sir Clinton suggested, returning to the body. "Go ahead, inspector."

Armadale began his search, reporting each object discovered.

"Raincoat pockets—nothing in either. Left-hand breast pocket of jacket—a handkerchief. Right-hand breast pocket—a note-case."

He handed this over to Sir Clinton, who opened it. "Fifteen-ten in notes. Nothing else. Well, it wasn't a case of robbery, apparently. Go on, inspector."

"Right-hand upper waistcoat pocket," the inspector droned obediently, "a pocket diary."

Sir Clinton took it, skimmed over the pages, and put it down.

"It's a calendar diary—blank. A book of stamps, with some stamps missing, in the cover. Not much help there. Go ahead."

The inspector continued his search.

"Other upper pocket—a pencil and fountain-pen. Lower waistcoat pocket, left hand, a silver match-box with monogram—S and N intertwined. Right-hand pocket—a penknife and a cigar-cutter. Trouser side-pockets—some money, mostly silver, and a nail-trimmer, and a couple of keys. Hip-pocket—a cigar-case."

He handed the various articles to the chief constable.

"Nothing in the ticket-pocket. Outside jacket pockets. Left-hand pocket—there's a pipe and a tobacco-pouch. Right-hand pocket—

ah, here's something more interesting! Letter-card addressed to 'N. Staveley, Esq., c/o Billingford, Flatt's Cottage, Lynden Sands.' So his name was Staveley? That fits the S on the monogram. And here's another bit of paper; looks like a note of some sort. No envelope to it."

He held out the two papers to Sir Clinton, who examined the letter-card first.

"Posted two days ago in London—W.1. H'm! Nothing much to take hold of here, I'm afraid. 'Dear Nick,—Sorry to miss you on Tuesday. See you when you get back to town.' No address, and the signature's a scrawl."

He turned to the single sheet of note-paper, and as he unfolded it Wendover saw his eyebrows raised involuntarily. For a moment he seemed in doubt; then, with a glance at the two fishermen, he carefully refolded the paper and stowed it away in his pocket-book.

"That will keep for the present," he said.

Over the chief constable's shoulder, Wendover caught a glimpse of a figure advancing along the sands from the direction of the hotel bathing-boxes. A towel over its shoulder showed the reason for the appearance of the stranger on the beach before breakfast. As it approached, Wendover recognised the gait.

"Here's Cargill, that Australian who's staying at the hotel, Clinton. He's come down for a bathe, evidently. You'd better do the talking for us."

Cargill had evidently recognised them, for he hastened his steps and soon reached the groyne.

"I shouldn't come any farther, Mr. Cargill," Sir Clinton said politely. "There are some tracks there which we may want to look at if we have time; and I'd rather not have them mixed up with yours, if you don't mind."

Cargill halted obediently, but looked inquisitively at the group on the rock.

"Is that where the murder happened?" he inquired.

"How do you know about it?" Sir Clinton replied, giving question for question.

"Oh, the news came up to the hotel with the milk, I expect," the Australian answered. "I heard it from a waiter as I came through on my way to bathe. The whole staff's buzzing with it. I say, who is it?"

"Couldn't say yet," Sir Clinton returned with an air of candour. Then he added: "I'm sorry we haven't time to talk it over just now, Mr. Cargill. This tide will be all round us in a minute, if we don't get a move on."

He turned to the fishermen.

"We'll shift the body into your boat now, and then you can row slowly along towards the village. Don't hurry; and don't go ashore till you see Inspector Armadale there. He'll take the body off your hands. You understand? Thanks."

The boat was brought close alongside the natural quay and the body of Staveley put aboard without mishap. At a sign from Sir Clinton, the boat put out into the bay. Armadale seemed a little at a loss over the procedure; but he made no audible protest. Cargill remained on the other side of the groyne, obviously taking the keenest interest in the whole affair.

Sir Clinton gave a last glance round the rock plateau; then, followed by his companions, he retreated to the upper sands. Cargill, thus left alone, hovered uncertainly for a moment or two, and finally sat down on the groyne, looking idly at the sand around his feet. Evidently he understood that he was not wanted, but it looked as though he had still some faint hopes of being allowed to join the party.

"We must carry all this stuff up to the car," Sir Clinton reminded his companions. "I'll take some of the casts; you can manage the rest, inspector. Wendover, the blow-lamp and the rest of the candles are your share, if you don't mind."

When they reached the car, he motioned Wendover into the driving-seat and signed to the inspector to get in also.

"I'm going for a short walk along the road towards the hotel," he explained. "Let me get a bit ahead, squire, and then follow on, slowly. I'm going to have a look at that extra wheel-track at close quarters. It won't take more than a moment or two."

He moved along the road to a point just before the groyne, and halted there for a few moments, examining the faint track left by the turning of a car. Then he continued his walk towards the hotel, scrutinising the ground as he went. At the end of a few hundred yards he halted; and, when Wendover brought up his car, Sir Clinton got into it, taking the seat in front.

"There are really two tracks there," he explained, as he closed the door. "Down by the beach, both of them are very faint, and I noticed rain-marks on top of them. Then, just a few dozen yards back from here, one of the tracks is strongly marked, while the second track remains faint. It's so lightly marked that I expect you missed it this morning, squire. Now what do you make of that?"

Wendover considered for a few moments.

"Somebody came down the road in a car before the rain and made the light track," he suggested. "Then he turned and came back in this direction; and when he had got this length the rain came on, and his tracks after that were in mud and not in dry dust, so they'd be heavier. That it?"

"I expect so," Sir Clinton acquiesced. "No, don't go on yet. I've something to show you before we go farther. I didn't care to produce it before all that audience down at the rock."

He put his hand into his pocket and pulled out the piece of note-paper found on Staveley's body. Wendover leaned over and examined it as the chief constable unfolded it.

"Hullo! The hotel heading's on the paper, Clinton," he exclaimed. "This is getting a bit near home, surely."

"It is," said Sir Clinton drily. "I'll read it, inspector. It's short and very much to the point, apparently. The date on it is yesterday. This is how it goes. There's no 'Dear So-and-so' or anything of that sort at the beginning.

> "'Your letter has come as a complete surprise, as you expected, no doubt. You seem to know all about what has happened, and I suppose you will do all you can to make the worst of things—at least I can't take any other meaning out of what you have written. I shall

come to Neptune's Seat tonight at 11 P.M. to hear what you have to say. But I warn you plainly that I will not submit to being blackmailed by you, since that seems to be what is in your mind.'

And the signature," Sir Clinton concluded, "is *Cressida Fleetwood*."

The inspector leaned forward and took the letter.

"*Now* we've got something to go on!" he exclaimed jubilantly. "That name, coupled with the hotel notepaper, ought to let us lay our hands on her within half an hour, if we've any luck at all."

Wendover had been thunder-struck by the revelation of the signature. His mind involuntarily called up a picture of Cressida as he had seen her less than twenty-four hours earlier, frank and care-free, and so evidently happy with her husband. A girl like that could hardly be mixed up with a brutal murder; it seemed too incongruous. Then across his memory flitted a recollection of Sir Clinton's description of the poker-sharp, and the implied warning against trusting too much to appearances; but he resolutely put them aside. A glance at Armadale's face tended to increase his bias, for it displayed a hardly restrained exultation. Quite evidently the inspector supposed that his case was now well on the road to a satisfactory solution.

"Damned man-hunter!" Wendover commented inwardly, quite forgetting that a few minutes earlier he himself had been every bit as eager as the inspector. "I don't want to see her fall into that brute's hands."

His imagination called up a picture of Cressida, with that fascinating touch of shyness changed to dismay, faced by the harsh interrogations of an Armadale determined to force from her some damning statement. The inspector would see no reason for kindly treatment in the case of a woman whom he seemed to have condemned already in his mind.

Wendover turned to Sir Clinton in the hope of seeing some signs of other feelings there. But the chief constable's face betrayed nothing whatever about his thoughts, and Wendover remembered that Sir Clinton had known the contents of the letter before he left the

beach. It had not affected him when he read it then, Wendover recalled; for there had been no change in his manner.

Suddenly the squire felt isolated from his companions. They
were merely a couple of officials carrying out a piece of work, re-
gardless of what the end of it might be; whereas he himself had
still his natural human sympathies to sway him in his judgments
and tip the scale in a case of doubt. Almost with surprise, he found
himself disliking Armadale intensely; a great, coarse-fibred creature who cared nothing for the disaster which he was about to un-
chain within an hour.

Wendover awoke from his thoughts to find Sir Clinton looking
at him with an expressionless face.

"Care to step off here, squire? Your face gives you away. You
don't like the way things are trending? Better leave us to finish the
job alone."

Wendover's brain could work swiftly when he chose. Almost in
a moment he had gauged the situation. If he dropped out, then the
two officials would go forward together and there would be no
human feelings among the hunters. If he stayed with them, he could
at least play the part of critic and shake the inspector's confidence
in any weak links of the chain which he was forging. Further than
that he could not go, but at least he could hold a watching brief for
Cressida. His mind was made up at once.

"No," he answered. "If you don't mind, since I'm in the thing
now, I'll stay in. You may need an impartial witness again, and I
may as well have the job."

The inspector made no attempt to conceal his disgust. Sir
Clinton showed neither approval nor objection, but he evidently
thought it right to give a warning.

"Very well, squire. It's your own choice. But, remember, you're
only a witness. You're not to go putting your oar in when it's not
wanted."

Wendover indicated his acquiescence by a curt nod. Sir Clinton
restarted his car and drove along with his eyes fixed on the clearly
marked tracks of the non-skid tyres. At the hotel entrance the stud-
ded print turned inward, and was lost on the gravel of the sweep
up to the hotel.

As he noticed this, the inspector made an involuntary gesture of satisfaction, whilst Wendover felt that the net had been drawn yet tighter by this last piece of evidence.

"That's a clincher, sir," Armadale pointed out with a frank satisfaction which irritated Wendover intensely. "She took a car down and back. This is going to be as easy as falling off a log."

"I suppose you noticed that that car never stopped at all on the road home," Sir Clinton remarked casually. "The tracks showed no sign of a stop and a restart once the machine had got going."

Only after he had run his car into the hotel garage did he speak again.

"We don't want any more chatter than we can help at present, inspector. There's no real case against anyone yet; and it won't do to rush into the limelight. I suggest that Mr. Wendover should ask to see Mrs. Fleetwood. If you inquired for her, every tongue in the place would be at work in five minutes; and by the time they'd compared notes with each other, it'll be quite impossible to dig out anything that one or two of them may really happen to know. Everything will have got mixed up in their minds, and they won't remember whether they saw something themselves or merely heard about it from someone else."

Wendover saw the force of the argument; but he also realised clearly the position into which he was being pushed.

"I'm not so sure I care about that job, Clinton," he protested. "It puts me in a false position."

The chief constable interrupted him brutally.

"Five minutes ago I offered you the chance to get off the bus. You preferred to stay with us. Therefore you do as you're told. That's that."

Wendover understood that his only chance of keeping in touch with the hunters now depended on his obeying orders. Gloomily he made his submission.

"All right, Clinton. I don't like it; but I see there are some advantages."

Accompanied by the others, he entered the hotel and made his way to the desk, while the two officials dropped into the background.

"Mrs. Fleetwood?" the clerk repeated, when Wendover had made his inquiry. "Yes, sir, she's upstairs. Didn't you know that Mr. Fleetwood broke his leg last night? The doctor's set it now. I think Mrs. Fleetwood's up in his room with him."

"What's the number?" Wendover asked.

"No. 35, sir. Shall I 'phone up and ask if you can see her? It's no trouble."

Wendover shook his head and turned away from the desk. As he crossed the hall, the other two rejoined him.

"It's on the first floor. We'll walk up," said Sir Clinton, turning towards the stairs. "You can do the talking, inspector."

Nothing loath, Armadale knocked at the door of No. 35, and, on receiving an answer, he turned the handle and entered the room. Sir Clinton followed him, whilst Wendover, acutely uncomfortable, hovered on the threshold. On the bed, with his features pale and drawn, lay Stanley Fleetwood. Cressida rose from an armchair and threw a startled glance at the intruders.

The inspector was no believer in tactful openings.

"I'm sorry to trouble you," he said gruffly, "but I understand you can give me some information about the affair on the beach last night."

Wendover, despite his animus against Armadale, could not help admiring the cleverness of this sentence, which took so much for granted and yet had a vagueness designed to lead a criminal into awkward difficulties in his reply. But his main interest centred in Cressida; and at the look on her face his heart sank suddenly. Strain, confusion, and desperation seemed to have their part in it; but plainest of all was fear. She glanced from her husband to Armadale, and it was patent that she understood the acuteness of the danger.

"Why," he admitted to himself in dismay, "she looks as if she'd really done it! And she's deadly afraid that Armadale can prove it."

Cressida moistened her lips automatically, as if she were about to reply; but, before she could say a word, her husband broke in.

"What makes you come here with inquiries? I suppose you've some authority? Or are you a reporter?"

"I'm Inspector Armadale."

Stanley Fleetwood made an evident effort to keep himself in hand, in spite of the physical pain which he was obviously suffering. He nodded in acknowledgment of the inspector's introduction, and then repeated his question.

"What makes you come to us?"

Armadale was not to be led into betraying anything about the extent of his information.

"I really can't go into that, Mr. Fleetwood. I came to ask a few questions, not to answer any. It's to your interest to answer frankly."

He turned to Cressida.

"You were on the beach last night about eleven o'clock?"

Stanley Fleetwood broke in again before Cressida could make a reply.

"Wait a moment, inspector. Are you proposing to bring a charge against me?"

Armadale hesitated for a moment, as if undecided as to his next move. He seemed to see something further behind the question.

"There's no charge against anyone—yet," he said, with a certain dwelling on the last word; but as he spoke his eyes swung round to Cressida's drawn features with a certain menace.

"Don't say anything, Cressida," her husband warned her.

He turned back to the inspector.

"You've no power to extract evidence if we don't choose to give it?" he asked.

"No," the inspector admitted cautiously, "but sometimes it's dangerous to suppress evidence, I warn you."

"I'm not very amenable to threats, inspector," Stanley Fleetwood answered drily. "I gather this must be something serious, or you wouldn't be making such a fuss?"

In his reply, Armadale reinforced his caution with irony.

"It's common talk in the hotel that there's been a murder on the beach. Perhaps the rumour's reached you already?"

"It has," Stanley Fleetwood admitted. "That's why I'm cautious, inspector. Murder's a ticklish business, so I don't propose to give any evidence whatever until I've had legal advice. Nor will my wife give any evidence either until we've consulted our lawyer."

Armadale had never seen a move of this sort, and his discomfiture was obvious. The grand scene of inquisition would never be staged now; and his hope of wringing damning admissions from unprepared criminals was gone. If these two had a lawyer at their elbow when he questioned them, he wouldn't stand much chance of trapping them into unwary statements. Wendover was delighted by the alteration in the inspector's tone when he spoke again.

"That doesn't look very well, Mr. Fleetwood."

"Neither does your intrusion into a sick-room, inspector."

Sir Clinton evidently feared that things might go too far. He hastened to intervene, and when he spoke his manner was in strong contrast to the inspector's hectoring.

"I'm afraid you hardly see the inspector's point of view, Mr. Fleetwood. If we had the evidence which you and you wife could evidently give us, then quite possibly we might get on the track of the murderer. But if you refuse that evidence just now, we shall be delayed in our work, and I can't guarantee that you won't come under suspicion. There will certainly be a lot of needless gossip in the hotel here, which I'd much rather avoid if I could. The last thing we want to do is to make innocent people uncomfortable."

Stanley Fleetwood's manners gave way under the combined action of his physical pain and his mental distress.

"Where do you buy your soap?" he asked sarcastically. "It seems a good brand. But it won't wash. There's nothing doing."

Inspector Armadale threw a glance at his superior which suggested that Sir Clinton's intervention had been a mere waste of time.

"When'll your lawyer be here?" he demanded brusquely.

Stanley Fleetwood paused to consider before replying.

"I'll wire him to-day; but most likely the wire will lie in his office until Monday. I expect Monday afternoon will be the earliest time he could get here, and perhaps he won't turn up even then."

Inspector Armadale looked from husband to wife and back again.

"And you'll say nothing till he comes?"

Stanley Fleetwood did not think it worth the trouble to answer.

"I think you'll regret this, sir. But it's your own doing. I needn't trouble you further just now."

Armadale stalked out of the room, suspicion and indignation written large in every line of his figure. Sir Clinton followed. As Wendover closed the retreat, he saw Cressida step swiftly across to her husband's side and slip to her knees at the edge of the bed.

CHAPTER VIII
THE COLT AUTOMATIC

AT THE FOOT OF THE STAIRS, Armadale excused himself.

"Better have some breakfast, inspector," Sir Clinton suggested. "You've been up all night, and you must be hungry."

Rather to Wendover's relief, Armadale rejected the implied invitation.

"I'll pick up a sandwich, probably, later on, sir; but I've something I want to make sure about first, if you don't mind. Will you be ready again in half an hour or so?"

Sir Clinton glanced at his watch.

"We'll hurry, inspector. After all, it's about time that we took Billingford out of pawn. The constable may be getting wearied of his society by this stage."

Inspector Armadale seemed to have no sympathy in stock so far as either Billingford or Sapcote was concerned.

"Staveley's body has to be collected, too," he pointed out. "I've a good mind to 'phone for some more men. We really can't cover all the ground as we are."

"I should, if I were you, inspector. Get them sent over by motor; and tell them to meet us at Lynden Sands. A sergeant and three constables will probably be enough."

"Very good, sir."

The inspector went off on his errand, much to the relief of Wendover, whose antagonism to Armadale had in no way cooled. Sir Clinton led the way to the breakfast-room, and impressed on his waiter the necessity for haste. As they sat down, Wendover saw inquisitive glances shot at their table by other guests in distant parts of the room. Evidently the news of the tragedy on the beach was common property by now.

"I don't think Armadale made much of that business," Wendover commented in a voice low enough to be inaudible to their nearest neighbours. "There's nothing so undignified as a bit of bullying when it doesn't quite come off."

Sir Clinton never allowed a criticism of a subordinate to pass unanswered.

"Armadale did his best, and in nine cases out of ten he'd have got what he wanted. You're looking at the thing from the sentimental standpoint, you know. The police have nothing to do with that side of affairs. Armadale's business is to extract all the information he can and then use it, no matter where it leads him. If an official had to stop his investigations merely because a pretty girl breaks down and cries, we shouldn't be a very efficient force in society."

"He met his match in young Fleetwood," Wendover pointed out, with hardly concealed satisfaction.

Sir Clinton gazed across the table with a curious expression on his face.

"For a J.P. you seem to be strangely out of sympathy with the minions of the law. If you ask me, young Fleetwood will have himself to thank for anything that happens now. Of course, he's gained two or three days in which he can discuss everything in detail with his wife, and they can concoct between them just what they propose to tell us eventually. But I never yet saw a faked-up yarn that would stand the test of careful investigation and checking. And you may take it that, after the way Armadale was received, he'll put every word he gets from them under a microscope before he accepts it as true."

Wendover nodded a gloomy assent to this view.

"I expect he will," he agreed. "Perhaps it's a pity that young Fleetwood took that line."

"I gave him his chance to make a clean breast of it, if he'd any reasonable tale to tell," Sir Clinton pointed out with a trace of impatience. "All I got was a piece of guttersnipe insolence. Obviously he thinks he can get the better of us; but when it comes to the pinch, I think—"

He broke off abruptly. Wendover, glancing round, saw that Mme. Laurent-Desrousseaux had come into the room and was moving in the direction of their table. As she came towards them, he compared her, half unconsciously, with Cressida Fleetwood. Both of them would have been conspicuous in any group; but Cressida's looks were a gift of Nature, whereas Mme. Laurent-Desrousseaux was obviously a more artificial product. Everything about her proclaimed that the utmost care had been spent upon her appearance; and even the reined-in manner of her walk suggested a studied movement in contrast to Cressida's lithe and natural step. Wendover noted that the wave in her red-brown hair was a permanent one, obviously too well designed to be anything but artificial.

"Now, why the deuce does one say 'foreigner' as soon as one sees her?" he inquired of himself. "Heaps of English girls wear dresses like that in the morning, though they may not carry them so well. And they have their hair waved, too. And her face isn't particularly Continental-looking; I've seen types like that often enough in this country. It must be the way she moves, or else the way she looks at one."

Mme. Laurent-Desrousseaux gave him a brilliant smile of recognition as she passed; then, seating herself at the next table, she took up the menu and studied it with a look of distaste on her features. Quite evidently the English breakfast was not much to her liking. After some consideration she gave her order to the waiter by pointing to the card, as if she mistrusted her pronunciation of some of the words.

Sir Clinton obviously had no desire to discuss police affairs any further, with a possible eavesdropper at his elbow. He went on with his breakfast, and, as soon as Wendover had finished, he rose from the table with a glance at his wrist-watch.

"We'd better pick up the inspector and get off to Lynden Sands. I'll bring the car round."

At the hotel door, a few minutes later, Armadale for some reason or other seemed to be in high spirits; but he gave no indication of the cause of his cheerfulness.

A few minutes' run along the coast brought them to Lynden Sands village, and the inspector directed Sir Clinton to Sapcote's house. The constable was evidently on the look-out, for as they were about to knock at the door he appeared and invited them into a room where Billingford was sitting. At the first glance, Wendover was prejudiced against the man. Billingford had the air of someone trying to carry off an awkward situation by a forced jauntiness; and, in the circumstances, this jarred on Wendover. But, on reflection, he had to admit to himself that Billingford's position was an awkward one, and that an easy demeanour was hardly to be expected under these conditions.

"Now, Mr. Billingford," the inspector began at once, "I've one or two questions to ask you. First of all, why didn't you tell the constable immediately that Staveley was a friend of yours? You must have recognised him whenever you saw the body on the rock."

Billingford's surprise was either genuine or else must have been very well simulated.

"Staveley, is it?" he exclaimed. "I didn't know it was Staveley! There was a cloud over the moon when I got to the body, and I couldn't see the face. It was quite dark then for a while—so dark that on the way there I splashed through a regular baby river on the beach. My trousers are all wet still round the boot-tops. Staveley, is it? Well, well!"

Wendover could make nothing of the man. For all he could see, Billingford might be genuinely surprised to hear of Staveley's death. But, if he were, his emotion at the loss of a friend could hardly be called excessive.

The inspector put his next question.

"Did you know if Staveley had gone out to meet anyone last night?"

Billingford's eyes contracted momentarily at this question. Wendover got the impression of a man on his guard, and thinking hard while he talked.

"Meeting anyone? Staveley? No, I can't say I remember his say-ing anything about it to me. He went out some time round about ten o'clock. But I thought he'd just gone for a turn in the fresh air. We'd been smoking a lot, and the room was a bit stuffy."

The inspector jotted something in his note-book before asking his next question.

"What do you do for a living, Mr. Billingford?"

Billingford's face assumed a bland expression. "Me? Oh, I'm a commission agent."

"Do you mean a commercial traveler?" Armadale demanded.

A faint smile crossed Sir Clinton's face.

"I think Mr. Billingford means that he lives by his wits, inspec-tor. Am I correct?" he asked, turning to Billingford.

"Well, in a way, yes," was the unashamed reply. "But commis-sion agent sounds rather better if it gets into the papers."

"A very proper tribute to respectability," Sir Clinton commented drily.

"What did you know about Staveley?" the inspector went on.

"Staveley? Nothing much. Used to meet him now and again. The two of us did business together at times."

"Was he a commission agent too?" the inspector inquired ironi-cally.

"Well, sometimes he said he was that, and other times he put himself down as a labourer."

"On the police charge-sheet, you mean?" Sir Clinton asked.

Billingford grinned openly.

"Never saw the inside of a gaol in my life," he boasted. "Nor did Staveley either, that I know about."

"I've no doubt my colleagues did their best," Sir Clinton said amiably.

The inspector came back to his earlier question. "Is that all you can tell us about him?"

"Who? Staveley? Well, sometimes we worked together. But it's not likely I'd tell you much about that, is it?"

"What was he doing down here?"

"Staying with me for a day or two. I was getting a bit jaded with rush-work in the City, so I came down here for a rest. And Staveley, he said he'd join me and we'd work out a new scheme for benefiting some members of the public."

The inspector nodded.

"Some easy-money business, I suppose. Now come to last night, and be careful what you say. Tell me exactly what you can remember. Begin about dinnertime."

Billingford reflected for a moment or two before answering.

"After dinner, things were a bit dull, so the three of us started to play poker to pass the time."

"Three of you?" Armadale interrupted. "Who was the third man?"

"Oh, he's an Australian by the twang. Derek Fordingbridge, he calls himself. Staveley brought him down. There was something about his having an estate round about here, and wanting to take a look at it."

"You hadn't met him before?"

"Me? Oh, only once or twice. I thought he was just another labourer in the vineyard, if you take me."

"A competitor of yours in the commission agent business? What was he doing in that line if he had an estate?"

"Search me!" Billingford answered guardedly. "I'm not one for asking too many questions about people's affairs. 'Do unto others as you'd be done by' is my motto."

Armadale evidently realised that he would get nothing by persisting on this line.

"You played poker, then. Anything further happen?"

Billingford seemed to be considering carefully before he ventured further. At last he made up his mind.

"About half-past nine, I think, someone came to the door. Staveley got up and went to see who it was. I heard him say: 'Oh, it's you, is it?' or words to that effect—as if he'd been taken by surprise. Then I heard a woman's voice say something. I didn't catch the words. And when Staveley replied, he dropped his voice. They talked for a bit, and then he shut the door."

"And after that? Did you find out who the woman was?"

"Not I. Some local piece, I expect. Staveley was always a good hand at getting hold of them. He'd a sort of way with him, and could get round them in no time. Made kind of hobby of it. Over-did it, to my mind."

"What happened after that?"

"Nothing much that I remember. We played some more poker, and then Staveley began grousing about the stuffiness of the place. Mostly his own fault, too. Those cigars of his were pretty heavy. So he went out for some fresh air."

"When was that?"

"Ten o'clock. I told you before. Perhaps 10.15. I can't be sure to a minute."

"And then?"

"I felt a bit wakeful. I lose a lot of sleep some nights. So I thought I'd go for a turn along the shore and see if that would cure it."

"When did you leave the house?"

"A little before eleven, I think. I didn't notice. It was after Fordingbridge had gone to bed, anyhow."

The inspector absent-mindedly tapped his note-book with his pencil for a moment or two. Then he glanced at Sir Clinton.

"That's all I want to ask you just now," he said. "You'll be needed at the inquest, of course. I suppose you're staying on for a while at Lynden Sands?"

"Oh, yes," Billingford replied carelessly. "If you want me at any time, I'll be handy. Always pleased to play 'Animal, Vegetable, or Mineral?' with you any time you like, inspector."

"I daresay you've had plenty of practice," Armadale growled. "Well, you can go now. Hold on, though! You can show us the way up to Flatt's cottage. I'll need to see this friend of yours, Fording-bridge."

"Meaning to check up my story?" Billingford suggested, un-abashed. "I've met this sort of sceptical spirit before. Somehow it always seems to develop in people who've worn a constable's hel-met in their youth. Compression of the credulity lobe of the brain, or something like that, perhaps."

Armadale made no reply, but led the way out of the house. Before they had gone more than a few yards, a police-sergeant came forward and accosted the inspector. After a few words, Armadale turned to Sir Clinton.

"Now we've got the constables, sir, I think we'd better get the body ashore and notify Dr. Rafford that we'll need a P.M. done. If you don't mind going round by the beach, I can put the sergeant here in charge; and then we can go on to Flatt's."

The chief constable made no objection; and the inspector paid no attention to Billingford's humorous protest against a further waste of his time. The whole party made their way down to the shore, where they found most of the idlers of the village assembled, awaiting the putting in of the boat.

Armadale signaled to the two fishermen; and very soon they rowed their craft to the little pier. The police kept the crowd back while the body was being landed. Then the inspector gave the sergeant some instructions; and under the guidance of Sapcote the squad set off into the village with the body.

Suddenly Billingford seemed to recognise the rowing-boat.

"Snaffled my boat, have you, inspector? Well, I like the nerve of that! If I'd borrowed your handkerchief without asking you, there'd have been a bit of a stir in official circles. But when you take and steal my boat, everybody seems to think it's just the sort of thing you _would_ do. Well, brother, we'll say no more about it. _I_ never care to rub things in. Live and let live's my motto."

Armadale refused to be drawn.

"We'll clean up the boat and return it in the afternoon," he said shortly. "Now come along. I haven't time to waste."

A short walk took them to Flatt's cottage, which stood near the point of the promontory between the village and the bay in which Staveley's body had been found. The road up to it was hardly better than a rough track, and pools of water stood here and there which evidently dated farther back than the rain of the previous night. The cottage itself was neatly kept, and seemed fairly roomy.

"Call your friend," Armadale ordered, as they reached the door.

Billingford complied without protest, and almost at once they heard steps approaching. As the door opened, Wendover received a shock. The man who stood before them was almost faceless; and his eyes looked out from amid a mass of old scars which gave him the appearance of something inhuman. The hand which held the door open lacked the first two fingers. Wendover had never seen such a wreck. When he took his eyes from the distorted visage, it was almost a surprise to find that the rest of the form was intact.

The newcomer stared at them for a moment. His attitude showed the surprise which his face could not express.

"What made you bring this gang here, Billingford?" he demanded. "Visitors are barred, you know that quite well."

He made a suggestive gesture towards his twisted face.

Armadale stepped forward.

"You're Mr. Fordingbridge, aren't you?" he asked.

The apparition nodded, and fixed its eyes on him without saying anything.

"I'm Inspector Armadale. I suppose you know that your friend Staveley was murdered last night?"

Derek Fordingbridge shook his head.

"I heard there had been a murder. I believe they borrowed the boat from here to use in bringing the body in. But I didn't know it was Staveley. Who did it?"

"Weren't you surprised that he didn't come home last night?" the inspector demanded.

Something which might have been a smile passed over the shattered face.

"No. He had a knack of staying out all night often enough. It wasn't uncommon. Was there a woman in the case?"

"I think we'll get on faster if you let me do the questioning," said the inspector bluntly. "I'm sorry I haven't any time to spare just now. Can you tell me anything about Staveley?"

"He was a sort of relation of mine. He married my cousin Cressida during the war."

Armadale's face lighted up as he heard this.

"Then how do you account for her being the wife of Mr. Stanley Fleetwood?" he asked abruptly.

Derek Fordingbridge shook his head indifferently.

"Accidental bigamy, I suppose. Staveley didn't turn up after the war, so I expect she wrote him down as dead. She'd hardly grieve over him, from what I know of his habits."

"Ah." the inspector said thoughtfully. "That's interesting. Had she come across him by any chance since he came down here?"

"I couldn't say. I'm hardly in touch with the rest of my family at present."

The inspector, recalling the fact that this was the claimant to the Foxhills estate, did not think it necessary to pursue the matter further. He turned back to the more immediate question.

"Can you tell me anything about Staveley's movements last night?"

"Nothing much. We played poker after dinner. Someone interrupted us—a friend of Staveley's. Then we played some more. Then I went to bed early. That's all."

"What about this friend of Staveley's? Was it a man or a woman?"

"A woman, I believe; but I didn't see. Staveley went to the door himself. That would be between nine and ten o'clock."

"When did Staveley go out?"

"I can't say. After ten o'clock, at any rate, for I went to bed, then. I'd a headache."

"When did you hear about the murder?"

"Before I got out of bed. I was told that two men wanted to borrow the boat."

The inspector paused before continuing his inquiry. When he spoke again, it was on a different point.

"I shall need to go through his luggage, of course. Can I see it?"

Derek Fordingbridge led the way into the cottage.

"It's in there," he said, indicating one of the rooms. "He'd only a suit-case with him."

The inspector knelt down and turned out the suitcase's contents with some care.

"Nothing here of any use," he said disappointedly when he had finished. "One or two odds and ends. No papers."

He rummaged in the drawers of the room-furniture with the same lack of success. As he rose to his feet, Sir Clinton turned to Fordingbridge.

"I'd like to see the fourth man of the party," he said thoughtfully. "Perhaps you wouldn't mind getting hold of him for me if he's here."

Wendover and Armadale showed some surprise; but Fordingbridge seemed to see nothing in it.

"That's rather sharp of you. It's just as well we aren't up against *you*. You mean the man who told me about the boat being wanted? Sorry I can't get him for you. He was a handy-man we brought down with us. Billingford had a row with him last night and fired him, so he took himself off this morning."

"What was his name?"

Billingford's look of innocence was intentionally overdone.

"His name? Well, I called him Jack."

"Jack what?"

"Just Jack. Or at times: 'Here! You!' He answered to either."

Inspector Armadale's temper began to show signs of fraying.

"You must know something more about him. Hadn't he a character when you employed him?"

"Oh, yes. A pretty bad one. He used to drink my whiskey."

"Don't be funny," snapped Armadale. "Didn't you get any references from an earlier employer?"

Billingford's eyes twinkled.

"Me? No. I've a charitable nature. Where would any of us be if we had our characters pawed over? Forgive and forget's my motto. It's easy enough to work on till someone does you in the eye."

"So you say you know nothing about him?"

"I don't quite like the way you put it, inspector. It seems almost rude. But I don't know where he is now, and I'll kiss the Book on that for you if you want it."

Armadale's expression showed clearly that he thought little would be gained by accepting Billingford's offer. He warned Derek

Fordingbridge that his evidence might be needed at the inquest; then, with a cold nod to Billingford, he led the way out of the cottage. Sir Clinton maintained silence until they were beyond earshot of the door, then, as though addressing the world at large, he said pensively:

"I wonder why they brought such a large card-index down with them from town."

Armadale was taken aback.

"Card-index, sir? Where was it?"

"I noticed it in their sitting-room as we passed the open door. It's one of these small cabinet affairs."

The inspector had no suggestion to offer; and Sir Clinton did not seem to be anxious to pursue the matter. A few yards farther on he halted, and pointed to something at the edge of one of the puddles.

"Doesn't that footprint seem a bit familiar, inspector? Just measure it, will you?"

Armadale's eyes widened as he looked.

"Why, it's that 3½ shoe!" he exclaimed, stooping over the mark.

"I noticed it as we were coming up, but it didn't seem to be the best time for examining it," Sir Clinton explained. "Now, inspector, that's a permanent kind of puddle. The chances are that this mark was made before last night's rain. It's on the very edge of the water now, not the place where a girl would step if she could help it. The puddle's filled up a bit since she made it."

"So she was Staveley's visitor last night?"

"It looks like it," Sir Clinton agreed. "Now measure it carefully, inspector."

Armadale produced his tape-measure and took various dimensions of the mark. When he had risen to his feet again, Sir Clinton looked back at the cottage. Billingford and his companion were on the doorstep, eagerly gazing towards the police party.

"Give it a good scrub with your foot now, inspector, if you've quite finished with it. We may as well give Mr. Billingford something to guess about. He's a genial rascal, and I'd like him to have some amusement."

The inspector grinned broadly as he rubbed his boot vigorously over the soft mud, effacing the print completely.

"I'd like to see his face when he comes down to look at it," he said derisively, as he completed the work of destruction. "We couldn't have got much of a cast of it, anyhow."

When they reached Sir Clinton's car, Armadale took leave of them.

"There's one or two things I've got to look into," he explained, "and I'll get some food between whiles. I'll come along to the hotel in about an hour or so, if you don't mind waiting there for me, sir. I think I'll have something worth showing you by then."

He threw a triumphant glance at Wendover, and went off up the street. Sir Clinton made no comment on his subordinate's remark, but started the car and drove towards the hotel. Wendover saw that nothing was to be got out of the chief constable, and naturally at the lunch-table the whole subject was tabooed.

Armadale did not keep them waiting long. They had hardly left the lunch-table before he presented himself; and Wendover noted with dismay the jubilant air with which the inspector came forward to meet them. He carried a small bag in his hand.

"I'd rather be sure that nobody overhears us, sir," he said as he came up to them. "And I've some things to show you that I don't want talked about in public yet."

He tapped the bag as he spoke.

"Come up to my room, then, inspector. We'll be free from interruption there."

They took the lift up; and, when they entered the room, the inspector turned the key in the door behind them as an extra precaution.

"I've got the whole case cut and dried now, sir," he explained with natural exultation in his voice. "It was just as I said this morning—as easy as falling off a log. It simply put itself together of its own accord."

"Well, let's hear it, inspector," Sir Clinton suggested as soon as he could edge a word into the current of the inspector's roam

"I'll give you it step by step," the inspector said eagerly, "and then you'll see how convincing it is. Now, first of all, we know that the dead man, Staveley, married this Fleetwood woman during the war."

Wendover flinched a little as he identified "this Fleetwood woman" as Cressida. This was evidently a foretaste of the inspector's quality.

"From what we've heard, one way and another, Staveley was nothing to boast about," Armadale went on. "He was a bad egg, evidently; and especially in the way that would rasp a wife."

"That's sound," Sir Clinton agreed. "We needn't dwell on it."

"He disappears; and she thinks he's dead," the inspector pursued. "She's probably mighty glad to see the end of him. After a bit, she falls in with young Fleetwood and she marries him. That's bigamy, as it turns out; but she doesn't know it then."

"One can admit all that without straining things much," Sir Clinton agreed. "Go on, inspector."

"The next thing is that Staveley turns up again. I don't suppose he appeared in public. That wouldn't be his game. These Fordingbridges have money; and, from what we've heard, Staveley wasn't scrupulous about transferring other people's money to his own pocket."

"Nothing that could be shaken, so far," Sir Clinton encouraged him. "Go ahead."

"Very well," the inspector went on. "He writes her a letter evidently trying to put the screw on her, and asking for an appointment on the quiet. She must have been taken a bit aback. She'd been living with young Fleetwood for the best part of a year. It's quite on the cards that she's—"

He broke off, glanced at Wendover's stormy countenance, and evidently amended his original phrase:

"That perhaps young Fleetwood and she weren't the only people who might be hit by the business when it came out."

"So that's your notion of the motive, is it?" Sir Clinton commented. "Well, it's ingenious, I admit. I didn't quite see how you were going to work up a case on the strength of a mere accidental bigamy, for nobody would think much about that. But one can't tell how it might look from the point of view of a mother, of course. Anything's possible, then. Go ahead."

"She writes him a letter making an appointment at an out-of-the-way place—Neptune's Seat—at a time when it's sure to be quiet—11 P.M. That was the note we found on the body. Secrecy's written all over it, as any jury would see."

He paused for a moment, as though he were not quite sure how to put his next piece of the case.

"She takes an automatic pistol with her; probably her husband had one. I'm not prepared to say that she meant definitely to murder Staveley then and there. Perhaps she only took the pistol as a precaution. Probably her barrister will try to pretend that she took it for self-defence purposes, Staveley being what he was. I don't think that. Why? Because she took her husband along with her; and he could have looked after Staveley for her."

Wendover was about to interpose, but the inspector silenced him.

"I'll give you the evidence immediately, sir. Let me put the case first of all. She puts on her golfing-shoes, because she's going on to the sand. She takes down her golf-blazer and puts it on over her evening dress. Then she goes out by the side-door and meets the car that her husband has brought round from the garage for her. That must have been close on eleven o'clock. Nobody would miss her in a big place like the hotel."

With unconscious art, the inspector paused again for a moment. Wendover, glancing at Sir Clinton's face in the hope of reading his thoughts, was completely baffled. The inspector resumed, still keeping to the historical present in his narrative.

"They reach the point of the road nearest to Neptune's Seat. Perhaps they turn the car then, perhaps later. In any case, she gets out and walks down towards the rock. Fleetwood, meanwhile, slips in behind the groyne and keeps in the lee of it as he moves parallel with her. That accounts for the kind of prints we saw this morning.

"She gets to the rock and meets Staveley. They talk for a while. Then she loses her temper and shoots him. Then the fat's in the fire. The Fleetwoods go back to their car and drive off to the hotel again. They don't take the car to the garage straightway. She gets out, goes round by the entrance leading to place where the guests keep their golfing togs. She takes off her golfing-shoes, strips off her blazer and hangs it up, and slips into the hotel, without being spotted."

Wendover had listened to this confident recital with an ever-increasing uneasiness. He comforted himself, however, with the hope that the inspector would find it difficult to bring adequate proof of his various points; but he could not deny that Armadale's reconstruction manifested a higher gift of imagination than he had been expecting. It all sounded so grimly probable.

"Meanwhile," the inspector resumed, "young Fleetwood leaves the car standing and goes into the hotel. What he was after I can't fathom—perhaps to establish some sort of alibi. In any case, he comes hurrying down the stairs at 11.35 P.M., catches his foot, takes a header, and lands at the bottom with a compound fracture of his right leg. That's the end of him for the night. They ring up Rafford, who patches him up and puts him to bed."

Armadale halted again, and threw a superior smile towards Wendover.

"That's my case stated. I think there's enough in it to apply for a warrant against the woman as principal and young Fleetwood as accessory."

Wendover took up the implied challenge eagerly, now that he knew the worst. This was the part for which he had cast himself, and he was anxious to play it well.

"There's a flaw at the root of your whole case, inspector," he asserted. "You make out that it was fear of exposure that acted as the motive. Well, by this murder exposure became inevitable—and under its worst form, too. How do you get round that difficulty?"

Armadale's air of superiority increased, if anything, as he heard the objection advanced.

"I'm afraid, Mr. Wendover, that you haven't had much experience of *real* murder cases. In books, of course, it may be different," he added, with an evident sneer. "Your real murderer may be stupid and unable to forsee the chain of events that the murder's going to produce. Or else you may have an excitable clever type that's carried away by strong feelings on the spur of the moment, so that all the cleverness goes for nothing and the murderer does the work in a frame of mind that doesn't give much heed to the possible consequences."

"And, of course, the murderers who are neither stupid nor excitable are the ones who never get caught, eh?" Sir Clinton interjected in an amused tone. "That accounts for us police being at fault now and again."

Wendover considered Armadale's thesis with care.

"Then, as Mrs. Fleetwood isn't stupid," he said frigidly, "you're assuming that she lost her head under some strong provocation?"

"It's quite likely," Armadale insisted. "No jury would turn down that idea simply because we can't state what the precise provocation was. They wouldn't expect a verbatim report of the conversation on the rock, you know."

Wendover could hardly deny this in his own mind; and his heart sank as he heard the inspector's confident declaration. He tried a fresh point of attack.

"You said you'd definite evidence to support this notion of yours, didn't you? Well, how do you propose to prove that Mrs. Fleetwood was there at all last night?"

Armadale's smile had a tinge of triumph in it. He bent over his bag and drew from it one of the wax casts, which he laid on the table. A second dip brought to light a pair of girl's golfing-shoes. He selected the proper one and placed it, sole upward, alongside the cast. Wendover, with a sinking heart, compared corresponding parts of the two objects. Even the most carping critic could not deny the identity.

"These are the woman Fleetwood's golfing-shoes, sir," the inspector announced a trifle grimly. "I found them in the lady golfers' dressing-room. I can bring a witness or two who'll swear to them, if need be."

Suddenly Wendover detected a possible flaw in the inspector's case; but, instead of unmasking his battery immediately, he made up his mind to lead Armadale astray, and, if possible, to put him off his guard. He let his full disappointment show clearly in his face, as if the evidence of the shoes had shaken his beliefs. Dropping the matter without further discussion, he took up a fresh line.

"And the golf-blazer? What about it? That left no tracks on the sands."

Armadale's smile of triumph became even more marked. He turned once more to his bag, slipped his hands into his rubber gloves, and then, with every precaution, lifted a dusty-looking Colt automatic into view.

"This is a .38 calibre pistol," he pointed out. "Same calibre as the cartridge-case we picked up on the rock, and probably the same as the bullet'll be when we get it from the body. I've examined the barrel; there's been a shot fired from it quite recently. I've looked into the magazine; it lacks one cartridge of a full load."

He paused dramatically before his final point.

"And I found this pistol in the pocket of the woman Fleetwood's golf-blazer which was hanging on her peg in the lady golfers' dressing-room."

After another pause, meant to let the fact sink home in Wendover's mind, Armadale added:

"You'll admit, sir, that a toy of this sort is hardly the kind of thing an ordinary lady carries about with her."

Wendover thought he saw his way now, and he prepared to spring his mine.

"Let's be quite clear about this, inspector. I take it that you went into that ladies' dressing-room, hunted around for Mrs. Fleetwood's coat-peg, and found the blazer hanging on it and the shoes lying on the floor below."

"Exactly, sir. Mrs. Fleetwood's card was there, marking the peg. I'd no difficulty."

Wendover made no attempt to repress the smile which curved his lips.

"Just so, inspector. Anyone else could have found the things just as easily. They were lying there, open to anyone; not even a key to turn in order to pick them up. And after dark that dressing-room is left very much to itself. No one goes there except by accident."

In his turn he paused before launching his attack. Then he added:

"In fact, some other woman might have gone there instead of Mrs. Fleetwood; worn her shoes and her blazer; and misled you completely. Anyone could take the blazer from its peg and the shoes from the floor, inspector. Your evidence is all right up to a point, I admit; but it doesn't incriminate the owner of the articles, since they were accessible to anybody at that time of night."

Wendover had expected to see a downfall of the inspector's pride; but instead, Armadale's face showed clearly that the shot had missed its mark. With a slight gesture, the inspector drew Wendover's eyes to the pistol.

"There are some fingerprints on this—quite clear ones, sir. I've dusted them, and they're perfectly good as a means of identification."

"But you don't suppose Mrs. Fleetwood will let you take her fingerprints if they're going to tell against her, do you?"

Armadale's face showed the pleasure which he felt in having forestalled criticism. He gingerly replaced the pistol in some receptacle in his bag, and then drew out, with all precaution, a table-knife which Wendover recognised as the pattern used in the hotel.

"This is the knife that the woman Fleetwood used to-day at lunch. The waiter who served her was told to keep it for me—he brought it on the plate without handling it. When I dusted it some of her fingerprints came up, of course. They're identical with those on the pistol. Any reply to that, sir?"

Wendover felt the ground cut away from under his feet. He could think of nothing to urge against the inspector's results. But, even then, Armadale seemed to have something in reserve. He put the knife back in his bag, searched the contents again, and produced a pair of pumps, which he placed on the table.

"I got the chambermaid to lift these while she was tidying up Fleetwood's room this morning. Put your finger on the soles:

they're still quite damp. Naturally; for you know how water oozes from sand if you stand long on the one spot. What's more, if you look at the place between the soles and the uppers—at the join— you'll see some grains of sand sticking. That's good enough for me. Fleetwood was the man behind the groyne. Now you won't persuade me that Fleetwood was off last night helping anyone except his wife—any woman, I mean—in that affair at the rock."

Wendover scrutinised the pumps minutely and had to admit that the inspector's statements were correct. Armadale watched him scornfully and then concluded his exposition.

"There's the evidence you asked for, sir. Fleetwood was there. His pumps are enough to prove that. I haven't checked them with the cast yet, for there's enough already; but I'll do it later on. His wife was there—golf-shoes, blazer, pistol, fingerprints, they all prove it up to the hilt, when you take in the empty cartridge-case we found on the rock. Then there's the car left standing out all night. Probably he meant to bring it in and broke his leg before he could come back to do the work. That's enough to satisfy any jury, sir. There's nothing to do now except apply for a warrant and arrest the two of them."

Sir Clinton had listened to the inspector's recapitulation of the evidence with only a tepid interest; but the last sentence seemed to wake him up.

"It's your case, Inspector," he said seriously, "but if I were in your shoes I don't think I'd be in a hurry with that warrant. It may not be advisable to arrest either of the Fleetwoods—yet."

Armadale was plainly puzzled; but it was equally evident that he believed Sir Clinton to have sound reasons for his amendment.

"You think not, sir?" he asked, a shade apprehensively.

Sir Clinton shook his head.

"I think it would be a mistake to act immediately, inspector. But, of course, I'll take the responsibility off your shoulders. I'll put it in writing for you now if you wish it."

Armadale in turn shook his head.

"No need for that, sir. You never let any of us down. But what's your objection?"

Sir Clinton seemed undecided for a moment.

"For one thing, inspector," he said at last, "there's a flaw in that case of yours. You may be right in essentials; but you've left a loose end. And that brings me to another thing. There are far too many loose ends in the business, so far as it's gone. Before we do anything irrevocable in the way of bringing definite charges, we must get these loose ends fixed up."

"You mean, sir?"

"I mean we'll have to eliminate other possibilities. Billingford is one. I hope to throw some light on that point to-night, inspector, about midnight. And that reminds me, you might get the light ready to throw—a couple of good flash-lamps will be enough, I think. Bring them along here about 11.30 P.M. and ask for me. Then there's the dame with the neat shoe. She's a loose end in the tangle. . ."

"I've been looking into that, sir."

Sir Clinton's approval was obviously genuine.

"Really, inspector, you've done remarkably well in the short time you've had. That's good work indeed. And what are the results?"

The inspector's face showed they had not been altogether satisfactory.

"Well, sir, that footprint wasn't made by any of the hotel visitors. I've gone into it fully. Only three ladies here wear 3½'s: Miss Hamilton, Mrs. Rivel, and Miss Staunton. The footprint in the mud up at the cottage was made between nine and ten o'clock last night. Between those hours, Miss Hamilton was dancing—I've even a note of her partner's name. She's the best dancer, it seems; and a lot of people were watching her for the pleasure of it. So she's cleared. Mrs. Rivel was playing bridge from immediately after dinner until half-past eleven; so it couldn't be her. And Miss Staunton twisted her ankle on the links yesterday and had Dr. Rafford up to look at it. She's hobbling about with a stick, sir; and as there was no sign of a limp on the tracks, that clears her."

Sir Clinton considered the evidence without vocal comment. The inspector, anxious to prove his zeal, continued:

"Just to make sure, I went over all the small-sized shoes. About half a dozen ladies wear 4's: Miss Ruston, Mrs. Wickham, Mrs.

Fleetwood, Miss Fairford, that foreign lady with the double-barreled name, Miss Leighton, and Miss Stanmore—the younger Miss Stanmore, I mean. But as it's a 3½ shoe by the measurements I took, they're all out of it. I'm making some quiet inquiries in the village, sir. It looks as if it might have been some local girl, from what we heard about Staveley's habits. I'll report as soon as anything turns up."

Sir Clinton had listened patiently to the inspector's recital, but his next speech seemed to suggest that his attention had been wandering.

"I think you'd better get some more constables over, inspector. Let 'em come in plain clothes and don't advertise them. And you can turn Sapcote on to watch that crowd at Flatt's cottage. I've just developed an interest in the fourth man—'who would answer to "Hi!" or to any loud cry,' as it says in *The Hunting of the Snark*. It's the merest try-on; but I shouldn't be surprised to learn that he's back again at the cottage. And, by the way, the two fishermen must have seen him when they went to borrow the boat. You might get a description of him from them."

"Very good, sir."

"And there's a final point, inspector. I don't want to overburden you, but what about the Peter Hay case? Anything further?"

Armadale's face showed that he thought he was being overdriven.

"Well, sir," he protested, "I really haven't had much time."

"I wasn't blaming you, inspector. It was a mere inquiry—not a criticism."

Armadale's face cleared.

"I've been to the sweet-shop, sir. Peter Hay hadn't bought peardrops there for a long while. In fact, they haven't any in stock just now."

"That's interesting, isn't it?"

"Yes, sir. And Dr. Rafford says that undoubtedly the body contains amyl nitrite. He seemed a bit taken aback when I put it to him. I don't think he'd spotted it off his own bat. But when I suggested it, he did some tests and found the stuff."

Sir Clinton rose to his feet as though to indicate that business was over. Armadale busied himself with the repacking of his bag. When he had finished, he moved over towards the door and began to unlock it. Before he got it open, Sir Clinton added a final remark.

"Don't you think it's a bit curious, inspector, that the Fordingbridge family should be mixed up, directly or indirectly, in these two affairs? Think it over, will you?"

CHAPTER IX
THE SECOND CARTRIDGE-CASE

THE CHIEF CONSTABLE had a fresh task on his hands as soon as Armadale took his leave. It seemed to him essential to get the body of the dead man identified by someone in addition to the group at Flatt's cottage. Stanley Fleetwood was unable to move, even if he had wished to do so; and Sir Clinton had no particular desire to confront Cressida with her late husband's corpse. Paul Fordingbridge had known Staveley well; and it was to him that the chief constable turned in this difficulty.

To his relief, Paul Fordingbridge showed no annoyance at the state of affairs. He consented at once to go with the chief constable to inspect the body and give his evidence as to its identity. Wendover accompanied them in the car; and in Lynden Sands village the formalities were soon over. Fordingbridge had no hesitation in the matter; he recognised Staveley at the first glance.

Until they were clear of the village again, Sir Clinton made no attempt to extract any further information; but when the car crossed the neck at Flatt's cottage and was running beside the bay, he slowed down and turned to Fordingbridge.

"There's a point you might be able to throw light on, Mr. Fordingbridge," he said tentatively. "Quite obviously, Staveley was supposed to have been killed in the war. Could you give me any information about his earlier history? You came in contact with him at times, I understand."

Paul Fordingbridge seemed in no way put out by the request.

139

"I can tell you all I know about the fellow easily enough," he answered readily. "You'll have to go elsewhere for any real information about his past; but, so far as I'm concerned, I met him here. My nephew, Derek, brought him home to spend his leave with us at Foxhills. That was in 1916. In the spring of '17, he was slightly wounded; and we asked him down again to stay with us when he was convalescent. He married my niece in April 1917. The marriage wasn't a success—quite the other thing. The fellow was a scoundrel of the worst brand. In September 1917 we learned privately that he had got into the black books of the military authorities; and my private impression—it's only that, for I really don't know—my private impression was that he ran the risk of a firing-party. What I heard was a rumour that he'd been given a chance to rehabilitate himself in the field. There was a big attack being mounted at the moment, and he was sent in with the rest. That was the last we heard of him. After the attack, he was posted as missing; and a while later still the War Office returned some of his things to my niece. It seems they'd found a body with his identity disc on it. Naturally we were relieved."

He halted for a moment; then, seeming to feel that he had put the matter in an unnecessarily callous way, he added:

"He was a thoroughly bad lot, you understand? I caught him once trying to forge my name to a cheque for a good round figure."

Sir Clinton nodded his thanks for the information.

"Then I suppose one has to assume that in some way or other he managed to escape, after exchanging identity discs with somebody who was really killed," he suggested. "It's not difficult to see how that could be done."

Wendover interposed.

"More difficult than it looks at first sight, Clinton. How do you imagine that he could conceal himself after the battle? He'd have to give some account of himself then."

"Oh, I expect he went amongst people who didn't know his substitute by sight. That wouldn't be difficult."

"He'd be picked up and sent back to his supposed unit very soon—the dead man's unit, I mean. And then the fat would be in the fire."

"Obviously he wasn't sent back, then, squire, if you prefer it so," Sir Clinton conceded, turning to Fordingbridge. "What we've heard just now accounts well enough for Staveley being associated with your nephew lately—I mean the man who's living at Flatt's cottage."

"Is there a nephew of mine at Flatt's cottage?" Paul Fordingbridge questioned coldly. "I don't know with certainty that I have a nephew alive at all."

"He calls himself Derek Fordingbridge, if that's any help."

"Oh, you mean that fellow? I've no proof that he's my nephew."

"I should like to hear something more about him, if you don't mind," Sir Clinton suggested.

"I've no objection—not the slightest," Paul Fordingbridge responded. "My nephew Derek was in the Army from 1914. He was captured on the West Front in the same battle as the one I've been speaking about. We learned later on that he'd been sent to the prisoners' camp at Clausthal. He got away from there almost at once and made a good try to get over the Dutch frontier; but they got hold of him at the last moment. Then he was sent to Fort 9, Ingolstadt. He hadn't been there a week before he got away again. My impression is that most probably he was shot in trying to get across the Swiss frontier, if not earlier; and they failed to identify him. We heard no more about him, anyhow; and when the prisoners were released after the Armistice, he wasn't among them. If this fellow were really my nephew, it's hard to see why he's let so long a time go by without communicating with us. If he really is my nephew, there's a lot of money waiting for him; and he's an enterprising chap, as you can see from his escape attempts. And yet we've had no word from him of any sort since before the attack in which he was captured."

"Lost his memory, perhaps?" Wendover suggested.

"It might be possible," Paul Fordingbridge answered in a frigid tone which damped further speculation on Wendover's part. Turning to Sir Clinton, he added:

"Unless there's any further information you want, I think I'll get down here and walk back to the hotel. I'd be glad of a chance to stretch my legs."

As Sir Clinton showed no desire to detain him, he stepped out of the car; and they soon left him behind.

"Barring the girl," Wendover confided to Sir Clinton as they drove on, "that Fordingbridge family seem a damned rum crew."

"You surprise me, squire. You even capture my interest. Proceed."

"Well, what do you make of it all?"

"I'll admit that my vulgar curiosity is piqued by their highly developed faculty of reticence. Miss Fordingbridge seems the only one of them who has a normal human desire to talk about her own affairs."

"Did you see anything else?"

"They seem a bit at sixes and sevens. But you've a much acuter mind than I have, so I suppose you spotted that quite a long time ago."

"I had a glimmering of it," Wendover retorted sarcastically. "Anything more?"

"Oh, yes. For one thing, Mr. Paul Fordingbridge seems to have a singularly detached mind. Why, even you, squire, with your icy and well-balanced intellect, seem to be more affected by his niece's troubles than the wicked uncle is. Quite like the Babes in the Wood, isn't it?—with you in the role of a robin. All you need are some leaves and a red waistcoat to make the thing go properly."

"It's hardly a thing to laugh at, Clinton."

"I'm not laughing," Sir Clinton said soberly. "Hanging's no joke. Remember the *Ballad of Sam Hall*—

"Then the parson he will come . . .

and all the rest of the gruesome ceremonial? It would be a bad business if the wrong person got hanged by mistake."

Before Wendover could reply, the car drew up before the front of the hotel.

"You can get out here, squire. There's no need to go round with me to the garage."

But as Wendover was prepared to get down, they saw the Australian, Cargill, hurrying towards them. He had been sitting on one of the garden-seats, evidently on the look-out for their arrival.

"I've been hunting for you for ever so long, Sir Clinton," he explained as he came up to the car. "I missed you at lunch-time; and when I tried to get hold of you, I found you'd gone off. I've got something that seems important to show you."

He fished in his waistcoat pocket and drew out a tiny glittering object which he handed over to the chief constable. Wendover saw, as it passed from hand to hand, that it was the empty case of a .38 cartridge.

"I've seen things of this sort before," Sir Clinton said indifferently as he glanced at it. "I doubt if the loser's likely to offer a reward."

Cargill seemed taken aback.

"Can't you see its importance?" he demanded. "I found it down on the beach this morning."

"How was I to know that until you told me?" Sir Clinton asked mildly. "I'm not psychic, as they call it. I just have to be told things plainly. But I shouldn't shout them, Mr. Cargill, if they really are important."

Cargill dropped his voice at the implied rebuke.

"You remember I was down bathing this morning before breakfast? And you warned me off the premises—wouldn't let me come nearer than the groyne. I sat down on the groyne and watched you for a while; then you went away. I wasn't in a hurry to bathe just then, so I sat for a bit on the groyne, just thinking things over and trying to put two and two together from what I could see of the footmarks on the sands. I suppose I must have sat there for a quarter of an hour or so. When I got up again, I found I'd been kicking up the sand a bit while I was thinking—shuffling about without noticing what I was doing with my feet. And when I looked down— there was this thing shining on the sand at my toes. It was half hidden; and until I picked it up I didn't spot what it was. By that time your party had cleared out. So I made a careful note of the spot, put the thing in my pocket, and set off to look for you. Unfortunately, you weren't to be found just then; so I've been waiting till I could get hold of you."

He looked at the chief constable eagerly as though expecting some display of emotion as a reward for his trouble; but Sir Clinton's face betrayed nothing as he thanked Cargill.

"Would you mind getting aboard?" he asked immediately. "I'd like to see just where you found this thing."

Then, as a concession to Cargill's feelings, he added:

"You must have pretty sharp eyes. I thought I'd been over that ground fairly carefully myself."

"Probably the thing was buried in the sand," the Australian pointed out. "I saw it only after I kicked about a while."

Sir Clinton turned the car and took the road leading down to Neptune's Seat.

"What do you make of it, Mr. Cargill?" he inquired, after a moment or two.

"I haven't thought much about it," Cargill answered. "It seems straightforward enough. Somebody must have been behind the groyne and fired a shot. It's within easy shooting distance of the rock where the body was found."

Wendover opened his mouth as if to say something. Then, thinking better of it, he refrained.

When they reached the shore, the tide was sufficiently far out to allow Cargill to show them the spot at which he had picked up the cartridge-case. Wendover still had a mental map in his head, and he recognised that the shot must have been fired by the man behind the groyne at the time when he was nearest to Neptune's Seat. If Stanley Fleetwood was even a moderate shot with an automatic, he could hardly have missed Staveley's figure at the distance.

Sir Clinton seemed to become more keenly interested when they reached the shore. His detached manner thawed markedly, and he thanked Cargill again for having brought the evidence to light.

"Oh, it was only an accident," the Australian protested. "I wasn't looking for anything. It just chanced to catch my eye. Does it throw any light on things?"

Sir Clinton obviously resented the question. "Everything helps," he said sententiously.

Cargill saw that he had been indiscreet.

"Oh, I'm not trying to stick my oar in," he hastened to assure the chief constable. "I just asked out of mere curiosity."

He seemed rather perturbed lest he should have appeared unduly inquisitive; and in a moment he changed the subject completely.

"By the way, I heard someone mention in the hotel that a man called Derek Fordingbridge is staying somewhere hereabouts. Know anything about him? I came across somebody of that name in the war."

"He's staying at that cottage across the bay," Wendover explained, pointing out Flatt's cottage as he spoke. "What sort of person was your friend?—in appearance, I mean."

"Oh, about my height and build, clean-shaved, hair darkish, if I remember right."

"This looks like your man, then," Wendover assured him. "But you'll probably find him a bit altered. He's had some bad wounds."

"Has he? Pity, that. I say, I think I'll just go across the bay now and see if he's at home. I'm half-way there already."

Sir Clinton offered him a lift in the car; but on finding that it would be taking them out of their way, Cargill refused the invitation and set off alone across the sands. Before he started, Wendover gave him a warning about the quicksand near the wreck, lest he should stumble into it unawares.

"That's an interesting find," Wendover volunteered as they climbed the beach. "I didn't say anything in front of Cargill, but it occurred to me that his cartridge-case clears up one of the difficulties of the evidence."

"You mean that Billingford couldn't tell the inspector whether there was a single shot or a pair?" Sir Clinton inquired.

"Yes. That looked funny at first sight; but if the two shots were fired almost simultaneously, then it would have been a bit difficult to say whether there was a double report or not."

"That's so squire. You're getting devilish acute these days, I must admit."

But, from his friend's tone, the compliment did not sound so warm as the words suggested. Wendover imagined that he detected a tinge of irony in Sir Clinton's voice; but it was so faint that he could not feel certain of it.

"I'm getting too much into a groove," the chief constable went on. "This was supposed to be holiday; and yet I'm spending almost every minute of it in rushing about at Armadale's coat-tails. I really must have some relaxation. There's some dancing at the hotel to-night and I think I'll join. I need a change of occupation."

Wendover was not a dancing man, but he liked to watch dancers; so after dinner he found his way to the ballroom of the hotel, ensconced himself comfortably in a corner from which he had a good view of the floor, and prepared to enjoy himself. He had a half-suspicion that Sir Clinton's sudden humour for dancing was not wholly explicable on the ground of a mere relaxation, though the chief constable was undoubtedly a good dancer; and he watched with interest to see what partners his friend would choose.

Any expectations he might have had were unfulfilled, however. Sir Clinton seemed to pay no particular attention to any of his partners; and most of them obviously could have no connection with the tragedies. Once, it is true, he sat out with Miss Staunton, whose ankle was apparently not sufficiently strong to allow her to dance; and Wendover noted also that three others on Armadale's list—Miss Fairford, Miss Stanmore, and Mme. Laurent-Desrousseaux—were among his friend's partners.

Shortly before midnight, Sir Clinton seemed to tire of his amusement. He took leave of Mme. Laurent-Desrousseaux, with whom he had been dancing, and came across the room to Wendover.

"Profited by your study of vamps, I hope, Clinton?"

Sir Clinton professed to be puzzled by the inquiry.

"Vamps? Oh, you mean Mme. Laurent-Desrousseaux, I suppose. I'm afraid she found me poor ground for her talents. I made it clear to her at the start that she was far above rubies and chief constables. All I had to offer was the purest friendship. It seems it was a new sensation to her—never met anything of the sort before.

She's rather interesting, squire. You might do worse than culti-
vate her acquaintance—on the same terms as myself. Now, come
along. We'll need to change before Armadale turns up, unless you
have a fancy to dabble your dress trousers in the brine down there."

They left the room and made their way towards the lift. In the
corridor they encountered Cargill, who stopped them.

"Thanks for directing me to that cottage," he said. "It turned
out to be the man I knew, right enough. But I'd hardly have
recognised him, poor devil. He used to be a fine-looking beggar—
and look at him now."

"Enjoy a talk with him?" Sir Clinton asked politely.

"Oh, yes. But I was a bit surprised to hear that he's quite a big
pot with an estate and all that. I only knew him in the war, of
course, and it seems he came into the cash later on. Foxhills is his
place, isn't it?"

"So I'm told. By the way, did you meet his friend, Mr. Billingford? He's an amusing artist."

Cargill's brow clouded slightly.

"You think so?" he said doubtfully.

Sir Clinton glanced at his wrist-watch.

"I'm sorry I've got to hurry off, Mr. Cargill. I'd no notion it was
so late."

With a nod, Cargill passed. Sir Clinton and Wendover hurried
upstairs and changed into clothes more suitable for the sands. They
were ready just as the inspector knocked at the chief constable's
door; and in a few minutes all three were in Sir Clinton's car on
the road to the beach.

"Got the flash-lamps, inspector?" Sir Clinton demanded as he
pulled up the car at a point considerably beyond Neptune's Seat.
"That's all right. We get out here, I think. We ought to be opposite
those two cairns we built, if I'm not out in my reckoning."

They moved down the beach and soon came to a long pool of
sea-water extending into the darkness on either hand. Sir Clinton
surveyed it for a moment.

"We'll just have to splash through, I suppose," he said, and set
an example. "It won't take you over your ankles."

A few seconds took them through the shallow pool and brought them to drying sands on the farther side.

"This is a low whale-back," Sir Clinton pointed out. "When the tide's full in, this is covered, like all the rest. Then, as the tide falls, the whale-back acts as a dam and there's a big sea-pool left on the sands between here and the road. That's the pool we've just waded through. Now we'll look for the next item."

Wendover and Armadale followed him across the sands to where a broad stream of water was pouring down towards the sea.

"This is the channel between our whale-back and the next one," Sir Clinton explained as they came up to it. "This water comes from the pool that we waded; and the cairns are on each side of it, lower down."

The night was cloudy, and they had to use their flash-lamps from time to time.

"What I wanted to note is the exact time when the stream just touches the cairns on each side. Just now, as you can see, the cairns are in the water; but the level of the stream's sinking as the head of water falls in the pool behind. Watch till the stream runs between the two piles of stone and then note the time."

Slowly the flow diminished as the water emptied itself from the pool behind; and at last they saw the rivulet confined to a channel between the two cairns.

"I make it five past twelve," Sir Clinton said, lifting his eyes from his watch. "Now I'm going over to Neptune's Seat. You stay here, inspector; and when you see my flash-lamp, run your hardest to the rock and join me."

He disappeared in the darkness, leaving the others rather puzzled as to the meaning of these manoeuvres. At last Wendover thought he saw the point.

"I see what he's getting at."

But just as he was about to explain the matter to the inspector, they saw the flash of Sir Clinton's lamp and Armadale set off at a lumbering trot across the sands with Wendover hurrying after him.

"It's simple enough," Sir Clinton explained when all three had gathered at Neptune's Seat. "You remember that Billingford's track was broken where the cairns are—no footprints visible for several yards. That was the place where he crossed the runnel last night. All we need to do is to note when the runnel is the same breadth at that point to-night—which we've just done—and then make a correction of about forty minutes for the tide being later this evening. It's not exact, of course; but it's near enough, perhaps."

"I thought you were after something of the sort," Wendover interjected. "Once I got as far as the runnel I tumbled to the idea."

"Well, let's take the results," Sir Clinton went on. "The runnel was in the right state to-night at five past twelve. Make the forty-one minute deduction—since the tide's forty-one minutes later to-night than it was last night—and you get 11.25 P.M. as the time when Billingford crossed that rivulet last night. Now the inspector took over seven minutes to run from the cairns to Neptune's Seat, for I timed him. Therefore, even if Billingford had run the whole distance, he couldn't have reached Neptune's Seat before 11.32 at the earliest. As a matter of fact, his track showed that he walked most of the way, which makes the possible time of his arrival a bit later than 11.32 P.M."

"So he couldn't have fired a shot at 11.19 when Staveley's watch stopped?" Wendover inferred.

"Obviously he couldn't. There's more in it than that; though I needn't worry you with that at present, perhaps. But this bit of evidence eliminates another possibility I'd had my eye on. Billingford might have walked into the runnel and then waded down the rivulet into the sea, leaving no traces. Then he might have come along the beach, wading in the waves, and shot Staveley from the water. After that, if he'd returned the way he came, he could have emerged from the runnel at the same point, only on this bank of the channel, and left his single track up to Neptune's Seat, just as we found it. But that won't fit in with the shot fired at 11.19 p.m., obviously. If he'd done this, then his last footmark on the far side would have been made when the runnel was full, and his first footmark on this side would have been made later, when the runnel had shrunk a bit; and the two wouldn't have fitted the banks neatly as we found to-night that they did."

"I see all that, clear enough, sir," said Armadale briskly. "That means the circle's narrowed a bit further. If Billingford didn't fire that shot, then you're left with only three other people on the list: the two Fleetwoods and the woman with the 3½ shoe. If she can be eliminated like Billingford, then the case against the Fleetwoods is conclusive."

"Don't be in too much of a hurry, inspector. How are you getting along with the shoe question?" Sir Clinton inquired a trifle maliciously.

"To tell you the truth," the inspector replied guardedly, "I haven't been able to get at the root of it yet, sir. Only two of the village girls take that size of shoe. One of them's only a kiddie; the other's away on a visit just now. It doesn't look like either of them."

"And the Hay case?" the chief constable demanded.

The inspector made an inarticulate sound which suggested that he had nothing fresh to recount on this subject.

"And the P.M. on Staveley's body?" pursued Sir Clinton.

Here the inspector had something to report, though not much.

"Dr. Rafford's gone into it, sir. The contused wound on the back of the head's nothing to speak of. The base of the skull's intact. That blow had nothing to do with his death. At the most, it might have stunned him for a minute or two. According to the doctor, Staveley was killed by the shot; and he thinks that the shot wasn't fired at absolutely close quarters. That fits in with the fact that I could find no singeing of the cloth of his rain-coat or his jacket round about the bullet-hole. Dr. Rafford found the bullet, all correct. Death must have been practically instantaneous, according to the doctor's view. These are the main results. He's written a detailed report for reference, of course."

Sir Clinton made no direct comment.

"I think that'll do for to-night, inspector. Come up to the car and I'll run you into the village. By the way, I want some of your constables to-morrow morning for a bit of work; and you'd better hire some labourers as well—say a dozen men altogether. Tell them to dig up the sand between Neptune's Seat and the sea to the depth of about a foot, and shift it up into a pile above high-tide mark."

"And how far are they to carry their diggings?" Wendover inquired.

"I really doubt if they'll be able to dig much below low-tide mark. What do you think?"

"And what do you expect to find there?" Wendover persisted.

"Oh, a shell or two, most likely," Sir Clinton retorted caustically. "Would you like to bet on it, squire?"

Wendover perceived that the chief constable did not intend to put his cards on the table and that nothing would be gained by further persistence.

CHAPTER X
THE ATTACK ON THE AUSTRALIAN

NEXT MORNING, BEFORE GOING TO THE LINKS, Sir Clinton went to the shore and superintended the start of the excavating work there; but when once the actual digging had begun, he seemed to lose interest in the matter. It was not until late in the afternoon that he paid his second visit, accompanied by Wendover. Even then he contented himself with the most casual inspection, and soon turned back towards the hotel.

"What *are* you after with all this spade-work?" Wendover demanded as they sauntered up the road.

Sir Clinton turned and made a gesture towards the little crowd of inquisitive visitors and natives who had congregated around the diggers.

"I've heard rumours, squire, that the Lynden Sands public thinks the police aren't busy enough in the sleuth-hound business. Unofficial opinion seems divided as to whether we're pure duds or merely lazy. They want to see something actually being done to clear up these mysteries. Well, they've got something to talk about now, you see. That's always gain. So long as they can stand and gape at the digging down there, they won't worry us too much in the things we really have to do."

"But seriously, Clinton, what do you expect to find?"

Sir Clinton turned a bland smile on his companion. "Oh, shells, as I told you before, squire. Shells, almost certainly. And perhaps the brass bottle that the genie threw into the sea after he'd escaped from it—the *Arabian Nights* tale, you remember. Once one starts digging in real earnest one never can tell what one may not find."

Wendover made a gesture of impatience.

"I suppose you're looking for something."

"I've told you exactly what I expect to find, squire. And it's no good your going off to pump these diggers, or even the inspector, for they don't know what they're looking for themselves. The general public can ask questions till it's tired, but it won't learn much on the beach. That'll tend to keep its excitement at fever-heat and prevent it looking any farther for points of interest."

As they neared the hotel they overtook Mme. Laurent-Desrousseaux, who was walking leisurely up the road. Sir Clinton slowed down to her pace, and opened a brisk conversation as he came abreast of her. Wendover, feeling rather out of it, inspected Mme. Laurent-Desrousseaux covertly with some disfavour.

"Now, what the devil does Clinton see in that vamp?" he asked himself as they moved on together. "He's not the usual idiot, by a long chalk. She'll get no change out of him. But what does he expect to get out of her? It's not like him. Of course, she's a bit out of things here; but she doesn't look the sort that would mind that much, somehow. And he's evidently laying himself out to get her good graces. It's a bit rum."

He could not deny that the personal attractions of Mme. Laurent-Desrousseaux were much above the average; and, despite himself, he felt a tinge of uneasiness in his mind. After all, even the cleverest men get caught occasionally; and it was plain enough that Sir Clinton was doing his best to make friends with the Frenchwoman.

They had just entered the hotel grounds when Wendover saw approaching them down the drive the figure of Cargill. The Australian seemed to have something to say to them, for he quickened his pace when he caught sight of Sir Clinton.

"I've come across something else that might be of importance," he said, addressing the chief constable without a glance at the others. "It's a—"

He broke off abruptly, with a glance at Mme. Laurent-Desrousseaux. It seemed almost as though he had not seen before that she was there, or as if he had just recognised her.

"I'll let you see it later on," he explained rather confusedly. "I'll have to hunt it out. I find I've left it in the pocket of another jacket."

Sir Clinton successfully repressed any signs of a curiosity which he might have felt.

"Oh, any time you like," he suggested, without betraying much interest in the matter.

By an almost imperceptible manoeuvre he broke the group up into two pairs, and moved on towards the hotel entrance with Mme. Laurent-Desrousseaux, leaving Wendover and the Australian to follow if they chose. It was almost dinner-time as they entered the building; and Wendover took the opportunity of shaking off Cargill, who seemed inclined to cling to him more than he wished.

Rather to Wendover's surprise, Sir Clinton showed no inclination, after dinner, to plunge into further investigations.

"We mustn't be greedy, squire," he argued. "We must leave the inspector a fair share of the case, you know. If amateurs like ourselves bustle around too much, the professional would have no practice in his art at all."

"If you ask me," Wendover retorted, "the professional's spending all his time barking furiously at the foot of the wrong tree."

"You think so? Well, if the cats up the tree insist on making a noise like a murderer, you can't blame him, can you?"

"I don't like his damned flat-footed way of going about his job," Wendover protested angrily. "One always supposed that people were treated as innocent until they were convicted; but your inspector interviewed that girl as if he were measuring her for a rope."

"He's built up a wonderfully convincing case, squire; don't forget that."

"But you admitted yourself that there's a flaw in it, Clinton. By the way, what is the flaw?"

But Sir Clinton did not rise to the bait.

"Think it over, squire. If that doesn't do the trick, then think again. And if that fails, shake the bottle and try a third dose. It's one of these obvious points which I'd hate to lay before you, because you'd be covered with confusion at once if I explained it. But remember one thing. Even if the inspector's case breaks down in one detail, still, the facts need a lot more explanation than the Fleetwoods have condescended to offer up to the present. That's obvious. And now, what about picking up a couple of men and making up a table of bridge?"

Wendover's play that evening was not up to its usual standard. At the back of his mind throughout there was the picture of Cressida and her husband upstairs, weighed down by the burden of the unformulated charge against them and preparing as best they could against the renewal of the inquisition which could not be long delayed. He could picture to himself the almost incessant examination and re-examination of the evidence which they must be making; the attempts to slur over points which would tell heavily against them; the dread of the coming ordeal at the hands of Armadale; and the terror of some masked battery which might suddenly sweep their whole defence away. He grew more and more determined to put a spoke in the inspector's wheel if it were at all possible.

Late in the evening he was aroused to fresh fears by the entry of a page-boy.

"Number eighty-nine! Number eighty-nine! Number—"

"Here, boy!" Sir Clinton signaled to the page. "What is it?"

"You Sir Clinton Driffield, sir? Message from Mr. Cargill, sir. He wants you to go up and see him. His number's 103, sir."

Sir Clinton was obviously annoyed.

"Tell him I'm here if he wishes to see me. Say I'm playing bridge."

The boy seemed to enjoy springing a sensation on them.

"Beg y'r pardon, sir, but he can't come. He's upstairs in bed. He's been shot. Mrs. Fleetwood brought him back in her car, sir, a few minutes ago; and they had to carry him up to his room. The doctor's been sent for."

Sir Clinton laid down his cards, and made a brief apology to the others for interrupting the game.

"You'd better come along with me, squire. We have to break up the table, in any case."

Followed by Wendover, he ascended to the Australian's room. They found Cargill lying on his bed with some rough bandages round his ankle, and evidently in considerable pain.

"Sorry to hear you've had an accident," Sir Clinton said sympathetically, as he bent down and inspected the dressings. "That seems good enough to serve until the doctor comes. Who put it on for you?"

"Mrs. Fleetwood," Cargill answered. "She seemed to know a bit about first aid work."

Sir Clinton, rather to Wendover's surprise, asked no leading question, but awaited Cargill's explanation. The Australian did not keep them in suspense.

"I sent a message down for you because you're the Lord High Muck-a-muck in the police hereabouts; and the sooner the police get hold of the beggar who tried to do me in, the better I'll be pleased. It's no advertisement for a new hotel to have one of its guests half murdered within a week of his arrival."

"True. Suppose you explain what happened."

Cargill seemed to see that he had hardly approached the matter in a tactful manner.

"I'm a bit sore at present, and perhaps I sounded peevish. But it's enough to make one lose one's rag a bit, I think. Here's what happened. This evening, after dinner, I strolled across the bay to pay a visit to my friend Fordingbridge at Flatt's cottage. We sat there for a while, playing cards; and then I thought I might as well be getting home again. So I said goodbye to them—"

"Who was there?" Sir Clinton interjected.

"Fordingbridge and Billingford," Cargill replied. "I said goodbye to them, and set off for home—"

"Did anyone see you off the premises?" the chief constable interrupted once more.

Cargill shook his head.

"I'm an old pal of Fordingbridge's, so he didn't trouble to come to the door with me. I put on my hat and coat and gave the cottage door a slam after me, to let them hear I was gone. Then I walked down that muddy path of theirs."

"You didn't notice if anyone followed you?" Cargill reflected for a moment.

"I didn't notice particularly, of course; but I can't think that anyone did. I mean I can't remember anything that suggests that to my memory, you understand?"

Sir Clinton nodded to him to continue his story.

"When I got down to the road, I turned off in this direction. Now, that's the point where I do remember someone behind me. I heard steps. After a yard or two, I looked round—you know how one does that, without having any particular reason. But it was a heavily clouded night, and the moon didn't light things up much. All I could see was a figure tramping along the road behind me— about a couple of dozen yards behind, I should think."

"No idea who it was, I suppose?" Sir Clinton questioned.

"Not the foggiest. I thought it might be one of the hotel people, so I slowed down a trifle for the sake of company. No one except some of the hotel crowd would be walking in this direction at that time of night. The next thing I heard was the sound of steps coming up behind me, and then there was the crack of a pistol, and down I went in the road with a bullet in my leg."

"Whereabouts were you at the time?"

"About fifty yards along the road from the path to Flatt's cottage, I should say. But you'll find the place all right in daylight. I bled a good deal, and it'll be all over the road where I fell."

"And then?"

"Well, I was considerably surprised," said Cargill drily.

"Very natural in the circumstances," Sir Clinton admitted, giving Cargill humour for humour. "What did you think had happened?"

"I didn't know," the victim continued. "You see, I'm a total stranger here. Fordingbridge is the only person in the place who's met me before. No one that I know of could have a grudge against me. That's what surprises me in the business."

He paused, evidently still pondering over the mystery.

"It beats me still," he continued, when his reflection had produced no solution. "But at that moment I hadn't much time to think over it. The next thing I heard was the sound of steps coming closer;

and that gave me a start, I can tell you. It looked too much like the fellow coming to finish his job at close quarters. He must have been a damn bad shot—or it may have been the dark that troubled him. But I'd no longing to have him put a pistol-muzzle to my ear, I can tell you. I just let out a yell."

He winced, for in the excitement of his narrative he had unconsciously shifted his wounded ankle.

"That seems to have been the saving of me; for of course I couldn't stand, much less get away from the beggar. I suppose the racket I raised scared him. You see, they heard me at Flatt's cottage, and there might easily have been other people on the road as well. So he seems to have turned and run at that. I kept on yelling for all I was worth; it seemed the most sensible thing to do. Just then, I heard the sound of a big motor-horn down the road at the corner where the path to the cottage comes in; and almost at once a couple of blazing head-lights came up."

"Mrs. Fleetwood's car, I suppose?"

"I believe that's her name. Pretty girl with dark hair? That's the one. She pulled up her car when she saw me all a-sprawl over the road; and she was down from the driving-seat in a jiffy, asking me what it was all about. I explained things, more or less. She made no fuss; kept her head well; and turned on an electric horn full rip. You see, I explained to her I didn't want to be left in the road there all alone. She'd proposed to go off in her car and get assistance, but I wasn't keen on the idea."

Sir Clinton's face showed his approval of this caution.

"In a minute or two," Cargill continued, "Fordingbridge and Billingford came up. They'd been roused by my yells and the electric horn. I don't know what the girl thought when she saw Fordingbridge in the light of the motor's lamps—it must have given her a start to see a face like that at close quarters in the night. But she's a plucky girl; and she never turned a hair. Billingford proposed taking me down to the doctor in the car, but she insisted on bringing me back here. More comfortable, she said. And between the lot of them they got me bundled on board her car, and she drove me home."

"You left the other two there, then?"

"Yes. She didn't invite them on board. Then, when we got here, she fixed me up temporarily"—he nodded towards the bandages—"and then she went off in her car again to hunt up a doctor."

Sir Clinton seemed to find nothing further to ask. Wendover stepped into the breach.

"Would you recognise this gunman if you saw him again?"

Cargill shook his head.

"In that light you couldn't have told whether it was a man or a woman, much less recognise 'em."

Before Wendover could say anything more, the door opened and Dr. Rafford came in, followed by Inspector Armadale.

"H'm!" said Sir Clinton. "I don't think we need trouble you any more just now, Mr. Cargill. By the time the doctor's fixed you up you'll not want to be bothered with an inquisition, I suspect. I'll drop in tomorrow and see how you're getting on. Good night. I hope it's not a bad business."

He turned to Armadale.

"You needn't worry Mr. Cargill, inspector. I've got the whole story, and can tell you what you need."

Wendover and Armadale followed him from the room, leaving the doctor to do his work undisturbed. Sir Clinton led the way to his own room, where he gave the inspector the gist of what they had learned.

"And now, inspector," he concluded, "perhaps you'll tell us how you managed to pop up so opportunely. How did you come to hear of this affair?"

"Mrs. Fleetwood brought me up in her car, sir. It seems she drove to the doctor's first of all, and, as he wanted a minute or two to collect bandages and so forth, she brought her car round to the place where I'm staying and asked for me. I was a bit taken aback when I saw her—couldn't make out what it was all about at the first glance. She got me on board and was off to the doctor's before you could say: 'Snap!' we picked him up and she drove us both up here. On the way she told me her side of the business."

"And that was?"

"By her way of it, she'd wanted to make sure of catching the first post in the morning—an important letter, she said. She'd taken her car and driven in to Lynden Sands post office to post it, for fear of the hotel post not catching the first collection. Then she was driving back again when she heard someone calling, just as she came to the corner at Flatt's cottage. She turned on her horn and came round the corner; and almost at once she saw, in the beam of her head-lights, Cargill lying on the road. So she stopped and got down. In a minute or so, up came the gang from Flatt's cottage; and between the lot of them they got Cargill into the car and she brought him home."

"Did she see anyone on the road except Cargill?"

"I asked her that, sir. She says she saw no one there. No one was on the road between Cargill and the corner."

"Slipped off the road, evidently. There are a lot of rocks by the roadside thereabouts, and a man could hide himself quick enough among them, if he were put to it," Sir Clinton pointed out.

The inspector seemed to find the suggestion unsatisfying.

"There's just one point you've overlooked, I think, sir," he criticised. "Remember what Cargill told you. With the light as it was, he couldn't tell whether it was a man or a woman who shot him."

Wendover flamed up at the inspector's insinuation.

"Look here, inspector," he said angrily, "you seem to be suffering from an *idée fixe* about Mrs. Fleetwood. First of all you insist that she murdered Staveley. Now you want to make out that she shot Cargill; and you know perfectly well the thing's absurd. You haven't got a shred of evidence to make your ideas hang together in this last affair—not a shred."

"I'm not talking about evidence just now, Mr. Wendover. There's been no time to collect any as yet. I'm just taking a look at possibilities; and this is quite within the bounds of possibility, as you'll see. Suppose Mrs. Fleetwood came out of Lynden Sands village and drove up the road towards Flatt's cottage. She could see the door of it as she came up the hill to the corner. You'll not deny that, I suppose?"

"No," Wendover admitted contemptuously. "That's quite possible."

"Then suppose, further," the inspector went on, "that just before she reached the corner the door of Flatt's cottage opened and a man came out. In the light from the open door he'd be fairly plain to anyone in her position—but not too plain."

"What's that got to do with it?" Wendover demanded brusquely. "Haven't you Cargill's own evidence that he knows nobody hereabouts except Derek Fordingbridge? Why should Mrs. Fleetwood want to shoot a total stranger? You're not suggesting that she's a homicidal maniac, are you?"

"No," Armadale retorted, "I'm suggesting that she mistook Cargill's figure for somebody else—somebody whom she'd a good reason for putting out of the way. She'd only get a glimpse of him as he opened and shut the cottage door. A mistake's quite on the cards. Is that impossible, so far?"

"No, but I shouldn't say that it mattered a rap, if you ask me."

"That's as it may be," the inspector returned, obviously nettled by Wendover's cavalier manner. "What happens after that? She shuts off her lights; gets down off the car; follows Cargill along the road, still mistaking him for someone else. She steals up behind him and tries to shoot him, but makes a muddle of it owing to the bad light. Then Cargill shouts for help, and she recognises that she's made a mistake. Off she goes, back to her car; switches on her lights and sounds her horn; and then pretends to have been coming up the hill in the normal way and to have arrived there by pure accident at that time. Is that impossible?"

"Quite!" said Wendover bluntly.

"Come now, squire," Sir Clinton interposed, as the tempers of his two companions were obviously near the danger-point. "You can't say anything's impossible except a two-sided triangle and a few other things of that sort. What it really amounts to is that you and the inspector differ pleasantly as to the exact degree of probability one can attach to his hypothesis. He thinks it probable; you don't agree. It's a mere matter of the personal equation. Don't drag in the Absolute; it's out of fashion in these days."

Wendover recovered his temper under the implied rebuke; but the inspector merely glowered. Quite evidently he was more wedded to his hypothesis than he cared to admit in plain words.

"There isn't much chance of our getting the bullet," he admitted. "It went clean through Cargill's leg, it appears. But if we do get it, and if it turns out to be from a pistol that a girl could carry without attracting attention, then perhaps Mr. Wendover will reconsider his views."

CHAPTER XI
MME. LAURENT-DESROUSSEAUX'S EVIDENCE

"I SHAN'T BE ABLE TO GIVE YOU a game this morning, squire," Sir Clinton explained at breakfast next day. "I've got another engagement."

He glanced towards Mme. Laurent-Desrousseaux's empty seat at the adjoining table, and suppressed a grin as he saw the expression on Wendover's face.

"Need you advertise yourself quite so much in that quarter, Clinton?" Wendover demanded, rather put out by the turn of events.

Sir Clinton's features displayed an exaggerated expression of coyness, as though he were a boy half inviting chaff on the subject of a feminine conquest.

"I find her interesting, squire. And good-looking. And charming. And, shall we say, fascinating? It's a very rare combination, you'll admit; and hence I'd be sorry not to profit by it when it's thrust upon me."

Wendover was somewhat relieved by the impish expression in Sir Clinton's eye.

"I've never known you to hanker after semi-society ladies before, Clinton. Is it just a freak? Or are you falling into senile decay? She's fairly obvious, you know, especially against this background."

Sir Clinton failed to suppress his grin.

"Wrong both times, squire, making twice in all. It's not a freak. It's not senile decay. It's business. Sounds sordid, doesn't it, after your spangled imaginings? 'Chief Constable Sacrifices All for Love,' and that sort of thing. It's almost a pity to disappoint you."

163

Wendover's relief was obvious.

"Don't singe your wings, that's all. She's a dangerous toy, by the look of her, Clinton. I shouldn't play with her too long, if I were you. What she's doing down here at all is a mystery to me."

"That's precisely what I intend to find out, squire. Hence my devotion. There were more brutal ways of finding out; but I don't share the inspector's views about how to elicit evidence. You see, she's studied in the best school of fascination, and she knows a woman can always get into a man's good graces by leading him on to talk about his work. So she's secured a number of horrific details about the dreadful powers of the police in this land of freedom from me. I think she'll part with the information I want when I ask for it."

Wendover shook his head disapprovingly.

"Seems a bit underhand, that," he commented.

"The finer graces do get shoved aside in a murder case," Sir Clinton admitted. "One regrets it; but there it is. You can't wear a collar and tie when you're going to be hanged, you know."

"Get on with your breakfast, you gruesome devil," Wendover directed, half in jest and half in earnest. "I expect the next thing will be your luring all your suspects on to the hotel weighing-machine, so as to have the right length of the drop calculated beforehand. Constant association with that brute Armadale has corrupted you completely."

Sir Clinton stirred his coffee thoughtfully for a moment or two before speaking again.

"I've got a job for you to do, squire," he announced at last in a serious tone. "About eleven o'clock I have an appointment with Mme. Laurent-Desrousseaux. We're going for a walk along the bay. Now, I want you to drive into Lynden Sands, pick up Armadale, and get back again so as to meet us somewhere about the old wreck. It was a spring tide yesterday, and the tide's just turning about this time in the morning; so we'll have to keep quite near the road in our walk across the sands. You can hail us from the road easily enough."

Wendover nodded an acceptance of the task.

"The inspector can bring along a tape-measure in his pocket, and, if he likes, he can drag the blow-lamp and wax with him also, though I doubt if we'll need them."

At the mention of the tape-measure, Wendover pricked up his ears.

"You don't imagine that she was on the beach that night, do you, Clinton? Armadale found out that her shoes were No. 4—half a size, at least, too big for the prints we haven't identified yet. Besides, she's quite a good height—as tall as Mrs. Fleetwood; and, you remember, the steps were much shorter than Mrs. Fleetwood's. The person who made these prints must have been much smaller than the Laurent-Desrousseaux woman. Have you found some more prints that you didn't tell us about?"

"All in good time, squire," Sir Clinton answered. "Take things as they come."

He sipped his coffee as though to show that he did not propose to be drawn. But Wendover was not to be put off.

"You couldn't have got a No. 4 shoe into these prints."

"No."

"And, from what I've seen of her feet, her shoes are a perfect fit."

"I've noticed you admiring them—quite justifiably, squire."

"Well, she couldn't wear a 3½ shoe."

"No. That's admitted. She hasn't such a thing in her possession; I'm sure of that. Give it up, squire. The fishing's very poor in this district. I'm not going to tell you anything just now."

Wendover recognised that he could not hope to extract any further information from the chief constable, and he consoled himself with the thought that a couple of hours at most would see this part of the mystery cleared up. After breakfast he went into the lounge, and passed the time in smoking and reviewing the state of affairs. He became so engrossed in this exercise that it was almost with a start that he realised the time had come to take out the car and pick up Armadale.

As he and the inspector drove slowly back from the village, they saw the figures of Sir Clinton and Mme. Laurent-Desrousseaux sauntering across the sands just below high-tide mark; and in a few moments the car came level with the walkers. Sir Clinton waved his arm, and Wendover and Armadale got out and walked down the beach.

"This is Inspector Armadale, Mme. Laurent-Desrousseaux," the chief constable said, as they came up. "He wants to ask you some questions about Friday night, when you were at that rock over there."

He pointed to Neptune's seat as he spoke. Mme. Laurent-Desrousseaux seemed completely taken by surprise. For a moment or two she stood glancing uneasily from one to another; and her eyes showed something more than a tinge of fear.

"I am much surprised, Sir Clinton," she said at last, her accent coming out more markedly than usual in her nervous voice. "I had supposed that you were friendly to me; and now it appears that, without making a seeming of it, you have been leading me into what you call an English police-trap, isn't it? That is not good of you."

Armadale had picked up his cue from Sir Clinton's words.

"I'm afraid I must ask you to answer my questions, ma'am," he said, with a certain politeness. Obviously he was by no means sure of his ground.

Mme. Laurent-Desrousseaux eyed him in silence for some moments.

"What is it that you desire to know?" she demanded finally.

Before Armadale could formulate a question, Sir Clinton intervened.

"I think, madame, that it will make things easier for us all if I tell you that the inspector is preparing a case against someone else. He needs your deposition to support his charge. That is the whole truth, so far as he is concerned. You need not have any fears, provided that you tell us all that you know about Friday night."

Wendover noticed the double meaning which might be attached to Sir Clinton's words; but he could not feel sure whether the chief constable wished to deceive or merely to reassure his witness. Mme. Laurent-Desrousseaux's face cleared slightly as she grasped the meaning of Sir Clinton's speech.

"If such is the case," she said cautiously, "I might recall to myself some of the things which happened."

Armadale seemed a trifle suspicious at this guarded offer, but he proceeded to put some questions.

"You knew this man Staveley, ma'am?"

"Nicholas Staveley? Yes, I knew him; I had known him for a long time."

Sir Clinton interposed again.

"Perhaps you would prefer to tell us what you know of him in your own words, madame. It would be easier for us if you would do so."

Mme. Laurent-Desrousseaux nodded her agreement. She seemed to have conquered her nervousness.

"It was during the war, messieurs, in 1915. I was Odette Pascal then, a young girl, an honest girl—what you English call straight, isn't it? It was later that I became Aline Laurent-Desrousseaux, you understand? I encountered this Nicholas Staveley in Paris, where I was employed in a Government office. He was very charming, very caressing; he knew how to make himself loved."

She made a gesture, half cynical, half regretful, and paused for a moment before she continued in a harder tone:

"It did not last long, that honeymoon. I discovered his character, so different from that which I had believed it. He abandoned me, and I was very rejoiced to let him go; but he had taught me things, and forced me to work for him while he had me. When we separated ourselves, in fact, I was no longer the gentle, honest little girl that I had been. All that was finished, you understand?"

Wendover saw that the inspector was taking notes in shorthand. Mme. Laurent-Desrousseaux paused for a time to allow Armadale to catch up.

"The rest is without importance. I became Aline Laurent-Desrousseaux, and I had not any need of Nicholas Staveley. During a long time I had no need of him; but from time to time I heard speak of him, for I had many friends, and some of them could tell a little; and always he was the same. Then is come the report that he was killed at the Front."

She paused again, with her eye on the inspector's pencil.

"The time passed," she resumed, "and I desired only to forget him. I believed him well dead, you understand? And then, from one of my friends, I learned that he had been seen again after the war. I disinterested myself from the affair; I had no desire to see him. But suddenly it became of importance to me to satisfy myself about him. It is much complicated, and has nothing to do with him—I pass on. But it was most necessary that I should see him and get him to consent to some arrangements, or an affair of mine would be embarrassed."

"Embarrassed," Armadale repeated, to show that he was ready to continue.

"I have consulted my friends," Mme. Laurent-Desrousseaux pursued. "Some among them have been able to help me, and I have discovered where he was living in London. It was most necessary for me to speak with him. Thus I came over to England, to London. But he is no longer there; he is gone to Lynden Sands, one says. So I procure his address—at Flatt's cottage—and I come myself to Lynden Sands Hotel."

Armadale's involuntary upward glance from his notebook betrayed the increase in his interest at this point.

"I arrive here; and at once I write him a letter saying I go to Flatt's cottage to see him on Friday night. There is no response, but I go to Flatt's cottage as I had planned. When I knocked at the door, Staveley appeared."

"What time on Friday night was that?" Armadale interposed.

"In my letter I had fixed a rendezvous at half-past nine. I was exact—on time, you say, isn't it? But it seemed that this Staveley could not see me alone there; others were in the cottage. Then he said that he would meet me later—at half-past ten—at some great rock beside the sea, the rock one calls Neptune's Seat."

"So you came away, and he went back into the cottage?" Armadale demanded.

Mme. Laurent-Desrousseaux assented with a slight bow.

"I came away," she continued. "To pass the time, I walked on the road, and perhaps I walked too far. It was late—after the hour of the rendezvous—when I arrived opposite the rock, this Neptune's Seat. I went down on to the sands and attained to the rock. Staveley was there, very angry because I was ten minutes late. He was much enraged, it appears, because he had a second rendezvous at that place in a few minutes. He would not listen to me at all at the moment. I saw that it was no time for negotiating with him, he was so much in anger and so anxious to deliver himself of me. I fixed another rendezvous for the following day, and I left him."

"What time did you leave him on the rock?" Armadale interjected.

"Let us see." Mme. Laurent-Desrousseaux halted for a moment to consider. "I passed some minutes with him on the rock—let us put ten minutes at the least."

"That would mean you left the rock very shortly before eleven o'clock, then?"

Mme. Laurent-Desrousseaux agreed with a gesture. "I went away from the rock by the same road as I had come," she went on. "I was much agitated, you understand? It was a great disappointment that I had attained to no arrangement at that moment, I had hoped for something better, isn't it? And that Staveley had been very little obliging—unkind, isn't it? It was very desolating.

"As I was crossing the sands, a great automobile appeared on the road, coming from the hotel. It stopped whilst I was waiting for it to pass; and the chauffeur extinguished its projectors. Then a woman descended from the automobile, and walked down on to the sands towards the rock."

Wendover could read on Armadale's face an expression of triumph. The inspector was clearly overjoyed at getting some direct evidence to support his case against Cressida; and Wendover had to admit, with considerable disquietude, that Mme. Laurent-Desrousseaux's narrative bore out Armadale's hypothesis very neatly.

"When I again regarded the automobile, the chauffeur also had vanished. He was not on the road. Perhaps he also had gone down to the *rivage*."

"Shore," Sir Clinton interjected, seeing Armadale's obvious perplexity at the word.

"I was standing there for some minutes," Mme. Laurent-Desrousseaux continued. "Against one like that Staveley one must utilise all weapons, isn't it?—even espionage. I had a presentiment that something might eventuate. Staveley and a woman, you understand? I was hoping that something, anything, might arrive to give me an advantage over him.

"I have forgotten to say that the sky was obscured by great clouds. It was a little difficult to see clearly. On the rock they discussed and discussed, but I could hear nothing; and in the end I grew tired of attending."

"How long did you stand there?" Armadale asked.

"It would be difficult to say, but perhaps it was about a quarter-hour. I was quite tired of attending, and I walked—quite slowly—along the road away from the hotel. I avoided the automobile, you understand? I desired no embarrassments. It was not my affair—isn't it?—to discover the identity of this woman. All that I desired was an arm against Staveley. There was nothing else at all.

"A little after, I returned; it seemed to me longer, perhaps, than it really was; and I was believing that they must be gone, those two. Then, all at once, I heard the report of a firearm down at the rock—"

"A single shot?" Sir Clinton questioned. "*Un seul coup de jeu?*"

"One only," Mme. Laurent-Desrousseaux answered definitely. "I hastened back along the road in the direction of the automobile. I had the idea of an accident in my head, you understand? It was very sombre; great clouds were passing on the moon. I could see with difficulty the woman's figure hasten up from the rock towards the automobile; and almost at once the chauffeur rejoined her. When they were getting into the automobile I was quite close; I could hear them speak, although it was too dark to see them except most dimly. The woman spoke first, very agitated."

Her three listeners were intent on her next words. Armadale looked up, his pencil poised to take down her report. Wendover felt a catch in his breath as he waited for the next sentences which would either make or break the inspector's case.

"She said," Mme. Laurent-Desrousseaux continued, "She said these very words, for they were stamped on my memory since they meant so much to me: 'I've shot him, Stanley.' And the chauffeur

demanded: 'Have you killed him?' And you can understand, messieurs, that I listened with all my ears. The woman responded: 'I
think so. He fell at once and lay quite still. What's to be done?'
And to that the chauffeur made the reply: 'Get you away at once.'
And he made some movement as if to put the motor in march. But
the woman stopped him and demanded: 'Aren't you going down to
look at him—see if anything can be done?' And to that the chauffeur made the response in anger: 'It's damn well likely, isn't it?'
Just like that. And he pursued: 'Not till I've seen you in safety,
anyhow. I'm not running any risks.'"

Wendover felt that his last shred of hope had been torn away.
This reported conversation might have been concerted between
Mme. Laurent-Desrousseaux and Armadale beforehand, so neatly
did it fit into its place in the inspector's case. He glanced up at Sir
Clinton's face, and saw there only the quiet satisfaction of a man
who fits a fresh piece of a jig-saw puzzle into position.

"Then," Mme. Laurent-Desrousseaux continued, "the chauffeur
set his motor in march and reversed the automobile. I stepped aside
off the road for fear that they should see me; but they went off
towards the hotel without illuminating the projectors."

She stopped, evidently thinking that she had told all that was of
importance. Armadale suggested that she should continue her tale.

"Figure to yourselves my position," she went on. "Staveley was
lying dead on the rock. The automobile had gone. I was left alone.
If one came along the road and encountered me, there would be
suspicion; and one would have said that I had good reason to hate
Staveley. I could see nothing but embarrassments before me. And
the chauffeur had suggested that he might return later on. What
more easy, if he found me there, than to throw suspicion on me to
discredit me? Or to incriminate me, even? In thinking of these
things, I lost my head. My sole idea was to get away without being
seen. I went furtively along the road, in trembling lest the automobile should return. No one met me; and I regained the gardens
of the hotel without being encountered. As I was passing one of
the alleys, I noticed standing there the great automobile, with its
lights extinguished. I passed into the hotel without misfortune."

"What time did you get back to the hotel, madame?" Armadale asked, as she halted again.

"Ah! I am able to tell you that, Monsieur l'Inspecteur, and exactly. I noted the hour mechanically on the clock in the hall. It was midnight less five minutes when I arrived."

"It's a twenty to twenty-five minute walk," Armadale commented. "That means you must have left the beach somewhere round about half-past eleven. Now, one more question, madame. Did you recognise the voices of the man and the woman?"

Mme. Laurent-Desrousseaux hesitated before replying.

"I should not wish to say," she answered at last unwillingly.

A frown crossed Armadale's features at the reply, and, seeing it, she turned to Sir Clinton, as though to appeal to him.

"The automobile has already been identified, madame," the chief constable said, answering her unspoken inquiry. "You can do no one any harm by telling us the truth."

His words seemed to remove her disinclination.

"In this case, I reveal nothing which you ignore? Then I say that it was the voice of the young Madame Fleetwood which I have heard in the night."

Armadale bestowed a glance on Wendover, as much as to say that his case was lock-fast. Mme. Laurent-Desrousseaux, now that she had got her narrative off her mind, seemed to be puzzled by something. She turned to Sir Clinton.

"I am embarrassed to know how you came to discover that I was at the rock on that night. May I ask?"

Sir Clinton smiled, and with a wave of his hand he indicated the trail of footmarks across the sands which they had made in their walk.

"Ah, I comprehend! I had forgotten the imprints which I must have left when I went down to the rock. It was dark, you understand?—and naturally I did not perceive that I was leaving traces. So that was it, Sir Clinton?"

Armadale was obviously puzzled. He turned to Mme. Laurent-Desrousseaux.

"What size of shoe do you wear, madame?"

She glanced at her neatly shod feet.

"These shoes I have bought in London a few days ago. The *pointure*—the size, you call it, isn't it?—was No. 4."

Armadale shrugged his shoulders, as though to express his disbelief.

"Measure these prints on the sand here, inspector," Sir Clinton suggested.

Armadale drew out his tape-measure and took the dimensions of the footmarks left by Mme. Laurent-Desrousseaux.

"And the length of step also, inspector," Sir Clinton suggested.

"They correspond with the tracks down to the rock, true enough," the inspector admitted, when he completed his task. "But only a 3½ shoe could have made them."

Sir Clinton laughed, though not sneeringly.

"Would you lend me one of your shoes for a moment, madame?" he asked. "You can lean on me while it's off, so as not to put your foot on the wet sand."

Mme. Laurent-Desrousseaux slipped off her right shoe and held it out.

"Now, inspector, there's absolutely no deception. Look at the number stamped on it. A four, isn't it?"

Armadale examined the shoe, and nodded affirmatively.

"Now take the shoe and press it gently on the sand alongside a right-foot print of Mme. Laurent-Desrousseaux—that one there will do. See that you get it square on the sand and make a good impression."

The inspector knelt down and did as he was told. As he lifted the shoe again, Wendover saw a look of astonishment on his face.

"Why, they don't correspond!" he exclaimed. "The one I've made just now is bigger than the other."

"Of course," the chief constable agreed. "Now do you see that a No. 4 shoe can make an impression smaller than itself if you happen to be walking in sand or mud? While you were hunting for people with 3½ shoes, I was turning my attention to No. 4's. There aren't so many in the hotel, as you know. And it so happened that I began with Mme. Laurent-Desrousseaux. She was good enough to go for a walk with me; and by counting her steps I gauged the length of her pace. It corresponded to the distance on the tracks."

Mme. Laurent-Desrousseaux was examining Sir Clinton with obvious admiration, not wholly unmixed with a certain uneasiness.

"You seem to be very adroit, Sir Clinton," she observed. "But what is this about the length of my pace?"

"The inspector is accustomed to our English girls, madame, who have a free-swinging walk and therefore a fairly long step. From the length of the steps on the sand he inferred that they had been made by someone who was not very tall—rather under the average height. He forgot that some of you Parisians have a different gait—more restrained, more finished, shall we say?"

"Ah, now I see!" Mme. Laurent-Desrousseaux exclaimed, not at all unsusceptible to the turn of Sir Clinton's phrase. "You mean the difference between the cab-horse and the stepper?"

"Exactly," Sir Clinton agreed with an impassive face.

Armadale was still puzzling over the two footprints. Mme. Laurent-Desrousseaux, evidently wearying of standing with one foot off the ground, recovered her shoe from him and slipped it on again. Sir Clinton took pity on his subordinate.

"Here's the explanation, inspector. When you walk in sand, you put down your heel first. But as the sand's soft, your heel goes forward and downward as you plant your foot. Then, as your body moves on, your foot begins to turn in the sand; and when you've come to the end of your step, your toe also is driven downwards; but instead of going *forward*, like your heel, it slips backward. The result is that in the impression the heel is too far forward, whilst the toe is in the rear of the true position—and that means an impression shorter than the normal. On the sand, your foot really pivots on the sole under the instep, instead of on heel and toe, as it does on hard ground. If you look at these impressions, you'll find quite a heap of sand under the point where the instep was; whilst the heel and toe are deeply marked owing to each of them pivoting on the centre of the shoe. See it?"

The inspector knelt down, and Wendover followed his example. They had no difficulty in seeing Sir Clinton's point.

"Of course," the chief constable went on, "in the case of a woman's shoe, the thing is even more exaggerated owing to the height of the heel and the sharpness of the toe. Haven't you noticed, in tracks on the sand, how neat any woman's prints always look? You never seem to find the impression of a clumsy foot, simply because the impression is so much smaller than the real foot. Clear enough, isn't it?"

"You are most ingenious, Sir Clinton," Mme. Laurent-Desrousseaux commented. "I am very glad indeed that I have not you against me."

Sir Clinton turned the point.

"The inspector will bring you a copy of the evidence you have so kindly given us, madame, and you will do us the favour to sign it. It is a mere formality, that; but we may need you as a witness in the case, you understand?"

Rather ungraciously, Mme. Laurent-Desrousseaux agreed. It was evident that she had hoped to escape giving evidence in court.

"I do not desire to offer testimony against the young Madame Fleetwood if it could be averted," she said frankly. "She was good to me once or twice; very gentle, very kind—not like the others in the hotel."

The inspector shrugged his shoulders, as though the matter were out of his hands; but he made no reply.

"You will, of course, say nothing about this to anyone, madame," Sir Clinton warned her, as they walked across the sands to the car.

At the hotel, Sir Clinton was met by a message from Cargill asking him to go up to his room. Wendover accompanied him, and when they had inquired about his wound and been reassured by a good report from the doctor which Cargill was able to repeat, the Australian plunged into the matter which he wished to lay before the chief constable.

"It's that thing I told you about before," he explained. "This is how it happened. I was so sore last night that I forgot all about it."

He felt under his pillow, and drew out a crumpled envelope.

"I was in the writing-room one day lately, and Mme. Laurent-Desrousseaux—that French high-stepper—was writing something at one of the tables. She made a muddle of her addressing of the thing, and flung a spoiled envelope into the waste-paper basket beside her. Then she addressed another envelope, sealed up her letter, and went out.

"I happened to have some jottings to make; and, as her waste-paper basket was just at my elbow, I leaned over and fished out the old envelope, to save myself the bother of getting out of my chair for a piece of paper. I scribbled down the notes I wanted to make, put the envelope in my pocket, and left it there. It wasn't for a while after that—yesterday—that I needed the jottings I'd made. I fished the envelope out, and was reading my notes, when suddenly my eye was caught by the spoiled address on the envelope."

He handed the paper across to Sir Clinton, who read:

Monsieur Nicholas Staveley,
Flatt's Cotage,
Lynden Sands.

"You see, she'd spelt 'cottage' with one 't,'" Cargill pointed out unnecessarily. "That's what made her throw away the envelope, I expect."

Sir Clinton took the envelope and examined it carefully.

"That's extremely interesting," he said. "I suppose I may keep this? Then would you mind initialing it, just in case we need it for reference later on?"

He handed Cargill a pencil, and the Australian scribbled his initials on one corner of the envelope. The chief constable chatted for a few minutes on indifferent matters, and then retired, followed by Wendover.

"Why didn't you tell him he was a day after the fair?" Wendover demanded, as they went down the stairs. "The only value that envelope has now is that it further confirms Mme. Laurent-Desrousseaux's evidence. And yet you treated it as if it were really of importance."

"I hate to discourage enthusiasm, squire," Sir Clinton answered. "Remember that we owe the second cartridge-case to Cargill's industry. If I had damped him over the envelope, he might feel disinclined to give us any more assistance; and one never knows what may turn up yet. Besides, why spoil his pleasure for him? He thought he was doing splendidly."

As they reached the first floor, they saw Paul Fordingbridge coming along the corridor towards the stairs.

"Here's someone who can perhaps give us more valuable information," Sir Clinton added in a low tone. He stopped Paul Fordingbridge at the head of the stairs.

"By the way, Mr. Fordingbridge," he asked, glancing round to see that there was no one within earshot, "there's just one point I'd like you to clear up for me, if you don't mind."

Paul Fordingbridge stared at him with an emotionless face.

"Very glad to do anything for you," he said, without betraying anything in his tone.

"It's nothing much," Sir Clinton assured him. "All I want is to be clear about this Foxhills estate and its trimmings. Your nephew owns it at present?"

"If I have a surviving nephew, certainly. I can offer no opinion on that point, you understand."

"Naturally," Sir Clinton acquiesced. "Now, suppose your nephew's death were proved, who are the next heirs? That's what I'd like you to tell me, if you don't mind. I could get it hunted up at Somerset House, but if you'll save me the trouble it will be a help."

"Failing my nephew, it would go to my niece, Mrs. Fleetwood."

"And if anything happened to her?"

"It falls to me in that case."

"And if you weren't there to take it by then?"

"My sister would get it."

"There's no one else? Young Fleetwood, for instance, couldn't step in front of you owing to his having married your niece?"

"No," Paul Fordingbridge answered at once. "The will took account of seven lives, and I suppose that was sufficient in the ordinary way. My sister, if she gets it, can leave it to anyone she chooses."

Sir Clinton seemed thoughtful. It was only after a slight pause that he took up a fresh line of questions.

"Can you tell me anything about the present management of the thing? You have a power of attorney, I believe; but I suppose you leave matters very much in the hands of lawyers?"

Paul Fordingbridge shook his head.

"I'm afraid I'm no great believer in lawyers. One's better to look after things oneself. I'm not a busy man, and it's an occupation for me. Everything goes through my hands."

"Must be rather a business," Sir Clinton criticised. "But I suppose you do as I would myself—get a firm of auditors to keep your books for you."

Paul Fordingbridge seemed slightly nettled at the suggestion.

"No. Do you suppose I can't draw up a balance-sheet once a year? I'm not quite incompetent."

It was evident that Sir Clinton's suggestion had touched him in his vanity, for his tone showed more than a trace of pique. The chief constable hastened to smooth matters over.

"I envy you, Mr. Fordingbridge. I never had much of a head for figures myself, and I shouldn't care to have that kind of work thrust on my hands."

"Oh, I manage very well," Paul Fordingbridge answered coldly. "Is there anything else you'd like to know?"

Sir Clinton reflected for a moment before replying.

"I think that's everything. Oh, there's one other matter which you may know about, perhaps. When does Mrs. Fleetwood expect her lawyer to turn up?"

"This afternoon," Paul Fordingbridge intimated. "But I understand that they wish to consult him before seeing you again. I believe they'll make an appointment with Inspector Armadale for to-morrow."

Sir Clinton's eyebrows lifted slightly at the news of this further delay; but he made no audible comment. Paul Fordingbridge, with a stiff bow, left them and went on his way downstairs. Sir Clinton gazed after him.

"I'd hate to carry an automatic in my jacket pocket continuously," he remarked softly. "Look how his pocket's pulled all out of shape by the thing. Very untidy."

With a gesture he stopped the comment that rose to Wendover's lips, and then followed Fordingbridge downstairs. Wendover led the way out into the garden, where he selected a quiet spot.

"There's one thing that struck me about Mme. Laurent-Desrousseaux's evidence," he said, as they sat down, "and that is: It may be all lies together."

Sir Clinton pulled out his case and lit a cigarette before answering.

"You think so? It's not impossible, of course."

"Well, look at it squarely," Wendover pursued. "We know nothing about the woman. For all we can tell, she may be an accomplished liar. By her own showing, she had some good reason for wanting Staveley out of the way."

"It wouldn't be difficult to make a guess at it," Sir Clinton interjected. "I didn't want to go beyond our brief this morning, or I'd have asked her about that. But I was very anxious not to rouse her suspicions, and the matter really didn't bear directly on the case, so I let it pass."

"Well, let's assume that her yarn is mostly lies, and see where that takes us," Wendover went on. "We know she was at the cottage all right; we've got the footprint to establish that. We know she was on the rock, too, for her footprints were on the sands, and she doesn't contest the fact of her presence either. These are the two undeniable facts."

"Euclidian, squire. But it leaves the story a bit bare, doesn't it? Go on; clothe the dry bones with flesh, if you can."

Wendover refused to be nettled. He was struggling, not too hopefully, to shift the responsibility of the murder from the shoulders of Cressida to those of another person; and he was willing to catch at almost any straw.

"How would this fit, then?" he demanded. "Suppose the Mme. Laurent-Desrousseaux herself was the murderess. She makes her appointment with Staveley at the cottage as she told us; and she goes there, just as she said she did. She meets Staveley, and he refuses to see her. Now assume that he blurts out the tale of his appointment at 11 P.M. at Neptune's Seat with Mrs. Fleetwood, and makes no appointment at all with Mme. Laurent-Desrousseaux for that evening. That part of her tale would be a lie, of course."

Sir Clinton flicked the ash from his cigarette on to the seat beside him, and seemed engrossed in brushing it away.

"She goes to the shore near 11 P.M.," Wendover continued, "not to meet Staveley, as she told us, but to eavesdrop on the two of them, as she confessed she did in her tale. She waits until Mrs. Fleetwood goes away; and then she sees her chance. She goes down to the rock herself then and she shoots Staveley with her own hand for her own purposes. She leaves the body on the rock and returns, as her footmarks show, to the road, and so to the hotel. What's wrong with that?"

"Nothing whatever, squire, except that it omits the most damning facts on which the inspector's depending. It leaves out, for instance, the pistol that he found in Mrs. Fleetwood's golf-blazer."

Wendover's face showed that his mind was hard at work.

"One can't deny that, I suppose," he admitted. "But she might quite well have let off her pistol to frighten Staveley. That would account for—"

He broke off, thought hard for a moment or two, then his face cleared.

"There were two cartridge-cases: one at the rock and one at the groyne. If Mme. Laurent-Desrousseaux killed Staveley, then the cartridge-case on the rock belongs to her pistol; and any other shot fired by the Fleetwoods—at the groyne. That means that Stanley Fleetwood, behind the groyne, fired a shot to scare Staveley. Then, when the Fleetwoods had gone, Mme. Laurent-Desrousseaux went down and shot him on the rock. That accounts for everything, doesn't it?"

Sir Clinton shook his head.

"Just think what happens when you fire an automatic. The ejector mechanism jerks the empty case out to your right, well clear of your shoulder, and lands it a yard or two behind you. It's a pretty big impulse that the cartridge-case gets. Usually the thing hops along the ground, if I remember rightly. You can take it from me that a shot fired from where Fleetwood crouched wouldn't land the cartridge-case at the Point where Cargill showed us he'd picked it up."

Wendover reflected for a while.

"Well, who did it, then?" he demanded. "If the shot had been fired on the rock, the cartridge-case couldn't have skipped that distance, including a jump over the groyne. And there were no other footmarks on that far side of the groyne except Fleetwood's."

Again he paused, thinking hard.

"You said there was a flaw in the inspector's case. Is this it, by any chance?"

Looking up, he saw the figure of Mme. Laurent-Desrousseaux crossing the lawn not far from them.

"That's very opportune," he said, glancing after her. "Any objection to my asking your witness a couple of questions, Clinton?"

"None whatever."

"Then come along."

Wendover managed matters so that it appeared as though they had encountered Mme. Laurent-Desrousseaux by a mere accident; and it was only after they had talked for a few minutes on indifferent matters that he thought it safe to ask his questions.

"You must have got drenched before you reached the hotel on Friday night, madame, surely? I hope there have been no ill-effects?"

"Yes, indeed!" Mme Laurent-Desrousseaux answered readily. "It was a real rain of storm—how do you say that in English?"

"Thunderstorm; heavy shower," Sir Clinton suggested.

"Yes? *Une pluie battante*. I was all wetted."

"When did the rain start, do you remember?" Wendover asked indifferently.

Mme. Laurent-Desrousseaux showed no hesitation whatever.

"It was after the automobile had started to return to the hotel—a few minutes only after that."

"You must have got soaked to the skin yourself," Wendover commiserated her. "That reminds me, had Staveley his coat on—his overcoat, I mean—or was he carrying it over his arm when you met him at the rock?"

Again the Frenchwoman answered without pausing to consider. "He carried it on his arm. Of that I am most certain."

Wendover, having nothing else to ask, steered the talk into other channels; and in a short time they left Mme. Laurent-Desrousseaux to her own affairs. When they were out of earshot, Sir Clinton glanced at Wendover.

"Was that your own brains, squire, or a tip from the classic? You're getting on, whichever it was. Armadale *will* be vexed. But kindly keep this to yourself. The last thing I want is to have any information spread round."

CHAPTER XII
THE FORDINGBRIDGE MYSTERY

"TUESDAY, ISN'T IT?" SIR CLINTON SAID, as he came in to breakfast and found Wendover already at the table. "The day when the Fleetwoods propose to put their cards on the table at last. Have you got up your part as devil's advocate, squire?"

Wendover seemed in high spirits.

"Armadale's going to make a fool of himself," he said, hardly taking the trouble to conceal his pleasure in the thought. "As you told him, he's left a hole as big as a house in that precious case of his."

"So you've seen it at last, have you? Now, look here, squire. Armadale's not a bad fellow. He's only doing what he conceives to be his duty, remember; and he's been wonderfully good at it, too, if you'd only give him decent credit for what he's done. Just remember how smart he was on that first morning, when he routed out any amount of evidence in almost less than no time. I'm not going to have him sacrificed on the Fleetwood altar, understand. There's to be no springing of surprises on him while he's examining these people, and making him look a fool in their presence. You can tell him your idea beforehand if you like."

"Why should I tell him beforehand? It's no affair of mine to keep him from making an ass of himself if he chooses to do so."

Sir Clinton knitted his brows. Evidently he was put out by Wendover's persistence.

"Here's the point," he explained. "I can't be expected to stand aside while you try to make the police ridiculous. I'll admit that

Armadale hasn't been tactful with you; and perhaps you're entitled to score off him if you can. If you do your scoring in private, between ourselves, I've nothing to say; but if you're bent on a public splash—why, then, I shall simply enlighten the inspector myself and spike your gun. That will save him from appearing a fool in public. And that's that. Now what do you propose to do?"

"I hadn't looked at it in that way," Wendover admitted frankly. "You're quite right, of course. I'll tell you what. You can give him a hint beforehand to be cautious; and I'll show him the flaw afterwards, if he hasn't spotted it himself by that time."

"That's all right, then," Sir Clinton answered. "It's a dangerous game, making the police look silly. And the inspector's too good a man to hold up to ridicule. He makes mistakes, as we all do; but he does some pretty good work between them."

Wendover reflected that he might have expected something of this sort, for Sir Clinton never let a subordinate down. By tacit consent they dropped the subject.

Half-way through breakfast they were interrupted by a page-boy with a message.

"Sir Clinton Driffield? Miss Fordingbridge's compliments, sir, and she'd like to see you as soon as possible. She's in her private sitting-room upstairs—No. 28, sir."

When the boy had retired, Sir Clinton made a wry face.

"Really, this Fordingbridge family ought to pay a special police rate. They give more trouble than most of the rest of the population of the district lumped together. You'd better come up with me. Hurry up with your breakfast, in case it happens to be anything important."

Wendover obviously was not much enamoured of the prospect opened up by the chief constable's suggestion.

"She *does* talk," he said with foreboding, as though he dreaded the coming interview.

They found Miss Fordingbridge waiting for them when they went upstairs, and she broke out immediately with her story.

"Oh, Sir Clinton, I'm so worried about my brother. He went out last night and he hasn't come back, and I don't really know what to think of it. What could he be doing out at night in a place like Lynden Sands, where there's nothing to do and where he hasn't any reason for staying away? And if he meant to stay away, he could have left a message for me or said something before he went off, quite easily; for I saw him just a few minutes before he left the hotel. What do you think about it? And as if we hadn't trouble enough already, with that inspector of yours prowling round and suspecting everyone! If he hasn't more to do than spy on my niece, I hope you'll set him to find my brother at once, instead of wasting his time."

She halted, more for lack of breath than shortage of things to say; and Sir Clinton seized the chance to ask her for some more definite details.

"You want to know when he went out last night?" Miss Fording-bridge demanded. "Well, it must have been late—after eleven, at any rate, for I go to bed at eleven always, and he said good night to me just before I left this room. And if he had meant to stay away, he would have told me, I'm sure; for he usually does tell me when he's going to be out late. And he said nothing whatever, except that he was going out and that meant to take a walk up towards the Blowhole. And I thought he was just going for a breath of fresh air before going to bed; and now it turns out that he never came back again. And nobody in the hotel has heard anything about him, for I asked the manager."

"Possibly he'll put in an appearance shortly," Sir Clinton suggested soothingly.

"Oh, of course, if the police are incompetent, there's no more to be said," Miss Fordingbridge retorted tartly. "But I thought it was part of their business to find missing people."

"Well, we'll look into it, if you wish," Sir Clinton said, as she seemed obviously much distressed by the state of things. "But really, Miss Fordingbridge, I think you're taking the matter too seriously. Quite possibly Mr. Fordingbridge went for a longer walk than he intended, and got benighted or something; sprained his ankle, perhaps, and couldn't get home again. Most probably he'll turn up safe and sound in due course. In the meantime, we'll do what we can."

But when they had left the room, Wendover noticed that his friend's face was not so cheerful.

"Do you notice, squire," the chief constable pointed out as they went downstairs, "that everything we've been worried with in this neighbourhood seems to be connected with this confounded Fordingbridge lot? Peter Hay—caretaker to the Fordingbridges; Staveley—married one of the family; and now old Fordingbridge himself. And that leaves out of account this mysterious claimant, with his doubtful pack of associates, and also the suspicious way the Fleetwoods are behaving. If we ever get to the bottom of the affair, it'll turn out to be a Fordingbridge concern entirely, either directly or indirectly. That's plain to a village idiot."

"What do you propose to do in this last business?" Wendover demanded.

"Get hold of a pair of old Fordingbridge's shoes, first of all. We might need them; and we might not have time to come back for them. I'll manage it through the boots, now. I could have got them from Miss Fordingbridge, I expect, but she might have been a bit alarmed if I'd asked her for them."

With the shoes in an attaché-case, Sir Clinton set out for the Blowhole, accompanied by Wendover.

"Not much guidance, so far," he commented, "so we may as well start at the only place she could mention."

When they reached the Blowhole, out on the headland which formed one horn of the bay, it was only too evident that very little trace was to be expected there. The turf showed no marks of any description. Sir Clinton seemed rather resentful of the expectant manner of Wendover.

"Well, what do you expect me to do?" he demanded brusquely. "I'm not an Australian tracker, you know. And there don't seem to be any cigar-butts or cigarette-ash or any of these classical clues lying around, even if I could use them if I'd found them. There's just one chance—that he's gone down on to the sands."

As he spoke, he stepped to the cliff-edge and gazed down on the beach.

"If those tracks on the sand happen to be his," he said, "then we've got at least one bit of luck to start with."

Wendover, coming to the chief constable's side, saw the footprints of two men stretching clean-cut along the beach until they grew small in the distance.

"We'll go down there and see what we can make of it," Sir Clinton suggested. "I've telephoned to Armadale to come out from Lynden Sands and meet us. It's handy that these tracks stretch out in that direction and not into the other bay."

They descended a steep flight of steps cut on the face of the cliff for the convenience of hotel visitors; and when they reached the sands below, they found the footprints starting out from the bottom of the stair. Sir Clinton opened his attaché-case and pulled out Paul Fordingbridge's shoes, which he had procured at the hotel.

"The boots told me that Fordingbridge had two pairs of shoes, both of the same pattern and both fairly new; so it should be easy enough to pick out his tracks, if they're here," he said, taking one shoe and pressing it into the sand to make an impression of the sole. "That looks all right, squire. The nail pattern's the same in the shoe and the right-hand set of footmarks."

"And the mark you've just made is a shade larger than the footprint," Wendover commented, to show that he had profited by Sir Clinton's lesson of the previous day. "That fits all right. By the way, Clinton, it's clear enough that these two fellows met up at the top of the stairs and came down together. If they'd met here, there would have been a second set of tracks for Man No. 2, which he'd have made in coming towards the foot of the stairway."

Sir Clinton nodded his agreement with this inference, put the shoes back in his attaché-case, and set out to follow the tracks across the sands. In a short time they passed Neptune's Seat, where Sir Clinton paused for a few moments to inspect the work of his diggers.

"That seems an interminable job you've set them," Wendover commented as they walked on again.

"The tides interfere with the work. The men can only work between tides, and each incoming tide brings up a lot of sand and spreads it over the places they've dug out already."

"What *are* you looking for, Clinton, damn it? It seems an awful waste of energy."

"I'm looking for the traces of an infernal scoundrel, squire, unless I'm much mistaken; but whether I'll find them or not is another question altogether. It's a pure grab in the dark. And, as I suspect I'm up against a pretty smart fellow, I'm not going to give any information away, even to you, for fear he infers something that might help him. He's probably guessed already what I'm after—one can't conceal things on the open beach—but I want to keep him guessing, if possible. Come along."

The tracks ran, clearly marked, across the sands of the bay in the direction of the old wreck which formed a conspicuous landmark on the shore. The chief constable and his companion followed the trail for a time without finding anything which called for comment.

"They don't appear to have been hurrying," Sir Clinton said, examining the tracks at one point. "They seem just to have sauntered along, and once or twice they've halted for a moment. I expect they were talking something over."

"The second man must have been a pretty big fellow to judge by the size of the footmarks," Wendover ventured cautiously. "Apart from that, there's nothing much to see."

"No?" Sir Clinton retorted. "Only that his impressions are very shallow—much shallower than Fordingbridge's ones. And his stride's not longer than friend Paul's, either. Also, the impression of the sole's quite smooth—looks like crêpe-rubber soles or something of that sort. If so, there's nothing to be got out of them. That kind of shoe's sold by the thousand."

Wendover made no reply, for at this moment he caught sight of the inspector plodding along the road above the beach. Sir Clinton whistled shrilly, and Armadale, catching sight of them, left the road and descended to the sands. In a few minutes he reached them, and Sir Clinton gave him a summary of the facts which had come to light since he had telephoned.

"There's just one thing that's turned up since I saw you last, sir," the inspector reported in his turn. "I've had Flatt's cottage watched, as you ordered; and there's a third man there now. He keeps himself under cover most of the time; but I gave Sapcote a pair of good field-glasses, and he recognised the fellow as soon as he saw him—knew him quite well. His name's Simon Aird. He used to be valet at Foxhills, but he got fired for some cause or other, and hasn't been near Lynden Sands since. Then I asked the fishermen if they'd recognised the man who opened the door to them when they went to borrow the boat, and they recalled that it was Aird. They hadn't thought anything about it, of course, until I questioned them."

"Now, that's something worth having," Sir Clinton said appreciatively. "But let's get on with the job in hand. That tide's coming in fast; and, if we don't hurry, it'll be all over these tracks. We never seem to get any time to do our work thoroughly in this place, with all that water slopping up and down twice a day."

They hurried along the beach, following the trail. It seemed to present nothing of particular interest until, as they drew near the old wreck, Sir Clinton's eye ranged ahead and picked up something fresh.

"See that new set of tracks—a third man—coming out from behind the old wreck's hull and joining the other two?" he asked, pointing as he spoke. "Keep well to the landward side as we come up to them, so as not to muddle them up with our own footprints. I think our best line would be to climb up on top of the wreck and make a general survey from above."

They followed his advice; and soon all three had climbed to the deck of the hulk, from which vantage-point they could look down almost straight upon the meeting-point of the three trails.

"H'm! " said Sir Clinton reflectively. "Let's take No. 3 first of all. He evidently came down from the road and took up a position where the hull of the wreck concealed him from the other two. The moon must have risen three or four hours before, so there would be light enough on the beach. You'd better make a rough sketch of these tracks, inspector, while we're up here. We shan't have much time before that tide washes everything out."

The inspector set to work at once to make a diagram of the various tracks on the sand below, while Sir Clinton continued his inspection.

"No. 3 evidently hung about behind the wreck for a long while," the chief constable pointed out. "You can see how the sand's trampled at random as he shuffled around trying to keep himself warm during his waiting. Now we'll suppose that Fordingbridge and No. 2 are coming up. Look at their tracks, squire. They came up almost under the lee of the wreck; and then they turned right round, as if they intended to retrace their steps. It looks as though they'd come to the end of their walk and meant to turn back. But they seem to have stood there for a while; for the prints are indistinct—which is just what happens if you stand long enough on wet sand. The water oozes, owing to the long displacement of the sand particles, and when you lift your foot it leaves simply a mass of mushy stuff where you stood, with no clean impression."

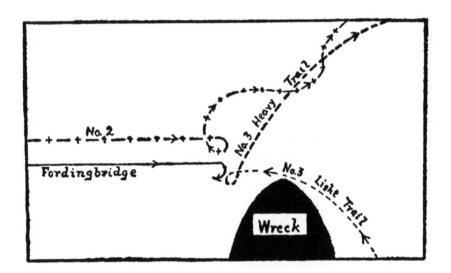

He glanced again over the tracks before continuing.

"I'd read it this way. While they were standing there, with their backs to the wreck, No. 3 started into activity. He came out from the cover of the hull and walked up to where they were standing. He must have gone quietly, for they don't seem to have turned to meet him. You see that, squire? Do you see anything else?"

Wendover was staring at the tracks with a puzzled look on his face. The inspector, who had just reached this point in his diagram, gave a smothered exclamation of surprise as he examined the sand below him. Wendover was the first to find his voice.

"Where's the rest of Fordingbridge's track?" he demanded. "It simply stops short there. He didn't turn; he didn't walk away; and—damn it, he can't have flown away. Where did he go to?"

Sir Clinton ignored the interruption.

"Let's take the tracks as we find them. After No. 3 came up behind the others, it's clear enough that No. 2 and No. 3 went off side by side, down towards the sea. Even from here you can see that they were in company, for sometimes the tracks cross, and No. 2 has his prints on top of No. 3, whereas farther on you see No. 3 putting his feet on top of No. 2's impression. Have you finished with that jotting of yours, inspector? Then we'll go and follow these tracks down the beach to the tide edge."

He dropped neatly down from the wreck as he spoke, and waited for the others to rejoin him.

"Both No. 2 and No. 3 must have been wearing crêpe-rubber shoes or something of that sort," the inspector remarked, stooping over the tracks. "And they've both got fairly big feet, it seems."

"No. 3 seems to have been walking on his toes," Wendover pointed out. "He seems to have dug deeper with them than with his heels. And his feet are fairly parallel instead of having the toes pointing outwards. That's how the Red Indians walk," he added informatively.

Sir Clinton seemed more interested in the general direction of the tracks. Keeping to one side of them, he moved along the trail, scanning the prints as he went. Armadale, moving rather more rapidly on the other side of the route, came abruptly to a halt as he reached the edge of the waves. The rest of the trail had been obliterated by the rising tide.

"H'm! Blank end!" he said disgustedly.

Sir Clinton looked up.

"Just as well for you, inspector, perhaps. If you'd hurried along at that rate at low tide you'd have run straight into the patch of quicksand, if I'm not mistaken. It's just down yonder."

"What do you make of it, sir?"

"One might make a lot of it, if one started to consider the possibilities. They may have walked off along the beach on the part that's now swamped by the tide. Or they may have got into a boat and gone home that way. All one really knows is that they got off the premises without leaving tracks. We might, of course, hunt along the water-line and try to spot where they came up on to high-and-dry ground; but I think they're fairly ingenious, and most likely they took the trouble to walk on shingle above the tide-mark if they came ashore. It's not worth wasting time on, since we've little enough already. Let's get back to the meeting-point."

He led the way up the beach again.

"Reminds one a bit of Sam Lloyd's 'Get off the Earth' puzzle, doesn't it?" he suggested, when they came back to the point where the three tracks met. "You can count your three men all right, and then—flick!—there are only two. How do you account for it, squire?"

Wendover scrutinised the tracks minutely.

"There's been no struggle, anyhow," he affirmed. "The final tracks of Fordingbridge are quite clear enough to show that. So he must have gone voluntarily, wherever he went to."

"And you explain his going—how?"

Wendover reflected for a moment or two before answering.

"Let's take every possibility into account," he said, as his eyes ranged over the sand. "First of all, he didn't sink into the sand in any normal way, for the surface isn't disturbed. Secondly, he didn't walk away, or he'd have left tracks. That leaves only the possibility that he went off through the air."

"I like this pseudo-mathematical kind of reasoning, squire. It sounds so convincing," Sir Clinton commented. "Go ahead. You never fail to combine interest with charm in your expositions."

Wendover seemed untouched by the warmth of this tribute.

"If he went off through the air, he must have managed it either by himself or with the help of the other two; that's self-evident. Now it's too far for him to have jumped backwards on to the wreck and climbed up it; we can rule that out. And it's hardly likely that he was enough of a D. D. Home to manage a feat of levitation and sail up into the air off his own bat. So that excludes the notion that he vanished completely, without any extraneous assistance, doesn't it?"

"'He who has truth at his heart need never fear the want of persuasion on his tongue'—Ruskin," quoted Sir Clinton, with the air of reading from a collection of moral maxims. "You've made the thing crystal-clear to me, squire, with the exception of just one or two trifling points. And these are: First, why did that very solid and unimaginative Mr. Paul Fordingbridge take to romping with his—presumably—grown-up pals? Second, why didn't he return home after these little games? Third, where is he now? Or, if I may put it compendiously, what's it all about? At first sight it seems almost abnormal, you know, but I suppose we shall get accustomed to it."

Armadale had been examining the tracks on the sand without paying Wendover even the courtesy of listening to him. He now broke in.

"If you'll look at No. 3's tracks, sir, you'll find that they're quite light up to the point where he came directly behind Fordingbridge; and then they get deeply marked on the stretch leading down to the sea."

"That's quite correct, inspector," Sir Clinton agreed. "And if you look again you'll find that when they're light, the toes turn out to a fair extent; but on the heavier part of the track No. 3 walked—as Mr. Wendover pointed out—like a Red Indian. Does that interest you?"

The inspector shook his head.

"I don't quite get it, sir."

"Ever been in France, inspector?"

"Just for a trip, sir."

"Ah, then you may not have chanced to come across Père François, then. If you met him, he might have helped you a bit in explaining these levitation affairs."

Wendover pricked up his ears.

"Who's your French friend, Clinton?"

"Père François? Oh, he was one of the pioneers of aviation, in a way; taught men to fly, and all that. 'Get off the Earth' was his motto."

"There's not much of the strong, silent man about you, Clinton," said Wendover glumly. "I never heard anyone to beat you for talking a lot and saying nothing while you're doing it."

"Père François not mentioned in the classics? Well, well. One can't drag in everything, of course. But don't let's dwell on it. What about the business in hand? We must have a theory to work on, you know. How do you account for Mr. Paul Fordingbridge's quaint behaviour, squire? That's really of some importance."

Wendover pondered for a time before taking up his friend's implied challenge.

"Suppose that No. 3 had a chloroformed pad in his hand when he came up behind Fordingbridge," he suggested at last, "and that he clapped it over Fordingbridge's mouth from behind; and then, once he was unconscious, they both carried him down to a boat."

"You can chloroform a sleeping man without any struggle," the inspector commented acidly, "but you can't chloroform a normal man without his making some sort of struggle. There's no trace of a struggle here."

Wendover had to admit the flaw.

"Well, then," he amended, "I suppose one must assume that he voluntarily allowed himself to be lifted down to the boat."

Armadale hardly troubled to conceal his sneer.

"And what earthly good would that be?" he demanded. "Here are his tracks stretching back for the best part of a mile over the sands. Lifting him for twenty yards or so at the end of that doesn't seem much use. Besides, as I read the tracks, that's an impossibility. No. 2's tracks are mixed up with No. 3's in the second part of the trail, and sometimes one was ahead and sometimes the other of them. Two men don't waltz round like that when they're carrying anyone, usually. It's impossible, for their footmarks show they were both walking straight ahead all the time; and if they were carrying a man between them they'd have had to reverse somehow if the front man changed round to the rear. That's no good, Mr. Wendover."

"What do you propose then, inspector?" Wendover inquired, without troubling to repress a nettled tone in his voice.

"I propose to take casts of their footprints and hunt up shoes to match, if I can."

"I shouldn't trouble, inspector," Sir Clinton interposed. "Look at the marks. They seem to me to be about the biggest size of shoe you could buy. The impressions are light; which seems to suggest a medium weight distributed over an abnormally large foot-area. In other words, these shoes were not fits at all; they were probably extra-sized ones padded to suit or else, possibly, put on above normal shoes. Compare the lengths of the steps, too. If these men had heights anything in proportion to the size of their shoes, they would be six-footers on any reasonable probability, whereas their pace is no longer than mine. There's no certainty, of course; but I'm prepared to bet that you'll get nothing by shoe-hunting. And by this time these shoes have been destroyed, or thrown away in some place where you'll never find them. These fellows are smarter lads than you seem to think."

Rather mollified by the inspector's failure, Wendover tried to draw the chief constable.

"What do you make of it yourself, Clinton?"

Somewhat to the surprise of both his hearers, Sir Clinton extended the range of the subject under discussion.

"Motive is what interests me at present," he confessed. "We've had the Peter Hay case, the Staveley affair, the shooting of Cargill, and this vanishing trick of Fordingbridge's. There must have been some incentive at the back of each of them. Eliminate Cargill's affair for the present, and the other three are all concerned with one or other of the Foxhills people. The odds against that happening by accident are a bit too heavy for probability, aren't they?"

"Obviously," Wendover admitted.

"Then it's reasonable to look to the Foxhills affairs for motives, isn't it?" Sir Clinton continued. "What's the big thing in the Foxhills group about which they might come to loggerheads? It stares you in the face—that old man's will. You've seen already that it's led to friction. Paul Fordingbridge won't recognise the claim of this nephew of his—we'll call him the claimant for short. He sat tight with his power of attorney and refused to abdicate. That suggests a few bright thoughts to me; and probably you feel the same about it."

He glanced at his watch, and with a gesture invited them to walk over the sands.

"By the way, though," he suggested, just as they were moving off, "you might note on your diagram, inspector, the difference between the light and heavy tracks of No. 3's feet. Make the trail of the deep footprints a bit darker." [*see* diagram, page 190]

The inspector did as he was requested.

"If you start with that assumption," Wendover pointed out, as they began to move across the sands, "then it ought to lead you to the idea of two camps in the Fordingbridge lot."

"Who's in your camps?" Sir Clinton asked.

"The claimant, Staveley, and Miss Fordingbridge would be in the one, since Staveley was living at the cottage and Miss Fordingbridge identifies the claimant. The other camp would be Paul Fordingbridge, with Mr. and Mrs. Fleetwood."

Sir Clinton nodded thoughtfully, and put a further question.

"On that basis, squire, can you find a motive for each of these affairs?"

"I think one might find some," Wendover contended confidently. "In the first place, Peter Hay had known the claimant very well indeed in the old days. Therefore his evidence would be invaluable to either one side or the other; and whichever side he did not favour might think it worth while to silence him. It was someone well known to Peter Hay who murdered him, if I'm not mistaken. In any case, it was someone in our own class. That was implicit in the facts."

"It's not beyond possibility, squire. Continue the analysis."

"Supposing Paul Fordingbridge were out of the way, who would oppose the claimant?" Wendover pursued.

"The Fleetwoods," said the inspector. "They're next in the succession. And Staveley was a witness of some value to the claimant, too, so he was put out of the way. Everything points to the same thing, you see, sir."

Wendover, bearing in mind the coming fall of the inspector's case, took this side-thrust amiably.

"Let's go on," he suggested. "There's the Cargill affair."

"I've got my own ideas about that," the inspector interjected. "Though I haven't had time to work them up yet."

"Cargill's about the same build as the claimant," Wendover continued, without noticing the interruption. "It seems to me quite on the cards that the attack on him was a case of mistaken identity. Or else—of course! He was a good witness for the claimant! He'd met him in the war, you remember. Perhaps that was why he was attacked."

"I think more of your first notion, sir," the inspector interrupted, with more than a tinge of approval in his tone. "As I said before, everything points the same way. You find Mrs. Fleetwood mixed up in the whole affair from start to finish."

Sir Clinton ignored this view of the case, and turned to Wendover.

"Doesn't it seem rather out of proportion when you assume that Paul Fordingbridge would go the length of murder merely in order to keep the claimant out of the money and out of Foxhills?" he inquired gently. "It really seems carrying things a bit too far when you take that as a premise."

"Well, what better can you suggest?" Wendover demanded.

"If I were set to make a guess, I think I'd hazard something of this sort," the chief constable returned. "Suppose that friend Paul has been up to some hanky-panky under his power of attorney—malversation of some kind. He wouldn't dare to sell Foxhills; but he might safely dispose of securities. There was no audit, remember; the competent fellow managed it all himself. And so long as no claimant turned up he was all right; for none of the rest of them seemed to need money badly, and no one protested against the estate being left hanging in the wind. But, as soon as this claimant hove in sight, friend Paul looked like being 'for it' if the claimant could establish his case. Everything would come out then. That would be a good enough motive, wouldn't it?"

"There's more in it than that, sir," the inspector broke in. "If he'd got himself into Queer Street, it might be handy if he could disappear when things looked like getting too hot for him. Perhaps the whole of this"—he turned and waved his hand towards the mysterious footprints—"is simply a blind to cover his get-away. Perhaps it's just something left for us to scratch our heads over while he gets under cover, sir."

Sir Clinton seemed slightly amused by the picture the inspector had drawn.

"I never held with head-scratching, inspector. It's a breach of good manners, and not even friend Paul shall tempt me to make a habit of it. I don't think he's very far away; but I doubt if you'll get your hands on him in a hurry. My impression is that he's gone to ground in a very safe hole."

The inspector seemed to be reminded of something.

"By the way, sir, that new fellow who's turned up at Flatt's cottage must have come down by car, probably during the night. They've got the car in the boat-house beside the cottage; I saw its bonnet sticking out as I passed this morning."

"Very sensible of Mr. Aird, inspector, since he seems to shun being recognised by his old friends round about here. If he'd come by train, someone would have spotted him at the station."

Without paying further attention to the matter, Sir Clinton changed the subject.

"When we get back to the hotel, inspector, I think we'll interview the Fleetwood family. They've had quite long enough to polish their speeches by this time. But I'll give you one hint—and I mean it, inspector. Don't be too sure about that case of yours. And don't let your zeal run away with you when you come to question the Fleetwoods. You're on very slippery ice; and, if you get their backs up too much, we may fail to get a piece of evidence out of them which is essential."

The inspector considered this in silence for a few moments. Quite obviously he did not like being handled in this fashion.

"Well, sir," he conceded at last, "if you think I'm likely to bungle something because I don't know what it is, why not give me a hint?"

"Mr. Wendover could do that, I think, if you cared to ask him, inspector."

Armadale turned round to Wendover with ill-concealed sulkiness.

"Have you something up your sleeve, sir?"

Wendover took no notice of the ungracious tone. He saw his way to achieve his end without the difficulties he had feared.

"You've got no case at all, inspector," he said roundly. "Sir Clinton told you long ago that there was a flaw in it. The whole thing's a wash-out. Now I don't want to have you walking straight into a mess, you understand; and you'll do that if you aren't careful. Suppose we let Sir Clinton do the talking at this interview? He'll get what he wants. You and I can ask any questions we choose after he's done. And after it's all over I'll show you the flaw in your case. Agree to that?"

"I really think Mr. Wendover's suggestion is sound, inspector," Sir Clinton interposed, as Armadale hesitated over accepting the situation. "It's a fact that you can't prove your case on the evidence available."

"Oh, very well, then," Armadale agreed, rather resentfully. "If you want it handled so, sir, I've no objection. But it seems to me that case will take a lot of breaking."

"It's quite on the cards that this interview will stiffen you in your opinions, inspector; but you're wrong for all that," Sir Clinton pronounced, in a voice that carried conviction to even the inspector's mind.

CHAPTER XIII
CRESSIDA'S NARRATIVE

REASSURED BY THE KNOWLEDGE that Sir Clinton had taken the examination of Cressida out of the inspector's hands, Wendover was eager to know if anything fresh would be elicited from the Fleetwoods which might help him to carry his theories to a further stage. Feeling sure that he could clear Cressida from the murder charge, he had difficulty in restraining his impatience during the half-hour which elapsed before they were shown into the Fleetwood suite.

His first glance at Cressida showed him that the strain of the last day or two had told heavily upon her. Her darkened eyes and the weariness of her whole attitude spoke for themselves of the long hours of tension and anxiety; and on her face he could read clearly the apprehension which she was vainly striving to conceal. What puzzled him most was an impression of conscious guilt which he sensed in some mysterious way without being able to analyse it clearly.

Stanley Fleetwood, lying on a couch with his leg in splints, seemed to present almost as difficult a problem. On his face also the strain had left its traces; and his whole expression inevitably suggested the bearing of an accomplice who, seeing that all is lost, still determines to brazen things out in the hope that some turn of the wheel may yet bring him into a safer position.

The third occupant of the room was the lawyer, a pleasant, keen-faced man, who was seated at a table with some papers before him. His face betrayed nothing whatever as to his views on the case.

"Mr. Wendover has no *locus standi* here, of course," Sir Clinton explained when the lawyer had been introduced to them, "but I think it might be advantageous to have a witness at this interview who is not officially concerned in the case. Have you any objection, Mr. Calder?"

The lawyer mutely consulted Cressida and her husband, and then gave his consent without ado. Stanley Fleetwood nodded his assent.

"I've consulted Mr. Calder," he said, when this matter had been settled, "and we've come to the conclusion that frankness is the best policy. We've nothing to conceal. Now, what is it that you want to know?"

Wendover's glance, traveling from one to the other, reached Cressida's face; and he could see plainly that she was in dread of the coming ordeal. It seemed as though she had made up her mind for the worst, and could see no hope of coming safely through the inquisition.

"Perhaps Mrs. Fleetwood could tell us what she knows about this affair?" Sir Clinton suggested. "Then, after we've had her account, Mr. Fleetwood could amplify her story wherever he came into the matter directly."

Cressida nerved herself for the task, but she seemed to find difficulty in controlling her voice. At last she pulled herself together with an obvious effort and began.

"If I'm to make the thing clear to you," she said, looking distrustfully from one to another in the group, "I'll need to go back a bit, so that you can understand the state of affairs properly. You know, of course, that I married Nicholas Staveley in 1917, when he was convalescing after a wound he got. It's common property that my marriage was a complete failure. It couldn't have been worse. In less than a month he'd shattered almost every ideal I had; and I loathed him more than I'd thought it possible for one person to loathe another. And he terrified me, too.

"He went back to the Front again; and the next we heard was that he'd been reported killed in action. It sounds dreadful to say it, I know, but I can't pretend I was anything but glad when I heard the news. He was a horrible creature, horrible in every way. Life with him, even for that short time, had been a waking nightmare; and it was an infinite relief to find myself free of him. Then, in 1926, I married Mr. Fleetwood."

She paused and glanced at the lawyer, as though to draw some encouragement from him. Evidently the sequence of her narrative had been concerted between them beforehand. Wendover's glance passed from her to Stanley Fleetwood; and he could see from the expression on Fleetwood's face how much he must have hated the dead man on Cressida's account.

"Last week," Cressida continued, in a slightly more controlled tone, "I got a letter signed 'Nicholas Staveley.' It was a dreadful shock to see that handwriting again. It seems that the report of his death had been a mistake; but he had let it pass for purposes of his own. It had suited him to disappear then. Now it suited him to reappear—so far as I was concerned. You can guess what that meant to me. It invalidated my second marriage; and it threw me into the hands of that brute. Or, at least, if it didn't actually put me into his hands, it gave him a weapon against me which he could use for his own ends. He was a selfish beast, and vindictive, too; and I saw that he meant to stir up all the trouble he could. His letter hinted quite plainly that blackmail was his object in reappearing at this moment. He knew I'd married again, and he saw his chance."

The lawyer produced a paper and handed it across to Sir Clinton.

"This is the letter," he explained.

Sir Clinton glanced through it and then put it down on the table.

"That's a pretty production," he commented. "I can understand your feelings, Mrs. Fleetwood. Please go on."

Cressida glanced across at the couch.

"Naturally I consulted Mr. Fleetwood," she continued. "We decided that the best thing to do was to arrange a meeting with the man and try to get him to let us put matters on some bearable kind of footing."

"What we wanted," Stanley Fleetwood interrupted, "was to persuade him to allow a divorce to go through quietly. Then we could have regularised matters with as little fuss as possible. From what I'd heard of him, he didn't seem the sort who would refuse a bribe, if it was big enough—"

He caught the lawyer's warning eye and halted abruptly.

"I understand," Sir Clinton interposed smoothly. "You wished to come to some agreement with him. We needn't discuss the terms. Will you go on, please, Mrs. Fleetwood?"

"I wrote him a letter," Cressida pursued, with rather more courage in her tone as she saw that Sir Clinton was obviously not directly hostile, like the inspector. "Mr. Fleetwood took it across to Flatt's cottage that afternoon—Friday afternoon—and dropped it into the letter-box. You'll understand in a moment that I didn't wish Mr. Fleetwood to meet this man face to face."

The inspector looked up from the note-book in which he was making a shorthand report of the interview.

"You might identify the letter we found on the body," he suggested.

Sir Clinton produced the letter, and Cressida examined it.

"Yes, that's it. I arranged to meet him at Neptune's Seat late in the evening, when no one was likely to be on the beach. I didn't want to have him coming about the hotel, naturally."

She halted for a moment or two, as though she felt she was coming to the difficult point in her tale.

"Perhaps you won't understand what I've got to say next. If I could let you know what sort of man he was, you'd understand better. There are some things one can't tell. But I want you to know that I was really in physical fear of him. I'm not easily frightened; but during the month or so that I lived with him he stamped fear into me—real physical fear, downright terror of personal violence, I mean. He drank; and when he had been drinking he seemed to grow almost inhuman. He terrified me so much that I left him, even before he went back to the Front."

Her face showed even more clearly than her words what it had meant to her. She halted for a space, unintentionally letting her effect sink home on her audience.

"When it came to meeting him," she went on, "Mr. Fleetwood insisted on going with me."

"Naturally," Stanley Fleetwood broke in. "I wanted to go alone to meet the fellow; but she wouldn't let me go either alone or along with her."

Cressida nodded.

"If they had met, nothing could have prevented a quarrel; and that man would stick at nothing. I was afraid of what he might do. Anything was better than letting them meet. But I was horribly afraid of meeting him alone, without any protection. I'd had enough experience of him already. So I borrowed a pistol from Mr. Fleetwood and took it with me to Neptune's Seat. I thought it would serve to frighten that man if he showed any signs of going over the score."

"What sort of pistol was it?" Armadale interjected, looking across at Stanley Fleetwood.

"A Colt .38. I have the number of it somewhere."

"I'll get you to identify it later on," Armadale said; and with a gesture he invited Cressida to continue.

"Mr. Fleetwood gave in about going with me to meet the man," Cressida went on, "but he insisted on taking me down to the shore in our car. I let him do that. I was glad to know that he'd be at hand. But I made him promise not to interfere in any way. He was to stay with the car while I went down alone to Neptune's Seat."

"I think the inspector would like to know exactly what you did before you left the hotel," Sir Clinton intervened.

"Mr. Fleetwood went round to the garage to get out the car. Meanwhile I went down to the ladies' dressing-room, where I keep my golfing things. I changed my slippers for my golfing-shoes—I was in an evening frock—and I slipped on my golfing-blazer. Then I went out through the side-entrance and joined Mr. Fleetwood in the car. He drove me down to the point on the road nearest Neptune's Seat. I left him there, got out of the car, and went across the sands to the rock.

"The man was there, waiting for me; and at the first glance I could see he'd been drinking. He wasn't drunk, you understand, but he wasn't normal. When I saw that, I was terrified. I can't explain these things, but he— Oh, I used to shiver at times even at the very thought of what he'd been like in that state; and when I met him down there, face to face, I was really in terror of him. I pulled the pistol out of my pocket and held it in my hand, without letting him see it.

"Then I spoke to him and tried to persuade him to come to some arrangement with me. It was no use—none whatever. You've no idea of the kind of man he was. He wanted money to keep his mouth shut. He wouldn't hear of any divorce, because that would loosen his hold on me if it went through, he said, and he meant to keep me in his grip. And then he said—oh, I'm not going to repeat what he said about Mr. Fleetwood and myself—horrible things, meant to hurt me and degrade me in my own eyes. And the worse he got in that way, the angrier he grew. You know what a drunken man's like? I know it only too well."

She made an involuntary gesture which betrayed even more than her words.

"At last he went beyond all bounds. I was trembling all over, partly from fear and partly from pure rage at the things he said. It was quite clear that I could do nothing with him in that state; so I turned to go. Then he muttered something—I'm not going to repeat it; you can imagine it for yourselves—and he pounced forward and gripped me when I wasn't expecting it.

"I lost my head completely. I didn't know what I was doing. I was almost beside myself with terror of him. Somehow the pistol went off in my hand, and down he fell at my feet and lay there without a movement. It was too dark to see anything clearly, and I was absolutely taken aback by what had happened. I said to myself: 'I've shot him!' And at that my nerves got the upper hand completely, and I turned and ran up the beach to the car. I told Mr. Fleetwood at once what had happened. I wanted him to go down and look at the man, but he wouldn't hear of it. He drove me back to the hotel, and we left the car in one of the side-alleys. I went in through the dressing-room, took off my blazer, and changed my golfing-shoes for my slippers. I was so much upset that I forgot to take the pistol out of the blazer pocket. And when I came out into the hotel corridor, I heard that Mr. Fleetwood had tripped on the stairs and hurt himself badly. That put the pistol out of my mind at the moment; and when, next day, I remembered about it, and went to get it, someone else had taken it away. That terrified me, for I knew someone was on my track."

She paused for a moment, and then added:

"That's really all I have to tell. It was the purest accident. I didn't mean to kill him. When I took the pistol with me to the shore, I only meant to frighten him with it. But he'd been drinking, and I wasn't ready for him when he attacked me. I was terrified, and my finger must have twitched the trigger without my knowing what I was doing. I'd never have shot him in cold blood, or even intentionally in a fit of anger. It was the merest accident."

She stopped there, evidently having said everything that she could bring herself to tell.

"One moment, Clinton," Wendover interposed as the chief constable turned to question Stanley Fleetwood in his turn. "There's just one point I'd like to have cleared up. Would you mind telling me, Mrs. Fleetwood, whether you can recall how Staveley was dressed when he met you?"

Cressida, looking up quickly, seemed to read the sympathy in Wendover's face, for she answered readily enough.

"It wasn't a very good light, you understand? He wore some sort of lounge suit, but I couldn't tell the colour of it. And when I got down to Neptune's Seat he was carrying a light coat of some kind over his arm; but as I came up he tossed that down on the rock beside him."

"He didn't put it on again, did he?" Wendover demanded.

"Not so far as I can remember," Cressida replied, after some effort to recall the point.

"You were caught in the rain before you got back to the hotel, weren't you?" Wendover pursued.

"Yes. It came down hard just after the car started."

Wendover's satisfaction at these answers was too plain to escape Cressida's attention. She looked at him with a faint gleam of hope in her expression, as though expecting him to come to her help; but her face fell when he turned to the chief constable and indicated that he had nothing further to say. Sir Clinton took his cue.

"Now, Mr. Fleetwood," he inquired, "you didn't stay by the car as you had arranged, did you?"

Stanley Fleetwood looked suspiciously at his interlocutor.

"As it happened, I didn't," he admitted, rather with an ill grace. "It was bad enough to let my wife meet that scoundrel at all. You couldn't expect me to stand off at a distance, could you? I'd promised her not to interfere; but that didn't hinder me from getting as near them as I could, just in case of accidents. I went down to the shore, keeping behind a groyne that runs down towards Neptune's Seat."

"So we supposed," Sir Clinton commented. "You haven't a second Colt pistol, have you?"

"No. One's all I have."

"So you didn't fire a shot from behind the groyne, by any chance?"

Both Fleetwood and Cressida seemed completely taken aback by this question. They glanced at each other; and then Stanley Fleetwood answered:

"No, of course I didn't. How could I, when I hadn't a pistol?"

"Of course not," Sir Clinton admitted. "Occasionally one has to ask questions as a matter of form, you know. Now, what happened after Mrs. Fleetwood's pistol went off? I mean, what did you yourself do?"

"I saw her hurrying up the beach towards the road, where she expected to find me; so naturally I bolted up the way I'd come and joined her at the car."

"And then?"

"She told me she'd shot Staveley. I shed no tears over him, of course; but I wanted to get my wife away as quick as I could, in case anyone came along, attracted by the noise of the shot. So I drove up towards the hotel. I didn't put on the lights of the car, because they might have been noticed by someone in the distance; and I didn't want to be traced through the car if I could help it. I'm being quite frank with you, you see."

"I wish we could persuade everybody to be *quite* frank," Sir Clinton confessed. "It would lighten police work considerably. What happened next, please?"

"As I was driving up, it suddenly struck me that we'd left all these tracks on the sand, and that when everything came out our footprints would be evidence connecting us with the business. So I made up my mind—I'm being perfectly frank with you—I made up my mind that after I'd dropped my wife at the hotel I'd take the car back again and see if Staveley was alive, If he wasn't, then I'd make hay of our tracks—rub 'em out somehow and get clear away if possible. Then it occurred to me that Staveley alive would be better than Staveley dead. If he was only hurt, then the whole affair might be hushed up somehow. Apart from that, frankly, I'd rather have had him dead. Anyhow, when I got to the hotel I bolted upstairs to my room to get a flask of brandy I keep for emergencies. I meant to revive him if he was alive, you see? And in sprinting downstairs again I slipped and crocked myself, and that finished any chance of getting down to the beach again. I'd left the car outside, of course, meaning to take it to the garage later on, after I'd been down to fix things up on the beach."

"That seems clear enough," Sir Clinton said in a tone which suggested that he had got all the information he wanted. "Have you any questions to ask, inspector?"

"There's just one point," Armadale explained. "Did you see anyone except Staveley between the hotel and the rock, either going or coming?"

Stanley Fleetwood shook his head.

"I saw nobody at all. Naturally I kept a sharp lookout on the way home."

Sir Clinton indicated that, so far as he was concerned, the matter was ended. As if to make this still clearer, he turned to the lawyer, Calder, who had taken practically no part in the proceedings.

"Are you by any chance Mr. Fordingbridge's lawyer?"

Calder seemed somewhat surprised by the question.

"My firm has had charge of the legal affairs of the Fordingbridge family for more than a generation," he explained a little stiffly. "But I don't see what that has to do with this business."

Sir Clinton ignored the stiffness.

"We're investigating Mr. Fordingbridge's disappearance just now," he explained, "and I would like you to give us some information which might help us. Can you spare a moment or two?"

Calder, though evidently not prepared for the move, made no objection; and, when Sir Clinton and his companions left the room, the lawyer followed them.

As soon as they had reached a place where there was some chance of privacy, Sir Clinton made his purpose clear.

"One possible explanation of Mr. Fordingbridge's disappearance has been suggested, Mr. Calder. He had large funds belonging to other people within his control under a power of attorney. Unless we can learn the state of these funds, we are rather at a loss to know what we're looking for. Now, quite unofficially, have you any information on the point, or can you make a guess as to the state of affairs? Every moment may count, you understand; and we don't want to bark up the wrong tree, if it is the wrong tree."

The lawyer evidently had no desire to implicate himself.

"There's always a possibility of malversation," he admitted, "in every case where a man has control of someone else's money."

"You were familiar with the affairs of the Fordingbridge estate, I suppose, before Paul Fordingbridge took them out of your firm's hands not long ago? I mean that, if I got hold of his papers, you could tell roughly if there had been any hanky-panky?"

"I think it's possible."

Sir Clinton considered for a time before speaking again.

"Suppose I get permission to examine his papers, either from the family or from the authorities, you could put your finger on any malversation if you had time to look into things?"

"Very likely, though it might take time."

"Then I'll get permission, one way or another. I suppose any papers will be at his house in London?"

"Probably."

"Then I'll go up to town with you this afternoon, Mr. Calder, and we'll look into things with your help."

The lawyer made no comment on the suggestion, and, as Sir Clinton showed no desire to detain him further, he went back to his clients. As soon as his back was turned, Armadale swung round on Wendover.

"I see what you're driving at now, sir," he declared in a rather scornful tone. "You think she'll get off on a manslaughter charge instead of a murder case. And, of course, if it's merely manslaughter, she's a nice-looking girl with a hard-luck story ready, and you're counting on a sympathetic jury to bring in a verdict that'll amount to an acquittal. That's it, isn't it?"

Wendover was genuinely amused.

"That's deuced ingenious of you, inspector," he admitted. "I hadn't thought of it in that light at all."

"Oh, hadn't you?" Armadale replied. "Well, in any case, you needn't count much on it. What's the evidence in favour of it? Nothing but a prepared statement by the accused and her accomplice, backed by a sharp lawyer. Any prosecutor would make hay of it in five minutes so far as credibility goes."

"I'm not depending on her statement, inspector. I had the whole affair cut and dried in my mind before she opened her lips. All that her statement did was to confirm my ideas on every point. Your case is a complete wash-out."

Armadale seemed quite unshaken by this blunt assertion.

"I'll be glad to listen to your notions, sir," he replied, in a tone which he would have used towards a spoiled child whom he wished to conciliate. "It'll be most instructive to hear what a layman thinks of this affair, sir."

Wendover was slightly nettled—as the inspector meant him to be—by the faint but unmistakable emphasis on the word "layman."

"Sometimes the looker-on sees most of the game," he retorted sententiously. "It's true enough in this case. You've missed the crucial bit of the evidence, inspector. Didn't you hear Mrs. Fleetwood tell you that, while she was interviewing him, Staveley had no overcoat on? And yet he was shot through his coat. The hole in the coat corresponded to the position of the wound on the body. Does that convince you?"

"You mean that he must have been shot later on, after he'd put on his coat? No, sir, it doesn't count for a rap, so far as convincing me goes. She and Fleetwood have had plenty of time to concoct their yarn and put in nifty little touches like that. What's that evidence worth? Nothing, when it comes from the criminals and when there's nothing to back it up independently."

Wendover's smile broadened into something resembling an impish grin.

"You've missed the crucial bit of evidence, inspector. Mme. Laurent-Desrousseaux could have given it to you if you'd asked her; but you didn't think of it. I did."

"And might I ask what this valuable bit of evidence is?" the inspector inquired, with heavy politeness.

Wendover had no objection now.

"It's the time that the rain began to fall on Friday night," he explained, with the air of setting a dull schoolboy right. "Mme. Laurent-Desrousseaux told me that the rain started all of a sudden, *after* the Fleetwoods' motor had gone away from the shore."

The inspector thought he saw what Wendover was driving at.

"You mean that Staveley put on his coat when the rain came down, and you're relying on his not having had it on beforehand when Mrs. Fleetwood met him? But you've only her story to go on."

"No, inspector. I've got an independent witness to the fact that he was carrying his coat over his arm at first. Mme. Laurent-Desrousseaux told me he was carrying it that way when she met him before eleven o'clock."

"He might have put it on as soon as she left him," objected the inspector, fighting hard for his case.

Wendover shook his head.

"It's no good, inspector. There's more evidence still. If you remember, Staveley's jacket was wet through by the rain, although he was wearing his rainproof coat over it. He was shot through the coat. He put the coat on after the rain started. But by the time the rain had started the Fleetwoods were away up the road to the hotel in their car. Further, if he put it on *after* the rain started, then the shot that Mme. Laurent-Desrousseaux heard was obviously not the shot that killed Staveley. See it now, inspector?"

Armadale was plainly disconcerted by this last touch.

"It's ingenious," he conceded gruffly, without admitting that he was convinced. "What you mean is that Staveley was carrying his coat while he talked to Mrs. Fleetwood. She fired her pistol and her shot missed him. She ran off to the car. Then, after the car had gone, the rain came down and soaked Staveley to the skin. After being nicely wet, he took the trouble to put on his coat, which had slipped his mind during the downpour. And then someone else came along and shot him for keeps. That's how you look at it?"

"More or less."

"H'm!" said Armadale, pouncing on what he thought was a weak spot. "I generally manage to struggle into a coat, if I have one, when a thunderstorm comes down. This Staveley man must have been a curious bird, by your way of it."

Wendover shook his head. In view of past snubbings, he was unable to banish all traces of superiority from his tone as he replied:

"It's all easily explicable, inspector, if you take the trouble to reason it out logically. Here's what really did happen. Mrs. Fleetwood's story is accurate up to the point when the pistol went off. It so happened that, as she fired, Staveley slipped or tripped on the rock, and came down on the back of his head. You remember the contused wound there? That happened in this first fall of his."

The inspector paid Wendover the compliment of listening intently to his theory. The old air of faint contempt was gone; and it was clear that Armadale was now seriously perturbed about the solidity of his case.

"Go on, sir," he requested.

"Staveley came down hard on the rock with his head and was stunned," Wendover explained. "He lay like a log where he had fallen. It wasn't a good light, remember. Now, just think what Mrs. Fleetwood could make of it. Her pistol went bang; Staveley dropped at that very instant; and there he was, to all appearance, dead at her feet. Naturally she jumped to the conclusion that she'd shot him, and probably killed him. She went off instantly to consult her husband, whom she'd left in the car. Not at all unnatural in the circumstances, I think."

The inspector's face showed that he was beginning to feel his case cracking; but he said nothing.

"Meanwhile," Wendover continued, "all her husband had seen was some sort of scuffle on the rock—in a dim light, remember—and he'd heard her pistol explode. Perhaps he'd seen Staveley fall. Then his wife cut back towards the car, and he ran up along the groyne to rejoin her. What could he think, except that his wife had shot Staveley? And she thought so herself; you've got Mme. Laurent-Desrousseaux's evidence for that, in the report she gave you of the Fleetwoods' conversation before they started the car."

"There might be something in it," Armadale conceded, in a tone which showed that he was becoming convinced against his will. "And what happened after that? Who really committed the murder?"

Wendover had thought out his line of argument very carefully. He meant to convince the inspector once for all, and prevent him giving Cressida any further annoyance.

"Don't let's hurry," he suggested. "Just let's look around at the circumstances at that moment. You've got Staveley lying on the rock, stunned by his fall—or at any rate sufficiently knocked out to prevent his getting up at once. In the crash, his wrist-watch has stopped at 11.19; but the glass of it hasn't been broken. You know how easily some wrist-watches stop with a shock; even if you play a shot on the links with a watch on your wrist the swing of the club's apt to stop the machinery.

"Then comes the rain. It soaks Staveley; but he's too muzzy to get up. The crack on the head keeps him quiet—or he may have been unconscious for a while. By and by he wakes up and scrambles to his feet; finds the rain pouring down; and mechanically he picks up his rainproof and puts it on. By that time the Fleetwood car is well on its way to the hotel. There was only one person near at hand."

"Mme. Laurent-Desrousseaux, you mean?" demanded the inspector. "You're trying to fix the murder on her, sir? She had a grudge against Staveley; and there he was, delivered into her hands if she wanted him. Is that it?"

Wendover could not resist a final dig at Armadale. "I shouldn't care to commit myself too hastily to an accusation against any-one," he said, smiling pleasantly at the crestfallen inspector. "Certainly not until I was sure of my ground, you understand?"

Armadale was so engrossed in a reconsideration of the evidence that apparently Wendover's mockery escaped his attention.

"Then your case is that the wrist-watch stopped at 11.19, when he fell the first time, but that the glass wasn't broken until he was shot down, later on?"

"That's what seems to fit the facts," Wendover averred, though without letting himself be pinned down definitely.

"It's one way of looking at the business, certainly," the inspector was forced to admit, though only grudgingly. "I can't just see a way of upsetting your notions right away. I'll think it over."

Sir Clinton had been listening with a detached air to the whole exposition. Now he turned to Wendover.

"That was very neatly put together, squire, I must admit. The handling of the watch-stopping portion of the theme showed how well you've profited by your study of the classics. I wish I had time to read detective stories. Evidently they brighten the intellect."

Wendover was not deceived by this tribute to his powers.

"Oh, of course I know well enough that you spotted the flaw long before I did. You told us, days ago, that there was one. It was when the inspector produced the pistol from Mrs. Fleetwood's blazer, I remember."

"There's a flaw in almost every case that depends purely on cir-cumstantial evidence, squire; and one can never guess how big that flaw is till one has the whole of the evidence together. It's safest to wait for all the evidence before publishing any conclusions; that's what I always bear in mind. Mistakes don't matter much, so long as you keep them to yourself and don't mislead other people with them."

He turned to Armadale, who was still in deep cogitation.

"I'm going up to town this afternoon, inspector, to look into that end of the Fordingbridge business. In the meantime, I want you to do two things for me."

"Very good, sir," said the inspector, waking up.

"First of all, put all that sand-heap we've collected through fairly fine sieves, and see that you don't miss a .38 cartridge-case if it happens to be there. Quite likely it may not be; but I want it, if it should chance to turn up."

"So *that's* what you were looking for all the time?" Wendover demanded. "I must say, Clinton, you came as near lying over that as I've known. You said you were looking for shells, or the brass bottle with the genie in it; and you insisted you were telling the truth, too; and that makes it more misleading still."

"Not a bit of it, squire. I told you the plain truth; and if you take the wrong meaning out of my words, whose blame is it? Did you never hear an American use the word 'shell' for an empty cartridge-case? And the genie's brass bottle, too. Could you find a neater description of a cartridge-case than that? Didn't the genie come out in vapour, and expand till no one would have supposed he could ever have been in the brass bottle? And when you fire a cartridge, doesn't the gas come out—far more of it than you'd ever suppose could be compressed into the size of the cartridge? And wasn't the genie going to kill a man—same as a pistol cartridge might do? I really believed that I'd produced a poetical description of a cartridge-case which would be fit to stand alongside some of Shakespeare's best efforts; and all you can say about it was that it misled you! Well, well! It's sad."

Wendover, now that he saw the true interpretation, could hardly protest further. He had to admit the ingenuity which had served to mislead him.

"Then there's another thing, inspector, which is much more important. You'll go at once to a magistrate and swear information against Mrs. Fleetwood on a charge of murder, and you'll get a warrant for her arrest. That's to be done immediately, you understand. You'll hold that warrant ready for execution; but you won't actually arrest her until I wire to you: 'Take Fleetwood boat on Thursday.' As soon as you get that message, you'll execute the warrant without any delay whatsoever. That's vital, you understand? And, of course, there mustn't be a whisper about this until the moment of the arrest."

As he heard these instructions, the inspector glanced at Wendover with the air of one who has pulled a rubber out of the fire at the last moment. Wendover, thunderstruck, stared at Sir Clinton as though he could hardly believe his ears.

CHAPTER XIV
THE TELEGRAM

ON THE DEPARTURE OF SIR CLINTON, Wendover found himself in a position of isolation. The Fleetwoods and Miss Fordingbridge kept to their own suite, and did not show themselves in the public rooms; but the whole hotel was astir with rumours and discussions among the guests on the subject of the recent tragedies; and Wendover shrank from associating too closely with anyone. He felt that he was in a position of trust, and he feared lest, under the strain of questioning, he might be betrayed into divulging, unconsciously, something or other which was best kept from the public. A reporter from a newspaper in the nearest town demanded an interview, in the hope of eliciting something; but Wendover had the knack of posing as a dull fellow, and the reporter retired baffled and uncertain as to whether his victim had any exclusive information or not. Armadale was the only person with whom Wendover might have talked freely; and Armadale was entirely antipathetic.

Wendover filled in his time as best he could by taking long walks, which kept him out of reach of the more inquisitive guests as much as possible. He reviewed the whole range of affairs from the beginning, in the hope of seeing his way through the tangle; but there seemed to be so many possible cross-trails that he had to admit to himself that even an approximate solution of the problem was beyond him, and that he could produce nothing better than the merest guesswork.

In the first place, there was the Peter Hay case. There, at least, the motive was plain enough. Someone had good reason to silence

217

Peter Hay and suppress any evidence which he might give with regard to the Derek Fordingbridge claim. But, unfortunately, at least two people might be supposed to have good grounds for wishing to suppress Peter Hay's evidence: the claimant and Paul Fordingbridge. Either of them would fit the facts neatly enough.

Then there was the Foxhills' housebreaking, and the theft of various articles. Obviously the silver was not the important part of the loot, since it was worth next to nothing; and the few odds and ends found in Peter Hay's cottage must have been planted there merely to confuse the trail. The real thing the thief had wanted was Derek Fordingbridge's diary. But here again the two possibilities were open. To a false claimant, the diary would be an invaluable mine of information; and, if the man at Flatt's cottage were an impostor, it was obvious that he would do his best to lay hands on such a treasure. On the other hand, if he were the real Derek, then Paul Fordingbridge would have every interest in suppressing a document which could be utilised to confirm his nephew's recollections at every point.

The problem of Staveley's death was a piece of the puzzle which defeated all Wendover's attempts to fit it into place. Who had an interest in removing Staveley? The Fleetwoods, according to the inspector's ideas; and Wendover could not help admitting that a jury might look at things from the inspector's point of view. Undoubtedly he himself had produced enough circumstantial evidence to clear Cressida of even a manslaughter charge, provided that one pinned the prosecution down to the period when she met Staveley on the rock; but Wendover had been thoroughly alarmed by Sir Clinton's instructions to Armadale; and he feared that he had missed some vital link in the chain of evidence which might overturn his whole case for the defence.

Then there was the alternative hypothesis: that Mme. Laurent-Desrousseaux had been the one to shoot Staveley. Again there seemed to be the double solution open, with no way of deciding which answer to choose. And, to make the matter still more complex, there was the second cartridge-case found at the groyne, which Stanley Fleetwood denied having used. Finally, Sir Clinton most obviously expected to find yet another empty cartridge-case somewhere on the sands. Wendover gave it up. Then a fresh thought struck him. Staveley, as the inspector had hinted, would be a good witness for the claimant; and therefore, making the same assumptions as before, Paul Fordingbridge had an interest in silencing him. But there was no evidence connecting Paul Fordingbridge with the matter at all. That seemed to be a blank end, like all the others.

The next link in the chain of events was the attack on Cargill. The more Wendover considered the matter, the clearer it seemed to him that Cargill had been shot in mistake for the claimant. The two men were very much alike, except for the awful mutilation of the claimant's face; and, of course, that would not show in the dark. Once the claimant was out of the way, then Paul Fordingbridge would be free from the impending disclosure of his malversations, if these had really occurred.

And, suddenly, a light flashed on Wendover's mind from a fresh angle. The claimant, Cressida, Paul Fordingbridge—that was the order of inheritance. If by some manoeuvre Paul Fordingbridge could clear out of his way, not the claimant only, but his niece as well, then he himself would come into the estate, and no one could ask any questions whatever. Cressida had been twice involved— once in the affair of Staveley; again when her car came up just after Cargill had been shot. Was it possible that Paul Fordingbridge had tried to kill two birds with one stone in the last crime? The inspector would have been a willing tool in his hands, since he believed Cressida quite capable of murder.

Then there was the disappearance of Paul Fordingbridge himself, with all the puzzle of the footprints. A man didn't fly; nor did he hand himself over to enemies without some sort of struggle. Had he a couple of confederates who had helped him to stage the whole willfully mysterious affair on the sands? And what did Sir Clinton mean by his hints about Père François and Sam Lloyd's "Get off the Earth" puzzle? Wendover recalled that puzzle: two concentric discs with figures on them, and when one disc was revolved on the central pivot, you could count one Chinaman more or less according to where you stopped the disc. Three men when the discs were in one position; two men when you gave a twist to one of the bits of cardboard. Had Sir Clinton some hanky-panky of that sort in his mind, so that the third man on the sands had no real existence? Wendover gave it up.

He returned to the hotel for dinner, and spent as much time as possible in his own room rather than run the gauntlet of inquisitive guests. It was not until after dinner on Wednesday that he was again drawn directly into the game. He was just putting on his coat to go out, in order to escape his inquisitors, when the inspector appeared, evidently in a state of perturbation.

"I've just had a wire from Sir Clinton, sir. My old landlady's let me down badly. I'd warned the post office people to send me any message immediately, but I was out when it came, and the old fool put it behind her kitchen clock and forgot all about it. It wasn't till I asked her that she remembered about it and gave it to me. Net result: hours wasted."

He handed a telegram form to Wendover, who read:

> "Heavy defalcations take Fleetwood boat on Thursday meet last train with car."

"Well, have you carried out your instructions?" he demanded.

"No, worse luck!" Armadale confessed. "Owing to that old fool's bungling, she's slipped through my fingers."

Wendover's whole ideas of the case were overturned by the inspector's admission. He had refused to allow, even in his own mind, that Cressida could be guilty; but this sudden flight could hardly be squared with innocence by any stretch of probability.

"Tell me what happened, inspector."

Armadale was obviously very sore. It was clear enough from his face that he felt he had muddled things just at the point when his own original theory was going to be vindicated.

"I'd put a man on to watch her here. He couldn't do much except hang about in plain clothes and attract as little attention as possible; so he chose the entrance-hall as his look-out post, where he could keep an eye on the lifts and the stairs together. To-night, after dinner, he saw her come down in the lift. She'd evening dress on, and nothing to protect her head; so of course he thought she was just moving about in the hotel. However, he followed her along a passage; and at the end of it she opened a door marked: *'Ladies' Dressing-Room.'* Well, of course, he could hardly shove in there; so he hung about waiting for her to come out again."

"And it was the golf dressing-room with the side-entrance from the outside?"

"Of course. By the time he'd tumbled to what was up, she'd slipped off. Her golf-shoes and blazer are gone. She's diddled us. I wouldn't have had this happen for ever so much."

Wendover did not feel called upon to offer any sympathy.

"What do you come to me for?" he demanded. "I know nothing about her."

Armadale put his finger on the last phrase in the telegram.

"It's his own car he wants, apparently. You can get it out of the garage, sir, with less fuss than I could."

Wendover agreed, and, finding that the chief constable's train was not due for half an hour, he went up into his room and changed his clothes. They reached the Lynden Sands station in good time; and, as soon as the train steamed in, Sir Clinton alighted, with an attaché-case in his hand.

"Well, inspector! Got your bird caged all right, I hope?"

"No, sir," the inspector confessed shamefacedly. "She's got clean away."

Sir Clinton seemed both staggered and perturbed by the news.

"Got away? What do you mean? You'd nothing to do but walk up and arrest her. Why didn't you do it?"

Armadale explained the state of affairs; and, as he told his story, the chief constable's face darkened.

"H'm! Your landlady's made the mess of her life this shot. And I thought I'd been in plenty of time! Come along to the car. There isn't a moment to lose. Flatt's cottage, first of all."

Wendover drove them up to the headland, and Sir Clinton jumped out of the car almost before it pulled up. He opened his attaché-case.

"There's a Colt for each of you. The first cartridge is up in the barrel, so mind the safety-catches. You may not need them; but you'd better be prepared."

He handed a pistol to each of his companions, and pitched the attaché-case back into the car.

"Now, come along."

When they reached the door of the cottage, the place seemed deserted.

"Drawn blank, it seems," Sir Clinton confessed, in a tone which showed he had expected little else. "We'll go through the place, just to be sure. This is no time to stand on etiquette."

He smashed a window-pane with his pistol-butt; put his hand through the hole and slipped the catch; then, lifting the sash, he climbed in. Armadale and Wendover followed close on his heels. Sir Clinton produced a flash-lamp from his pocket and threw its light hither and thither until he found the oil-lamp which served to light the room. Armadale struck a match and lit the lamp. Then he followed Sir Clinton into the other parts of the house.

Wendover, left to his own devices, glanced round the sitting-room in search of he knew not what. His eye was caught by the large filing-cabinet which stood on one side of the fireplace; and he pulled out a drawer at random, lifted one of the cards, and examined it.

> "11-2-16.—Left for France. At dinner: Cressida, J. Fordingbridge, P. Fordingbridge, Miss Kitty Glen-luce (age 23, fair-haired, dispatch-rider; told some stories about her work) . . ."

He picked out another card at random and read:

> "15-4-17.—Staveley's wedding. Bride dropped bouquet when signing register. Wedding march Mendelssohn.

Bride given away by P. Fordingbridge. Bridesmaids were . . ."

He had no time to read further. Sir Clinton and the inspector were back again, having found no one else on the premises. The chief constable had a bottle in his hand, which he handed to Wendover, pointing to the label.

"Amyl nitrite?" Wendover asked involuntarily. "So that's where the stuff came from that killed Peter Hay?"

Sir Clinton nodded. His eye fell on the table, on which a manuscript book was lying. He picked it up and opened it, showing the page to his companions.

"Derek Fordingbridge's diary, isn't it?" the inspector inquired.

"Yes. And there's their card-index, with everything entered up in chronological order—every bit of information they could collect about the Foxhills crowd from any source whatever. That made sure that if they had to meet any questions from a particular person about *his* dealings with the real Derek Fordingbridge, they could turn up their index and know exactly what to say. It was far safer than trusting to any single man's memory on the spur of the moment. I expect they've been copying out entries from the stolen diary and putting them into the filing-cabinet. We haven't time to waste. Come along. The police, next. Sapcote must collect them for us and bring them along, inspector."

As Wendover drove, it was hardly more than a matter of seconds before Sapcote had been instructed to collect all the available constables and bring them to the hotel.

"That's our next port of call, squire. Drive like the devil," Sir Clinton ordered, as he ended his instructions to the constable.

But they had hardly cleared the village before he gave a counter-order.

"Stop at the cottage again, squire."

Wendover pulled up the car obediently, and all three jumped out.

"Get the oars of that boat," Sir Clinton instructed them. "And hurry!"

The oars were soon found and carried down to the car, which Wendover started immediately. A few hundred yards along the road, Sir Clinton pitched the oars overboard, taking care that they did not drop on the highway.

Wendover, intent on his driving, heard the inspector speak to his superior.

"We found that cartridge-case you wanted, sir, when we put that sand through the sieves. It's a .38, same as Mrs. Fleetwood's pistol. I have it safe."

Sir Clinton brushed the matter aside.

"That's good, inspector. We'll have that gang in our hands before long. But Lord knows what damage they may do in the meanwhile. I'd give a lot to have them under lock and key at this minute."

At the hotel, Sir Clinton wasted no time on ceremony, but darted up the stairs to the Fleetwoods' room. As they entered, Stanley Fleetwood looked up in surprise from a book which he was reading.

"Well—" he began in an angry tone.

Sir Clinton cut him short.

"Where's Mrs. Fleetwood?"

Stanley Fleetwood's eyebrows rose sharply.

"Really, Sir Clinton—"

"Don't finesse now," the chief constable snapped. "I'm afraid something's happened to Mrs. Fleetwood. Tell us what you know, and be quick about it. Why did she leave the hotel to-night?"

Stanley Fleetwood's face showed amazement, with which fear seemed to mingle as Sir Clinton's manner convinced him that something was far wrong. He pulled himself up a little on the couch.

"She got a letter from her uncle making an appointment at the Blowhole."

Sir Clinton's face fell.

"That's worse than I thought," he said. "Let's see the letter."

Stanley Fleetwood pointed to the mantelpiece; and the chief constable searched among two or three papers until he found what he wanted.

"H'm! There's no date on this thing. It simply says, 'Meet me at the Blowhole to-night at'"—he paused and scrutinised the letter carefully—"'at 9 P.M. Come alone.' It is 9 P.M., isn't it?"

He passed the letter to the inspector.

"It seems to be 9 P.M.," Armadale confirmed, "but it's a bit blotted. This is Mr. Fordingbridge's writing, I suppose?" he added, turning to Stanley Fleetwood.

"Quite unmistakable; and the signature's O.K.," was the answer.

Sir Clinton was evidently thinking rapidly.

"We'll try the Blowhole first, though there'll be nothing there, I'm afraid. After that, we'll need to look elsewhere. This letter came by the post in the usual way, I suppose?"

"I don't know. It came to my wife, and she showed it to me."

"Well, I've no time to wait just now. It's a pity you can't come along with us."

Stanley Fleetwood lay back on the couch and cursed his crippled state as the three hurried from the room. At the Blowhole they found nothing. The great jet was not playing, and the only sound was the beating of the waves on the beach below the cliff. The moon was just clearing the horizon mists, and there was enough light to show that the headland was bare.

"They've got away," Sir Clinton commented, when they saw they had drawn blank. "They had that car of theirs; I saw the boat-house was empty when we were at the cottage. That means they may be anywhere within twenty miles by this time. We can't do much except send out a general warning. You do that, inspector, when we get back to the hotel. But it's the poorest chance, and we must think of something nearer home if we're to do anything ourselves."

He pondered over the problem for a minute, and then continued:

"They won't go back to the cottage at present. It wouldn't be safe. If they want to lie up for even a few hours, they'll need a house of some sort for the work. And it'll need to be an empty house in a quiet place, unless I've misread things."

He reflected again before concluding.

"It's a mere chance, but Foxhills and Peter Hay's are the only two empty places here. But Miss Fordingbridge sometimes goes up to Foxhills, so Peter Hay's is more likely. We'll go there on the chance. Come along."

At the hotel, they found that Sapcote had assembled all the available constables and dispatched them along the road. He had telephoned a message to this effect before leaving himself. Armadale got his headquarters on the telephone and ordered a watch to be kept for any suspicious car; but, as he was unable to supply even the most general description of the wanted motor, the chance of its discovery seemed of the slightest.

He came out of the telephone-box to find Sir Clinton and Wendover waiting for him in Sir Clinton's car.

"Get in," the chief constable ordered. "We've got to waste a minute or two in going down the road to meet that gang of constables and giving them orders to follow on. Put both feet on the accelerator, squire, and do anything else short of spilling us in the ditch. Every minute may count now."

Wendover needed no urging. They flashed down the road towards Lynden Sands, pulled up as they met the body of police, and were off again as soon as Sir Clinton had given the constables their orders to make direct for Foxhills. A very few minutes brought the car to the Foxhills gate, where Wendover, at a sign from Sir Clinton, stopped the car. The chief constable jumped out and examined the road surface with his pocket flash-lamp.

"Thank the Lord! A car's gone up the avenue. We may be in time to nab them yet."

CHAPTER XV
THE METHOD OF COERCION

WHEN CRESSIDA RECEIVED her uncle's note that afternoon, she was both relieved and puzzled. Within less than a week she had been subjected to shocks and strains of such acuteness that she had almost lost the power of being surprised by anything that might happen; and Paul Fordingbridge's letter caused her hardly any astonishment, which she would certainly have felt had she been in a more normal condition. All that she gathered from it was that, after disappearing in a mysterious manner, he had returned and evidently needed her assistance. She was not particularly attached to him; but she was not the sort of person who would refuse her help to anyone in an emergency, even though that person had shown her very little sympathy in her own recent troubles.

She had a very fair idea of the rumours which had been running through the hotel, and she had no desire to advertise her meeting with her uncle. The final phrase in the note: "Come alone," was quite enough to suggest that he wished to keep the encounter secret. And she knew well enough that a plain-clothes constable had been detached to watch her; she had seen him once or twice when she had been passing through the entrance-hall, and had no difficulty in detecting the interest which he took in her movements. Unless she could contrive to give him the slip, he would follow her out to the Blowhole. Then she thought of the lady golfers' dressing-room, with its convenient door to the outside of the hotel, and a method of evasion suggested itself. She took the lift down; walked boldly past the watcher; turned down the passage and entered the

227

dressing-room. Then, picking up her hat, blazer, and golfing-shoes, she slipped out of the side-entrance and hurried down one of the paths till she reached a place where she could change her slippers for her outdoor shoes.

Leaving the slippers to be picked up on her way back, she crossed the hotel gardens and made her way out on to the headland where the Blowhole lay. The night was clear enough, but the moon was still very low, and the light was dim. As she came up towards the Blowhole, a figure came forward to meet her.

"Is that you, uncle?" she asked.

As soon as she spoke she was aware of someone who had risen behind her from an ambush. An arm came round her from the rear, pinning her hands to her sides; and a soft, wet pad was brought down on her face. She felt a burning liquid on her lips, and, as she gasped under the mask, a sickly, sweet-scented vapour seemed to penetrate down into her lungs. As she struggled to free herself and to cry out, the man before her stepped forward and helped his companion to hold her.

"Don't choke her altogether, you fool!" she heard her new assailant say, but his voice sounded faint; and in a minute she had lost consciousness.

When she came to herself once more, it was to find herself lying on a bed from which all the bed clothes had been removed. Her head swam at the slightest movement, and she felt deadly sick. With complete incuriosity, she noticed some figures in the room, and then again she slipped back into unconsciousness.

The sound of voices roused her once more, after what seemed to be a span of eternity, and she slowly began to recollect the events which had led to her present condition. As she gained more control over herself, she attempted to move, but she found that her wrists and ankles were fettered, and her further vague attempts to get her bearings satisfied her that some kind of gag had been thrust between her teeth and lashed at the back of her head.

For a while she lay, feeling sick and dizzy and unable to think clearly; but gradually, as the narcosis passed slowly off, she grew better able to take in her surroundings. She had just reached the stage when she could concentrate her attention when one of the figures in the room came to the side of the bed, and stooped down to examine her in the light of a candle. The features seemed faintly familiar; but in her drugged condition it was some moments before she could identify the man as Simon Aird, at one time valet at Foxhills.

"Got your senses back, miss? You've been a longish while over it. Better pull yourself together."

Even in her bemused condition she recognised something in the tone of his voice which told her that he was not friendly. She lay still, fighting hard to recover her normal personality. Aird watched her with cold interest, without making any attempt to disturb her. At last the fumes of the anaesthetic seemed to clear from her brain.

"Feelin' sick, miss?" Aird inquired callously. "That's the chlorry form, I expect. You'll be all right in a jiffy or two."

Her head still swam, but she managed to turn slightly so that she could see the two other figures in the room. One of them, with his back to her, was unrecognisable. The other, whose face she could see, was a total stranger.

Aird saw her glance, and interpreted it aloud. "Lookin' for your uncle, miss, I expect?"

His mean little eyes seemed to twinkle at some obscure joke.

"He couldn't come to meet you, miss, as arranged. He was unexpectedly detained. Ain't that so, boys? Mr. Paul Fordingbridge was unexpectedly detained, and couldn't come to meet 'is niece?"

The joke, whatever it was, seemed to be shared by the other two, for they laughed coarsely. Aird was encouraged to proceed to further flights of humour.

"You've got an expressive face, miss—always 'ad. Why, I can read you like a book. You're worryin' your pretty 'ead to know 'ow you came 'ere, isn't that it? Trust Simon Aird to understand what a girl's thinkin' about. A pretty girl's as plain as print to me—always was. But I'm keepin' you on tenterhooks, I see, an' that's not polite. I'll soon tell you. We found you up yonder on the headland, near the Blowhole, drunk and incapable. That was a dangerous thing to do, miss. I can't think 'ow you came to be doin' it. Lord! In that state, there's no knowin' what mightn't 'ave 'appened to you—it's dreadful just to think of it! But you fell into good 'ands, miss. We took you up an' lifted you into our car, which 'appened to be near by; and we brought you 'ere with as much care as if you'd been worth your weight in gold, miss. No pains spared, I assure you."

Through the numbness engendered by the anaesthetic, fear had been growing in Cressida's mind, until now it had overwhelmed every other feeling. She knew she was completely in the hands of these three men; and even what she had seen of them was enough to fill her with the acutest dread. Aird's oily phrases went ill with the expression in his little piggish eyes.

"It's a great thing to be a bit of a psycho-what-d'ye-call-it, miss. I can tell to a dot just exactly what's passin' through your mind," he went on. "You're wonderin' where you are at this minute. I 'ave much pleasure in enlightenin' you. You've 'ad the extraordinary good luck to be brought to the 'eadquarters of Aird & Co., a purely philanthropic syndikit formed for the good purpose of purifyin' morals, and rescuin' heiresses from the clutch of their fancy men, and teachin' them to lead saintly lives in future. Your case is the first we've 'ad brought to our door, so we can give it our excloosive attention. And we shall!"

He sniggered, apparently much amused by his own conceit. Cressida felt the menace behind all this forced jocularity. Aird brought the candle nearer to her face, and made a pretence of studying her features.

"Ah!" he continued. "You're feelin' nervous, miss? It's as plain as a pike-staff to the eye of the trained mind-reader like me. You're all of a flutter, like. And no wonder, miss. You that's been livin' in sin with that young Fleetwood for the best part of a year, with your own true husband alive and mournin' all the while. Shockin'! Such goin's on! But never fear, miss. You 'ave fallen into good 'ands, as I said once before. Aird & Co., expert matrimonial agents, will take up your case and make an honest woman of you yet."

Behind his joviality, Cressida could feel some dreadful menace. She turned her face away, so as to hide from herself his little gloating eyes.

"That'll do, Aird," said a fresh voice, quite unknown to her. "I'll explain things. You talk too much."

The man who had his back turned to her came across to the bed and took the candle from Aird. Then, stooping down, he let the light play over his own features, while his hand forced Cressida's head round so that she gazed straight up into his face. At the first glance she thought she must still be under the influence of the chloroform, for what she saw was torn almost out of human likeness.

"Allow me to introduce myself," said the wreck. "Your future husband, also your cousin: Derek Fordingbridge. Not recognise me again? Well, I suppose I've changed since we said good-bye last."

He let the candlelight play across his shattered face for some moments, so that she might miss no detail of the horror. Then, as she closed her eyes, he released his grip, and she turned her head away to escape the sight of him.

"You'll get used to me in time," was his only comment. "Here's the situation. Our uncle chooses to keep me out of my money. If I go to law over it, most of the cash will be wasted in legal expenses. He won't suffer, but I shall. Now, you're the next in the line of inheritance; so, if I drop out, it comes to you. And if you marry me, then what's yours is mine—I'll see to that part of it. You understand the idea? You marry me and I drop my claim; and between us we collar the dibs. Uncle won't object, I'll guarantee; and dear Auntie Jay will be delighted."

He paused and examined the expression of loathing on Cressida's face.

"I don't wish to go to extremes," he said coldly, "but you're going to do as you're told. Make no mistake about that."

He drew back slightly, allowing Aird to come nearer.

"Aird will take the gag out and let you speak; but he'll keep his hand on your throat, and the first attempt you make to cry out you'll get throttled pretty sharply. Understand?"

Aird obeyed instructions, and Cressida passed her tongue over her bruised lips. She was in deadly terror now, and her mind was working swiftly. A glance at the three men bending over her was sufficient to show her that she need expect no mercy from them. She was completely in their power; and if she refused to give in to them, they might— But she thrust to the back of her mind all the possibilities which she could read so clearly on the face of Aird.

Then, as a thought shot through her mind, she strove her hardest to keep out of her expression the relief that she felt. If she submitted immediately, and promised to carry out the order, that would perhaps save her for the time being; and, when it came to implementing her promise, the marriage ceremony would have to be performed in public, or at least in the presence of some clergyman or official; and there would be nothing to prevent her refusing then. They could not coerce her in a church or before a registrar. Nowadays forced marriages are found only in books.

The pressure of the gag had hurt her mouth, and she had some difficulty in framing words in which to make her submission.

"I can't help myself. But you're not my cousin Derek."

The faceless creature laughed.

"That's a quick courting!" he sneered. "But one doesn't need to be a psycho-what-d'ye-call-it, as Aird says, to see what's in your mind."

His voice became tinged with a menace beside which Aird's seemed childish.

"You think you've only got to say 'Yes' now; then, when it comes to the point, you'll turn on us and give the show away? We're not such fools as all that. I've got a string that I'm going to tie to your leg. It'll bring you running back to me and no questions asked."

He paused for a moment, as though expecting her to speak; but, as she said nothing, he continued in the same tone:

"You think that the worst we could do to you would be to hand you over to Aird, there, or to share you amongst us. You can make your mind easy. It's not going to be that."

The wave of relief which passed over Cressida at this hint was followed by a chill of apprehension as she realised the full implication of his words. He did not keep her on tenterhooks long.

"Ever heard of hydrophobia? Know much about it? No? Well, then, I'll tell you something. You get bitten by a mad dog. First of all you feel tired and restless; and naturally you can't help being worried a bit. Then, after a day or two, things get a bit more definite. You can't swallow, and you get a thirst that torments you. Then, they say, you get spasms even at the thought of drinking; and you get into a state of devilish funk—unspeakable terror, they say in the books. After that you get fits—frothing at the mouth, and all the rest of the jolly business. And, of course, eventually you die after considerable agony, if you get the proper dose. I'd hate to see a pretty girl like you afflicted in that way. Dreadful waste of good material."

He paused deliberately, letting this picture sink into her mind, and scanning her face to see the effect which he had produced.

"No mad dogs here, of course; but they have them in France. I've a French medical friend who's kindly supplied me with some extract taken from one of them."

Again he paused, to let anticipation do its work.

"If you get injected with this extract, or whatever it is, there's only one hope. Within a certain number of days you've got to get to a Pasteur Institute and put yourself under treatment there. Nothing else is any good. And, if you overshoot the time, even the Pasteur Institute can do nothing for you. You just go on till you froth at the mouth, get cramp in the throat, and die that rather disgusting death."

He looked down at Cressida's face, with its eyes dark with horror; and something which might have been a smile passed over his shattered countenance.

"My French medical friend supplied me with both the bane and the antidote—at least, enough of the antidote for a first dose. You see the point? Perhaps I'd better be precise. Here's a hypodermic syringe."

He produced a little nickel case from his pocket, and drew from it a tiny glass syringe, to which he fitted a hollow needle.

"I'm going to fill this with some of the mad dog extract and inject it into your arm. Once that's done, your only chance is to get Pasteur Institute treatment within a certain time or else rely on me to give you a first dose of the antidote before the time's up.

Once the time's past without treatment, nothing can save you. I couldn't do it myself, even with the antidote. You'd simply go through all the stages I've told you about, and then die."

He fingered the tiny syringe thoughtfully.

"Now do you see the ingenuity of my plan? I'm going to inject some of the stuff into your veins now. Then we'll keep you here until the very last moment of your safety. Then you'll come with me and get spliced by special license. By that time it'll be too late to get to an institute; you'll have no chance whatever except the dose of antidote that I've got. And you won't get that from me until we're safely married without any fuss. You'll stand up in public and say: 'I will!' without any objection, because it'll be your one chance of escaping the cramps and all the rest of it. Ingenious, isn't it? Shall I repeat it, in case you've missed any of the points? It's no trouble, I assure you."

Cressida glanced from face to face in the hope of seeing some signs of relenting; but none of the three showed the faintest trace of pity.

"Be sensible, miss," said Aird, with the air of one reasoning with a wayward child. "A pretty girl like you wouldn't want to be seen frothin' at the mouth and runnin' round bitin' people. It wouldn't be nice."

His unctuous tone brought up all Cressida's reserves of strength.

"You'd never dare do it," she gasped.

"You think so?" the faceless man inquired indifferently. "Well, you'll see in a moment or two."

He rose with the hypodermic syringe in his hand and went out of the room. She could hear him doing something with a sink, and the sound of water. At that her nerve gave way.

"Oh, don't do it! Please, please don't! Anything but that! Please!"

For the first time she realised that this hideous scheme was seriously meant; and the pictures which flashed through her mind appalled her. To pass out of life was one thing; but to go out by the gate of madness—and such a form of madness—seemed an unbearable prospect. To die like a mad dog—anything would be better than that!

"Oh, don't!"

She gazed up at the faces of the two men who stood beside her in the hope that in this last moment they might flinch from carrying the foul business through. But there was no comfort in what she saw. Aird was evidently drinking in her torment with avidity. It was something which seemed to give him a positive pleasure. The stranger shrugged his shoulders, as though suggesting that the matter had been irrevocably settled. Neither of them made any answer to her hysterical pleading.

The man with the hypodermic came back into the room; and she hid her face as he crossed to the side of the bed. Her arm was roughly grasped, and she felt him pinch her skin before he drove the needle home. Then came a sharp pang as he injected the contents of the syringe.

Then, just as she wavered on the edge of fainting from the nervous strain she had undergone, the whole scene changed. There was a crash of glass, and a voice which seemed faintly familiar ordered sharply:

"Hands up!"

A scuffle, two shots, a cry of pain, and the fall of a heavy body to the floor; more sounds of rapid movement in the room; a voice shouting directions; another shot, outside the house—all these impinged on her consciousness without her grasping exactly what had happened. With a last effort of will she wrenched herself round on the bed, so that she could see the room.

Sir Clinton, pistol in hand, was stooping over the third man, who lay groaning on the floor. At the open window she could see Wendover climbing into the room; and, as he jumped down, Inspector Armadale dashed in through the open door. Rescue had come just too late; and, as she realised this, her power of resistance gave out, and she fainted.

Sir Clinton made a gesture to Wendover, putting him in charge of the unconscious girl, while he himself turned back to his captive.

"I've smashed your shoulder with that shot, I think, Billingford," he commented. "You're safe enough, my man, now that I've taken your gun away from you. You'll stay where you are until my constables come for you. Mr. Wendover will keep an eye on you—and he'll shoot you without the slightest compunction, I'm sure, if you give trouble."

Billingford seemed engrossed in more immediate afflictions.

"Oh! It hurts damnably!" he muttered.

"Glad to hear it," Sir Clinton declared unsympathetically. "It'll keep you quiet. Well, inspector?"

Armadale held up a bleeding hand.

"They got me," he said laconically. "It's only a flesh-wound. But they've cleared off in their car—hell-for-leather."

Sir Clinton turned to Wendover.

"You look after that girl. The constables will be here in a few minutes. Shoot Billingford in the leg, if he shows the slightest sign of moving, though I don't expect he'll do much. I've got to get on the track of those two who broke away."

Followed by the inspector, he hurried out into the night.

CHAPTER XVI
THE MAN-HUNT ON THE BEACH

MUCH TO THE INSPECTOR'S SURPRISE, Sir Clinton did not drive furiously when they had got into his car, which had been left standing at some distance from the cottage. It was only when they almost ran into the approaching squad of police that he understood his superior's caution.

"Two of you get on board," said Sir Clinton, as he pulled up. "Four more go up to the cottage; and the rest of you make the best time you can down to the hotel and wait there for orders."

When the two constables had got into the car, he drove off again; and this time the inspector had no reason to complain of slow speeds. His heart was in his mouth as Sir Clinton took the turn out of the avenue into the main road.

"You've got the number of their car, haven't you?" the chief constable demanded. "Then tell one of the constables to telephone a warning about it to headquarters from the hotel. I'm going to drop him there. And tell him to send a party with a car up at once to the cottage to get Mrs. Fleetwood down comfortably. You'd better get Billingford brought down also—not in the same car."

The inspector transmitted these instructions just in time to allow the constable to alight from the car as Sir Clinton pulled up at the hotel gate. Without hesitation, the chief constable swung the car off along the road to Lynden Sands and opened the throttle to its fullest.

"Sure they're going this way, sir?" Armadale asked.

237

"No, just taking a chance. They'll want to get clear of the car as soon as possible, I expect, since it's recognisable now that we've got the number. I may be all wrong, of course."

The big car tore on in the moonlight, and the speed left the inspector little inclination for talk. He gasped once or twice as they swung round corners, and his main feeling was one of thankfulness that at that hour of the night they were not likely to meet anything on the road. One last turn, which made Armadale and the constable grip frenziedly at the nearest hand-hold, and they came out on the edge of the bay.

"Look!" the inspector ejaculated. "You've pulled them in, sir."

Not three hundred yards ahead, the hunted car appeared in the moonlight, traveling much slower than Armadale had expected, but apparently gaining speed as it ran.

"They've parted company," Sir Clinton snapped. "The car's slowed down to let one man off. There's only the driver on board now."

Suddenly, at a point where the road ran level with the beach, their quarry left the highway and plunged down on to the sands.

"He's trying to gain something by cutting straight across the beach, sir, instead of following the curve of the road."

Armadale, expecting Sir Clinton to do the same, gripped the side of the car in anticipation of the shock when they left the road; but the chief constable held to the highway.

"He's making for Flatt's cottage, to get the boat and leave us standing," he said. "He'll get a surprise when he finds the oars gone."

The inspector had no time to admire his chief's forethought. The hunted car was now running on a line which would bring it between the old wreck and the edge of the incoming tide; and on the hard sands it was making tremendous speed. Armadale, leaning forward in the excitement of the chase, saw the long cones of its headlights illuminate the hull of the wreck for a moment; then the beams swung up into the air; the car seemed to halt for an instant, and then rolled over sideways along the sands. And then it vanished as though the ground had swallowed it.

"The quicksand!" ejaculated Armadale, as he realised what had happened.

Sir Clinton shut the throttle and let his car slow down.

"Hit some rock projecting slightly from the sand, I expect," he commented. "Probably the front axle or the steering-gear went, and he came to smash. Well, that's one of 'em gone."

He chose a place carefully and turned his own car on to the sands, running down to near the wreck.

"Don't go too near," he advised. "One can't be sure of the danger-zone."

They got out and went down to the scene of the disaster. A glance at the car-tracks showed the correctness of Sir Clinton's guess. The hunted car had struck a low projecting rock with its near front wheel; and from that point the wheel-marks were replaced by the trace of the whole vehicle, overturned and sliding along the beach. The trail ended abruptly; and where the car had sunk they saw an area of repulsive black mud.

"Ugh!" said the inspector, examining it with disgust. "Fancy going down into that stuff and feeling it getting into your eyes and mouth. And then choking in that slime! It gives me the creeps to think of it."

He shuddered at the picture conjured up by what he saw before him.

"Do you think there's any chance of recovering the body?" he inquired after a moment or two.

Sir Clinton shook his head.

"I doubt it. You'll need to try, of course; best do it with grappling-irons from a boat, I suppose. But I shouldn't think you're likely to succeed. It doesn't matter much, anyhow. He's got his deserts. Now for the other man. Come along!"

They went back to the car and got aboard. Sir Clinton seemed to have decided on his next move, for he drove along the sands in the direction of the hotel. Rather to the inspector's surprise, they did not turn off on to the road at Neptune's Seat, but went still farther along the shore, making for the headland on which the Blowhole was situated.

Armadale was still in ignorance of much that had happened in the last hour. When they had reached Peter Hay's cottage, Sir Clinton had detached the inspector to search for the car which had brought their quarry; and, as this had been carefully concealed, Armadale had spent some time in hunting for it. In the meanwhile, Sir Clinton and Wendover had gone cautiously to the cottage. The next thing the inspector heard was the sound of shooting; and two men had come upon him before he had time even to think of disabling the fugitives' car. They had shot him in the hand, flung him down, and escaped in the car before he had time to do anything to hinder them. His entry into the cottage had failed to enlighten him as to what had been going on; and Sir Clinton had hurried him off again almost before he had time to get his bearings.

"That's as far as we can go with the car," Sir Clinton announced, opening the door and getting out.

The moon shone out just at that moment, as a passing cloud slipped away from its face; and Sir Clinton, gazing along the shore, uttered an exclamation of satisfaction.

"We're in luck, inspector! See him? Yonder, just under the cliff. He hasn't been able to get far."

He pulled out his automatic.

"I've often wondered how far these things carry. I don't want to hurt him, and it seems safe enough at this range. A scare's all we need, I think. He's making for the mouth of the cave below the headland."

He lifted the pistol and fired in the direction of the figure. At the sound of the shot, the fugitive turned and, seeing his pursuers, ran stumblingly over the rocks where the edge of the tide was washing close up against the cliff.

"No hurry," Sir Clinton pointed out, as Armadale and the constable quickened their steps. "We've got him trapped by the tide. There's only one bolt-hole—the cave. And I hope he takes it," he added, with something of sinister enjoyment in his tone which surprised the inspector.

They moved leisurely in the direction of the cave-mouth; and, as they did so, the fugitive gave one backward glance and then splashed waist-deep through the water which was foaming into the entrance. He ducked under the low arch and vanished. As he did so, Sir Clinton halted, and then, after a careful inspection of the incoming tide, he led the way back to the car.

"It's as cheap sitting as standing," he commented, settling himself comfortably in the driving-seat. "We'll need to wait here until the tide shuts the door on him by filling that tunnel he's gone through. After that, I suspect he'll be the most anxious of the lot of us."

"But there's another exit from that cave," Armadale pointed out. "He's probably climbing up the tube of the Blowhole just now, sir. He might get clean away by the top of the headland."

Sir Clinton pulled out his case and lit a cigarette in a leisurely fashion.

"I'm sure I hope he does," he replied, much to the inspector's surprise. "Just wait a moment and you'll see."

He smoked for a minute or two without troubling to make his meaning clear; and then the *souffleur* itself gave the answer. Armadale's ear caught the sound of a deep gurgle from the heights above their head; then came a noise like a giant catching his breath; and at last from the Blowhole there shot up the column of spray, towering white and menacing in the moonlight. As it fell, Sir Clinton pressed the self-starter.

"That bolts the back door, you see, inspector. I only hope he's been caught on the threshold. Now, I think, we can go back to the hotel and see if we can pick up one or two useful things."

He turned the car on the last strip of sand before the rocks and swung it round towards Neptune's Seat. After a little searching, he found a spot from which he could ascend to the road without straining his springs.

"I had the curiosity to examine that Blowhole cave at low tide once, inspector," he explained as he drove up towards the hotel. "The thing works this way. The entrance is low, and the tide fills it soon. The air in the cave can still get out by a narrow tunnel leading up to the Blowhole. But in a minute or two this second tunnel's mouth gets filled up, and there's no escape from the cave. The sides are smooth, and the tide rises quickly, so that fellow will either drown or else he'll creep into the Blowhole tunnel to escape. The tide rises a bit farther, and compresses the air in the cave. At that stage the *souffleur* begins to work. Intermittently, you get the air-pressure in the cave big enough to blow through the Blowhole tunnel, carrying the layer of water there in front of it; and that mixture of water and compressed air makes the jet. So, you see, if that fellow's in the cave, he must be swimming round like a rat in a pail; and if he's in the tunnel, he must be suffering agonies as the jet comes up and tears at him. You know what sort of force it has. And if he can't cling on to the rocks of the tunnel, he'll be battered against the sides as the jet carries him before it, and he'll probably be severely injured by the time it spits him out at the top."

"Good Lord!" said the inspector, as the realisation of the thing crept into his mind. "That's a nasty trap to fall into. He's going to get his gruel, sure enough."

They had reached the hotel, and Sir Clinton dispatched the constable to bring ropes, if any were available.

"You don't seem eager to get him out, sir," the inspector ventured, as they were waiting.

"I don't know exactly what happened at Peter Hay's to-night," Sir Clinton returned, "but I saw enough to know it was something uncommonly bad that they were trying to do to that girl, inspector. It must have been something worse than the normal way of putting the screw on a woman. Our friend in the Blowhole didn't mind doing that. And, somehow, that makes me feel a bit indolent when it comes to rescuing him. Let him go through it. Besides, the longer he's there—if we happen to get him out alive—the more his nerves will be shaken, and the easier it will be to wring some truth out of him. You can tackle him at once, before the effect wears off. And I shan't feel inclined to ask you to be moderate in your questioning this time. We must get all we can out of him while he's got the jumps. I've no doubt whatever that Billingford will turn King's evidence if he gets half a chance—he's that sort. But the other fellow was deeper in, and we may get more out of him if we can catch him at the right moment. So I'm not really in much of a hurry. This isn't a case where my humanitarian instincts are roused in the very slightest."

He broke off, seeing Wendover coming out of the hotel.

"Everything fixed up comfortably, squire?" he asked.

Wendover nodded affirmatively; then, as Sir Clinton invited him to join them, he amplified his news.

"We got Mrs. Fleetwood down here quite comfortably; and she's upstairs now. Very shaken up, of course; but she's a plucky girl, and she hasn't had any bad collapse of her nerves so far, though one might have expected it."

"I've a good mind to see her myself now," Sir Clinton said thoughtfully. "Did she say anything about what they'd done to her?"

"No. But she asked me to send for Rafford immediately. I didn't like to worry her with questions."

Sir Clinton's face darkened.

"It's a nuisance we have to go and fish that creature out of the Blowhole. I'd much prefer to leave him there to go through it. He deserves as long a spell as we can give him. But I suppose there would be a howl if we left him to die. Besides, I want to hang him if I can. By the way, what about his jovial colleague, Billingford?"

"He's here too," Wendover explained. "We thought we'd bring him to the hotel and wait for your instructions. He's safe enough."

"That's all right. Now here's the constable with the ropes, so I think we'll have to move on."

Sir Clinton showed no desire to hurry; nor did Wendover when he had learned the state of affairs. Both of them were in the mood to prolong the agony so far as decency permitted. Wendover could not get out of his mind the expression he had seen on Cressida's face at Peter Hay's cottage; and when it came back to his memory he felt that the man in the Blowhole tunnel was getting only a fair retribution for his crime.

As they came near the mouth of the *souffleur*, the great fountain shot up into the night air and broke in spray in the moonlight. Sir Clinton hurried forward and bent down to listen to the orifice.

"He's there, all right, and still alive," he reported. "A trifle un-nerved, to judge by his appeals. I suppose we'll have to yank him out now."

Armadale also had been listening to the cries from below.

"If we get him out in that state," he said, with satisfaction, "there won't be much that he'll keep back when we start question-ing him. He's all to pieces."

Before they could do any more, the *souffleur* spouted again. Wendover, whose imagination was keener than that of the inspec-tor, was suddenly appalled by the picture conjured up by that wild fountain jetting from the ground. Down below their feet he could see with his mind's eye the miserable wretch clinging for life to some inequality in the tunnel, while the continual blasts of the *souffleur* tore and battered at him, and the rush of water made him fight for his breath. A rat in a trap would be happy compared with that.

"Oh, let's get him out!" he exclaimed. "It must be devilish down there in the dark, waiting for the next spout."

"If you're set on seeing him hanged, squire, we'll do our best," Sir Clinton conceded, with no sympathy in his tone.

But, even by doing their best, they had great difficulty in res-cuing their quarry from the grip of the death-trap. When at last they got him to the surface, he was more dead than alive; and three ribs had been cracked by the last torrent which had flung him against the side of the conduit.

As they lifted him into safety, Sapcote hurried up from the hotel; and, after a glance at the torn and haggard face, he recognised the prisoner.

"That's Aird, sir. Used to be valet at Foxhills once."

"Well, you can have Mr. Aird, inspector," Sir Clinton intimated. "If you give him some brandy, he'll probably wake up enough to part with any information you want. Don't let your sympathy over-come you. We must get enough out of him to hang him if we can; and it depends on putting him through it while his nerve's gone."

He moved away without another glance at the broken figure on the ground, and, followed by Wendover, turned his steps towards the hotel.

"I suppose he calculated on being able to climb to the top before the jet began to play," he continued. "Well, he seems to have paid for his mistake," he concluded grimly.

At the hotel door, Wendover expected that they would go straight to the Fleetwood suite; but, rather to his surprise, Sir Clinton summoned one of the constables and gave him some instructions in a low voice. Then, accompanied by Wendover, he ascended the stairs.

"I want to see Cargill for a moment," he explained, as they passed the first floor. "I've something to say to him."

Rather puzzled, Wendover followed him to the Australian's room.

"I happened to be passing," he said, as he entered in response to Cargill's permission, "and I dropped in to see how you've been getting on. Leg all right now?"

"It's a bit better," Cargill replied. "Won't you sit down?"

"Got enough to read?" Sir Clinton inquired, stepping over a pile of books which lay near Cargill's couch and picking up one of them. "I've got one or two I can lend you."

Wendover was taken completely by surprise; for, without altering the tone of his voice, Sir Clinton bent suddenly forward and imprisoned Cargill's wrists.

"See if you can find a pistol anywhere near, squire. It's as well to be on the safe side."

He whistled shrilly; and, before the Australian had recovered from the surprise of the attack, two constables had rushed into the room and made any attempt at a struggle impossible. Sir Clinton relaxed his grip.

"I shouldn't kick about, if I were you, Cargill. All you'll succeed in doing is to reopen that wound of yours. The game's up, you see; and you may as well take it quietly. We've got some of your friends."

Cargill's face showed an eagerness at the words.

"Has my brother got off?"

"You mean the pseudo-Derek, I suppose? Yes, he's gone to ground"—Cargill's expression showed a relief which was quenched as Sir Clinton continued—"in the same place as you put Paul Fordingbridge."

Cargill's head sank at the news.

"I'm afraid I can't stay," Sir Clinton said, with almost ironical politeness. "You've given me such a lot of work to do, you know, lately. I shan't trouble you with questions, because I think we shall get all we want from your confederates. If you need anything we can give you, please ask the constables for it. Good evening."

In the corridor, Wendover broke into a flood of questions; but Sir Clinton brushed them aside.

"There's time enough for that by and by," he said brusquely. "I must get to the bottom of this business first. We'll go along and ask if Mrs. Fleetwood can see us for a moment or two."

Wendover was glad to find, when they entered the Fleetwood suite, that Cressida seemed to be getting over the worst of the shock. Her face lighted up as she saw them come in, and she began at once to thank them. Sir Clinton brushed the thanks aside.

"There's nothing in it," he said. "I only wish we'd been sooner."

At the words, Cressida's expression changed, as though some dreadful thing had been recalled to her. Sir Clinton put his hand into his pocket and drew out the glass syringe.

"What part did this thing play?" he asked gently.

The sight of it brought back all Cressida's terrors.

"Oh, you *were* too late!" she exclaimed despairingly. "I'm still dazed by it all, and that brings it back."

Under Sir Clinton's sympathetic interrogation, she was soon able to tell them of the ordeal she had gone through. When she had finished, the chief constable bent forward and took up the hypodermic syringe from the table.

"You can sleep quietly to-night," he said. "There was nothing in this affair except tap-water. I saw the fellow filling it at the sink as I passed the window. I'd have stopped him then, but there were only two of us against three of them, and I had to wait till they were all in one room. I must say the hypodermic puzzled me. I couldn't make out what they were after, unless it was more drugging. But there was nothing in the syringe. I saw him washing it out under the tap before he filled it. At the worst you may have a sore arm; but the only germs in the syringe were some that might be in tap-water. The whole affair was a piece of bluff from start to finish. But it's no wonder it took you in. They must have staged it well. Be thankful it's no worse, Mrs. Fleetwood."

"Oh, I am! You don't know what a relief it is, Sir Clinton. I meant to go off first thing to-morrow to the Pasteur Institute for treatment. I wasn't very frightened, once I got out of the hands of these horrible men, because I knew I could be saved if I got treatment in time."

"That's very sensible of you. But you need have no fears about hydrophobia, at any rate. It was simply a bluff and nothing more."

Cressida thanked them again, and, in order to escape from her gratitude, Sir Clinton said good night, promising to return next morning to tell her anything that she might wish to know.

Wendover had been horrified by the story; and he began to wish that after all they had left Aird to his fate in the tunnel.

"Brutes like that aren't fit to live," he declared bitterly, when the door had closed behind them.

"Some of them won't live much longer, squire, if I can manage it," Sir Clinton assured him, in a tone that left no doubt in the matter.

In the hall below, they encountered Mme. Laurent-Desrousseaux, and at the sight of Sir Clinton her face showed something more than the mere pleasure of meeting an acquaintance. She came forward and intercepted them.

"I am most fortunate," she explained, with a smile which betrayed her real gratification at their meeting. "I depart to-morrow morning by the first train, and I was fearing that I might not encounter you to make you my adieux. That would have been most impolite to friends so cordial as you have been. And, besides, I am so very happy that I would wish to be very amiable to all the world. All the embarrassments that I feared have been swept away, and everything has arranged itself happily."

Sir Clinton's face lost the hard expression which it had borne a few moments before.

"I hope that it is my good fortune to be the first to congratulate you on your approaching marriage, madame. You have all my wishes for great happiness."

Mme. Laurent-Desrousseaux's manners did not allow her to throw up her hands in astonishment, but her face betrayed her surprise.

"But it is marvelous!" she exclaimed. "One would need to be a sorcerer to know so much! It is quite true, what you say. Now that Staveley is dead, I can espouse such a good friend of mine, one who will be kind to me and whom I have been adoring for so long. I can hardly believe it, I am so happy."

Sir Clinton smiled.

"And you would like everyone else to be happy too? Then you will perhaps begin at once. Go upstairs, madame, and ask to see Mrs. Fleetwood. Say that I sent you. And when you see her, tell her that you married Staveley in 1915. You do not need to say any more."

Rather puzzled, but quite anxious to do as he told her, Mme. Laurent-Desrousseaux bade them both farewell, and they saw her ascending the stair. Sir Clinton gazed after her.

"Easy enough to guess that riddle. One gets a reputation on the cheap sometimes. Her association with Staveley; then her complete separation for years; then this sudden need to meet him again in order to sidetrack some 'embarrassments': obviously she had married him, and needed a divorce if she was to marry again. I wish most problems were as simple."

"And, of course, if she married Staveley in 1915, as she seems to have done, he committed bigamy in marrying Mrs. Fleetwood?"

"Which means that Mrs. Fleetwood *is* Mrs. Fleetwood, and that she's legally married now. She won't be sorry to hear it. That's why I sent Mme. Laurent-Desrousseaux up there now. First-hand evidence is better than documents; and, of course, the documents will be forthcoming if they're required in future. Evidently those three scoundrels didn't know this latest twist in the affair, or they wouldn't have tried the trick they did last night. They'd have done worse, probably, when they got hold of her. If she'd been dead and out of the way, there would have been no one except old Miss Fordingbridge to contest that impostor's claim—and she was so besotted with him that she'd never have dreamed of doing so."

He paused for a moment or two, as though considering the case; but when he spoke again it was on a different point.

"You sometimes jeer at me for playing the mystery-man and refusing to tell you what I infer from the facts that turn up. It's sometimes irritating, I admit; and now and again I suppose it makes me look as if I were playing the superior fellow. But it's really nothing of the sort. In affairs of this kind, one never can tell what the next turn of the wheel may be; and one might quite well blurt out something which would give the cue to the very people you want to keep in the dark."

"You do irritate me often enough, Clinton," Wendover admitted. "I can't see why you shouldn't put your cards on the table. A fact's a fact, after all."

"I'll give you just one example," said Sir Clinton seriously. "Suppose I had blurted out the fact which I'd inferred about Mme. Laurent-Desrousseaux's marriage. It was implicit in the story she told us; but luckily no one spotted the key except myself. Now, just think what would have happened to-night if that had been common property. These scoundrels would have known that Mrs. Fleetwood was legally married to young Fleetwood, since the ceremony with Staveley was illegal. Therefore, instead of trying the business of the forced marriage, they'd simply have pitched her over the cliff at the Blowhole. She'd have been dead by this time; for their only interest in keeping her alive was to force this marriage with the claimant and sidetrack difficulties in that way. Suppose I'd blurted out my inference, and sent that girl to her death by my carelessness, how should I be feeling at this moment? None too comfortable, so far as I can see."

Wendover had to admit that the secrecy policy had justified itself.

"It would have been a dreadful business," he confessed.

Inspector Armadale's figure appeared from one of the corridors, and, catching sight of Sir Clinton, he came over to where they were standing. His face showed that he had good news to tell.

"I've got practically the whole business out of them, sir. Billingford gave everything away that he knew about; and the other chap's nerve was completely gone, so that he couldn't resist questioning. It's as clear a case as one could wish for."

He paused, as though puzzled by something, and then added:

"It beats me how you tumbled to the fact that Cargill was one of the gang, though."

Sir Clinton ignored the underlying inquiry.

"Was he the brains of the show?" he asked. "I've only a suspicion to go on there."

"Yes, he did the planning for them."

"And the gentleman with no face collaborated with Aird in the actual murders? That's a guess, I may say, so far as the Staveley affair's concerned, though I'm fairly sure of my ground in the other cases."

"You're right in that case too, sir. Aird and the impostor fellow were the actual murderers. Aird'll hang for certain."

"It'll make a very nice case for you, inspector; and I'm sure you'll work it up well for the Public Prosecutor. I can seen a laurel wreath somewhere in the background."

"But it's you who did most of it, sir. Nobody understands that better than I do," the inspector objected, evidently afraid lest Sir Clinton thought him capable of accepting the credit without protest.

"I came into the thing on a strict understanding that I was to be a pure spectator, you remember. I'm afraid that at times I got a shade too zealous, perhaps; but it's your case and not mine. If we'd made a mess of it between us, you'd have had to stand the racket; so obviously a success goes down to your account. The subject's closed."

Wendover, seeing the inspector's difficulty in framing a suitable reply to this, intervened to change the subject.

"I see the main outlines of the affair easily enough, Clinton," he said, "but I'd like to hear just how you worked it out as you went along. Any objections to telling me? It'll go no farther, of course."

The chief constable's face betrayed a tinge of boredom.

"You've lived with this case for the best part of a week. Haven't you had enough of it by this time?"

Wendover persisted in his demand; but Sir Clinton, instead of complying, glanced at his watch.

"There's one detective story I'm very fond of, squire: *The Hunting of the Snark*. I rank it high in the scale, especially on account of the number of apt quotations one can make from it. Here's one:

> The method employed I would gladly explain
>   While I have it so clear in my head,
> If I had but the time and you had but the brain—
>   But much yet remains to be said.

It's far too late to start a long story to-night. I'm dead sleepy. If you remind me about it to-morrow, I'll do my best; but I will not sit up all night even to please you."

The inspector seemed as much disappointed as Wendover at his superior's decision.

"I'd like to hear it too, sir, if you don't mind."

Sir Clinton suppressed a yawn with difficulty.

"I don't mind, inspector. Meet us at Neptune's Seat at eleven o'clock to-morrow morning. It'll be interesting to hear how far wrong I've gone in some of my guesses; and you can tell me that, since you've got so much out of these two precious scoundrels to-night. And now I'll drive you into Lynden Sands—save you the trudge. After that I really must get to bed."

CHAPTER XVII
THE THREADS IN THE CASE

"THIS HASN'T BEEN A TIDY CASE, in the strict meaning of the words," Sir Clinton mused, as he chose a comfortable spot on Neptune's Seat and settled down on it. "It's really an *omnium gatherum*. It began long before we appeared on the scene; and the inspector has the facts about the earlier stages, whilst I've nothing better than guesswork."

"What we're interested in, chiefly, is what you thought about it at different stages in the game," Wendover pointed out. "If you start with the Peter Hay case and go on from there, you can tell us what you saw and what we missed. And at the tail end you can give us your guesses about the earlier stage. The inspector can check them from the confessions he got."

Sir Clinton agreed with a gesture, and began without more ado. It was evident that he was by no means eager to recapitulate, and was doing so merely out of good nature.

"The Peter Hay case was crystal clear so far as one side was concerned. It required no marvelous insight to see what had happened. It wasn't by any possibility a one-man murder. At least two men must have been on the spot to overpower Peter and tie him up. They—or at least one of them—was a better-class fellow, or Peter Hay would have been in his shirt-sleeves instead of having his jacket on. And the jacket implied that he knew they were coming that evening, too. Further, the fact that they had amyl nitrite ready in their pockets is enough to prove two things. They weren't casual strangers, for they knew about his liability to cerebral

252

congestion. And they premeditated killing him in certain circumstances. We worked out pretty definitely the course of events which led to his death, so I needn't go over that again. I suppose we were right in the main points, inspector?"

Armadale, primed with the information he had extracted from Aird, was able to confirm this.

"They used surgical bandages because they hoped to leave no marks on the skin, I suppose?" Sir Clinton inquired.

"That was the idea, Aird admitted, sir. He thought they'd succeeded, and he was surprised to find they'd made a mess of it."

Sir Clinton smiled, apparently at the thought of Aird's discomfiture.

"Well, if they bungled one side of the affair, they certainly managed to leave us in the dark about the second side: the motive behind the murder. It wasn't robbery, obviously. It wasn't bad feeling—everyone we examined had a good word for Peter Hay. It couldn't be homicidal mania—not with two of them mixed up in it. That left, so far as I could see, only one probable motive at the back of the thing. Either they wanted to force Peter Hay into something he didn't like, or else he knew something about them which they were afraid of.

"Peter Hay wasn't the blackmailing type, from all we learned about him. That notion wouldn't hold water for a moment. So, if he had to be silenced, then the information he had must have been something he'd come across quite innocently. What it was I couldn't guess. In fact, the whole idea was very vague in my mind, since there didn't seem anything definite to support it. That was the stage I'd reached when we sat in the garden and discussed the thing.

"But there was one thing that seemed to lead on to something fresh—the silver we found in Peter Hay's drawer. That silver was the murderers' mistake—the silly thing that gives them away. No sensible person would ever have tried to throw a suspicion of breach of trust on Peter Hay. The thing was absurd on the face of it, from what we learned of his character. But these fellows weren't looking at it objectively. They would have abused their trust in

Hay's shoes; and naturally they saw nothing *outré* in faking a petty theft and trying to throw it on his shoulders. That made me think.

"Why suggest a robbery at Foxhills? For that was what they evidently intended the police to swallow. As a matter of fact, they'd have been much better to have left the thing alone. It was a mistake to fake evidence; it always is. However, they'd done it, and I wanted to know why they'd done it. So, when the Fordingbridges arrived, we went off to Foxhills.

"I wasn't surprised to find that the murderers had tried to make the thing convincing by filling that sack with silver odds and ends. I'd almost expected something of the sort. But I don't suppose any of us were misled to the extent the murderers hoped. They thought we'd be delighted to find confirmation of Peter Hay's dishonesty—stuff ready packed up for transport. But what one obviously asked oneself was the question: 'What's all this meant to cover?' And the answer was, so far as I could see: 'The removal of some inconspicuous object whose absence won't be noticed in the excitement over the silver.'

"It wasn't long before I got an inkling of what that inconspicuous object was. Miss Fordingbridge was able to tell us. But, notice, if Miss Fordingbridge hadn't happened to come up to Foxhills when we paid our visit, we'd never have known that the diary was missing. We'd have missed the main clue in the whole affair. That was where we were really lucky, and where Aird & Co. had very hard lines.

"There was the diary gone a-missing, anyhow; and the obvious question to ask was: '*Cui bono?* Who stands to score by its removal?'

"You heard the story of the missing nephew and the power of attorney given to Paul Fordingbridge. You could hardly help drawing the obvious conclusion that here at last was a possible motive appearing behind the Peter Hay case. The stake on the table was the assets of the Fordingbridge estate; and that was quite big enough to make murder worth while, if you happened to have a turn for that sort of thing.

"But when you come to ask: '*Cui bono?*' you find that the problem's like one of those quadratic equations we used to get at school, where there are two answers and one seems just as good as the other.

"Suppose the claimant was an impostor, and see where that leads you. Derek Fordingbridge had spent a lot of time with Peter Hay in earlier days. The chances were that Peter Hay was the only man who could give evidence about their joint doings, and that evidence might form the basis of a damaging examination of the impostor. Further, the diary would be a priceless thing for an impostor to lay his hands on. It would supply him with any amount of irrefutable evidence which he could draw on for his sham recollections. Clearly enough, if the claim was a fraudulent one, then the theft of the diary and the silencing of Peter Hay would fit in very neatly.

"On the other hand, suppose the boot's on the other foot. Assume that Paul Fordingbridge had some very strong reason for wishing to retain control over the funds, and see where that leads you. Remember that he showed no desire whatever to investigate this claim. He simply denied straight off that the claimant was his nephew, without waiting for any evidence on the point. That seemed to me a curious attitude in a trustee; perhaps it struck you in the same way. And he appeared to be very little put out by Peter Hay's death, if you remember—treated it very much as a matter of course. It doesn't take much thinking to see that what holds good for a fraudulent claimant would hold good for a fraudulent trustee also. The diary and Peter Hay would be two weak spots for him too. They'd help a genuine nephew to establish an almost irrefutable case if he could pass tests applied both by the diary and by Peter Hay's recollections.

"So, whichever way one looked at it, there seemed to be something to be said. And, consequently, I got no further at that stage than being able to say that three things were possible. First, the claimant might be a fraud, and Paul Fordingbridge merely an obstinate old beggar. Second, the claimant might be genuine, and Paul might be a dishonest trustee. Or, third, both the claimant and Paul might be wrong 'uns.

"Miss Fordingbridge had known her nephew intimately, and she had identified him straight off, it's true. But we've heard of that kind of thing before. You remember how Roger Tichborne's mother identified Arthur Orton as her son, and stuck to it through thick and thin. Hallucinations of that sort do occur. And one couldn't help noticing Miss Fordingbridge's talk about spiritualism and so forth, all tending to show that she had a sort of fixed idea that her nephew would turn up sooner or later. That discounted the value of her identification a good deal, but it didn't discredit it completely, of course.

"Now go back a stage. The thing was a two-man job at Peter Hay's. Therefore, whether the claimant or Fordingbridge was our man, we had to find a second fellow for the accomplice's part. The claimant we knew nothing about at that stage; and I proposed to look into his affairs later. If Paul Fordingbridge was one of the murderers, on the other hand, then, who was his accomplice? 'Cui bono?' again. If the claimant could be kept out of the succession, who was next on the list? Stanley Fleetwood's wife."

Careless of the inspector's feelings, Wendover broke out at this point:

"You won't persuade me you were such an ass, Clinton, as to suppose that young Fleetwood helped in a murder merely for the sake of cash or any other reason?"

"It wasn't my business to make pets of anyone, and exclude them from suspicion merely because I liked them in private life, squire. Many murderers are most amiable persons—Crippen, for example. 'A fair field and no favour' is the only motto for a conscientious detective.

"Before we had time to delve further into the Peter Hay case, however, the Staveley murder occurred. There's no need to go into the whole business; it's fresh in your minds; but I'll tell you the main points that struck me when we'd finished our examination of the scene of the murder.

"First, Staveley had banged his wrist and stopped his watch at 11.19. But, of course, that didn't prove he'd been killed at that moment. Second, his clothes were wet under his rainproof; and, he'd been shot through both rainproof and jacket, it must have rained before he was shot. Third, since the car-tracks had gone back on a dry road for a while before the rain came on and made them clearer, Staveley was killed after the car had gone off; and the people in the car weren't mixed up in the actual killing. Fourth, there was only one cartridge-case to be seen—the one on the rock. There was no cartridge-case at the groyne when I searched the place. Besides, that track at the groyne belonged to the man in the car, and he was cleared completely by the rain question. If I was right in my inferences, then the murder must have been committed by one of three people: the woman with the neat shoes, Billingford, *or someone who had left no tracks on the sand.*

"The letter we found in Staveley's pocket showed the business; and you worked up the case against them that Mrs. Fleetwood had been to meet him on the previous night at the rock; and, as she was acting in conjunction with a man, there wasn't much trouble in inferring that young Fleetwood might have been on the spot also, as soon as we heard that the Fleetwoods' car had been out all night. You, inspector, jumped to the conclusion that the Fleetwoods were at the back of the business; and you worked up the case against them very convincingly. But, as I told you at the start, the case wasn't sound. I wanted all the data I could get, of course, so I didn't discourage you too much; and you eventually dragged out a lot of interesting material about the events of the night.

"Meanwhile, we'd come to a blank end with the Fleetwoods and had turned to Billingford. My impression was that he seemed genuinely surprised by the news of Staveley's murder; but he might have been acting, for all one could tell. What we did get out of him was the general impression that Flatt's cottage was inhabited by a gang of rogues. How many were there? Three, if one took Billingford at face value; four, if one believed the story the claimant blurted out when we questioned him at the cottage.

"Anyone could see that the fourth man was a dark horse. He might be the murderer whom they were shielding, possibly. But there was another explanation of his disappearance; he might be someone well known to the local people, and whom it was desirable to keep under cover. How would that fit in with things? Suppose the claimant was an impostor; he wouldn't be very anxious to meet the villagers more than he could help, for fear of dropping on someone who might trap him and expose him. The less he saw of his neighbors the better; and his disfigurement gave him a fair excuse for keeping indoors in the daytime. Staveley was well enough known to the villagers also; and perhaps he had good reason for not wishing his presence known. If the fourth man was in the same boat, then none of them would care to go shopping and so forth, and yet supplies had to be got daily. Hence it might be convenient to have a man like Billingford as the nominal host, to act as go-between for them in their public transactions. That's how it appeared to me. Naturally, I was curious about the fourth man, and I got you, inspector, to set a watch and see if he could be recognised.

"That left me with a fair suspicion that these fellows were hatching some devilment or other at the cottage. Then I noticed the card-index; and I saw light to some extent. A card-index implies the need for ready reference. The claimant, if he were a fraud, would need to cram himself with all the available facts about the doings of the real Derek Fordingbridge—just as Arthur Orton crammed up all the facts about Roger Tichborne. And a card-index would be the handiest repository of all the news they could collect. As you saw for yourself, squire, that guess of mine was right.

"Assume that state of affairs—I had no certain knowledge then— and things begin to fall into their places. I've given you my notion of why Billingford was needed. What about the other three?

"The claimant was obviously needed to represent Derek Fordingbridge; and he'd been cast for the part on two grounds. First, his face was so much damaged that no one could swear to his original appearance. He might quite well have been Derek or anyone else, so far as that went. Then the loss of his fingers made him invaluable also, because he couldn't be expected to write like the real Derek nowadays, with a mutilated hand. All that was wanted in addition was a good memory to cram up the immense amount of facts that they needed in order to meet questioning.

"Then there was Staveley. What was he doing in the affair? Well, obviously, he had a lot of information about the Foxhills people which he must have picked up while he stayed there with the real Derek on leave, and also some more facts which he must have learned from Mrs. Fleetwood from time to time.

"And, finally, there was the fourth man. I suspected that he might turn out to be a second information-mine; and when I heard the report you gave me, inspector, about the fishermen and Sapcote having recognised him as an ex-valet at Foxhills, I felt I was getting on to fairly sure ground.

"Well, there were four of them to share in the loot if they pulled it off. But a third's better than a quarter-share any day. If they had pumped Staveley dry of his information, and had got notes of it all on that card-index, what further need had they for friend Nicholas? None whatever.

"And suppose they could involve the Fleetwoods in a murder case and get them hanged, wouldn't that remove one possible set of objectors to the claimant dropping into the funds? So I didn't exclude the possibility that they knew—although they denied it—that Staveley was going to meet Mrs. Fleetwood at Neptune's Seat that night. When I say 'they,' I really mean the faceless fellow and Aird.

"There was a further long shot possible. I'm not sure if it really entered into their plans; but I give it you for what it's worth. Suppose they suggested a walk along the sands to Billingford that evening, and arranged matters so that he would reach the rock just after the murder had been committed and they had cleared out. Wouldn't that have been a tight corner for Master Billingford? With any luck he might have been hung for the murder, since he'd no evidence but his own to rely on to prove he wasn't on the spot when the shot was fired. And then there would be only two of them, instead of four, to share out the loot if they got it.

"You see now how I was beginning to look at the affair. But I was considerably worried by the woman with the neat shoe. Her part in the business would have to be cleared up eventually; but for the moment I had to put it aside.

"And then our friends made their second blunder—trying to prove too much, as usual. Friend Cargill came on the scene, innocently going down to bathe. He sat down on the groyne and proceeded to dig up a .38 cartridge-case, which he presented to me like an honest fellow anxious only to help the police. Well, all three of us had been over that particular bit of sand and had seen no cartridge-case before he arrived on the scene. Also, as I pointed out to you, squire, an automatic ejects its cartridge-case sharply and jerks it well behind you, especially on hard sand where the thing can jump along. It was obvious that no one could fire a shot from Fleetwood's position at the groyne and leave his ejected shell lying close under the groyne, where Cargill assured me he'd kicked it up. So naturally I began to look at Mr. Cargill with more than common interest; and, as you saw yourselves, he's got a build rather like the claimant's, so I wondered if they were related.

"Then our friend Cargill told us his yarn about meeting Derek Fordingbridge in the war; and off he went to meet his dear old friend. And later on he volunteered eagerly that he'd had a talk with the dear old fellow. By that time I was more than a bit suspicious of the dear old friend; and naturally some of that suspicion spilled over on to Cargill. If the claimant was an impostor, then the man who recognised him was a liar; and, as I had no use for aimless liars in a case of this sort, I inferred that Master Cargill was one of the gang, posted at the hotel for intelligence purposes—to keep an eye on the Fordingbridge group. And that cleared up one of the main difficulties I'd had—namely, how the murderer had known to use a .38 automatic so as to match the Fleetwood pistol. Of course, if you assume that Cargill had taken the opportunity of rummaging in Fleetwood's room, or had drawn him into talk about pistols, they would be sure of their ground on that point. That had been a troublesome point to me; for I didn't like to stretch coincidence to the extent of assuming it was mere accident that made the Fleetwood pistol and the bullet in the body both of the same calibre.

"It remained to check Billingford's story as far as possible, and you know how the runnel helped us in that. What the facts of the case proved beyond any reasonable doubt was that at 11.19 P.M. Billingford was about three-quarters of a mile from Neptune's Seat. With the sound of the sea in his ears, it's most unlikely that he could hear a pistol-shot at that distance. And his tracks showed him walking along quite steadily there. Then, at a point far nearer the rock—a point that I suppose he may have reached about 11.35 P.M. the trail showed that he began to run. Now that fitted in with his story. At that second point he might quite well have heard a shot fired on the rock, just as he said he did. He couldn't possibly, on the facts we established, have reached the rock before about 11.37 or 11.38; and by that time the murder was done and the murderer had got away.

"By that time I felt fairly sure of my ground; and I got that digging in the sand started, just on the off-chance that we might get hold of the shell of the cartridge which really did kill Staveley. It wasn't absolutely necessary for the case; but, if it turned up, then it would help to confirm my notions. As it was bound to be below tide-mark, there was no point in trying to locate its exact position, since it might have been washed about by the waves in the falling tide after the shot was fired. So I simply had the whole strip of sand dug up and dumped down above the high-water mark for future examination.

"Meanwhile, I'd been on the hunt for the dame with the neat shoe—a No. 4, as you remember. There were several of the guests wearing shoes of that size; but I picked out Mme. Laurent-Desrousseaux first of all because she seemed likeliest. Staveley had served in France; she was a Frenchwoman; she was at Lynden Sands Hotel, where she most obviously was out of place and knew no one. It seemed best to find out something about her.

"I talked to her. She was a bit lonely, it seems, and quite ready to go for a walk now and again. I know my own length of pace; so, by counting hers in a given distance and comparing with the numbers of my own, I made a fair guess at her step-measurement. It fitted in with the prints of the neat shoe on the sands. Gentle treatment did the rest, as you saw. She told us her story quite honestly, and it threw a good deal of light on the affair. I inferred from it just what you yourself inferred later on, squire: the shot fired by Mrs. Fleetwood at 11.19; Staveley's fall on the rock; and the bolt in the car to the hotel. And, in turn, this checked Billingford's story

quite neatly, because he couldn't have heard the shot at 11.19, being
so far away. It was the second shot, about 11.35, that he heard.

"Now, let's reconstruct what really happened; and remember
that, although it was full moon, it was a cloudy night, and the light
was bad all through. We'll begin with Staveley leaving the cottage.
He's in a bad temper; been drinking as well as playing poker. He
gets to the rock and waits for Mme. Laurent-Desrousseaux. She's
late; and his temper gets worse. She arrives and tells him she wants
to get a divorce arranged. Between his temper and the chance he
sees of making her pay sweetly for the favour she asks he treats
her brutally, and sends her off both pained and angry. Then Mrs.
Fleetwood arrives, and that meeting culminates in the shot she
fired at 11.19 by accident. Then you get the talk between the Fleetwoods at the car, overheard by Mme. Laurent-Desrousseaux; their
drive back to the hotel; and her hurry to get away from what she
thinks is the scene of a murder. That leaves Staveley on the rock,
stunned by his fall; and Billingford sauntering across the sands towards the runnel. In the meantime, Aird and the gentleman without a
face have got out the boat belonging to Flatt's cottage and are row-
ing for Neptune's Seat, which is just above tide-level.

"Down comes the rain. Staveley gets soaked; and perhaps the
chill revives him. He staggers up and puts on his rainproof. Then
in comes the boat, and they shoot him without having to land on
the rock at all. The ejector jerks the cartridge-case into the water,
where it sinks into the sand and gets covered up by the wash of the
waves. The murderer and his pal row off into the dark. Meanwhile
Billingford has heard the shot, and he, not knowing anything about
this little plot, rushes up—rather pluckily—to see what it's all about,
and he finds the body on the rock. That explains the two shots and
the general chronology of the affair.

"Now, by this time friend Cargill had made his second error.
He'd been keeping his eye on things at the hotel, and he'd got hold
of that envelope which Mme. Laurent-Desrousseaux addressed to
Staveley and dropped in the waste-paper basket. He thought he
could give me a fresh scent to follow up, and he was just going to

produce it when he realised that Mme. Laurent-Desrousseaux herself was with us; so he suppressed it then and handed it over later on. All it did was to confirm me in the idea that he was one of the gang.

"Up to that point everything seemed plain sailing. I had, as I believed—and as it turned out in the end—got the thing cut and dried against the gang at the cottage. The case wasn't complete; but, short of getting some direct evidence from one of the two actual murderers, I didn't see how I was to make it absolutely watertight. They'd been a bit too clever for a jury, I feared. And, of course, the Peter Hay case was getting clearer also, once you could assume that these fellows would stick at nothing.

"Then, out of the blue, came the shooting of Cargill. That wouldn't fit in with the rest of the business. Cargill wasn't a pawn like Staveley and Billingford. He was watching one end of the business for them—keeping an eye on us for one thing; and, besides, I was becoming more and more sure that he was a brother of the faceless fellow, and possibly the brains of the gang. They had a use for him; they wouldn't shoot him. But, then, who did?

"And at that point I took a long cast back and raked up again a possibility I'd dismissed at an earlier stage. Suppose that both the claimant *and* Paul Fordingbridge were wrong 'uns, what then? Suppose friend Paul had been at some hanky-panky with the funds he held in trust for his nephew. Then, whether the claimant was an impostor or not, it would be very convenient for friend Paul if the claimant left this vale of tears. And the claimant and Cargill were much alike in build; and Cargill was shot after leaving the cottage. There might be something in it. And when I found that friend Paul carried a pistol in his pocket, and didn't care who knew it, by the look of his jacket, I began to think furiously.

"I didn't blame Paul for carrying arms. In his position, with that gang at the cottage in the offing, I think it was a wise precaution; for he must have known that he was the main stumbling-block in the claimant's road. But I don't think that he kept within the limits of precaution. I think he decided to get ahead of them by knocking out the claimant—and after that he would be able to live in peace as heretofore.

"However, I never had time to probe that matter any further, for the next business was the disappearance of friend Paul. I think I have a fair notion how that was managed.

"They approached him and asked for an interview. He sent the claimant a scrap of paper:

'Meet me at the Blowhole to-night at 11 P.M. Come alone.'

The last two words give you the key to friend Paul's feelings about them. One man he could keep an eye on, and he didn't propose to have any more present. Of course, they filed that note and used it again later, as you'll remember.

"Probably the claimant met him at the Blowhole and suggested a walk over the open sands as a good way of avoiding eavesdroppers. Paul would feel safer in the open. By the time they reached the old wreck the claimant would have got him interested, or else his natural fears would be dissipated. At the hulk the claimant obviously turned, as though to go back across the sands, and Paul turned with him. Then, from behind the hull, Aird stole out and did *le coup du Père François*."

"What's that?" Wendover demanded. "You talked a lot about Père François and Sam Lloyd's 'Get off the Earth' puzzle, I remember."

"If you happen to be in Paris late at night, squire, and a rough-looking customer asks you the time or begs for a match, you'd better look out for his friend—*le Père François*, they call him—who may be coming up behind you with a long strip of flannel in his hand. While the first man holds you in talk, the Père François lassoes you with his flannel rope and pulls the two ends so that it catches your throat. Then he sinks down suddenly and turns his back to you, slipping the rope over his shoulder as he turns. This pulls you down back to back with him; and when he rises to his normal height again, there you are on his back like a sack on a coalheaver's back, with your feet off the ground. The first man then goes through your pockets at his leisure, and if you choke to death before he's done, so much the worse for you. You can't struggle with any effect.

"That I suspect, was how they caught friend Paul; and Aird just carried him on his back to the quicksand and dumped him in. From Aird's footmarks it was clear he'd been carrying a heavy weight; the prints were deep and the feet almost parallel after he'd done his Père François trick. See now what I meant by 'Get off the Earth'? Naturally there were no signs of a struggle, since all the struggle was off the ground. And, of course, they'd take care to wear shoes that left no clue—common type and largest size. And they got away either in a boat or by wading along in the water, so as to leave no tracks. I could see no way to bring the affair home to them. The only sure method depended on our wringing evidence out of one of them somehow; and I didn't see how it could be managed just then. Also, I hadn't much of a case against Cargill beyond suspicion; and I wanted him too, if it could be managed.

"The next thing was the arrival of the Fordingbridge lawyer; and from him I learned that we might get on the track of any malversations by Friend Paul if I went up to London. I wanted to know definitely where I stood in that matter, because, if I was wrong there, then the whole latter part of my notions would collapse. So I made up my mind to go to town.

"But I was very uneasy. Now that Paul Fordingbridge was out of the road for good, Mrs. Fleetwood was the only person between the claimant and the cash. If she disappeared in her turn, then Miss Fordingbridge would have welcomed her long-lost nephew with pure joy and gratitude for his preservation, and there would have been no one left alive to object to his coming into Foxhills and the rest. Therefore, I was inclined to take some steps to see that she came to no harm while I was away.

"The obvious thing to do would have been to warn her. But that would have meant giving my case away to the Fleetwoods; and I don't feel inclined to chuck confidences around if it can be avoided, as I've pointed out before. Further, the police were not altogether in good odour with the Fleetwoods; and I wasn't sure if I'd make much impression on them by a mere warning, with nothing to back it. So I hit on the notion of putting a man on to watch Mrs. Fleetwood; and, as a further precaution, I fixed up that code-wire so that if I wanted it I could have her arrested at a moment's notice, and then she'd be safe in police hands and out of reach of the gang.

"I went up to London and found, as I'd expected, that friend Paul had been playing ducks and drakes with all the securities he could handle without exciting too much suspicion. He seems to have been speculating right and left, most unsuccessfully. So I'd been right about his motives, anyhow.

"But I couldn't get out of my mind the risk I was letting that girl run; and at last—I suppose Miss Fordingbridge would say it was telepathy or something—I got the wind up completely, and wired to have her arrested. After that I felt safer.

"As you know, they'd been too quick for me. They fished out the note that Paul Fordingbridge wrote to the claimant and they sent it to her as if it came from Paul himself, after altering the hour on it. She thought her uncle was in trouble; went to help him; dodged the constable; and fell straight into the trap they'd set for her. You know all the rest. And probably by now you understand why I was quite content to let Mr. Aird have his full dose in the funnel of the *souffleur*. There's nothing like a confession for convincing a jury, and I meant him to hang if it could be managed. I didn't want to run any risk of his getting off merely because it was all circumstantial evidence."

"Thanks," said Wendover, seeing that the chief constable had finished his outline. "To quote from that favourite detective story of yours:

> In one moment I've seen what has hitherto been
> Enveloped in absolute mystery.

There's just one point I'd like to hear you on. What about Staveley's resuscitation after his being killed in the war? Did you get to the bottom of that by any chance?"

Sir Clinton hesitated a little before answering.

"I don't much care about pure guesswork, squire; but, if you'll take it as that, then I don't mind saying what I think. Suppose that is what happened. Staveley and Derek Fordingbridge went into action together; and Staveley was under a cloud at the time. He'd probably had enough of the war, and was looking for a way out. Derek Fordingbridge gets killed in that battle, and is probably badly damaged in the process—made unrecognisable we may suppose. Staveley sees him killed, and grasps at the chance offered. He takes Derek's identity disc off the body and leaves his own instead. Probably he takes the contents of the pockets too, and puts his own papers into the dead man's pockets. They were friends; and, if anyone saw him at work, he'd have his excuse ready. No one would think he was robbing the dead. Then he goes on—and simply hands himself over to the enemy. He's a prisoner of war—under Derek's name.

"He manages to escape, and the escape is put down to Derek's credit. But, of course, Derek never turns up again; and naturally people suppose that he must have died of exposure in his last attempt, or been shot at the frontier, or something of that sort. Meanwhile Staveley, once out of Germany, drops his borrowed identity, probably changes his name, and disappears. I suspect he was in very hot water with the military authorities, and was only too glad of the chance to vanish for good.

"After the war, he evidently got in amongst a queer gang, and lived as best he could. Billingford's evidence points to that. And somewhere among this shoal of queer fish he swam up against our friend Cargill. My reading of the thing is that somehow Staveley gave away—perhaps in his cups—something of what I've given you as my guess; and Cargill, remembering his disfigured brother, saw a grand scheme to be worked by putting forward his brother as claimant to the Foxhills property.

"It wasn't half so wild a plan as the Tichborne business, and you know how that panned out at the start. So the three of them set to work to see the thing through. Staveley, I suspect, got hold of Aird, who had invaluable information about all the affairs at Foxhills in the old days. Then they went to work systematically with their card-index and noted down everything that Aird and Staveley could remember which would bear on the case.

"That accounts for the delay in the claimant turning up. It probably was quite recently that Staveley fell in with Cargill. And evidently the delay points to the fact that Staveley wasn't the originator of the notion, else he'd have got to work much earlier. It was only when he fell in with Cargill, who had a brother suitable to play the part of the claimant, that anything could be done. Then they must have spent some time in unearthing Aird.

"Well, at last they're ready. They come down to Lynden Sands with their card-index handy. Now, the claimant doesn't want to appear in public more than he can help, for every stranger is a possible danger to him. He might fail to recognise some old friend, and the fat might be in the fire. Nor does Staveley want to show himself; for his presence might suggest the source of the claimant's information. Aird's in the same position. And when they learn that the Fordingbridges are at the hotel, Cargill is detached there to keep an eye on them. Thus they need a go-between; and Billingford is brought down to serve that purpose. Also, as soon as the claimant makes his first move there will be sure to be a lot of gossip in the village, anecdotes of the claimant's history floating round, and so forth; and Billingford will be able to pick them up and report them to the rest of the gang. They'd have been safer to leave Staveley and Aird in London; but I suppose they were afraid something might be sprung on them and they wanted their references handy.

"Peter Hay, I suspect, they fastened on as being the most dangerous witness. Probably Aird made an appointment for the claimant, and they called at the poor old chap's cottage at night. He evidently refused to have anything to do with them; and he was too dangerous to leave alive; so they killed him. Then they went after the diary—probably Aird knew about that, or else Peter may have let the information out somehow—and they took Hay's keys to get into Foxhills. The silver plant was an obvious muddle. They hadn't Cargill at the back of them at the time, and they made that mistake on the spur of the moment.

"By that time they'd got in touch with Miss Fordingbridge. Aird would know all about her spiritualistic leanings, and they played on that string. But soon they learned they were up against Paul

Fordingbridge; and they began to see that it would be easiest to put him out of their road.

"Meanwhile Staveley took it into his head to work on his own by trying to blackmail the Fleetwoods. And you know what came of that. The rest of the gang thought they could kill two birds with one stone—at least, the gang minus Billingford, for really I don't think Billingford was much more than a tool.

"Now, inspector, how far does that square with all the confidences you extracted last night from that precious pair of scoundrels? Do I get a box of chocolates or only a clay pipe in this competition?"

The inspector made no attempt to suppress the admiration in his tone.

"It's wonderfully accurate, sir. You're right on every point of importance—even down to what happened in the war."

"That's a relief," the chief constable admitted with a laugh. "I was rather afraid that I'd

> . . . Summed it so well that it came to far more
> Than the witnesses ever had said!

And now I think I'll go back to the hotel and try to make my peace with the Fleetwoods. I like them, and I'd hate to leave a false impression of my character on their minds. Care to come along, squire?"

COACHWHIP PUBLICATIONS

COACHWHIPBOOKS.COM

THE TWO TICKETS PUZZLE

J. J. CONNINGTON

ISBN 978-1-61646-305-2

Coachwhip Publications

Also Available

MURDER IN THE MAZE

J. J. CONNINGTON

ISBN 978-1-61646-113-3

COACHWHIP PUBLICATIONS

COACHWHIPBOOKS.COM

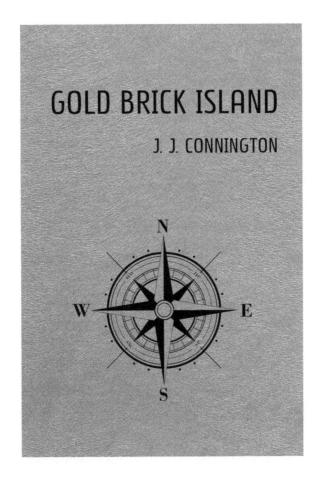

GOLD BRICK ISLAND

J. J. CONNINGTON

ISBN 978-1-61646-307-4

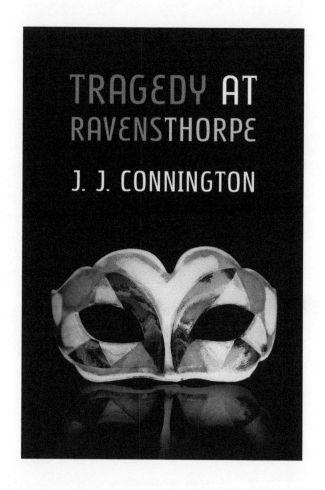

TRAGEDY AT RAVENSTHORPE

J. J. CONNINGTON

ISBN 978-1-61646-308-2

COACHWHIP PUBLICATIONS

COACHWHIPBOOKS.COM

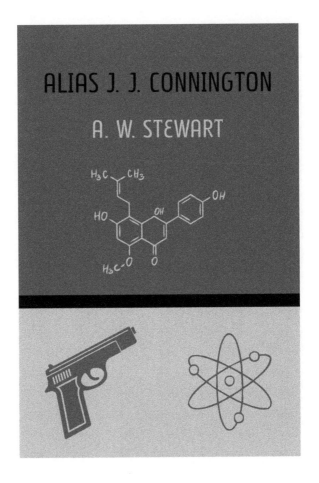

ISBN 978-1-61646-322-8

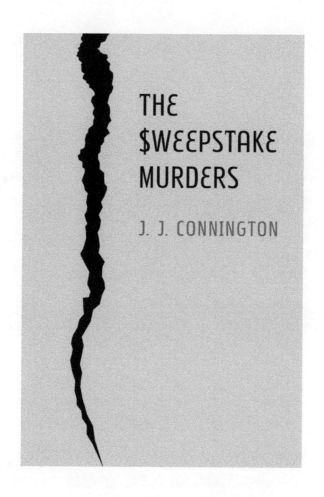

THE
$WEEPSTAKE
MURDERS

J. J. CONNINGTON

ISBN 978-1-61646-321-X

Lightning Source UK Ltd.
Milton Keynes UK
UKHW041142180219
337534UK00001B/324/P

9 781616 463205